MADEMOISELLE

CHANEL

ALSO BY C. W. GORTNER

The Tudor Vendetta

The Tudor Conspiracy

The Queen's Vow

The Tudor Secret

The Confessions of Catherine de Medici

The Last Queen

MADEMOISELLE
CHANEL

C. W. GORTNER

WILLIAM MORROW
An Imprint of HarperCollins*Publishers*

P.S.™ is a trademark of HarperCollins Publishers.

HarperCollins books may be purchased for educational, business, or sales promotional use. For information please e-mail the Special Markets Department at SPsales@harpercollins.com.

A hardcover edition of this book was published in 2015 by William Morrow, an imprint of HarperCollins Publishers.

FIRST WILLIAM MORROW PAPERBACK EDITION PUBLISHED 2015.

Designed by Jamie Lynn Kerner

Library of Congress Cataloging-in-Publication Data has been applied for.

ISBN 978-0-06-235643-7

20 21 22 OV/LSC 10

For Melisse, the only person I know who loves Chanel more than I do, and for Jennifer, who always believes

My life didn't please me, so I created my life.
—GABRIELLE "COCO" CHANEL

MADEMOISELLE
CHANEL

PARIS

The herd gathers below. I can hear them, all the journalists and eager celebrities, and select critics who received my embossed invitation. I hear their excited voices, a buzz that creeps up the mirrored staircase to where I wait in my disordered atelier.

About me, the twelve models are already dressed in my new creations, wreathed in clouds of cigarette smoke and my signature perfume. I've asked for silence as I lie on my back checking their hem lengths and snipping at stray threads. I cannot think when they chatter, but there is no stopping them. They tug the jeweled belts of my black gowns, clanking their brace-lets and clicking their pearls; they reflect the agitation I feel but cannot show.

I rise to my feet, letting my scissors dangle on their ribbon around my neck. I know the speculation going on below: Will she do it? *Can* she do it? She is seventy-one. She hasn't designed a dress in fifteen years. After falling so low, how can she possibly rise again?

How, indeed.

None of this is new to me. I have faced it all before. The expectation of failure, the craving for adulation; these are the hallmarks of my life. I light another cigarette and survey the models before me. "You," I tell a dark-haired girl who reminds me of myself at her age. "Too many bracelets. Remove one." Even as she flushes and does as I ask, I hear my beloved Boy whisper in my ear, "Remember, Coco, you're only a woman."

Only a woman who must continue to reinvent herself if she is to survive.

I catch sight of myself in one of the room's mirrors—my Gypsy skin and mouth red with lipstick, my thick brows and flashing gold-brown eyes, my body all angles and edges in my braided pink suit. There is nothing left of the pliant skin of my youth. And my hands, covered in precious rings, are as raw as a stonemason's, knotted, marred by a thousand needle pricks—the hands of the Auvergne peasant I am at heart, the foundling, the orphan, the dreamer, the schemer. My hands reflect who I am. I see in them the struggle that has always existed between the humble girl I once was and the legend I deliberately created to hide my heart.

Who is Coco Chanel?

"ALLEZ," I CALL OUT. The models line up at the head of the staircase to my salon. I have overseen this ritual so many times before, straightening a sleeve at the last minute, adjusting the tilt of a hat, the fold of a collar. As I wave the models forward, I draw back. I will not make my appearance until the applause has faded—*if* there is applause.

I cannot be sure anymore, not after all this time.

Coiling my knees to my chest, my cigarettes at my side, I silence the chimes of my bijoux and perch at the top of my mirrored stairs, becoming a hidden spectator, solitary, as I have always been.

And as I behold my uncertain future, I will reflect on my past and do my best to tell the truth, though myth and rumor clothe me as much as my signature crêpe de chine or tweed.

I will try to remember that for all my triumphs and mistakes, I am still only a woman.

ACT ONE
NOBODY'S DAUGHTER
1895–1907

"I DO NOT REGRET HAVING BEEN DEEPLY
UNHAPPY TO BEGIN WITH."

I

The day Maman died, I was lining up my dolls in the cemetery. They were poppets of cloth and straw I had made when I was a child, dirty and misshapen now because I was almost twelve. I gave them different names at different times. Today, they were Mesdames les Tantes, named for the black-clad women in our garret nearby, watching my mother gasp out her final breaths.

"You sit here and you here," I said, forcing their little bodies into position against the toppling headstones and imagining I was ordering about les Tantes. The cemetery was my haven, a patch for the dead on the edge of the village where my mother had brought me and my siblings after Papa left us. We had moved so often, I did not think of it as home. Papa often disappeared for months at a time, a marketplace vendor who took to the road with his wares.

"I was born for the road," he would say when Maman nagged him. "For generations, we Chanels have been wanderers. Do you expect me to change what is in my blood?"

Maman sighed. "Not entirely. But we are married now, Albert. We have children."

Papa laughed. He had a big laugh, and I loved hearing it. "Children learn to adjust. They don't mind if I travel. Isn't that so, *ma* Gabrielle?" he asked, turning to wink at me. I was his favorite; he'd told me so, swooping me up in his burly arms and scattering ash from his cigarette over my thick black braids as I laughed. "Gabrielle, *mon petit chou*, my little cabbage!"

Then he'd set me down, and he and Maman would argue. It inevitably ended with her shouting "Then go! Go away as you always do and leave us to our misery!" and I covered my ears. I hated her then. I hated her tears and scrunched-up face, her clenched fists as Papa stormed from the house. I feared he might never come back because of her. She didn't see that he left because he had to—her love was like smoke without flame. It left him nothing to breathe.

Still, I always waited for Papa, though this last time he left, a gossip in Lorraine eventually spotted him and the news winged its way to our village: Albert Chanel was working in a tavern and had been seen with a woman—a harlot. I didn't know what a harlot was, but Maman did. She went cold. Her tears dried. "He is a bastard," she whispered.

Packing up our meager belongings, she brought me, my two sisters, Julia and Antoinette, and my brothers, Alphonse and Lucien, here to Courpière, where her three widowed aunts clucked their tongues and said, "We warned you, Jeanne. We told you, the man is no good. His sort never are. What will you do now? How will you support this tribe he's left you to raise?"

"Papa is coming back," I yelled, rattling their chipped teacups. "He *is* good. He loves us!"

"This child is a hoyden," Maman's aunts declared in unison. "She has his bad blood. No good will come of her, either."

Coughing and clutching a cloth to her mouth, Maman sent me out to play. She grew thinner by the day, vanishing before my eyes. I knew she was sick but I did not want to admit it. I glared at the aunts and marched out, as I had seen Papa do so many times.

Mesdames les Tantes stayed away after that. But when Maman's cough settled in her chest and she could no longer work as a seamstress's assistant, they crept back into the house. They overran everything, turned everything black, and saw Maman to her bed, from which they said she would never rise again.

"Will Maman die?" asked my sister Julia. She was thirteen, only a year older than I was, but perpetually frightened by the winter winds that gnawed the village, by the clatter of carts splashing mud on our ragged skirts and the suspicious glances of the townsfolk. But most of all, she was afraid of death, for what would become of us, left alone in the world with les Tantes, who had watched in pitiless silence as our mother wasted away?

"She won't die," I said. Maybe if I said it, it would be true.

"But she is very sick. I heard one of les Tantes say she's not long for this earth. Gabrielle, what will happen to us?"

I felt a lump in my throat, like the stale bread Maman gave us when there was nothing else to eat. She would send me to the baker with the few centimes she had saved but told me not to beg, for we had our pride. Still, the bread the baker gave me was always hard.

This lump was like that. Swallow, I told myself. I must swallow it.

"She will not die," I said again, but a sob escaped Julia as she looked over her shoulder to our sister Antoinette, only five, happily tugging weeds from between the tombstones. "They will get rid of us," she said, "send us to an orphanage or worse because Papa is never coming back."

I bolted to my feet. I was too thin, as les Tantes often scolded, an urchin who looked as if she'd never had a full meal—as if such a feat were something Maman could conjure up like the miracle of the fishes and the loaves. Grabbing up one of my dolls, I shook it at Julia. "You must never say that. Papa *is* coming back. You will see."

Julia squared her narrow shoulders. It took me aback, the abrupt defiance in her, for though she was the eldest, Maman always said that Julia was too timid. "Gabrielle," she said somberly. "This is no time for make-believe."

No time for make-believe . . .

My sister's words echoed in my head as we trudged back to our house, summoned by one of the aunts yelling from the garret window.

In the parlor, the faded drapes were drawn and the table swept clean of the stuff of Maman's work—the bobbins, needles, and half-cut patterns for gowns she made for others, but could never afford for herself. The aunts had laid out our mother's corpse.

"Her suffering is over . . . Her pain is no more . . . Our poor Jeanne is at peace." One of the aunts beckoned with her claw. "Come, girls. You must kiss your mother good-bye."

I froze in the doorway. I couldn't move as Julia went to the table and leaned over it, setting her lips on Maman's purple mouth. Antoinette began to wail. In the corner, six-year-old Lucien banged his tin soldiers together, while nine-year-old Alphonse stared in bewilderment.

"Gabrielle," les Tantes said. "Come here this instant." Their voices flapped around me like ravens, swooping and pecking. I stared at my mother's body, her hands folded on her chest, her eyes shut and sunken cheeks like wax. Even from a distance, seeing her like that made me think that when people said the dead were at peace, they lied.

The dead didn't feel. They were gone forever. I would never see Maman again. She would never stroke my hair from my brow and say, "Gabrielle, why can't you keep your braids neat?" She would never check on us in our bed to make sure we were warm at night, never come trudging up the stairs with her baskets and give sugar cakes to keep the little ones happy so Julia and I could help her with her work. She would never again show me the difference between a slip stitch and a blanket stitch, never laugh in her quiet way when Julia sewed the edge of her own skirt to the garment she was supposed to be mending. Maman was gone and we were here alone, with the aunts and her body, without anyone to comfort us.

I whirled around and ran. I heard les Tantes shouting behind me, banging their canes on the floor. Lucien joined Antoinette's chorus of cries, but I did not look back. I didn't stop, flying down the staircase and out the door, running until I was back in the cemetery. I dropped to my knees before the tombstone where I'd left my dolls. I wanted to cry. I had refused to kiss my mother good-bye, so I must cry for her, to let her know I had loved her.

But no tears would come. Kicking my dolls aside, I crouched against the tombstone and waited as dusk fell, staring toward the dusty road that led from the village.

Papa would come. He must. He would never abandon us.

II

Three days later, Papa arrived and we gathered in the shabby parlor at the same table where Maman's body had lain. He'd missed the funeral—"My job, I had things to do," he explained as the aunts clucked—but he was here now, and I clung to his hand, inhaling the smell of his sweat and tobacco. He had come to us just as I said he would, and we were safe.

"What shall you do now?" les Tantes declared. "With a wife in the ground and this tribe she's left for you to raise on your own?"

Papa was quiet for a moment before he said, "What do you suggest, mesdames?" I jolted in my chair beside him. "I have my job at a tavern," he added, "with no room for children."

"A tavern," said one of the aunts, "is no place for children, room or not. Aubazine is the only place. Let them gain the skills to support themselves and avoid their mother's fate."

As I saw the scarce color drain from Julia's cheeks, I realized this Aubazine must be an orphanage, or worse. "But we are not orphans," I protested, and I took pleasure in les Tantes' horrified expression. They didn't care about us. They wanted us gone, but Papa would not let them. He would show them how wrong they were.

I turned to my father. "Papa, tell them we must live with you." I heard an imploring note in my voice that I tried to hide. But he didn't seem to know what to say. Then he muttered, "Gabrielle, the grown-ups are talking. You must trust we have your best interests at heart."

We? I stared at him.

He went on: "Aubazine, eh?" He was looking over my head toward the aunts, lined up like my childish dolls in the cemetery. "And you think the nuns will . . . ?"

"Absolutely," they replied, with determined bobs of their chins. "They cannot do anything else. The holy sisters of Aubazine have devoted themselves to such a cause."

"Hmm." Papa's grunt sent a shiver down my spine. "And the boys . . . ?"

"There are always families to take in boys," said the aunts, and I clutched at my father's hand, seeing now the cruel resolution in les Tantes' eyes.

"Papa, please," I said, forcing him to look at me. "We'll be no trouble. We always sleep together, so we don't need extra room. Julia can take care of Antoinette and Lucien, and Alphonse and I can help you. We helped Maman all the time. I used to help her sew, and I . . . I did errands for her. I'm good at it. I can work for you. We'll be no trouble at all," I repeated, speaking faster as I noticed a distance in his eyes that made my heart pound.

He took his hand away. Not with harshness. His fingers just unraveled from mine, like poorly spun threads. I was holding on to emptiness—it felt as if he had already gone as he said quietly, "I cannot. There is no room."

He stood. As I gazed up at him, frozen on my chair, he turned to the door. I lunged to my feet, running to him, trying to catch hold of his hand again as I cried, "Please don't leave us!"

He cast a vague smile over my head at my aunts as he carefully avoided my grasping fingers. "Mesdames," he said, "you will see to it, yes? The necessary clothes and the rest of it."

The aunts nodded in agreement. He looked down at me. *"Mon petit choux,"* he murmured. He ruffled my hair before he walked out. I couldn't move, hearing his footsteps fade down the stairs. Behind me, one of the aunts snapped, "She has no shame. Defiant till the end."

I didn't wait. Before they could swoop over to grab me, I bolted after Papa. But when I ran into the street, I didn't see him anywhere. I spun about, searching for his figure striding away, clapping his hat to his head.

He had disappeared, as though he'd never been here at all. The world darkened around me. I suddenly felt cold all over. In that moment, I realized Julia had been right.

The time for make-believe was over.

III

Les Tantes wouldn't let me leave to look for him, coming downstairs to haul me back up to the garret, kicking and struggling, locking the door and ordering us to pack our belongings. They pulled out the tattered cloth valise we'd used so many times before, and flung it open on the bed.

"I will not," I told them. "I hate you. My mother is dead because of you. You killed her."

Even as Julia whispered, "Gabrielle, please stop," I glared at the aunts until one of them spat out, "If you don't do as we say, we'll give you to the ragman. Would you like to spend your days sorting through trash? You told your father you knew how to work. So, go. Work."

My brothers cowered in the corner. Julia tugged at my arm. "Gabrielle," she implored, "come. Let's pack. It won't take long." Turning my back on the aunts as they gathered about the table to watch us, I sorted through the few items of clothing I had, makeshift articles darned and patched by Maman so they would last longer.

The next morning, a stranger arrived—an old man in a beret with a cigarette clamped between his teeth. We barely had a moment to hug Alphonse and Lucien farewell before the aunts hustled us into the man's cart, where he told us to sit in the back, on a pile of hard burlap sacks of flour.

"Stay still," he ordered, and I saw one of the aunts ladle coins from a purse into the man's hand—a small tapestry purse I recognized as my mother's.

The cart jolted forward. Julia gathered Antoinette against her as the man cracked his whip over his bony mule's back and led us onto the rutted mountain road. We jostled and clung to each other. Whatever was left of my courage withered inside me. Finally, toward dusk, the cart turned onto a dusty path and brought us before a set of stout wooden gates in a high wall.

I barely saw the stone tower or ring of buildings beyond, so alarmed was I by the sight of a flock of women in black habits and white wimples. As the man unloaded the sacks of flour for them, the nuns brought us inside, separating us in the courtyard. Julia and I were led to one wing, while Antoinette was taken to another, for she was still a child, the nuns said, and must reside with the other children.

Julia was ashen with fatigue. "We don't belong here," I said to her, and one of the nuns accompanying us turned her face to me to murmur, "In a perfect world, no child does. But this is where you are, and in time, you will adjust."

She took us into a dormitory where a hundred faces like ours turned to stare at us. I clenched my fists. "It's only for a short time," I announced, though nobody asked. "Our papa is coming for us, you'll see."

Julia shushed me. "Gabrielle, stop saying that."

I cried when the candles were blown out and the vast room swelled with the snores and sighs of the others, stuffing my head under the pillow so no one could hear. By day, everywhere I turned, I saw only black or white and shades in between, the black of the nuns' habits, flowing as if they glided on air, and of our uniforms, plain and sturdy. The starched white of linens, piled in cupboards or stretched taut on our narrow cots, glimmering like halos on the nuns' headdresses; and all the grays, shifting in the light on the flagstone floors and in the monotone voices of those charged to watch over us.

In those first weeks, I was miserable. I missed my brothers and the upheaval of being tumbled together. I missed Maman. It had been a rough-and-tumble life, but I still missed it.

"We're safe," Julia said one night. "Don't you see? Nothing bad can happen here."

I didn't want to see. I couldn't accept it, because if I did it meant Papa was truly never coming back. It meant he had abandoned us.

"It's awful," I said. "I hate it."

"No, you don't." Julia reached across the space between our cots to squeeze my hand. "Isn't it better we're here? What would we do, alone in the world, with no one to care for us?"

I turned away. "Just try," I heard her say. "You are the strong one; Maman always said she depended on you. Promise me you will try, Gabrielle. Antoinette and I need you."

I loved my sisters and so I did try. In the next weeks, I did my utmost to smile and be attentive, waking before dawn to the clamor of bells to trudge up the steep staircase and over the river-stone pathway into the chapel to hear prime. Then we were taken to the dining room for breakfast, followed by lessons, lunch, and afternoon chores, until we returned again to the chapel for vespers, back to the dining room for dinner, and to bed when it fell dark only to rise at dawn and do it all again. Nothing exciting ever happened, but as time wore on, nothing bad happened, either. No aunts came to scold; no landlords banged on the door to demand the late rent. All of a sudden, for the first time in my life, I knew where I was supposed to be and what was expected of me. I had a routine, unchanging and monotonous, but also surprisingly reassuring.

And as the weeks turned to months, without realizing it, Aubazine became my home.

It was the first place I had lived where everything was clean—astringent purity in the lye soap we bathed with every morning, in the sprigs of rosemary freshening the linens, and in the lime wash water for scrubbing the cloisters. No mice scurried behind peeling walls, no lice or fleas infested our hair and sheets, no dirt from the street seeped through broken windows or under doors. In Aubazine, life might be uneventful, regulated, and predictable, but it was pristine.

I marveled at how much I could eat. We had three meals a day—hot porridge and soup; fresh goat cheese and warm bread from the ovens; fruits and vegetables from the gardens; salty hams and roast chickens; and at Christmastime, sweet raisin pudding. I couldn't get enough; I had to learn to disguise my hunger as I did my discontent, fending off offers of friendship and cleaving to Julia, who said, "See? It is nice here."

It *was* nice, much as I didn't want to admit it. It was also a challenge. Because we had moved so much, our education had suffered. I discovered I had no aptitude for lessons, not like Julia, who filled her notebooks with precise letters that made mine look splotchy. The nun who oversaw our class, Sister Bernadette, had me stay an extra hour every day, though I always felt as if my hand had extra thumbs.

"You must apply yourself, Gabrielle," Sister Bernadette remonstrated. "You don't like to write so you don't make the effort. We must always try, if we are to succeed."

Try, try, try: it was all anyone said to me. It unsettled me because I'd gone from being the strong one, as Julia claimed, to someone who didn't seem to be good at anything.

Reading, however, entranced me. After I mastered children's fables and began to read more, I haunted the convent library, sifting among the tomes. Books took me to places I'd never imagined and I devoured every one I could, from the laments of saints to the tales of heroes and myths. I even began to enjoy the twice-daily procession to the chapel because the designs in the pathway were so interesting, obscure symbols linked to the convent, such as the five-pointed star. But like my lessons, prayer itself was a torture.

Closing my eyes, I tried to talk to God. I asked Him if Papa was coming back and if I would see my brothers again. I wanted to feel Him. The nuns kept telling us, God hears you. He listens when you pray. But I never felt anything but the hard wood kneeler under me. No matter how much I tried, all I heard was my own voice, echoing inside me. I peered about at the other girls to see their faces lifted as if to heaven, full of trust. Julia seemed transported to somewhere else, as if God spoke directly to her.

Why didn't I feel this same comfort? Why did God ignore my prayers? I searched for a way to prove my worth. I began to see that in their orderly world, the nuns valued those who applied themselves with a minimum of fuss, in particular those who could sit still for hours monogramming articles for other women's trousseaus. The sisters of Aubazine excelled at sewing and were paid for the work, which helped fund the orphanage.

Oh, the endless in and out of thread and needle! I imagined heaps piling up to the rafters, all the sheets and pillowcases, stockings and pinafores, petticoats and smocks. How could there be so much need for so many things? Yet it never ceased, like water pouring over a mill. I stopped feeling my callused fingers and pinpricks on my hands, attacking each new task, each day, with a ferocity that Sister Bernadette wished I would show in my grammar. Only here could I excel. Maman had often said I had a sure hand for sewing.

One day, I was given an entire sheet to hem. At the end of the day, Sister Thérèse, who supervised the workroom, walked up and down the aisles to inspect our work. She paused, took up my folded sheet. "Such fine stitches. Who taught you to sew like this, Gabrielle?"

"My mother. She was a seamstress. I used to help her sometimes."

"I can see that. You're quite skilled. How old are you now?"

"Nearly fourteen, Sister." As I spoke these words, I startled myself. How had the last two years passed so quickly?

She reached out to examine my hands. "You have small hands. Perfect for sewing." She smiled at me. "If you continue to improve, you could be a mercer's assistant one day or perhaps even a seamstress yourself, with your own shop. Would you like that?"

I had never thought of it. To me, being a seamstress meant my mother's lot, mending other people's clothes, paltry work that never earned enough. Now that I had decent food every day, I never wanted to be hungry again. But to have my own shop . . .

"Yes, Sister," I said quietly. "I think I would like that."

"Good. I'll have you embroider a handkerchief next time. A good seamstress must be knowledgeable in every aspect of her trade." She gave me a stern look. "That means grammar and math, too, so I'll expect you to heed your lessons with Sister Bernadette."

As she moved back down the aisle, I sagged in relief. If Sister Thérèse thought I might succeed in making my own way, perhaps I could.

I only became more determined as I saw Sister Thérèse shaking her head over Julia's pillowcase. My sister might be able to write, but those hands that were so skilled with a pen proved clumsy with the needle. As Julia gave me a dejected look from her seat, blond-curled Marie-Claire, who shared our dormitory and was a favorite with the nuns, always polite while ridiculing them behind their backs, hissed at me, "That stitch on your sheet is uneven. You'll never be a seamstress. You'll never be anything."

She resented me because I refused to join her circle of admirers and I despised her in return because she teased Julia mercilessly. I had tried to protect my sister, but as her hips widened and breasts sprouted (unlike mine, I was still as flat as a sole) so did the other girls' envy. While Antoinette lived in the children's wing, Julia was fifteen, practically a woman, and her beautiful features and timid air made her a target. Marie-Claire and her friends stuffed menses rags in her shoes and danced in circles around her, chanting that she was a bleeder, until I barreled into them and threatened to knock out their teeth.

I now examined the stitch Marie-Claire had mentioned. Fury suffocated me when I saw she was right; it was uneven. All of a sudden, I wanted to shred the sheet with my scissors but instead I leaned over to her and said, "I know what you do at night under the sheets. You'll grow up to be a harlot. They'll have to exorcise you like the devil sisters of Loudon."

Though I still didn't know what a harlot was, reading had taught me it must be dirty, and the horrified flush on Marie-Claire's face assured me of as much. I gave her a smug smile.

Marie-Claire wasted no time in telling Sister Thérèse: "Gabrielle Chanel is a beast. She says I'm possessed and called me a harlot."

"Gabrielle!" exclaimed Sister Thérèse and she marched me to the abbess's chamber.

"Is this true what I hear?" asked the abbess, a plump woman with a belt of keys affixed to her waist.

"Yes, Reverend Mother," I said, thinking that just as I had discovered my purpose, I was about to be cast out for my wickedness.

"Well, no proper lady uses words like that. And where did you learn such things?"

"The library, Mother. I . . . I like to read."

"'Read'?" echoed the abbess. She didn't realize that by now I could have recited the exploits of Charlemagne and the history of the convent from its founding by Étienne the Penitent to its desecration in the revolution, and I didn't want to boast, as that, too, would be improper.

"Do you read often, my child?" Her question was flat. I couldn't tell if she meant to encourage or ensnare me with my answer.

I lowered my eyes. How could I tell the truth, that reading was my escape because I had never asked to come here?

"Only so I may strengthen my faith," I finally murmured.

"I see." Relief softened her tone. "To seek God's truth is commendable, providing it does not lead to temptation. There can be no room for aspiration in a humble girl's heart. We must learn to submit always to our Almighty's will."

Her words were like wire, choking off my breath. If to aspire was a sin, did that mean I was doomed already? Had I not prayed to find something I was good at?

She dismissed me. "Henceforth, your access to the library is restricted; see that you read less and pray more. And no more talk of devils; do I make myself clear?" she added as I turned to the door. "You frighten the other girls. You must exercise moderation. It seems to me that you *think* too much, Gabrielle. You must learn to accept."

She might as well have asked me to yoke the moon with my rosary. But I took care from that day forth to appear penitent. Restrictions were often relaxed after a certain amount of time, and fusty Sister Geneviève who oversaw the library always nodded off after lunch at her stool. She never heard me as I tiptoed past with a book hidden under my pinafore. I read in corners when everyone else was in the courtyard, skipping rope. I read at night under my covers by the sliver of a candle stub that could have lit the dormitory aflame. I read at mass, pretending the book was a hymnal, risking my immortal soul. The other girls knew, but none dared tell on me. They knew what I had said to Marie-Claire. They, too, had secrets to hide.

All I needed to do was look.

SISTER THÉRÈSE GAVE ME a handkerchief as a test, showing me a pattern of camellia flowers from a book. "I want you to embroider this around the edges. Can you do that?"

I nodded, studying the pattern until I memorized its shape. Ignoring Marie-Claire's intermittent stares as she hemmed a smock, I threaded my needle and began to stitch the pattern into the linen. It was painstaking. I had only embroidered for my mother a few times, mostly easy motifs along sleeve cuffs, while this was intricate, with rounded corners that required precision. I made several mistakes that I had to undo; glancing up to find Marie-Claire smirking, I clenched my teeth. I was going to accomplish this if it killed me so I could wave it in her face. But once I finished the first camellia and Sister Thérèse came to look—"Oh, yes, Gabrielle, that is lovely"—I lost all sense of Marie-Claire and everyone else. The workroom with its rafter ceiling and white plaster walls, the large crucifix over the door and the rows of tables over which the girls bent, disappeared. It was only me with my needle, creating camellias as if by magic. When I looked up in a daze, I found I was the only one left.

As I stood, wincing at my sore buttocks from sitting for hours, Sister Thérèse rose from a stool in the corner. She floated to me, gathering shadows under her hem. "Are you finished?" she asked, and I nodded, suddenly aware I'd forgotten everything but what was before me, missing my prayers and, by the looks of it, dinner as well. Now she'd tell me I had failed her test, too.

She took up the handkerchief, turning it over to check the tiny knots of thread, then reviewed the pattern before she breathed, "Perfect," and to my disbelief, I saw tears in her eyes. "Just perfect, my child. Never have I had a girl here who can sew like you."

I didn't know what to say. Her praise was so unexpected that I could only look at the handkerchief in her hands and mutter, "It . . . it wasn't hard once I figured out how to do it."

"Not hard? It is one of the most difficult patterns I could find! The camellia is a blessed symbol of our order, grown in our very gardens, but few can reproduce it like this." She paused. Her next words were spoken so softly, I almost didn't hear them: "Does God speak to you?"

I met her gaze. Here at last was my opportunity, my chance to earn lasting reward. If I lied, I could become a novice and then a nun, immured and safe forever. But Sister Thérèse looked so eager that I couldn't bring myself to deceive her.

Without speaking, I shook my head.

She sighed. "It's not a punishment. God loves us all. He can't ask every one of us to serve Him. He needs us in the world, too."

Looking up, I whispered, "I am afraid." I had never admitted it to anyone, not even Julia. Fear had become my enemy because it might take root inside me and never leave.

Sister Thérèse smiled. "You needn't be. Don't you know we will see to your care even after you leave us? The most promising among you will be sent to other convents on your eighteenth birthdays, to perfect your skills in the hope that apprenticeships can be found. It is our duty. We do not want our girls to lose their way."

"You will?" I said hesitantly.

She nodded. "We will do all we can. You need not fear; I know it in my heart. A skill like this can save you, my child. God does indeed love you, Gabrielle. Never doubt it."

IV

On Sunday afternoons in the spring and summer, we were released past the locked gates into the countryside. I had never understood the reason for locking us in. There was nowhere to run; forests and the mountains surrounded Aubazine. With our allotment of two pairs of shoes and stockings, two chemises, a cloak, gloves, and a wool hat, and the one uniform we wore until it strained at the seams, where could we possibly go?

Still, the girls eagerly awaited the ceremonial unbolting of the gates. The noise was deafening as we tumbled into the fresh air with ecstatic cries no amount of chiding by the nuns could stifle, bounding to the summit overlooking the valley. Picnic baskets were uncovered, bread and cheese passed around. Even the nuns sat together to lift their shuttered faces to the sun.

It was during one of these excursions in late July, shortly before my eighteenth birthday, that Julia suddenly said to me, "You'll be leaving soon."

I glanced at her. We sat dangling our bare feet in the rushing waters of the river, which fed the convent's fishpond and now ran full with melting snow. It was the only time we were allowed to shed our stockings and shoes outside the dormitory.

"My birthday isn't until August. And if you haven't left by now, why would I?" In fact, I wondered why she hadn't. Her eighteenth year had come and gone in September and we both waited nervously for the day the abbess would summon her. But it hadn't happened.

"Have you decided to take the veil?" I added, not certain how I would feel if she told me she had. She seemed resigned to spending the rest of her days in Aubazine, but since my talk with Sister Thérèse, I wondered about life beyond these walls. Her reassurance about my skill with sewing had given me confidence, and though I still worried about my uncertain future, I was starting to anticipate the day when I could embark on it.

She sighed. "If only I could." She paused. "And you? Sister Thérèse is always praising your work. Even Sister Bernadette seems less demanding with you."

"Sister Bernadette has given up. She's resigned to the fact that I'll never learn proper grammar or penmanship."

"You haven't answered me, Gabrielle."

I met her stare. "No," I finally said. "I don't have a vocation, either. It's not for me." I was about to tell her what Sister Thérèse had said. For a reason I myself had not understood, I hadn't revealed her assurance that I could make a living. I realized why as Julia said, "They don't know what to do with me. I'm not good at sewing, so where can I go? If they let me out now . . ." Her voice faded. Like me, she, too, had apparently been worrying about the future. "But you," she said, with a tremulous smile. "You can do anything. You have a gift."

I burst out laughing. The sudden sound of it startled me almost as much as it did her. It made a raucous noise like my father's, too loud and coarse to have come from my narrow chest. Like the nuns, I didn't laugh often. "Honestly, Julia, where did you get such an idea? Just because I can turn a hem and embroider a pattern is hardly proof of anything."

"But it is." Her declaration was solemn, as it had been that day in the cemetery when our mother died. "You may not see it yet, or maybe you don't want to, but Sister Thérèse certainly does, and so does the Reverend Mother."

"Hah." I wiggled my toes; they were starting to freeze but I didn't want to pull them out. "The Reverend Mother won't allow me to use the library. She set me to extra hours of prayer and memorizing the Epistles. The last thing she thinks I have is a gift." Even as I spoke, I found myself waiting with unexpected breathlessness for her reply. Sister Thérèse had said I was more skilled than any other girl she had taught. Was that the same as having a gift?

Julia said, "The Reverend Mother only tries you because she knows you are different. She knows you question everything. And she knows you still sneak books out of the library."

"She does not!"

My sister arched her brow. "Sister Geneviève isn't blind. Everyone knows you read every spare minute you can find. That candle under your blankets isn't invisible, nor is the tent you make of your sheets with your knees to hide what you're doing."

"Well, at least I'm not doing what Marie-Claire does," I snorted.

Julia sighed again. "They'll send you to another convent, and from there you'll find a position. You won't end up like Maman. Or me."

I seized her hand in mine. "No matter what, I will never leave you or Antoinette. If you don't have a vocation, then we must find something else for you to do. And you mustn't let Marie-Claire or her friends push you around. They only do it because they think you are weak."

She looked at our entwined hands. "I am not like you, Gabrielle."

"Then you must learn to be. Everyone takes advantage of those who are weak."

The nuns called for our return. As girls slipped forth with rumpled skirts from climbing over the rocks, Julia and I gathered our shoes and stockings, and trudged down the hill to where the nuns awaited.

Joining the procession back to the convent, I said to Julia, "I don't know whether I have a gift or not, but I'll do whatever I can to see us safe."

"Yes," she said, without turning to me, "I have no doubt you'll try."

MY EIGHTEENTH BIRTHDAY DAWNED like any other day: the tolling of the bell tower waking us, the somnolent assembly to the chapel, the

breaking of our fast and dispersion to lessons and chores. As I sat embroi-
dering a pillowcase, I kept glancing at the doorway, expecting my summons
by the abbess. I was so distracted that I hardly paid heed to my work until
Sister Thérèse chided, "Gabrielle, what has gotten into you? Look at this
mess you've made. It's so unlike you."

Glancing at the cloth in my hand, I found a tangle of threads and
clumps.

"Unstitch it all and start again," Sister Thérèse ordered. "At once."

Since my triumph with the handkerchief, I rarely made a mistake.
When I did, no one was harder on me than myself, my compulsion for
perfection keeping me at my task until I succeeded; but all of a sudden, I
couldn't bear to sew anymore. "I don't feel well," I said. "The porridge this
morning hasn't agreed with me. May I be excused to use the privy?"

"Yes, yes, but do hurry back." Sister Thérèse waved me out.

Rushing into the corridor, I pulled at my high collar. I couldn't get
enough air into my lungs. Taking to the cloisters, I paced. I'd walked these
labyrinthine passages countless times, rounding the cloisters that circled the
fountain. The scent of white camellias from the gardens suffused the air. Everything was as familiar as my own body, down to the mosaics in the walkway,
so trodden upon during hundreds of years they were almost indiscernible.

For an inexplicable reason, today I paused to stare at the mosaics, trying
to make sense of the pattern, as if it might ease the simultaneous relief and
disappointment crushing me inside. The abbess had decided I wasn't ready.
As she had done with Julia, she intended to retain me here until I declared
a vocation or I was old enough to be evicted.

"They represent the number five."

I spun about, startled to find I was no longer alone.

"Didn't you know?" said the abbess, a wry note in her voice. "I thought
you'd read everything we had to offer by now and were fully aware of the
meaning of those figures."

I looked back at the mosaics. "Five?" Now, I saw the repetition, the
same five figures or five-pointed stars, duplicated over and over. "Why that
number?"

"Had you been paying as much attention to your catechism as you do to other matters, you would know it is our most holy number, the perfect embodiment of God's creation: wind, earth, fire, water, and, most important of all, spirit. Everything we see around us contains these five elements. Five is the most sacred number in the firmament." She motioned. "Come. I sent to the sewing room for you but Sister Thérèse returned word that you were unwell."

She didn't ask the cause of my discomfort. Following her in silence, my heart pounding hard in my ears, I had to stop myself from placing a hand to my chest to subdue it.

In her chamber, she pointed me to the stool before her desk. Once I sat, she paced to the window. She didn't speak for such a long moment, I began to fear she was going to confront me with my continued disobedience, ordering that I never set foot in the library again. Then she said abruptly, "I have welcome news. Though you may doubt His compassion, God has seen fit to look upon you and your sisters with favor."

She wanted me to take the veil. She had decided my life for me. Suddenly, the walls closed in around me. I was grateful for the care the nuns had given me, the stability and refuge, and the chance to discover myself. I had also accepted that my father was never coming for us, nor had he intended to. But I still had my sisters to support. I couldn't do it as a nun.

She turned around. "I wrote to your family. It took me some time to locate them, but they have returned word that they are willing to receive you."

"Family?" I echoed. "I have no family, Reverend Mother."

I meant it. Though I had long ceased to expect anything of Papa, I had not forgotten how my mother's sisters had sent us away, out of sight and out of mind, inconveniences for which no one wanted to assume responsibility.

"Oh, but you do." She retrieved a paper from her desk. "Your father's sister Madame Louise Costier has written to say she can place you and Julia with her own younger sister, Adrienne, in the boarding school at our blessed convent of Notre Dame in Moulins, near where the family resides. You can spend holidays with them and, in time, seek an apprenticeship that might lead to a permanent position."

Upon this announcement, she waited for my response. My hands clenched in my lap. It was exactly what Sister Thérèse had told me: the news I had been waiting for. But without even glancing at the letter the abbess held like a portent from heaven, I said firmly, "I do not know any Madame Louise Costier. You must have been misinformed, Reverend Mother."

Part of me deliberately refuted her, though I knew no one could fool the abbess. Another part of me had to see the evidence with my own eyes, for how could I have family willing to receive me? Where had they been these past seven years?

"I surely have not. You may not be aware of it, but your father's parents are alive and reside in a town outside Moulins. Louise is their eldest daughter; she assures me that had she known you and your sisters were here, she'd have come to visit you."

My nails dug into my palms. *Visit?* She would have come to visit but not take us in? I was right; I did not want to see her. As far as I was concerned, Louise Costier must be as bad as my other aunts, another heartless soul cut from the same unyielding cloth.

My anger must have shown, for the abbess said, "I see you are as contrary as ever. I do fear for you, as your nature is never to be satisfied. Yet Sister Thérèse assures me God sees past my concerns." She still didn't offer the letter, though by now I had to hold myself back from lunging up to tear it from her fingers. "You will prepare for your departure. Inform Julia of your good fortune and see that I hear no reports that you fill her head with these unseemly doubts. Am I understood?"

"Yes, Mother." I stood, not feeling my legs move. As I turned toward the door, I abruptly went still, overcome by the enormity of what had occurred. Once the convent gates opened to let me out, they would close behind me forever, unless I came back begging to take the veil. When I first arrived, all I had wanted to do was leave. Now that the moment was upon me, I hesitated. What if I failed? What would happen to me, to Julia and Antoinette? A needle was not much of a weapon; it certainly had not saved Maman. How could it save me?

I braved a look over my shoulder. Perhaps for the first time since I had darkened her threshold, the abbess detected that fear I kept tethered inside.

"What of Antoinette?" I asked.

"She, too, will go to Notre Dame in Moulins once her time here is over." The abbess paused. Her voice softened. "You must remember my warning, Gabrielle: There is no place for aspiration in a humble girl's heart. Sometimes, it's the simplest things we should most long for."

I left her at her desk, with the letter from an aunt I had never met still in her hand.

V

She was my reflection, a mirror image of my own self, if I'd been pampered since birth, enjoying the good fortune of not only two parents but also of a doting older sister with a loving husband—the genteel embodiment of what a girl should be.

Her name was Adrienne Chanel. I wanted to hate her at first sight.

She wafted out to welcome us after our three-day journey to Moulins and our new convent boarding school. I might have taken dismal note of another circle of walls, another spindly bell tower and grounds within double gates, had I not been riveted by her slim figure with its cloud of hair as black as my own. She acted as if she had known us our entire lives, greeting us with an embrace and a kiss on both cheeks, so that for hours afterward I smelled her lavender scent on me.

"How wonderful you're here at last," she declared. I watched her face with its thick-lashed eyes and wide mouth for any sign of hesitation. I could hardly blame her for not coming to our rescue, as we were the same age. She had been a girl when our mother died. Yet I found myself longing to find fault with her. "Now, we're together as a family and need never be apart again."

I saw Julia's entire person lean toward Adrienne's sun. I should have been relieved—for my sister had done little but utter terrified doubts about our future—but again, that unfathomable coil in the pit of my being, which I didn't yet recognize as envy, beset me.

Even if I had, I would have bitten off my own tongue rather than admit it. I'd never envied anyone. How could I now find myself longing to be like my gracious aunt?

In the weeks that followed, I could not escape her. As we were both eighteen, I had to bed in Adrienne's dormitory, which I soon learned was the place for "charity girls," while the exclusive dormitory in the opposite wing housed the daughters of respectable families who paid to have them educated. It was Aubazine all over again, with the same resentments and rivalries. And I knew I'd be a target because I was new, clearly impoverished, angry—in a word, *different*.

Adrienne cleared my path of obstacles without any apparent effort. "Pay no mind to them," she said as we walked to class with Julia at our heels. The rich girls with their preposterous bonnets and plump cheeks turned up their noses and said, "I smell roast chestnuts," alluding to our peasant blood. At Aubazine, I'd have whirled on them. However, Adrienne merely paused to regard them before she lilted, "Why, Angélique, such a fetching *capote* you have on." The recipient of this unexpected compliment flushed, embarrassed by her own cruelty as she muttered, "Thank you, Adrienne. Your sister Madame Costier made it."

"Did she really?" Adrienne smiled. "Well, it's enchanting. It suits you perfectly."

"Enchanting?" I said in disbelief as we walked on. "Why would you say such a thing? That bonnet didn't suit her in the slightest. She looks like a mule with a dead stork on her head."

Adrienne laughed. Even her laughter was sublime, its refinement truly differentiating us, despite our uncanny similarity of appearance. "Oh, Gabrielle, you are droll. She does look absurd, doesn't she? But we cannot always say what we think. What kind of world would it be if we all went around admitting our dislikes?"

"A better-hatted one?" I grumbled, though I had to admit she made sense. Her ability to win over even the most recalcitrant with her charm was a quality that I found not only maddeningly elusive in myself but also dangerously appealing.

At night after the doors closed on the dormitory and the girls settled into their various cliques, she glided to my bed to slide between my sheets. "Tell me a story," she whispered.

Unsettled by her proximity, I said, "What makes you think I know any stories?"

"Don't be coy." She reached over to pinch my nose. "Julia already told me you read everything you could in the library at Aubazine. You must know many stories."

Julia had been confiding in her. Why wasn't I surprised?

"All the stories I know are about martyrs or saints," I said, refusing to surrender to her enticement. "You've surely read the same yourself. There is a library here, as well."

"Oh, I never read if I can help it," she said, and I pounced on this admission of her ignorance with sheer delight.

"You don't read?"

"No." She reclined on our shared pillow, her hair draped about her face. "I don't care for books. I prefer to listen to stories; it is more exciting that way. I can hear the characters as if they're right there in front of me, on a stage."

My enthusiasm that I had uncovered a fault in her crumbled. "Well, I don't know any," I persisted, watching her from the corner of my eye as I'd watched the girls in Aubazine. "Does Aunt Louise actually make hats?" I finally asked.

"She doesn't make them," explained Adrienne. "She helps decorate hats for local mercers and tailors. In the busy season, she gets work from Vichy, because the shops don't have enough hands to get their orders completed on time. Have you ever been to Vichy?" she asked, and when I glowered at her, she nudged my ribs. "Don't frown so much. You'll get lines on your forehead and you really are quite pretty. Besides, you'll visit Vichy soon enough. Louise goes twice a year to deliver consignments and buy trimmings. I often go with her. You'll love it."

I barely heard her promise of a trip to Vichy. "You—you think I'm pretty?" I detested my own desperate question even as I braced myself for another of her offhand replies.

Instead, she righted herself on one elbow to stare at me. "I do. You have such fine, distinct features yet you don't look like anyone else."

"Julia says I look like you. She says we are more like sisters than she is."

"Does she?" Adrienne seemed genuinely surprised. "Well, there is a certain family resemblance, I suppose. How could there not be? Your father is my oldest brother! Of course we look like sisters. We have the same dark eyes and olive skin, and all this crazy hair." She gave a chuckle. "But that's only on the outside. Inside, I think we must be quite different."

Again, I was discovering Adrienne had unexpected facets to her personality.

She settled back against me. "I think you must find all this terribly provincial."

I was speechless. Had she forgotten I'd just left a convent in the middle of nowhere?

"What do you yearn to be when we leave here?" she asked. "We have only two years left. I think you should become an actress. Or perhaps a *grande cocotte*. Yes, that would suit you! You could go to the Opéra with pearls about your throat, and bring men to their knees with a mere glance of your bold black eyes."

I had to laugh. I couldn't help it. Pressing a hand to my mouth, I rocked the little bed with my stifled guffaws. When my mirth subsided, I found her regarding me patiently.

"I have no desire to be a—what did you call it?"

"A *grande cocotte*," she said. "A courtesan."

"Yes, well, I have no desire to be one or bring men to their knees. That, I should think, is something you could do well enough for both of us."

"Oh, no." She shook her head. "I only wish to marry for love."

So, she had a spark of foolishness after all. Marrying for love was a fantasy only the naive would indulge; even I knew that.

"I've always dreamed of meeting a man who will fall deeply in love with me," she went on, unaware of my scorn. "Someone handsome and gallant, not rich necessarily, or even of exalted birth—although that couldn't hurt—but kind and considerate, who wants to marry me because he cannot live without me."

"I see," I said dryly. "And does this gallant knight of yours have a name?"

"Not yet." She turned a smile to me. "But he will, I have no doubt. We will meet and—"

"He will bring you to your knees," I cut in, and when I saw her flinch, I added more gently, "Or you to his. In the end, it's the same thing. Or so I hear."

She brightened. "What about you? I told you my dream. Now you must tell me yours."

"I . . . I don't have any dreams," I said haltingly. "I only know I want to *do* something."

"Do?" she echoed, as though the notion was unfamiliar.

"Yes. Be someone." I hadn't ever contemplated such an idea before, hadn't even realized it skulked inside me, and I thought she would laugh at me, for my dream was even more ridiculous than hers. I was poor and female. Working *for* someone would be sufficient accomplishment, if I ever got that far.

But she appeared to consider me as if it was possible. "I think you will," she said at length. "I believe you can do whatever you choose. You simply require the opportunity."

"And opportunities are like stories in books," I retorted. "All we need do is pick one."

"I believe you just did. You want to be someone." She kissed my cheek before she folded back the covers to return to her own bed.

VI

Varennes-sur-Allier wasn't much of a village. I had known others like it in my childhood—a scrabble of whitewashed houses and shops huddled together, encircled by a road that exuded massive quantities of dust whenever a coach rattled past on its way to better places.

There was an ancient church near the travelers' inn and railroad station where Uncle Costier worked. In the village itself, surrounded by crop fields, men doffed their berets and black-clad widows eyed us as we made our way to Aunt Louise's house—a simple stone structure with a red-tile roof, reached by a pathway through a vegetable patch. In the doorway, a tidy woman waved to us. Her resemblance to my father, to Adrienne and me, was startling. Of course, she was Papa's sister, too, just as Adrienne was, so why did I feel this sudden urge to run away? Did I not want to be part of their lives? Deep inside, I did, but the reminder that these very people had not once come to find us stifled me. I had a thousand questions. Why had they left us alone? Did they have news of my father or brothers? Yet I said nothing. Aubazine had taught me to be guarded.

"Oh, my goodness, look at you!" exclaimed Tante Louise. "So like my brother Albert yet as petite as your mother. And you, Julia: why you're as lovely as a cameo." Kissing my sister and me on our cheeks, she swept us inside her home with its upholstered furnishings and cupboard displaying porcelain plate and silverware—clear signs that she'd married into a class higher than the one into which she'd been born.

She served tea with napkins, and little cakes with frosting. "Are you hungry, my dear? Go on, eat some more. Poor thing, you look half starved. Don't they feed you enough at the convent? They do? Well, then, you're not eating as you should. Look at Julia here, she's far more flesh on her bones. You're too thin. Now, let me see: I have this nice fresh bread and smoked ham. The ham was cured right here in Varennes! Come now. Eat some. No, more. Now, don't be shy. This is not the convent, my dear. Here, you may eat your fill."

With my stomach engorged, I was hurried into the parlor, a corner suited to feminine sensibilities. Here, there was a bit of a mess for such an otherwise neat household, baskets of multicolored trims, remnants of lace, and spools of ribbons strewn everywhere save for the woven-backed chairs. On the worktable were several bonnets in various stages of adornment, lined up like plump children awaiting inspection.

"Gabrielle has been dying to see these!" Adrienne said. "She's been so curious about how you make the *capotes*. I saw Angélique at the convent wearing one and Gabrielle has been asking about it ever since. She is quite determined."

An exaggeration, of course, but a clever one that caught Tante Louise's attention. She swerved her bright, birdlike gaze to me. "Is that so? Do you sew, my dear?"

"Yes," I mumbled, swallowing a belch that tasted of cured ham. "In the convent, I—"

Julia piped up, "She was the best seamstress in Aubazine. The nuns always praised her work. She can trim a handkerchief, mend a sleeve, or turn a hem so that it looks perfect, like new. Isn't that so, Gabrielle?"

I nodded uncertainly. Hearing my sister extol my skills made me uncomfortable.

"Oh, that is high praise, indeed," said Louise. "The nuns are notoriously hard to please. Such perfectionists! Would you like to work on a hat with me, my dear? Go on, don't be shy. Here, take this one." She thrust a bonnet into my hands. "It's not finished yet and I've so many to attend to before the season starts in Vichy." She directed an exasperated look at Adrienne. "I ask you, how hard can it be for those merchants to learn their own trade? By my word, they wait until the last minute, taking orders from all and sundry, they're so eager, and then they run about in a panic because they cannot be paid until the order is delivered to the customer's satisfaction and . . ."

Her babble of woes faded as I contemplated the thing she had set into my palms. It wasn't *finished*? To me, it looked as if it were about to grow legs and walk clucking into the garden, laden with carnation baubles, streamers, and sprigs of orange plume.

I became aware of the sudden silence, and glanced up to see the three of them watching me expectantly. The polite thing to do was say it was perfect and return it to its overdressed siblings. What did I know about hats? Yet I found myself staring at it closely, everything fading around me, disappearing, as it had in Aubazine when I'd toiled over camellias on a handkerchief. I reached out tentatively, as though the hat might squeal in protest, and plucked off the plume.

Better. But it still did not look right. Turning it around, I removed one of the streamers. Ah, much better. Now, the actual shape showed. With the palm of my hand, I flattened one bauble and wriggled the others off. Threads dangled now; searching the table, I found a pair of scissors and snipped them. *Now*, it looked like something a woman could wear.

After turning it around several times to assess it, I was satisfied. Its basic form couldn't be helped, for it was the ubiquitous lady's headpiece, with ribbons to affix it under the chin and a shallow depth intended to make it sit perkily on the head. Hardly ideal, but it worked for what it was. Turning around, I found my aunts and sister still staring at me. I thought I saw shock on their faces. A tremor went through me. I had just ruined a hat that Louise had no doubt worked on for weeks, ordered by a customer, entrusted to her by the milliner.

Louise gaped at me. Adrienne giggled. "See? I told you, she's quite determined."

"Yes, I do see." Louise's voice was tight. "Obviously, her talent is raw." She paused, inspecting the refurbished *capote* as if she couldn't decide whether to scold or applaud. "And these others . . . ? What would you do with them?"

"Nothing." I tried to force out a smile. "They're all lovely."

Louise gave me a searching look. "Please, don't humor me. What would you do?"

"Strip them bare and start again," I replied, without understanding from where my brazen confidence sprang.

"Why?" asked Louise, to my disconcertion. "Do you find them ugly, perhaps?"

I felt as I had in the abbess's chamber, cornered by a question with no easy answer. "Not ugly. But . . . uncomfortable. Do we really need to walk around with a basket of fruit on our heads?"

"A basket of fruit!" Louise let out a nervous chortle. "Oh my. I think we should start slowly. These bonnets are the latest style. It's the summer, after all. A hat must keep the sun off one's face and yet announce to the world that one is a lady."

And a lady must be seen coming from a mile away, I wanted to reply. Instead, I said quietly, "Why not use one or two pins, instead?"

"Pins?" Louise echoed.

"Yes. Hat pins. With simple stones, to set off the hat's shape without covering it up. It is still a hat. It should look like one. Shouldn't it?"

Louise turned from me to survey her hats. Excess was clearly her preference when it came to hats and food. Yet in her soul, she remained a frugal peasant of the Auvergne; and to her credit, and my astonishment, she turned to one of her cabinets and pulled out a drawer. She set it before me on the worktable. "Are these suitable?"

The drawer was filled with hat pins of every imaginable size and shape, some far too ornate to ever be noticed in an already overblown bonnet, but others that were less so. I selected a bone one with a fake blue sapphire. "May I?" I asked.

Louise stepped aside. I searched the hats for the least garnished and settled on a straw-braided boater with an azure band. Taking it up, I slid the pin through the band and then rummaged in the detritus around me for suitable adornment. When I found what felt right—a white linen flower that reminded me of the camellia of Aubazine—I took up needle and thread to attach it to the rim, nestling it against the side like a fallen bloom. "There. See?"

Adrienne didn't wait for her sister's verdict. Seizing it from me, she put the boater on and cocked her head, a hand at her hip. "Well? Does it suit?"

The consternation on Louise's face faded. "Why, it does. It does, indeed. It's so . . . different." She turned to me. "Where did you learn to do this?"

I shrugged. I didn't know, but I found myself echoing the abbess's words: "Sometimes, it's the simplest things we should most long for."

I hadn't meant to repeat the very phrase that had seemed more a warning than an encouragement. Nevertheless, as I viewed the boater on Adrienne's head, I realized that like the sheets, handkerchiefs, and other items I'd sewn in Aubazine, I was proud of this, too. It wasn't my choice of a hat, but I could wear it. I wouldn't be ashamed to be seen in it.

"I'm keeping it," Adrienne said. "I'll show it off next time we go to Vichy," and as Louise spluttered that the hat was already bought and Adrienne couldn't possibly be seen parading about Vichy in another lady's property, I looked past them to where Julia dawdled on a stool, nibbling on one of the frosted cakes.

Her smile needed no interpretation. I could hear her saying, "Didn't I tell you so?" as loudly as if she had shouted it out to the uncaring world.

For the first time since leaving Aubazine, I felt a stirring of hope.

Perhaps I did have a gift, after all.

VII

Moulins wasn't dreary compared with Aubazine. It boasted several taverns, cafés, and shops, and brigades of reserve officers were garrisoned outside town. I'd seen them on parade, marching down Moulins's one main street preceded by drumrolls and tinny trumpets—stalwart youths encased in epaulettes, braided waistcoats, and shiny leather boots.

There was also a boys' grammar school across the road from the convent. Every afternoon when the bells rang, the boys scampered out with their satchels slung over their shoulders, each one wearing the belted black overblouse with its round white collar, under which peeped shorts that reached just above knobby knees and high socks hugging skinny calves that looked like mine, their feet in tie-up ankle boots. I watched the boys from my dormitory window swaggering and shoving at one another, fascinated by their liveliness, their tugging at their colored ties and their yanking of hats from tousled heads as they raced down the lane, whooping like corsairs.

But I saw it only through a window. Girls couldn't go anywhere alone. We had to leave together in chaperoned packs, herded by the nuns, to various ceremonies in the church nearby and to sing in the choir for civic functions.

I liked singing. I liked the sensation of hearing my voice rise and imagining it was a bird taking flight, so that I could see all of Moulins and beyond, past the sedate villages, over the serpentine rivers to the waters of the Seine itself, dissecting the glamorous city of Paris.

To escape to Paris had become my obsession. The library of Notre Dame was much the same as Aubazine's, and I was weary of religious tracts. Through Adrienne—who encouraged my whim—I discovered a thriving black-market trade within the convent, a furtive exchange of cigarettes, ribbons, and gardenia-scented soap among the rich girls, who were willing to buy us articles we requested in return for our menial labor. So I ironed and mended their uniforms; I fetched water from the well and heated it in the kitchens, lugging it up flights of stairs to pour it into their copper tubs. In return, they brought me the only thing I desired: more stories.

Not actual books. These were too expensive and impossible to hide in the dormitory, which the nuns periodically swept through in search of contraband. Instead, I huddled under the covers at night to read serials published in Parisian newspapers, ongoing sagas that the rich girls had their mothers cut out and stuff into their weekly care packages, which I sewed into makeshift booklets that fit flat under my cot. Most were dreadful, high-strung tales of noble-hearted courtesans who perished of unrequited love or evil queens who poisoned their foes.

I enjoyed the queens more. Courtesans seemed to revel in suffering for suffering's sake, while the queens simply did what had to be done. Yet no matter how trite, even the worst stories had a kernel of truth to impart, illuminating the mysteries of the world. The more I read, the more anxious I became for my own life to begin. If I'd had the choice, I'd have walked barefoot to Paris, where anything seemed possible, even for a nobody like me.

In 1903, Adrienne and I turned twenty and were finally released. Julia, who had stayed two years longer than she should have, announced she had decided to reside with our grandparents and help them with their stall in the marketplace.

I was dismayed. I knew she had visited them. In the past few months, she had not accompanied me to Louise's house so she could make the trip to the town where they lived. She had even asked me to go with her, but I refused. Without my ever asking her, Tante Louise had confided that she made inquiries and found that our brothers Alphonse and Lucien had been given away to farmer families after we left for the convent, spending their childhood working in the fields. No one knew where they were now; my fury was kindled anew against all those who'd forsaken us. Tante Louise had made her amends, but she was the only one I cared to forgive. I admired Julia, for she was indeed stronger than she believed if she could care for the very people who had abandoned us. Personally, I had nothing to say to our grandparents. They were old now, settled in their ways, so I felt it best to remain at a distance.

"Why do you want to live with them?" I now asked my sister. "There's no future for you there. You'll grow old selling their vegetables."

"Where else can I go?" She sighed. "You know I don't sew well enough to take a job like you and Adrienne. I'll only be in your way. Besides, they cannot manage on their own. Antoinette can join me when her time comes to leave the boarding school; she will need a place to live and work. Louise also says she'll visit me often. You needn't worry about me anymore."

"But you and Antoinette can live with me!" All of a sudden, my anger boiled up. "Julia, you're always saying you're not good at anything, but how will you know if you don't try? Stay with me and we'll figure out the rest. *They* never cared about us. They never tried to see us!"

She smiled sadly. "Gabrielle, you only say that now because you must, but you know that in time, I'll be a burden to you. I am content to sell vegetables and tend to two old people. I don't blame them; what else could they do? We were children then, extra mouths to feed. Now I can be of use, so please, let's not quarrel. I want us to say good-bye like sisters." She kissed my cheek, holding me close. "Be brave," she whispered. "You are the strong one. You always were."

I found myself fighting back tears as she boarded the carriage to the village where my father's parents resided. I wanted to force her to stay, although I knew it was useless. Julia might not have my courage but she was as obstinate as any Chanel when she set her mind to something. I realized then, as the carriage pulled away, that I should have felt abandoned, as I had when we were left in Aubazine. But in truth, much as I despised myself for it, I felt only shameful relief.

Julia knew me better than I knew myself. She knew that becoming my burden would sour our love for each other, and that she could not bear.

As for Adrienne and me, the nuns and Louise had put their heads together and found us a position in Moulins in an establishment with the grandiose name of House of Grampayre, though it was only a modest lingerie and hosiery shop catering to local ladies and the garrisons. The proprietress, Madame G., as Adrienne and I dubbed her, repaired the usual assortment of women's apparel, as well as the torn, soiled *passementerie* of the officers' uniforms. In addition to our work, she offered us a cramped attic room near the shop that we could rent, she declared, "for a pittance."

That would have been fine had she not paid us a pittance of a wage. Her hours were tyrannical. From seven in the morning to nearly eight at night, we spent the entire time, save for a brief break for lunch, in an airless back room, sweltering over heaps of gowns with rent hems and split seams, cloaks that needed new buttons or linings replaced, and untold quantities of other wear and tear. Our backs ached constantly; at night, we huddled in our room over the tiny stove we tended with fearful obsessiveness, lest the fire got out of hand. After three months, I announced to Adrienne (who was becoming a shade of her former self) that we had to seek another means of subsistence. We couldn't go on like this, hoarding our weekly pay only to return it to Madame G. for rent, subsisting on the vegetables, cured ham, bread, and cheese that Louise gave us every Sunday, our one day off, which we spent traveling to and from her home.

"Other means?" Adrienne asked. "But Louise found us this post. How can we leave it?"

"I didn't say we should leave it," I replied, though as I rubbed my swollen knuckles I thought leaving it would be a blessing. "I mean, we have to find an extra income. I want to buy some plain hats that I can decorate and sell here. I think that if I have a few examples to show, and offer Madame G. a percentage of the profits, she might let me sell them."

I could think of no other solution. Although Tante Louise still adorned her *capotes* like centerpieces for a banquet, she had delivered the boater I had redone as is. She told me when the customer picked it up from the shop in Vichy, she deemed it "charming" and ordered two more in different colors, made from scratch. Louise set about instructing me on how to test an iron with a flick of spit to not scorch ribbon; how to pinch fabric between my thumbs to create a pleat or employ a board to fashion a drape; and other tricks of the trade that could turn something unremarkable into an article of beauty worthy of admiration—and money.

Money might not be something a respectable girl should strive for, as the nuns so often drilled into our heads, but it was a necessity and I had none. If I was going to make my way to Paris, I needed money—as much as I could earn.

"Oh, I couldn't possibly take on another job," moaned Adrienne. Our newfound independence was wearing thin on her; she often complained that perhaps she should accept her lot and move in with Louise, until I reminded her that if her prospects for meeting her knight were sparse in Moulins, in Varennes-sur-Allier all she would find was a goatherd with rotten teeth.

"What about auditioning at La Rotunde?" I suggested. We had gone to the pagoda-shaped coffeehouse overlooking the square on a few occasions, escorted by the young officers who flirted with us when they dropped off their torn coats or trousers for mending. It was not a genteel place; people went there to indulge in raucous sing-alongs led by chanteuses hired to entertain and ensure that the customers drank as much as they could. Or rather, the men drank while we sat beside them, hats firmly in place and chemises buttoned to our chins, demure and inaccessible. We might not have rich families, but never could we be mistaken for those brazen professionals who haunted the perimeters of the café, their bared shoulders swaying, though they were probably better paid than we were and could set their own hours.

"You want us to *serve* drinks?" Adrienne said, appalled.

"No, silly. To sing. We sang often enough in the convent choir and

we've been to La Rotunde enough times to know the repertoire by now."
Standing up and wincing as I banged my head on the eaves—we had to
crouch about the room like hunchbacks—I assumed the pose. One hand
on my bony hip and the other cocked somewhere near but not directly
upon my breast, I cleared my throat before I launched into my rendition of
"Qui qu'a vu Coco dans l'Trocadéro?"

"I've lost my poor Coco, my lovable dog," I sang out, "lost him, close
to the Trocadéro. He's far away, if he's still running. My biggest regret is
the more my man cheated on me, the more my Coco remained faithful.
You didn't happen to see my Coco? Coco near the Trocadéro?" I motioned
to Adrienne, who joined me in the refrain: "Co at the Tro, Co at the Tro,
Coco at the Trocadéro. Who has seen Coco? Oh, my poor Coco. Who has
seen my Coco?"

As the song faded, I flipped my wrist. "Well?"

"Awful," she said. "They'll throw pits at us and beg us to stop," and
we collapsed into laughter, easing the tension that sometimes grew taut
between us.

"But are we so awful they wouldn't pay?" I finally said, catching my
breath. I waited as a war of emotions played across her expressive face, another way in which we were different. Unlike me, Adrienne wore her heart
on her sleeve.

"No. Not so much so that they wouldn't pay. I've heard worse. I'm sure
they have, too."

"Then it's settled. We'll go tomorrow after work and apply. Just a few
evenings a week, until we save enough to buy my hats."

"If Louise or the nuns hear of it, they'll be outraged," Adrienne warned.
"La Rotunde is no place for a respectable girl. To go in company for an
aperitif, perhaps, but not to work."

"If we don't tell them, how will they ever find out?"

I went to sleep that night in blissful hope. I could do this, I told myself.
I wasn't born of peasant stock for nothing. Since fortune was dragging its
heels, I would lure it out with my hard work. Then who knew what I might
achieve?

But my plan didn't seem so easy once it was set in motion. La Rotunde's owner hired us on the spot, no doubt because we were fresh-faced girls straight out of the convent. On the night of our debut, I was so nervous I stammered out my Trocadéro song standing stiff onstage, as the patrons hissed and flung olive and cherry pits from their glasses at me, while Adrienne wove her way through the tables, tremulously holding out our empty purse.

I grimaced when I beheld our haul. "Less than three francs. That won't buy me a train ticket to Vichy, let alone a hat."

I practiced every night, roaming the attic and singing aloud as Adrienne shoved her head under the pillow, until I felt I had mastered the requisite sauciness and hand gestures. The next night, I did better, and the night after that. Within a few weeks, the owner graduated us to Friday evenings, when the crowd was composed of officers let out for the weekend from the barracks. That first Friday, I commanded the stage, and if my voice warbled on each high note, at the conclusion of the song I heard the unbelievable thumping of hands on the tables and enthusiastic shouts: "Coco! Coco! Coco!"

God save me, they demanded an encore.

I hoarded my savings in a tin hidden under the attic floorboards. When I realized I had enough, I told scowling Madame G. that Adrienne and I needed a few days off because Louise had taken ill. Then we boarded the coach to Varennes, as we couldn't afford the train.

At last, I was going to buy my hats.

VIII

Vichy was the first city I had ever seen—a resort town with wide boulevards, hotels, and casinos, patronized, Tante Louise explained, by wealthy visitors eager to partake of the famous healing waters of the spa. After breakfast in the cheap *auberge* where we slept three to a bed, we went with Louise as she delivered her completed wares to the various shops who hired her, then spent the afternoon perusing the shops for her gewgaws and my hats. I could buy only three, but I was as delighted as if I'd bought twelve. As the summer dusk settled over Vichy, Louise allowed us to take a stroll by ourselves while she rested her sore feet in our room, though she admonished us to not speak to anyone, especially men, or venture into any of the cabarets and alehouses that attracted the less respectable denizens of the city.

I'd never heard such a noise, never seen such hordes of people, all seeming to speak at once. Hooking her arm protectively in mine, Adrienne guided me down the sidewalks like a duchess surveying her palace, for she had been here before.

"Isn't it divine?" she breathed, her slim figure in a forest green, puff-sleeved shirtwaist jacket fitted to her waist and a tailored skirt with whale buttons running up the side (a creation made entirely by Louise out of scraps and remnants). "It's so civilized."

I had never been more aware of how isolated I had been in the convent. To me, Vichy was like a carnival ride, moving too fast for me to ever grab hold, and so I squared my shoulders and said, "It is a bit garish." As I spoke, we sidestepped a group of young officers lounging outside a café, smoking. They whistled as we passed, causing me to shoot a scathing look at them. Louts. I contended with dozens like them at La Rotunde.

"That seems to be your favorite word of late," said Adrienne. "But even you have to admit, it's also exciting. Don't bother lying to me; I can see it on your face. You've been staring at everything just like that elegant man behind us is staring at you."

I paused, and glanced warily over my shoulder. The officers clasped hands to their chests in mock swoons, crying out that they'd been pierced by arrows shot by a pair of heartless Dianas. But there was indeed an elegant man dressed in a brown velvet sack coat and cream-colored trousers with perfect creases, a gold watch chain dangling from his patterned vest. He held a bowler hat in his hand.

He did appear to be staring at me. In fact, he was smiling.

I whipped around to look away.

"Oh, look," giggled Adrienne. "You're blushing."

"I am not!"

"You are. You've gone red as a beetroot." She looked back, even as I hissed, "Don't encourage him!"

"He seems taken with you," she said as I tugged her forward, quickening our pace, mortified. "He's just being forward," I said. "He sees two girls out alone, and thinks we're . . ."

"*Grandes cocottes?*" teased Adrienne. "I told you no one looks like you. You've entirely won over the patrons of La Rotunde, no matter how badly you sing, and you attract attention here already despite that funereal ensemble you insist on wearing."

"I like black," I retorted. I'd copied the schoolboys from Moulins, belting my long blouse and pairing it with an ankle-length skirt, loose shirtwaist jacket, and collarless chemise. On my head, I'd donned a square sailor's hat with a black band; I'd filched a mother-of-pearl pin from Louise's drawer but rather than affix it to the hat, I'd inserted it in my lapel. I'd thought I looked smart, until we strolled down the boulevard and came upon the Vichy swans in their curvaceous skirts and matching jackets in shimmering jewel tones, their frothy hats crowning towers of upswept hair. I began to feel like a sorry little duckling. Not because I wished to look like them—I would never be able to move in such costumes—but because it occurred to me the dandy behind us must have been smiling at my feeble attempts to fit in.

"He's coming after us," said Adrienne, breathless with excitement.

I hauled her into the nearest establishment, another smoke-infused café.

"Order us something," I said, pushing her to the counter as she searched her small bag. We hadn't expected to buy anything. Only as she turned to me in desperation did I realize she probably didn't have money and I had spent all of mine on the hats. Then I saw her eyes widen.

I didn't need to look to know that the dandy had followed us inside.

"May I be of some assistance, mesdemoiselles?" he asked. He had a cultured, sardonic tone that betrayed the fact that he never found himself in a café with no money.

"Unless you care to buy us two coffees and cake, I think not." I meant to dissuade him with my sharp reply, for why should he waste his time on us when he surely could find other, more available women?

Instead, he smiled, revealing well-kept teeth under his groomed mustache. "I'd be delighted." He moved past Adrienne to the counter. She raised an anxious eyebrow at me. I shrugged. Let the cad buy us a snack; it wasn't as if we were doing anything indecent. But I could see her already quivering over the potential consequences of my rash invitation. Hadn't Tante Louise forbidden us to talk to, much less drink coffee with, a stranger?

"Shall we?" He pointed to an empty marble-topped table. He also drew out each of our chairs and waited until Adrienne and I had sat before he slid us forward to the table.

Though I took pains to hide it, I was impressed.

As the waiter served our coffee, I took advantage of the moment to inspect him. I noted at once that he must be wealthy: he had small manicured hands with perfect nails, and his topcoat alone cost more than Adrienne and I earned in a year. He was not handsome. Up close, he had a distinct smell of strong cologne that I disliked, and a long face with rounded cheeks, a prominent nose, and thin lips. His close-set brown eyes, though, gleamed with intelligence. I had seen his sort before at La Rotunde, though not often—a man of means, out on the town in search of illicit entertainment.

If he thought coffee and cake would gain him entrée, he was mistaken.

"Allow me to introduce myself," he said as Adrienne sipped from her cup with almost frantic haste and I deliberately left mine untouched. "My name is Étienne Balsan and I believe we have—"

"Balsan!" Adrienne almost choked on her coffee.

He smiled. "You have heard my name perhaps, mademoiselle?"

"No, I . . . I mean, yes, of course, I have, but I . . ."

I stared from across the table. What had gotten into her? It wasn't as if he was the Marquis of Richelieu.

He nodded, running one of his manicured hands through his fine light auburn hair (it was thinning on top, I noted) before he turned his gaze to me. "As I was about to say, I believe we have met before."

"We most certainly have not," I answered. Adrienne kicked me under the table. I forced out a terse smile. "What I meant to say was, we have not because I would remember you."

"Oh?" He leaned back, his cup held with precision, his little finger curled. "You would?"

"Gabrielle," said Adrienne, "this gentleman is—"

"Yes," I interrupted, without taking my eyes from his. "I would. And I have never seen you before in my life, begging your pardon, monsieur."

"My pardon?" He chuckled. "Oh, I think it is I who must beg yours, mademoiselle. You see, I fear I've mistaken you for a lovely chanteuse named Coco who has been entrancing the crowds at La Rotunde in Moulins. I'd hoped that you were her so I might congratulate you, as I find her interpretation of *'Qui qu'a vu Coco dans l'Trocadéro?'* the most delightful I've heard." He drank from his cup. "You must hear it sometime for yourself. She has exquisite talent."

I felt my embarrassment turn my cheeks red; taking my cup, I sipped the dark coffee and scalded my tongue. He smiled again, extending the plate of almond cakes to Adrienne. Was he mocking me on purpose? I couldn't tell, but whatever he intended I didn't care for his manner, and was about to tell him as much when Adrienne suddenly burst out, "You have not mistaken her, Monsieur Balsan. She is Coco from La Rotunde."

"She is?" He feigned shock. "But how can this be?"

With an artificial gaiety that made me want to strangle her, Adrienne said to me, "Do tell him the truth, Gabrielle. Don't be cruel. He has heard you sing and praised you for it."

"Not to mention paid," he added. "I always tip very well."

I set my cup back on its saucer. I would not insult him, since it was obvious he was indeed rich but I knew that because he'd seen me in a music hall, he assumed I had loose morals.

"And I sing well for tips, too," I said, "as you yourself have declared. Or would you have me give away my exquisite talent for free, monsieur?"

Adrienne sat with her mouth agape. To my surprise, he said softly, "Touché, mademoiselle. I regret to have caused you offense."

"No offense," I said. I retrieved the last three cakes on the plate and folded them into my handkerchief, then stood. "It has been a delight, monsieur, but I'm afraid we are expected elsewhere. We thank you for your hospitality and bid you good evening."

He stood at once, bowing. "The delight has been all mine, mademoiselle."

"I'm sure it has." I smiled at Adrienne. "Shall we?"

She stumbled up from her chair, a faint trace of coffee on her upper lip as she quavered, "Excuse us, monsieur. We are indeed late and we—"

I turned to the café entrance without looking back, though I had to hesitate at the doors until I heard Adrienne rush up behind me, heels clattering. Once we were outside, I strode down the boulevard to the *auberge*, not stopping until she grasped my arm and pulled me to a halt.

"Gabrielle, are you mad? Do you realize who he is?"

"I do. He is Étienne Balsan and he assumes too much for an alleged gentleman."

She gripped my arm tighter. "Étienne Balsan and his brothers are heirs to one of the largest fortunes in France. His family owns factories in Lyons; they produce all the wool cloth for military uniforms. Why, they practically own the town of Châteauroux and have any number of exquisite châteaux. He is not any alleged gentleman, Gabrielle. He is a very rich one!"

"Just because he's rich doesn't mean he has any decency. You heard what he said, about how well he tipped. I am not one of those women; I do not sell more than my songs."

Adrienne released my arm and took my hand in hers, uncoiling my clenched fingers to set a cream calling card with embossed lettering between them.

"Here is his card," she said. "He must be mad, too, because he wants to see you again. He said you are as irrepressible as he could expect and will call on us in Moulins next week." I looked at her, silent, as she added, "I suggest you be less rude when he does. Men like him do not come around often. You never know where an acquaintance like this might lead."

I almost said I had a very good idea of where Balsan wanted it to lead but held my tongue. Adrienne still nurtured her silly dream of marrying some knight, while I doubted anyone besides the butcher's son would ever see us as more than playthings.

It was the summer of 1904.

Though I pocketed his card and promptly forgot him, I had just met my savior.

IX

Étienne Balsan did appear at the shop, sending Madame G. aflutter when he delivered several shirts for repair—though I didn't find a single rip or tear on them and thus was not swayed. Nevertheless, he persisted on calling on me after work to take me on carriage rides, strolls about the square, and suppers. He often brought his well-heeled friends, sons of affluent families who, like him, served in the military—though, unlike him, they were eager for war to break out with the Prussians or Germans.

Balsan smirked as they stamped their boots and declared that only in war could a true gentleman prove his mettle. "They wouldn't know a cannon from a trumpet until the Huns were upon them," he said, leaning to me. "Such fools does money breed."

Despite my misgivings, I found his dry wit amusing. But I was not attracted to him. He did not press his advantage, either. We passed the next months in a whirlwind of drinking and dining, with Adrienne and I eating better than we ever had, squired about town by some of the barracks' most eligible bachelors. One in particular, Baron Maurice de Nexon, became enraptured with Adrienne and she reciprocated his interest, for he met all of her qualifications for knighthood. But she had several others panting at her heels and her sudden popularity kept me up until dawn in our room as she anxiously deliberated over whom she should most favor.

I also gained my share of attention. My doubts over my looks began to diminish as I heard such fervent declarations from Balsan's friends that I was almost tempted to believe them. But I did not, having developed a well-honed suspicion of flattery. With a carefree laugh, I brushed aside these scions of the high bourgeosie even as I toiled in the House of Grampayre and sang several evenings a week at La Rotunde. I refused to be seen as another impoverished seamstress, willing to forgo her virtue for a rich man's bed. Every centime I earned went into my tin under the floorboard. I also continued to decorate my hats, though Madame G. refused to sell such "atrocities" in her shop and I had to wear my creations myself, hoping in vain to attract notice from some milliner.

Balsan attended my nightly performances. I had only to peer out through the layer of smoke over the crowded tables to find him at his spot near the stage, his legs crossed to reveal his exquisite Italian-made boots, sometimes in his pressed blue uniform with its epaulettes and sash, other times in a tailored suit, but always with a smile on his lips.

Afterward he would take me out for a late supper. It was during these intimate evenings that I began to learn about him. He told me of how he'd been sent to an exclusive boarding school in England where he developed a passion for Thoroughbred horses and demonstrated singular disregard for his studies ("I sent a telegram to my family from my dog Rex, advising them that I'd failed all my courses," he laughed). Later, he rebelled against the expectation that upon his father's death, he'd assume a position in the family cloth business.

"I only enlisted in the military because of my uncle," he explained as we lingered over coffee. "He said that breeding horses is a hobby, not an occupation, and I must support our name with some accomplishment. Oh, how I hated hearing that," he sighed, lighting a cigarette and passing it to me. Having noticed how the other chanteuses at La Rotunde employed cigarettes to make themselves appear seductive (and how their artful blowing of smoke rings earned them extra tips), I'd trained myself to master the vice, enduring the burn in my lungs and coughing until I could do it with ease. Adrienne despised it, calling it a filthy habit, but I had made more money because of it. Men loved seeing a woman with smoke coming out of her nose, for some reason.

"I hate military service," Balsan went on. "I first enlisted in the foot regiment, which was intolerable. I wanted to be with horses, so I had myself transferred to the cavalry instead—if I must serve my family name, let it serve me, as well—and was dispatched to Algeria to the African Light Cavalry, which was boring, unbearably hot, and boring."

"You said twice that it was boring," I remarked.

"Did I?" He rolled his eyes. "That's because it was. I was so bored, in fact, that I ended up sleeping while on duty and was thrown into lockup. But then our horses began to suffer from a skin ailment the veterinarians couldn't cure. I made a pact with my superior. If I could treat the horses successfully, they would transfer me to a post in France. I distilled an ointment used in England for such ailments. I had no idea if it would work, but it did, and so here I came, to the Tenth Light Horse of Moulins—which, I might add, was as boring as Africa until I met you."

I feigned a careless smile, though his story fascinated me. That he'd forgone a lucrative post in his family business to indulge in his obsession for horses and challenged his uncle's expectations—it made my head spin. I, who had nothing, with no name to speak of, found his contemptuous disregard of his advantages both shocking and intoxicating.

"As soon as I've completed my service," he said, "I'm going to do as I please. I am twenty-six and my inheritance is mine; my uncle can't take it from me, no matter how much he threatens. I'm going to buy a château and breed the best racing horses this country has seen. I don't care what anyone thinks. We have one life. I intend to live it by my rules."

Although I still did not find him particularly attractive, my feelings toward him deepened in ways I could not explain. Perhaps because I had never met anyone like him, his brazen confidence and nonchalant air burrowed inside me until I found myself eagerly awaiting his arrival, the rest of my existence taking on a grayer hue when he was not there.

Adrienne probed me about him. "Has he expressed his intentions?" she asked as we lay tumbled on our cot, having spent the night dancing with Balsan and his friends. "I see how he looks at you. He watches you every moment. He doesn't seem to care that you sing in the café or mend petticoats. Do you think he might love you? Has he tried to kiss you yet?"

I felt her trembling; I had the impression she had already been kissed more than a few times. Her questions only roused my anxiety, for Balsan had not so much as touched my hand. He had reason, even if I did not afford him opportunity. He must know that others in his circle had tried in his stead; I was also young and pretty enough, if not beautiful, to entertain several admirers, as Adrienne did. Yet I did not want to. I had no interest in those boastful men. Balsan was the only one who appealed to me, so why did he not stir any of the feelings I had heard Adrienne go on and on about with her baron?

I wondered if there was something wrong with me. I had never wanted to belong to any man save my father. Had he imparted such a harsh lesson that I could not bring myself to rely on anyone? Did I not want to get married and have a family of my own? Adrienne had made it her entire reason for living, but I—I felt none of those yearnings, though surely these were the only acceptable ambitions for girls like us.

"Balsan and I are just friends," I finally said, and I turned away, silencing her questions.

But I soon found myself watching Balsan as much as he watched me, for a sign that I meant more to him than a casual dalliance. He asked me about my past, expressing an interest that made me more insecure, for when gentlemen did that, Adrienne had said, it usually meant they were debating our suitability.

In my eagerness to appear more than what I was, I spun outrageous stories of how my father had gone to America to build his fortune after my mother died, leaving me and my sisters with caring aunts, who had us educated by the nuns. I never mentioned Aubazine or my lost brothers or that I had turned my back on my grandparents. After I heard these falsehoods reel from my lips, I waited, breathless, for him to burst out laughing and chide, "Coco, what a liar you are!" But he never did. He accepted everything I told him and I began to see how easy it was to conceal my past. After all, other girls must find themselves in my position, especially as I took pains to elaborate that I'd chosen to earn my own way, because the alternative—to be sent to a matchmaker or wed one of the boys whose families knew mine—was unacceptable.

"Though of course," I added airily, "I hope to marry someday."

"Of course." He leaned to me. "It seems we both share an intolerance for expectations. Perhaps we are destined for each other, *ma petite* Coco."

It was the first time he had alluded to a possible future together and it roused equal parts hope and consternation. My plans had not come to fruition; I had not sold a single hat. No milliner in Moulins would give me the time of day. I was still under Madame G.'s thumb, singing my throat raw in the café, and though the money in my tin slowly increased, if no one wanted to buy my hats, what could I do? At this rate, I feared I would become my mother—enslaved to work that paid enough to keep a roof over my head but never enough to raise me out of the gutter. Balsan could change my fortunes with a snap of his fingers, but did I want him to? I had no illusions that he might propose; men like him did not take girls like me for a wife. And while becoming his mistress would resolve my financial difficulties, could he make me happy?

I evaded my own conflicted emotions, never asking him to state clearly his intent. After nearly two years of working in Moulins, I decided staying was pointless. Adrienne and I had to make a change, and after much cajoling, I persuaded her to move with me to Vichy, where we would rent a room and find work in the more sophisticated cafés of that city. We had experience now, I argued; surely, that counted for something. She was reluctant until Balsan assured her that he thought it was a delightful idea and he would provide us with sufficient means to establish ourselves. Moreover, her besotted baron declared that he would follow her to the ends of the earth and Vichy was hardly that far.

"But won't it be like . . . ?" she fretted as I threw our few belongings into our suitcases, after having enjoyed the satisfaction of delivering our notice to Madame G.

"Like what?" I barely paid attention to her, prying up the floorboard to remove my tin box and counting the money inside, half hoping it might have reproduced on its own.

"Well, like . . ." She lowered her voice. "Like those women who sell themselves."

I couldn't believe what I was hearing. "Are you saying that if we accept Balsan's help, it makes us prostitutes?"

"Not exactly," she said, though her troubled expression contradicted her. "Only that, well, it is *his* money, and if we accept it, it does carry a certain expectation . . ."

I restrained the impulse to remind her that not long ago she had suggested I might aspire to be a *grande cocotte*. Now she was worried about accepting assistance from a man we had known for months, with whom I had done nothing improper?

"It's not the same thing," I retorted, for while I thought her fears absurd, her suggestion carried a disquieting truth. "Étienne Balsan is a friend. It's a loan. We will pay him back."

"Louise is very upset," she went on, gnawing at her lip. "She told me when I went to see her that this move of ours is most ill-advised and Vichy is no place for us to be on our own. She said if we are so unhappy here, we should move to Varennes to live with her."

"And do what?" I banged my tin on the floor, making Adrienne flinch. "Help her decorate those silly hats and tend to the goat? Honestly, Adrienne. You've a baron in love with you and me at your side. If you want to go to Varennes, do so. But I am going to Vichy—with or without you."

Her eyes filled with tears. I had to hold her in my arms as she snuffled and choked out between sobs that not everyone had my courage, and sometimes I could be a perfect brute.

"I know," I said, wondering why I didn't share this paralyzing fear of independence that she, my sister Julia, and so many other girls felt. "But we've been to Vichy before and you can do all the things you do here, and visit Louise, too, as we'll earn enough to buy the train ticket."

"It won't be the same," she muttered but she stood by with our valises while I haggled with Madame G. over our final wages.

Balsan had bought us third-class tickets for Vichy, at my insistence; I didn't want to accept more charity than necessary. He left for a month-long visit to Lyons to see his family but promised to come see us once he returned.

Third class was better than the coach, but we still arrived in Vichy after standing the entire time, the few available seats taken by others. And the room I had rented during a previous trip with Balsan didn't look nearly as nice as when I'd first seen it. The one lopsided window opened onto an alley swarming with leavings from nearby restaurants; it smelled of damp and garbage, and I had to squash an enormous cockroach under my foot and kick it under the bed before Adrienne saw it. But we had livable furnishings, including a cracked mirror over the sagging bureau, and as Adrienne regarded it in miserable resignation, I said, "At least we don't have that awful stove to worry about," and proceeded to unpack with determination. "We'll be fine, you'll see," I kept saying. "In a few weeks, we'll have more work than we know what to do with."

It didn't turn out that way. Most of the cafés had a surfeit of chanteuses and queues of hopefuls at their back doors, as did the local shops. We managed to find part-time work taking in mending but the pay was no better than Madame G.'s, and though I emptied my precious tin to purchase an appropriately corseted costume for auditions, no proprietor of the boulevard cafés offered to hire me. Finally, as the summer season ended and Vichy emptied of its spa guests, I received my only offer from an off-the-boulevard cabaret named Le Palais Doré, though the only thing that could be described as golden about it were the nicotine stains on its walls.

Here I sang every night in the *beuglant*: ten of us, arranged in a chorus, subject to howling sailors on leave and other riffraff. I fended off more hands and slobbery lips than I could count and walked home every night, despite the drunkards on every corner. As soon as I opened the door to find Adrienne wilted on the bed with the daily mending at her feet, I adopted a bright smile and declared I'd made more tips in a night than in an entire week at La Rotunde.

"That is wonderful," she said, unconvincingly, and we cobbled together a cold meal out of three-day-old bread and fatty ham the charcuterie sold us at a reduced price.

Then one day, when I arrived home, nearly at my own wits' end, I found her waiting in her now-soiled linen travel suit, her suitcase packed and crumpled hat on her head.

"I'm going back to Moulins. I love you like a sister, Gabrielle, but I cannot take this anymore." Her voice caught. "Maurice hasn't visited me once, and if I stay away too long—"

"No. Say no more," I whispered, embracing her.

I accompanied her to the train station, bought her a third-class ticket home, and waved from the platform as the train pulled away in a jangle of gears and a cloud of black fumes.

Only as I trudged back to our grungy room did I realize I'd been abandoned once again.

However, this time I was truly alone.

X

Balsan's absence had first bewildered, then hurt, then outraged me, so that I squashed his memory like the numerous cockroaches infesting my room.

One night, as I performed in the *beuglant* in some awful number, dressed in a humiliating shoulder-baring costume that the proprietor demanded we wear and pay for in installments out of our wages, I saw Balsan enter the cabaret. I recognized him at once, even from across the room, like a kick to my stomach. As the lyrics of the song warbled, bitter in my mouth, he looked around, clearly aghast, at the rowdy stomping of boots and streams of chewing tobacco into spittoons. Then he slowly turned to the stage.

He must have spotted me, the gaunt one, my bodice held up with pins because I had lost so much weight, but I pretended not to see him. I finished the song and fled the lurid catcalls that followed, rushing backstage to tear off my costume, even as the manager barked, "You're not done! It's your turn to take around the purse for tips."

The purse he always dipped into, taking a substantial cut. I just glared at him and stormed out the back door, not caring if I dirtied my sole pair of shoes in the alley where customers relieved themselves.

I felt sick as I raced to my room. Flinging my coat aside, I looked at myself in the mirror. I had avoided it for weeks, not wanting to see the results of my stubbornness. Now, as I finally let myself take in my reflection, a scream rose in my throat.

I had the face of my childhood again: huge lightless black eyes hovering above pinched cheeks. Whirling away, I reached for my bag and near-empty pack of cigarettes (I smoked incessantly, the cheapest dregs I could buy, because it helped curb hunger).

A knock came at the door.

I froze, not moving, until the match I'd lit singed my fingers. I wouldn't answer. He could knock until his knuckles bled. He could go to hell, back to his privileged existence, to his damn horses and empty promises.

"Coco," he said, his voice clear, for the door was almost as thin as me. "I know you're in there. Open up. I want to see you. I've been looking for you everywhere."

That did the trick. Lunging at the door, I threw it open and before he could step over the threshold, I yelled, "Everywhere? Where did you look? I've been here the entire time, in the very room we rented together. You wanted to see me? Well, here I am. *Look at me!*"

I would have slammed the door on him had he not stuck his foot in the way. As he came inside I backed away, so enraged I could have strangled him with my bare hands.

He said softly, "My God. What have they done to you?"

I crumbled where I stood, covering my face with my hands as sobs overcame me. I had not experienced grief like this since my father left. It came pouring out, all the loss and bewilderment, the disbelief that no matter how much I tried, how strong I thought I was, the world would always be stronger—a tomb of illusions that would bury me under its weight.

"You're leaving now," I heard him whisper, his hands about me, catching me by the waist and forcing me to him as I cried and tried to push him away. "You're coming to live in my new château. Enough of this pride. I want you with me."

XI

What girl doesn't want to be taken care of?

That was what I kept telling myself when Balsan took me to Moulins to say my good-byes. After the ordeal in Vichy, even Moulins seemed like heaven, but I was only there to visit my aunts. I wore the new black linen jacket and skirt he had bought me—my other clothes tossed on the rag heap—and sat demurely as he assured Louise that I would want for nothing.

Adrienne clapped in delight, as if Balsan had gotten down on his knee to present me with a ring. In the few months we'd been apart, she had reclaimed her self-possession, aglow because Maurice de Nexon had indeed been pining for her, though she didn't explain why he had not come to see her in Vichy. Louise had found her a suitable chaperone, renowned for her matchmaking skills, who suggested a trip to Egypt for Adrienne and the baron, along with several other couples, to remove the lovers from their environment and see if marriage was truly something they wished to pursue. Adrienne later confided to me as we walked through the town square that Nexon's family expected him to wed a girl of rank, but he'd told them he desired only her, so she was prepared to do battle to win his family over.

"I couldn't be happier for you," I said, even if I wondered at her willingness to endure the inevitable disrepute of being seen as the baron's mistress. I also wondered at Louise's willingness to allow it, chaperone or not, even as I realized I was about to do the same with Balsan, though he'd not said as much. I could hardly judge a situation that I myself was willing to accept. Moreover, Adrienne was in love, while I did not feel anything remotely like that for Balsan. Gratitude, yes, and relief that he had found me, for I'd have perished on my own; but much as I searched my heart, I felt nothing approximating Adrienne's desire for Nexon. Indeed, I feared further intimacies, though it was inevitable. Once again, as Adrienne regaled me with her hopes, I wondered if I was incapable of the unquenchable ardor she described.

Tante Louise wished me *bonne chance* and averted her eyes, acknowledging with that one gesture that she was relieved to see me go. I had turned out to be my father's child, intent on forging my own path; it was better for everyone to remove me from Adrienne's sphere. I was only a niece, while Adrienne was her sister, upon whom Louise must focus all her attention if Adrienne was to win the baron's hand. I had become a liability, an unwanted reminder of where girls could end up. As in my childhood, I must be shuttled away, out of sight.

This realization hardened my heart. I departed Moulins without a second glance, though my sister Antoinette lived in the convent and Julia an hour away in my grandparents' house. I wanted to see them but I didn't care to explain. Tante Louise would inform them soon enough of how I had strayed from any hope for respectability. I knew it was what she thought; I saw it in her eyes. She did not believe Balsan would ever marry me.

Neither did I. But I had made my decision, for better or worse.

THE HOME BALSAN HAD BOUGHT near Compiègne was a seventeenth-century château with an impressive name—Royallieu—but unimpressive upkeep. A relic with musty furnishings and drapery-shrouded windows and doorways, it had no heating other than massive soot-streaked fireplaces. Rooms had sat uninhabited for years, occupied by heavy chairs and tables cloaked in sheets. The water ran brown in the tubs and sinks. Rodent droplets soiled the corners.

Balsan seemed strangely unperturbed, given his personal fastidiousness. He remarked that he would refurbish the château in time but for now must direct his efforts to the horses he'd bought, their stables, and clearing the encroaching forest so he would have courses to race on and meadows for polo.

I found him somewhat changed, though I couldn't tell precisely how. He had rekindled past friendships, admitting that the reason he took so long to come to Vichy was because he'd made an impromptu trip to Paris to conduct "overdue business." He didn't explain what his business concerned and I didn't ask. I sensed that a mistress who asked too many questions was not the arrangement he had in mind.

Whatever arrangement he did have in mind took some time to reveal itself. He let me choose a bedroom for myself with an adjoining bathroom and parlor, where I could read and make my hats. It was a luxury, no matter if the water came in fits and bursts or the pipes moaned like invalids. I basked in the sheer breadth of my suite, the sense that I could come and go as I pleased, carrying armloads of books from the well-stocked library (included in the château's purchase) and spending hours on end spilled on the carpet with my imagination free to roam.

Balsan gave me money to buy more hats and trimming supplies. A flare of creativity had me working throughout the night, until my finished hats occupied every surface of my parlor and the next room, as well. Balsan took it all in stride, with a smile on his face; he was gone most of the day, occupied with his projects.

We saw each other in the evening for dinners served by unobtrusive servants. I chattered about my latest creations and the novels I'd read in one sitting, devouring the fresh-cooked food. After Vichy, I would indeed never let myself go hungry again.

"Who would think you do all that?" he said, lighting his after-dinner cigarette. "I thought you slept until noon and bathed until three."

"Well, that, too," I admitted. "But I'm not entirely idle." The truth was, I felt a twinge of discomfort about subsiding on his largesse. I'd worked all my life. Sitting around all day wasn't something I could get used to. I occupied my time with books, for reading was not a passive occupation if one did it properly, and my hats, but already, in just a few weeks, I'd begun to experience an unsettling aimlessness. As I considered what else I might do to earn the privileges Balsan had bestowed, I felt subtle panic. What he must desire I was not yet prepared to give and in a sudden rush I said, "You could teach me to ride."

He smiled lazily. "That would be fun. You're not scared of horses?"

"Of course not," I retorted, though I'd never been on one. "I assume it's easy enough."

He chuckled, stubbing out his cigarette. "Then as soon as my horses arrive, I will teach my little Coco how to sit a saddle. It would be good, I think, as I plan to invite some friends here and most of them like to hunt."

An odd note had crept into his voice. He went off into the library while I returned upstairs to work on my hats. But my usual consuming focus deserted me. I found myself pacing, staring out the window at the impenetrable night, the silhouettes of trees outlined against the indigo sky.

When the door opened behind me, I knew what he had come for. Turning around, I found him on the threshold. He stepped inside, closing the door. As he lifted a hand to remove his shirt collar, I wrenched my eyes up to his face.

"Shall we?" he said.

I stood still, a cigarette smoldering between my fingers.

"Only if you want to," he added, removing his silver cigarette case from his trousers pocket and setting it by the lamp on my bedside table. "I don't want to force you."

"No, of course I do," I said. My heart started to pound as I fumbled at the fastenings of my dress. He watched me with almost casual disregard as I slipped the dress off and then my chemise. I stood with my arms crossed over my breasts, my undergarments bunched around my thighs. Now that the moment I had dreaded was upon me, I had no idea what he expected.

Images of the choristers at Le Palais Doré swinging their hips and leaning over tables to expose their cleavage raced through my mind. Was he anticipating some kind of brazen floor show?

Instead, he folded back my bedcovers and removed his shirt and trousers. His chest was surprisingly thin, like a boy's, white skinned and narrow. I didn't like the sight of his oddly fleshy nipples and dropped my gaze to his hips—wider than I thought men had—and thick hairy legs. It was as though he were a misshapen centaur: scrawny on top but heavy on the bottom. When I caught sight of the small, limp penis hanging from an auburn thicket at his groin that was darker than the hair on his head, I felt revulsion. He looked much better with his clothes on.

Slipping into the sheets, he patted the space beside him. I moved to the bed thinking I must look preposterous, with my underpants crammed around my thighs and my small breasts exposed. I scrambled under the sheet as fast as I could.

He reached over to stroke me, running his hands around my chest, pinching my nipples. I closed my eyes and tried not to think, but I kept seeing the web in the corner of the ceiling with the resting spider I watched every day, catching flies and patiently rolling up their still-thrashing bodies in her deadly cocoons. I'd named her Margot. She was sitting there now, immobile, waiting for her feast, and I felt like her victims as Balsan began kissing my throat.

It was not like what I'd read about in novels. I wasn't expecting that; I had surmised by now that such fictional ecstasies must be more mundane in reality, for how could an act so common, which everyone called *le petit mort*, be the summit of one's experiences? Still, I did expect to feel *something*. The fact that I did not disturbed me. When he progressed from my throat to my breasts, lapping at them like a babe at a mother's teat, I had to stifle a sudden giggle. It seemed so . . . farcical, so unlike us.

"Do you like it?" I heard him murmur, one of my nipples in his mouth, and I supposed I should, so I let out a fake moan. He seemed to like that, for he became excited, nipping and licking, until I felt his hard penis nudge my thigh and I shifted my legs to evade the sensation. He took my gesture as permission to mount me abruptly, sighing, "Ah, Coco, I've waited so long."

It hurt! I gasped at the unexpected fire of it, as he lowered himself upon me, thrusting, making clenched sounds through his teeth. I thought it would never end, and then it did, suddenly. With a cry, he pulled out and spilled a warm sticky liquid onto my stomach.

I looked down under the sheet at the slime. Then I saw smears of blood on the sheet and the insides of my thighs, and raised my eyes to his.

"You did not tell me," he said, not accusatorily, but with some surprise. "Had I known, I wouldn't have been so insistent."

I made myself shrug. "It had to happen sometime. I'm glad it was you."

He kissed me and disengaged himself from our position, reaching over the bed to his trousers to fetch his silver cigarette case. He lit two cigarettes, then passed one to me. We lay side by side without touching, smoking, before he sighed. "Well, that was delightful. Good night, Coco. Thank you."

I managed a weak smile as he dressed and left me. From her corner, Margot slipped down the strands of her web to nibble on her shrouded victims.

It wasn't something I cared to repeat, but as this was the price required, I could endure it.

XII

His friends arrived, disrupting the placid monotony of the house. Balsan had returned to my bed only twice. I still felt nothing, but he didn't seem to notice. He always smoked a cigarette with me afterward and then left me alone. I welcomed his consideration, as it gave me time to bathe and wash away the smell of his cologne and the mess he'd made on my stomach. After my bath, I would read or adjust a hat, avoiding the thought that something must indeed be wrong with me, that I could find no pleasure in an act he clearly enjoyed. But I could not keep from wondering if every couple was like this, enacting the same ritual with passionless precision? Inexperienced as I might be, I doubted it. It seemed to me that people like Adrienne and Nexon would not go through such trials to marry, only to reap such a paltry reward.

The arrival of people I didn't know increased my feeling of being caught unaware. Hearing the commotion downstairs, I detected the voice of a woman among them and threw open my wardrobe doors to rake through the dresses Balsan had bought me—flouncy affairs with ribbons and lace that drowned me. I suspected that whoever the woman was, she would certainly outshine me, for these dresses did nothing but turn me into something I was not. With a burst of determination, I pulled out an ensemble I had made for myself.

Bored one day, with nothing else to do, I had put it together on a whim. Taking one of Balsan's old evening shirts, I trimmed the waist and added a rounded collar. I left the shirt to fasten up the front but rather than customary studs, I sewed on cloth-covered buttons. Pairing it now with a slim camel-colored skirt bought during one of my trips to Compiègne for hat supplies, I belted a loose beige sweater—also of Balsan's, shrunk during a laundry mishap—about my waist and buckled on low-heeled cream-colored shoes.

I took a quick appraisal in the tarnished glass. The ensemble was undoubtedly eccentric, with overt mannish tones; I looked like a girl playing dress-up in her father's clothes, but the illusion also conveyed a trim line that appealed to me, adhering to my angular figure. I would certainly make an impression, I thought, and my tentative smile widened in the mirror.

Better to be remarked upon than ignored.

I descended the stairs to the living room, where Balsan and his company had gathered.

They were sleek and well dressed; a pall of cigarette smoke hovered over them as they sipped whiskey from tumblers and chatted. At my appearance, they turned as if on cue to look at me, not with overt judgment or condemnation, I saw with relief, but rather curiosity, as though I were a trophy Balsan had on display. He strode to me, taking me by the hand.

"Coco, allow me to present you." His recital of names flew from my head the moment it was uttered; later I'd come to know some of them well, but at the time I was too flustered, smiling and nodding until we came before a voluptuous woman in flounces and ringlets, her thick-lashed green-blue eyes assessing me with unabashed interest.

"And this is Émilienne d'Alençon, the famous actress."

She released a bubble of champagne laughter. "Famous to you, darling Étienne, but not to this fey creature. She doesn't know me." She smiled at me, revealing small, ivory-colored teeth. "*Enchanté, ma chère.* I see you are everything Étienne claims."

The way she spoke of him betrayed intimacy. As I realized they must be more than friends, Balsan chuckled and said, "Émilienne was my mistress. That business in Paris I mentioned; she was it."

He stated it matter-of-factly, the way he thanked me after we went to bed. Émilienne cuffed his arm playfully with her astonishingly smooth hand. "You're a rogue. You left me without paying and I intend to pass the bill. No man, no matter how charming, throws over Émilienne d'Alençon without closing out his account."

Balsan laughed, returning to his male guests. Émilienne smiled at me again, more warmly this time. She was remarkable, with impeccable pale skin that managed to appear rosy without being florid, her red-gold hair swept up in the current mountainous style, curls framing her oval face. Her ruffled gown was of azure silk with a woven *chinois* pattern of storks and waterfalls that I would have found lurid on any other woman. The jewels about her throat and wrists were breathtaking, but too lavish; I had never seen anyone wear so many jewels in daytime. Everything about her was excessive, theatrical, yet it only enhanced her attractiveness.

I recognized that I was in the presence of more than an actress. Émilienne d'Alençon must be one of the *grandes cocottes* Adrienne had told me about.

"How do you like it here in Royallieu?" Linking her arm in mine, she guided me away from the others, to the double glass doors that opened onto the veranda. "It is rather a frightful place, isn't it? As if Marie Antoinette herself had stopped here on her way to the guillotine."

I had to smile. She had that effect. I sensed nothing she said could ever cause offense.

"It does need some renovation," I replied.

She gave a delighted purr. "Indeed, it does. But Étienne is so wrapped up in his horses he'll ignore the house until it falls about his ears. Thank God, he has you." She paused, looking me up and down. "Given your style, I should think you could take over the renovations for him. He allows you access to his money, I presume?"

I barely knew what to respond. Finally, I mumbled, "I assume he would, if I asked."

"Then you must." She leaned close. "Get whatever you are due, my dear. Youth and love fade in time, but money never loses its luster." She swept me onto the veranda. "Ah, such marvelous air, so crisp and sweet, not like the ghastly stench of Paris! Shall we take a walk?" As I started to agree, she stopped suddenly. "Oh, I've left my chapeau inside. Would you be a love and fetch it for me?"

I turned back into the house to find her hat—it was difficult to miss, one of those monstrosities with overlapping rosettes and heaps of feathers. I would never have acted the servant for anyone else, yet I brought her the hat eagerly, watching her set it on her head and assisting her with the multiple pins required to hold it in place.

"Such fuss," she said. "What we women must do to appear at our best. I'm grateful for this weekend, when I can dispense with the armor." She curved her wrist, waving her hand gracefully over her person. "But not the hat; a lady must protect her complexion." As she turned to gaze at the gardens, she added, "I hear you're clever with your needle. Étienne was telling me when he came to Paris that you make the most fetching hats."

I went still. She eyed me in amusement. "Well, ma chère? Do you?"

"I do. It's . . . a hobby of mine."

"Well, we must see this hobby of yours. I'm always interested in new hats; fashions in Paris go out of style with such bewildering frequency that one day, you're the height of mode and the next you're rushing to the dressmaker to spend a king's ransom. The price of fame: when everyone is watching, one can never afford a mistake."

I found that I liked her very much. She must have sensed my admiration, for she took my arm in hers once more. "I would adore it if we became friends. Balsan is dear to me, despite his dismissal of my services, and he is infatuated with you. I don't think I've ever seen him so enthused."

He was?

I gave her a smile. "I'd like that, too," and it occurred to me that I'd never had a friend before, unless I counted Adrienne, who seemed so far from me now. She had left for Egypt with her baron, to prepare for a life I had decided I didn't want. What would we talk about if we saw each other again? Infatuated as Balsan might be, I had no illusion that either of us was in love.

Émilienne led me down the veranda's steps. We didn't speak, but as we strolled over the overgrown garden paths, I felt the pressure of her hand on my sleeve, so light it almost didn't touch me at all, and for the first time in as long as I could recall, I was content.

WHILE ÉTIENNE AND THE MEN PARADED ABOUT in jodhpurs, Émilienne and I sipped coffee on the veranda, nibbled on chocolate, and conversed about her life in Paris, where she acted on the stage and had an apartment overlooking the Tuileries. She spoke as if I had been to Paris and knew all the places she mentioned—the opera, theaters and cafés, the bistros and shops—and I pretended that I did, ashamed to admit that I'd barely seen anything of the world.

She had eschewed her opulent gowns and platter-size chapeaux for the weekend, lounging about in embroidered silk robes with wide sleeves and diamond-studded clasps, her hair rippling down her back. She had hair like a Madonna, so long and full she drifted about in its cloud. But no matter how casual her attire (or casual for her; to me, she still appeared if she was dressed for a gala), I noticed she never removed her corset.

When I finally got up the nerve to ask her if it hurt to be encased in whalebone all day, she replied, "It's an exercise in torture, but we must endure, for it has its rewards. Don't tell anyone, but I'm not as young as I used to be, *ma chère*, and illusion must be maintained." She regarded me pensively. "Do you never wear a corset?"

Of course I had, though as little as possible, and not since my departure from singing in cafés. I shook my head. "I do not like them," I said, and again I thought she would see right through me to the girl who had never been anywhere and didn't know how to dress.

She sighed. "Such is the resiliency of youth. You're practically invisible when you turn to the side. So flat and lean—I envy you. Though a corset would give a lift to your bosom, and men like Balsan—well, they prefer women with a few curves."

Was that my defect, my lack of curves?

Then, unexpectedly, she asked to see my hats. I had been dreading the moment, fearing that with her sophistication, she would find my creations poor substitutes. But I took her upstairs to my parlor, where (though I'd been keeping her at bay) I'd spent hours arranging my hats so they'd appear in the best light. My chest knotted as she wafted to the rows on the table by the window. She didn't speak, drifting her fingers over the hats without touching them. I had no idea what she thought. I was about to blurt out that I only made hats to stay busy and didn't expect anyone to like them, when she cast a glance over her shoulder. "May I try one?"

She had paused by my most ornate creation, a rounded hat with an upturned scoop, black silk camellias, and black feathers sewn around its brim. It was my least favorite. I hadn't found its perfecting touch, yet when she took it up and pivoted to the mirror, I suddenly realized it was ideal for her. Émilienne was not like me; she wasn't small boned. Though not fat, she was tall and plump, her body molded into that unnatural hourglass shape accentuated by her corset, a fleshy thrust of breast and a wasp waist rounding into full hips. The hat would emphasize her statuesque figure without overwhelming her. Placing the hat on her head, she tilted it to one side. A tiny frown puckered her brow.

I hastened to her, righting the hat so it sat directly on her brow and the scoop curled upward. "It's meant to be worn like this?" she asked, uncertain.

I nodded. "It's supposed to frame your features."

"But then, one's hairstyle must . . . ?"

"Be simple. It won't sit right if the hair is piled too high."

"No horsehair frames to elevate one's chignon?" She met my eyes in the mirror. "That would indeed be revolutionary. We spend hours each day having our hair styled. If we could forgo the effort, imagine what else we could do with our time?"

I smiled. The hat did suit her, but only in *my* opinion. As she turned to look at the others, I ventured to add, "A hat is an accessory; it should enhance our face and our clothes. I don't think walking around with a platter on our heads is either comfortable or attractive."

"I see. And you make these hats . . . how?"

"With basic forms. I decorate them myself, but the forms are already made."

"Yet none are traditional bonnets and you employ no other adornments, just these few feathers and a touch of colored cloth here or there. Again, revolutionary . . ." She returned to her reflection. After several moments, she said softly, "Why, *ma chère*, your hats are extraordinary. So unusual yet also refined, like you. Have you considered selling them?"

I contemplated lying to her, but instead heard myself say, "I tried when I was in Moulins. I once decorated a hat that a woman in Vichy found charming, but no one else expressed interest. Now, I mostly do it for me. I . . . I enjoy it."

"Evidently. And these intriguing outfits you wear, do you make them, too? You do? How extraordinary."

It was the second time she had said "extraordinary." It made me glow inside.

"You know, there's an excellent haberdashery in Paris on rue Lafayette; they sell many different types of these forms. I could bring some with me on my next visit, if you'd like?"

I could have kissed her. "I would, very much. In Compiègne, there's not much variety."

"Well, one cannot compare Compiègne to Paris. What would Balsan say?" Émilienne paused, considering. "It would be like comparing a donkey to a Thoroughbred." Laughing, she removed the hat. As I reached to take it from her, she said, "How much?"

I froze. I had no idea what a finished hat cost these days. "Consider it a gift," I said.

She clucked her tongue. "*Ma chère*, you must name a price. Nothing a woman has should ever be given away for free."

"Ten francs," I blurted out. It seemed an inordinate amount, but she merely arched her brow. "Is that all? Sold. I'll wear it the next time I go for tea in the Tuileries. The others ladies will seethe with envy and demand to know where I purchased such a marvelous chapeau."

As I turned trembling to the table, wondering how to wrap up the hat for her, she set a hand on my shoulder, her clean scent tinged with attar of roses permeating my being.

She murmured, "I believe you're destined for great success, Coco Chanel. And I'm going to help you achieve it."

XIII

I missed Émilienne when she left, my hat on her head, waving gaily and promising to return. I stood forlorn at the château entrance with Balsan's hunting hounds sniffing at my feet, watching her carriage drive away to the train station.

I'd heard such promises before. As I turned to trudge into the house, Balsan said, "There's no reason to look so glum. Émilienne charms everyone but she likes very few. If she said she's coming back to see you, she will."

He didn't understand my dejection, my haunting conviction that everyone was destined to leave me, one way or another. I couldn't believe Émilienne would come back, because if she didn't, it would crush me. I plunged into my work, walking around with a scowl as the scent of her faded from everything she had touched. Balsan took note of my mood. He kept away from my bed, busy with his horses, until I could not abide myself anymore and emerged one morning to stalk up to him as he spoke with his grooms.

"I want to learn to ride today," I announced.

He regarded me. "Like that?"

I bristled at once, my nerves rubbed by his sardonic air, by the complacency he seemed to exude at all times, though not long ago I had admired it. "Yes. Like this. Is there a problem?"

He passed his gaze over me. I wore a short jacket over a simple blouse, a skirt, and boots, my wide boater placed squarely on my head.

"You'll have to learn sidesaddle," he said.

"Fine." I strode into the stables as he instructed a groom to prepare the mare. Getting onto the beast proved more difficult than I had thought. Though I used the mounting block that Balsan set before me, my skirt wasn't wide enough to hike as high as I needed it to go without exposing my thighs. Once I settled precariously upon the saddle and had been shown how to set my foot in the stirrup, using my other leg for balance, I felt utterly ridiculous.

"Hold fast to the reins but not so tight that you cut her mouth," Balsan told me. "We'll go slowly at first."

I wanted to tell him I didn't need coddling, but as the mare lurched forward, following Balsan astride his prize gelding, I swayed like a sack of flour. I had never felt so ungainly or imperiled in my life. The ground seemed miles below me. It didn't help that as I grappled with the reins, the mare snorted and swiveled her great head to try to nip me.

We rode around the newly fenced-in meadow. It was hardly more than a short excursion but by the time we returned to the stables, I was soaked in sweat, chafed about my buttocks, and thoroughly disgusted with myself.

"There. That wasn't so bad," Balsan said as he helped me to dismount, no doubt relieved that I had shown some initiative and not spent another day indoors moping and filling my room to the rafters with more hats. "Tomorrow, you'll do better."

With a glare, I marched back into the château. I certainly would. I would not accept anything less. But not like this. If I was going to ride, I must have the use of both my legs, not be relegated to perching atop the mare like a figurine on a cake.

Rummaging through his closet in his room—where I almost never ventured—I searched his attire for something suitable I could use to make a riding outfit. He had more clothes than anyone else I had known, hundreds of jackets and waistcoats, trousers and shirts, though he was not vain. Rather, his limitless wealth allowed him to acquire as he pleased, and most of what he bought he never wore. Once I located a slightly frayed pair of his jodhpurs, I returned to my room and went to work. It took the rest of the day and most of the night, but when I arrived at the stables the next morning he took one look at me and laughed, "Coco, you really go too far!"

I ignored his mirth and the wide-eyed stares of his hired help. With my new jodhpurs fitted to my figure and a wide-brimmed felt hat, I clambered onto the mare with ease. Sitting astride, I took up the reins and said to a still-grinning Balsan, "*Now,* I'll do better."

And so I did. I spent the next weeks riding every day, until the improvised jodhpurs began to wear in the seat and I could gallop without my heart in my throat. When Balsan informed me that he planned another of his gatherings for the upcoming weekend, it bolstered my confidence. I went to Compiègne where he kept a tailor on account, to order two riding ensembles made for me in tweed and linen.

The tailor sniffed. "Mademoiselle, ladies do not wear trousers."

"They're not trousers," I said. "They're riding breeches. And this lady will wear them." I punctuated my tone with finality. By now, everyone connected to Balsan knew he had a *maîtresse* in his household. Even Adrienne, who wrote on occasion to provide the latest news on her ongoing battle to marry Nexon, had sent a letter indicating that Louise and unnamed others in our family were "troubled" by my behavior, going to live with a man and do—well, precisely what Adrienne did, only without the promise of marriage. I ignored her concern. What I did was my own affair. It always had been, since I was a child. Family wasn't going to see to my future, or at least not any future I'd consider, but in time Balsan might.

Nevertheless, the monotony of Royallieu started to wear on me. It was ironic after the deprivations I had endured that I couldn't find it in myself to revel in a luxury most girls would have killed to possess. The freedom I envisioned seemed as out of reach as it had during those dreary days of singing for my supper. Indeed, though I ate like a queen, slept in feathery comfort, and worked for my own delight, invisible tethers still bound me. I was beholden to someone else for the very food on my plate and I began to resent it. My discontent was a vague shadow that crept upon me at night, as

I stood swathed in smoke from my cigarettes, my ashtray overflowing and floor and worktable littered in ribbon and cloth. The black square of the window reflected the same blackness in my heart.

What else did I want? How much more could I ask for? I had no answer. There was no soul-lightening certainty. All I knew was that I couldn't be Balsan's mistress forever. I didn't love him in the way I should. In time, Balsan would tire of me. He would realize I felt only friendship for him and seek a more enthusiastic companion. Though he had given no indication that he wearied of my company or expected more than I could give, he was still a man and not unappealing. He'd had Émilienne for a lover and, while rare, she was not unique. Others like her would leap at the opportunity to supplant me, and in truth, though I feared being sent away to survive on my own, I would not miss his desultory lovemaking or this guilty feeling that I stole something from him by taking what he offered and not reciprocating in any discernible manner.

Riding therefore became my obsession. Not a passion, for I preferred to keep my feet on the ground, but because it provided an outlet for my restlessness, another unlikely achievement that might serve me later, though I couldn't see how.

It would be another two years before I found my answer. When it arrived, it was more sudden and unexpected than anything that had come before.

ÉMILIENNE ARRIVED THAT WEEKEND, radiating warmth and accompanied by a coterie of her actress-courtesan friends, a hive of intrepid beauties—none of whom, to my surprise, was here to test their claws or wrench Balsan from my tepid embrace.

They wanted to buy my hats.

As they crowded into my workroom to coo over my offerings, Émilienne leaned to me and murmured, "My dear, are you sure you are all right? You look thinner than the last time I was here. You're not going consumptive, are you?"

I averted my gaze, mumbling, "I'm fine," and went to attend to her friends, who had seen Émilienne in my hat in the Tuileries and virtually "mobbed her," as she put it, for an invitation to visit this eccentric haberdasher she had been hiding from them. That I was a woman only made them gasp and covet my creations more.

"Imagine," one declared, flouncing about with one of my feathered hats on her head, "what Monsieur Worth will say when he hears that we're not wearing *his* hats. *Mon Dieu*, the scandal! It'll be the talk of every salon in Paris."

Scandal, I discovered, was the bait that kept the courtesans' admirers in constant thrall, an aphrodisiac as powerful as oysters, Émilienne assured me, for what man with blood in his veins did not yearn for the forbidden, along with the sublime?

"I wouldn't know," I said. We reclined on the settee in my room, which she cushioned with her embroidered mantilla and a plethora of pillows. Her friends had gone out to stroll the gardens with the men; Émilienne arrived in my room with her hair unbound to declare that we must have this afternoon to ourselves.

Now, she surveyed me with her catlike eyes. "You wouldn't know? My dear, you seem positively wretched these days. Are you not happy that I brought my friends to buy your wares?" She motioned with her kimono-draped arm to my empty worktable, where a lone plain black square hat, one of my favorites, remained. On the floor were piled boxes from the haberdashery on rue Lafayette, containing the basic forms she had bought me. "Look, they've cleared out your stock. Now you've a fresh batch, so you can make new hats and I can bring another horde to buy them the next time I visit. Before you know it, your name will be on everyone's lips."

"Yes, of course I'm happy," I said with a strained smile. "It's only that..." I wasn't sure if I should broach the fog of discontent, which had settled upon me, the sense that I drifted in a world where I had no purpose or any chance for true happiness.

She immediately inclined to me. "Oh, no, *ma chère*. Tell me it is not so."

"What?" I stared at her, bewildered. "What is not so?"

She sighed. "I knew it: this strange melancholy and lack of appetite, the thinness and pallor. My dear, you are *enceinte*."

It took a moment for me to grasp her meaning. When I did, I was astonished. "You think I'm pregnant? Oh, no, Émilienne. I assure you, I am not."

"No?" She frowned. "Is it not possible?"

I paused. "Yes," I said at length, for I saw no reason to lie. She knew who Balsan and I were to each other. "I suppose it is. But I am not." The manner in which I spoke must have betrayed more than I intended, for she became contemplative in a way I had not seen before. Then she reclined, her kimono falling open to reveal her curvaceous body in a cream silk negligee, today without her corset. "I see."

"You do?" As I did not, I was curious to hear what she had divined.

"Have you considered instructing him, perhaps?" she asked, still in that intimate tone. "Men can be trained. They learn rather readily, in fact, if you take the time to show them. With patience and persistence, I have found they can accommodate our needs quite satisfactorily when given the chance."

She was not talking about financial needs, that much I understood. But I was so dumbfounded by the unexpected turn in our conversation, I couldn't say a word.

"He performed well enough for me," she added, with an arch of her plucked eyebrow. "Maybe not the best I've had, but certainly not the worst." She grimaced. "I don't keep those who refuse to accommodate, not with so many others waiting at the door."

I finally found my voice. "You think I should train Balsan? Like a dog?"

"Why, yes. He does not please you. You must do something to change his perspective. Not every woman is the same. He might not know that, being a man, but we do. How else is he to learn if you do not teach him?"

My laughter escaped me in an incredulous burst. "Show him? I hardly know myself!" and as soon as I spoke, I realized I had just stepped into my own unwitting snare.

Her tongue moistened her lips. "You have never . . . ?" When I failed to respond, though this time I knew perfectly well what she implied, she added, "Experienced pleasure in bed?"

"I do like to sleep," I said faintly. I wasn't about to admit to my furtive explorations with my fingers, the quick quiver and gasp that constituted the sum total of my pleasure in bed.

"Oh, my dear, you are indeed an innocent. What a delight. It is very rare among our kind. Do you think what he does, or does not do, is all there is?"

"I haven't thought of it much at all," I lied. "Though I must say, it was . . ."

"Disappointing?" She reached out to caress my arm. I shivered, though I did not find her touch unpleasant. "It often is," she said, "the first time. We mustn't let such disappointment dissuade us. We are not wives, after all; they are not our husbands. We have other choices."

The subtle stroking of her fingers melted through my sleeve, seeped under my skin, sinking into my very marrow. I recoiled a little, not in revulsion, for I liked the way she smelled, clean with soap, like we'd smelled in Aubazine, not suffused in the flowery fragrances that characterized the demimondaine. Her unblemished skin was clean, too, like fresh snowfall, and her breasts enticed under the lace of her negligee, the tips of her pink nipples showing. But I was afraid. *This* was the power she had mentioned: the forbidden that her lovers yearned for. It was the reason she had become one of the most successful courtesans in Paris. Émilienne d'Alençon was seduction incarnate, and now she directed her power at me. I had no idea how to react.

She, of course, understood. "Do you want me to show you, *ma chère?*" she asked, but it wasn't a question. It was an affirmation that did not require my approval, and as she bent to me and put her lips on mine, I sat quiescent, waiting to see what I would feel.

It was like Chantilly cream, her kiss—warm and moist, with a touch of froth, and sweet as sugar. As her hands flowed over me, unfastening buttons, removing my clothes as if these were made of air, I was not disgusted in the least. I wasn't overcome by desire, either, only sufficiently impressed by her resolve to not feign outraged modesty. Oddly enough, I had no qualms that we were women. I had seen girls in Aubazine slip into each other's beds on occasion and imagined the nuns did the same. I had no judgment. I believed that what people did was what people did, and who was I to condemn, providing no one forced me to do the same?

I was not forced. As she gently pushed me onto my back on her shawl to tease me with her agile tongue and fingers, kindling a heat that first took me aback, until it had me gasping and tangling my hands in her hair, I surrendered to sensation. My body became my own, no longer a utensil to measure fabric or submit to Balsan, but an instrument capable of astonishing joy, and, at the end, as her mouth found my cleft, infinite gratification.

When she raised her flushed face from between my legs, her hair tousled and lips glistening, I could barely draw enough breath to whisper, "I . . . I was wrong."

"Indeed," she murmured. "You see? Choices, my dear, are a woman's weapon."

XIV

Émilienne and I became lovers, though it wasn't the word I used at the time. To me, the term still carried connotations from my endless reading of novels, of yearning and delirious reunion. She left after her visits to return to Paris for months on end, coming back on occasional weekends with another herd of friends avid to sample my hats as she spent another secret afternoon pleasuring me. Words of love never crossed her lips or mine, and as much as I enjoyed her touch, her laughter and wit, I was not *in* love with her.

That much, I knew. Love, it seemed, was an emotion I could not feel.

And as often happens when familiarity sets in, she began to alarm me. One day after we had indulged, bathed together, and settled on the settee to chat, she remarked that I would make a magnificent debut in Paris should I have the inclination.

"You are so gamine, so unusual," she said. "Men will think you half boy, half girl, and want to buy you everything. You could give every one of us a run for our money, while accumulating quite a fortune yourself." She smiled lazily, languid with the aftereffects of sex and oleander-perfumed bathwater. "Have you not considered it? You've told me yourself, you're not happy here, and Balsan . . . well, you do realize he has other interests."

I started, drawing away my bare feet from where they touched hers. We reclined facing each other; all of a sudden, I found her proximity oppressive. I knew what she meant. Balsan sometimes went away for weeks to see his family in Lyons or to Paris to meet with friends, and not once had he invited me. I welcomed his absences, for it gave me time on my own, to work, ride, and read; to lounge in every room of the château without concern for the cigarette ash or clutter I left behind. When he returned, he was always happy to see me, aroused even. But I had never expected him to be faithful, considering how I felt about him.

Still, to hear it spoken aloud unnerved me. Reaching for my cigarette case, I lit one and exhaled smoke with exaggerated confidence. "Of course I know he has other women, but I never said I am unhappy."

"Not in so many words. But I can see you are not. Why not come to Paris? I'll introduce you, make you my first apprentice." She plucked at her throat. "There will come a time when I must submit to the inevitable and let another assume my place. Why shouldn't it be someone I choose?"

I could tell she was sincere. Honesty was a virtue she prized, even if she rarely tendered it to the men she enticed with her charms. Paris had always been my dream. I should consider it. After all, she was right, no matter how much I resisted it. The restlessness that had been an occasional interloper was now my constant companion, so that even at times the usually impervious Balsan muttered that I needed to get out more and cease fiddling with "those infernal hats."

Yet even as I contemplated it, I knew I could never be like Émilienne, even as she said, "And you, my dear, aren't getting any younger. What are you now? Twenty-seven?"

"Twenty-five," I said.

"Yes, yes." She waved her hand, as if a few years were of no account. "But still, at an age when most women have either wed, become someone's soon-to-be-discarded mistress, or resigned themselves to spinsterhood. Surely you desire more than those dismal fates?"

I nodded. "I do. But not what you offer." As I saw her expression harden, I added gently, "It has nothing to do with disapproval. It's just not for me. I don't want to be a courtesan."

She reflected on this in silence. "*Eh, bon*. Then, what do you want? And don't tell me it's to stay here forever and be Balsan's special friend, for I shan't believe you."

I shrugged, drew on my cigarette. "That's the problem, isn't it? I don't know. I think I would like to earn my own way. I've never been afraid of hard work."

"And what do you think I do? If it's not work, I don't know what it is." She paused, contemplating me. "I see. You mean, actually work. What, as a shopkeeper, perhaps?"

It came from out of nowhere, the suggestion, and she meant to be snide rather than helpful, but all of a sudden, I thought it the best idea I had heard yet.

"Why not? Your friends adore my hats; you tell me everyone who sees them asks where you bought them. I save every franc I earn. Why shouldn't I open a shop of my own?"

Émilienne pursed her lips. "Opening a shop requires more than a few francs."

"I could ask Balsan," I said, though as soon as I imagined his reaction, I lost heart. "He could help me, couldn't he?"

"It's not a question of whether he could, but if he will. I should think he'd find the idea unorthodox, to say the least." She stood. "I must get dressed. They'll be back from their hunting excursion soon and we should be downstairs sipping coffee like ladies, *n'est-ce pas?*"

She left me sitting alone with my cigarette between my fingers. That was all we spoke of my situation; and to her credit, not once did Émilienne again mention that I succeed her as a courtesan. Yet the idea she so carelessly tossed aside began to take seed in me.

My own shop. Why not?

AS SOON AS THE OCCASION PRESENTED ITSELF, I petitioned Balsan. I had meant to broach it carefully after we shared one of our brief interludes.

Instead, I blurted it out without warning over supper, as the butler brushed the tablecloth of crumbs. "I want to open a hat shop."

He regarded me with a quizzical look. "Shop?" he echoed.

"Yes," I said, and my rehearsed explanation came pouring out, about how much Émilienne and her friends loved my hats and how I'd saved my earnings, but that I was restless and needed something else to do. And, well, a shop would be perfect because then I could sell my hats in a place where everyone would see them and it would provide me with a way to—

He cut me off brusquely. "Just because Émilienne and her friends indulge your quaint hobby doesn't mean you should open a shop." He spoke as if "shop" were a word that left a bad taste in his mouth, and for the first time, I glimpsed the wealthy bourgeois he was at heart, born to money and reared on it, an endless resource he need not consider.

"You think what I do is a hobby?" I said through my teeth. Nothing was more certain to rouse my ire than the intimation that I was not capable of making decisions for myself.

"Well, isn't it?" He tapped a cigarette on the table and waited for his butler to extend the lighter. "Your hats are lovely and you've found a certain success with women of Émilienne's ilk, but how can you think I'd support such a déclassé venture? Women do not work unless they must and most never succeed unless they do it like Émilienne—on their backs."

I bolted to my feet, nearly overturning my chair.

He blew out a ring of smoke. "Stop looking at me like that. Don't I give you enough? If you need more, you need only ask. I've never denied you anything."

"I don't want your money," I spat out.

"Oh? I must have misunderstood. I thought that was precisely what you wanted."

Whirling about, I stormed from the room, ignoring his laughing calls that I come back and cease behaving like a child. He meant no harm; it was just who he was. He couldn't conceive of any woman wanting more than what he'd given me, because most women wouldn't.

I wasn't most women. And the fury that sent me hurtling up the stairs to my room, where I locked my door and refused to see him for the rest of the night, started to harden inside me, dulling my appreciation for him like tarnish on silver.

I did not want to hate him. I liked him too much for that.

Somehow, some way, I had to find my own means of escape.

TO EASE MY SOUR MOOD, Balsan persuaded me to join him on one of his racecourse trips away from Royallieu. I wanted to refuse, to underscore the point that I had my own mind and would do as I pleased, but the thought of leaving the château proved too strong. I couldn't abide the seclusion another second; the last thing I wanted was to become a harpy with an offended air.

So off to Longchamp we went, to parade among the Parisian elite while their inordinately expensive racehorses thundered down the tracks and everyone who was anyone strove to be seen. Not much had changed as far as fashions were concerned. It was 1908, nearly a decade into the new century that the newspapers heralded as the zenith of a revolutionary age. But women still pranced about in cinched dresses that constricted their ribs and made sitting down a torment, with elaborate loaves adorned in silk cabbages propped on their heads.

To my surprise, I reunited with Adrienne, who was in Longchamp for the races with her new guardian, Madame Mauzel, the matchmaker who'd arranged the expeditious trip to Egypt. At first, I didn't recognize my young aunt mincing along the edge of the white-fenced track with madame beside her—a slim figure encased in white and cream, beribboned and corseted within an inch of her life. But as she paused to stare at me, standing alone in my soft-brimmed fedora, simple blouse with a short silk tie at my collar (one of Balsan's, which I'd cut and adjusted), my belted black jacket, ankle-length camel hair skirt, and low-heeled boots, Adrienne's face lit up.

"Gabrielle!" she cried, causing me to glance around in momentary confusion until I realized she addressed me. I hadn't heard my given name since I'd left Moulins, and as Madame Mauzel appraised me with a wry expression, my aunt enveloped me in her arms.

"Look at you," she breathed, "as elegant as ever. Oh, how I have missed you! You never write. It's very hurtful. Don't you miss me?"

Now that she was before me, I realized I had indeed missed her. Her gentleness and airy grace—she'd not changed, though her love for Maurice had elevated her to prestige, judging by the expensive cut of her dress and the sparkling gemstone bracelets on her wrists.

"Are you married?" I asked, thinking she was and had not invited me to the wedding.

Madame Mauzel snorted, while Adrienne hooked her arm in mine and guided me toward no destination in particular. "Not yet," she said. "Now, how are you? Tell me everything. You must be so in love with Balsan, living with him in his château and accompanying him here—I envy you. Maurice and I must do everything in secret; it's so clandestine, the way we carry on in order to show his family it's truly love that binds us. I don't live with him, and see him at all times with Madame Mauzel. We never have a moment to ourselves, because no lady would allow a man such liberties."

I kept quiet. If this was the case, then I was no lady. But it soon became apparent she wasn't interested in my life. As far as she was concerned, I had settled with Balsan. Why ask more? She was too embroiled in her struggle for respectability and so I let her relate her whispered secrets, her desires and dreams and all those things love was supposed to be. I learned that despite her polished façade and her determination to wed her baron, his family still refused, citing her unsuitability, which pained her deeply even as Maurice continued to declare his devotion. I wondered at her assertion that they never saw each other alone; it seemed unlikely he would remain so intent had he not taken the liberties she professed to deny him. Then again, how would I know what lovers did or did not do for each other? Perhaps anticipation was the very fuel that drove him. It had been years now and they were still together. In her fervent quest to gain the title of baroness, Adrienne was proving rather resilient.

Finally, after she told me everything that weighed on her, she had to catch her breath and in the ensuing silence, while Madame Mauzel watched us, I heard myself say, "I'm going to open a shop." It just came out. I didn't plan it, but the seam of disapproval creasing madame's lips spurred me on. "Balsan has promised to help me. I'm seeking a suitable locale, which is why we are traveling."

"A shop?" Adrienne looked perplexed. "Whatever for?" Then, as she saw my own expression, she added hastily, "Oh, your hats. Are you still making them?" as if the concept was a baffling surprise, a remnant of our tawdry past which surely I should have set aside by now.

"I am. In fact, I've sold quite a few in Paris and now wish to go into business for myself." I paused, gauging the heavy silence. "It's not as though I'll wed anytime soon, if ever," I went on, twisting the imaginary knife in Madame Mauzel's gut. "I must work. I'm excited about it."

"Oh, that's . . . marvelous," Adrienne said, her ingrained admiration overcoming her initial dismay. "You always were so bold, Gabrielle. I think it's a marvelous idea, isn't it, madame?" She glanced at her chaperone. "A lovely little shop, how charming."

"Yes," said madame dryly. "Charming. Have you settled on any particular city yet? I would imagine Paris must be terribly expensive for such a venture."

"Money," I replied, "is not an issue. But no, I've not yet found the perfect location. We're considering various places." I enjoyed watching madame's gullible face assume a begrudging air, for in the end, money was the only deity she worshipped, and she knew very well that Balsan had plenty of it.

"Well, you must let me know when you do open the shop," said Adrienne. "I want to come see it and perhaps assist you like we always dreamed." She ignored madame's gasp. "It's not as if I'm going to wed anytime soon, either," she added, with a slightly hysterical peal of laughter. "So I might as well keep myself occupied until I do, if you still want me."

I nodded. "Of course. I will need help at some point, I'm sure." I basked in the prospect, which of course remained only that for the moment. I didn't care. I wanted madame to swallow her tongue and Adrienne to return to Moulins with tales of how well I was doing. Let Louise and the rest of them chew on that for a while.

"Here, you can write me at madame's." Adrienne extracted a little notebook with an attached silver pen from the tapestry purse madame carried, scribbling out the address. Ripping out the paper, she handed it to me. "I reside with her, though I still visit Louise on Sundays. Oh, Gabrielle"—she embraced me—"I'm so glad we could see each other. Do promise me you'll write. I'm so happy for you. I always said you could do whatever you set your mind to."

Her enthusiasm was sincere; Adrienne wanted everyone to be content, even when she was not, and I decided as we said our good-byes that when the day came, I would send for her. I had the feeling my dream of opening a shop was more likely to come true than marriage to her baron.

As I returned to the grandstands to find Balsan, who'd stayed behind to yell encouragement at his jockey, I felt lighter somehow. There might be many things I wanted to change, but I wouldn't have traded my life for Adrienne's. At least I still had aspirations.

Balsan was at the bar, sharing a drink with his friends and gesticulating with that rare passion he reserved for anything concerning his horses. I recognized two of his companions, Comte Léon de Laborde and Miguel Yuribe, wealthy associates who visited Royallieu regularly. As I approached, they turned to welcome me; I had become an honorary member of their club, my ability to ride astride and hunt with them, coupled with my flair in attire, having endeared me to them. They all called me "*la petite* Coco" and I now laughingly returned their greetings while Balsan beckoned me with a dejected, "We came in fourth. That jockey made Troika run too fast at the start, and lost momentum toward the finish, the stupid gnome." It was then that I noticed a striking man with them, someone I had not seen before.

He was almost swarthy, thick black hair slicked back from his brow with pomade, though a few strands fell in disarray over his forehead. He had smoky green eyes, deep set and solemn—eyes that captured my attention even as I took note of his impeccable suit of tobacco-colored tweed that looked soft to the touch. His trim figure filled out its expensive cut. He extended his square hand to me. I shook it, thinking he greeted me as he would a man, and felt a hint of callus on his palm. Compared with Balsan's pampered manicure, this was the clasp of a workingman, only no workingman could have afforded that suit.

"Have you not met?" said Balsan, and when the man replied in a low voice, "I don't think we have," Balsan frowned. "But I could have sworn . . . you have been to Royallieu since Coco arrived, haven't you? No? Oh, well. Arthur Capel, this is Gabrielle Chanel. Gabrielle, may I present Monsieur Arthur Capel, an English friend of mine with eccentric taste in transportation."

"Coco, to my friends," I said, forcing out a smile, for he still held my hand.

"Boy to mine," he replied, with a slight upturn of his mustached mouth. "It's an honor to meet you, Coco Chanel." He spoke perfect French, without a hint of an accent.

I found myself wondering what Balsan had told Capel about me. Our situation was *irrégulière*; apart from the gatherings at the château, Balsan had made no effort to integrate me into his wider social circle. Yet he must have had questions asked about me. Had he boasted to his friends that he had saved a waif from the streets and made her his mistress?

Capel's handsome features were unreadable, even as his stare seemed to look right through me. Or not through me, I thought with a jolt, but *at* me. He regarded me as if I was someone he actually saw, removed from my role in Balsan's life or whatever else he'd been told.

It disconcerted me. I might have thought he was assessing me, seeing a loose woman for the taking, only I could not tell if he was.

I withdrew my hand. His palm was dry. He didn't leave a drop of his sweat on my fingers, though it was sweltering outside. The man was as cool as a glass of ice.

"Show her your motorcar," Balsan urged. "As you can see by her clothes, she delights in breaking tradition, and that claptrap machine of yours is about as nontraditional as one can get. Go on, we've another race to watch. Coco doesn't really care about the races, do you, *chérie*?"

So riveted was I by Capel that even Balsan's use of an endearment failed to stir me. He never showed affection in public yet I almost expected a possessive pat on my rump as I followed Capel's broad-shouldered walk around the stands. We moved past parasol-shaded tables where ladies sat with their children, waving fans and sipping lemonade, to the area where horses and carriages were stationed.

"Have you ever seen a motorcar?" he asked, pausing so I could step next to him. In the full sunlight, his eyes had flecks of amber in their verdant hue and I saw he was not swarthy naturally but rather disdained a hat and had been bronzed by the sun—another trait that set me to wondering about his provenance. If he had one of the new motorized vehicles that were only just becoming available, he must have means. Yet he had a certain air about him that reminded me of the peasants I'd known in my childhood. He seemed almost taciturn, as if he preferred silence because to reveal his inner thoughts always came with a price.

"Only in newspapers," I told him. "But I'm curious."

"Are you?" His expression softened, turning his somber demeanor into one of undeniable appeal. "That's not a quality you find often." He didn't add "among women" but the words hung unspoken between us as he took me before a blazingly red coupe with metallic fenders so polished I could see my own distorted image in them. It was open topped and ungainly, with large spindle wheels, like a water beetle on stilts.

Capel ran his hand over the bonnet. "She overheats; the radiators are a problem in these models, but the American Henry Ford is devising a better one. This is the future, mademoiselle. In five years at most, the horse and buggy will be a thing of the past and even trains will see a loss of revenue and passengers."

I was fascinated, rounding the vehicle as though it might roar to life at any moment. "Can it go fast?" I asked, lifting my gaze to his.

"Do you want to see?" he replied, and I heard a nearly imperceptible trace of Émilienne in his voice—an invitation I should rebuke. He *was* flirting and it was presumptuous. Just because I was an unwed woman who slept with Balsan, he shouldn't assume I was available to any *gentilhomme* with a fancy suit and an expensive toy. But I nodded anyway, allowing him to open the little side door and see me settled on the quilted leather seat.

After he turned a crank at the front, the motor sputtered and caught with a loud thrumming that vibrated through me. Taking his place before the high steering wheel, he pressed down with his leg on a pedal and the car shot forward, not as fast as a horse at full gallop, but with startling force nevertheless.

The speed as he drove me down the road surrounding the racetrack, avoiding horse-drawn carts and carriages, zipping past amazed bystanders, was intoxicating. It was what I imagined sex should be yet never was— breathless and exhilarating, making me want to cry out from the sheer joy and throw up my arms to let the wind tear back my sleeves.

Then the car coughed, jolted, and rolled to a stop. Smoke billowed from the hood. "See?" he said, leaping over his door to fling open the side of the bonnet and wave away the smoke with his hands. "She overheats. It takes a few minutes to cool her down."

I retrieved my blown-off fedora from the tiny compartment behind my seat (how ingenious, I thought, finding another fold-up seat like a little sofa back there) and handed it to him. "Use this," I suggested, and his face broke into the first smile he'd given me, revealing teeth as strong and square as his hands.

The car took more than a few minutes to cool down. He had a stoppered bottle of water under his driver's seat that he had to pour into the engine. As the smoke faded, he lit a cigarette and extended his gold-plated case to me. He didn't ask if I smoked, though it wasn't something a lady did in public. Raking back my disheveled chignon, I accepted and we leaned against his car, not touching, smoking as we looked upon the landscape. Behind us, faint shouting from the racecourse indicated Balsan had either lost or won his wager. Crushing the butt of his cigarette under his heel, Capel said, "Let's see if she starts."

For a telling moment, I hesitated. I did not want to see Balsan. The realization speared me where I stood. I felt heat creep into my cheeks and nodded, returning to the car. He cranked it back to life and drove us more sedately back to the racecourse.

Balsan and his friends were in the lot with the others, the races finished for the day. He waved as we drove in and Capel opened the door for me. I slipped out past him, tugging at my skirt, thinking I must look a fright yet not caring if I did.

"I would like to see you again," he said quietly.

I half-turned to meet his penetrating gaze. "He's going to Pau next," I heard myself say, in a husky voice I scarcely recognized as my own. "He has a hunting lodge there. I was going to return to Royallieu, but . . ."

Capel did not reply. I went to Balsan, who guffawed that I resembled a scarecrow and wasn't this fad for motorcars an obnoxious waste. I smiled and replied—well, I don't remember what I said. Whatever it was, it no longer mattered.

How could I have explained that nothing between us mattered anymore?

XV

Boy caught me by surprise.

There was no other explanation for it. I had denied my heart to every man after my father ravaged it. I had defied expectations, living with a wealthy aristocrat I didn't love, but I now found myself brimming with an inchoate longing that would have been ludicrous had it not been mine.

He came with us to Pau. In Balsan's rustic château surrounded by dense forests, I came to know Capel as I had known no one else—though not physically. He was a perfect gentleman in this regard, though his sultry eyes would gleam as the nights turned long and the Jurançon wine flowed. Then the men staggered off drunk to bed, leaving us alone with Balsan, who always drank more than his share but never seemed to tip over from it.

I was amazed that Balsan failed to sense the current in the air, ambling about, sharing anecdotes, while Boy nodded and left his own glass untouched and I smoked cigarette after cigarette until my mouth went as dry as paste. Was he so blind that he couldn't tell I ached to see him gone so Boy and I could sit together instead of apart like suitors at a chaperoned ball? Did he not see the very ties that bound us were stretched to their limits, worn seams on a coat that no longer fit?

I'd been correct in assuming that Boy was like a peasant in his attitude toward self-confession. Yet in those weeks at Pau, I learned that he was two years older than I, the only son, with three sisters, born to a humble Catholic family, half French through his late mother, his father an enterprising Irish businessman who'd scaled the rungs of employment until making his fortune as an agent for railway and shipping companies. Boy had spent his childhood in Paris, where his father moved the family upon his success. Educated according to exalted standards—the best private boarding school in England, trips throughout Europe and the Middle East, even to America as he grew older—he mingled with the new bourgeoisie and the haut monde of old society, as antiquated rules began to disintegrate and money, no matter how it was gained, became society's sole calling card. As much as he loved motorcars, Boy also loved polo, an affinity he shared with Balsan. More important to me, and most unusual for a man of his means, he loved to work.

That made him magnificent in my eyes. Though groomed for a life of privilege, Boy wanted to earn his own way. He had assumed various positions in his father's firm until he garnered enough experience to strike out on his own, investing in coal, improved engines for trains, railroad expansions, elite polo clubs, and anything else that caught his eye and promised a return on his money.

"I don't want to be one of these men," he said as we sat before the ebbing fire after Balsan finally made his exit, "who indulge in leisure for leisure's sake. It's all fine to frolic and ride horses all day, to take life as it comes because, eh"—he shrugged with mocking nonchalance—"why worry? But I need to work. I must own something that is mine." He turned his arresting eyes to me. "You understand? You know that I am not like Balsan."

He needn't have asked. They couldn't have been more different, Balsan's laissez-faire attitude seeming trivial, the workings of an outdated automaton, compared with Boy's modernized purpose. "What we do not earn ourselves," he said, "is never truly ours. It can always be taken away. But even if we lose everything we work for, the achievement is ours forever."

How could I not be infatuated? He was the great stroke of fortune

I'd awaited without knowing it existed—someone I couldn't have possibly dreamed of because there was no one like him to model my fantasies on. In those long autumn nights and prematurely crisp days, he filled me with stories I'd always wanted to hear, even if I had not known how to find them. Yet not once did he indicate he was interested in anything more than friendship, except to occasionally take my hand and squeeze it when he became overly impassioned during our talks.

In turn, I shared the story of my deprived childhood, of the brimstone of Aubazine, the garret in Moulins, and the humiliation of Vichy, and of my yearning for something more, always more, until I finally confessed my dream of one day opening my own shop. I spoke tentatively, as cautious as if I was unwrapping a fragile heirloom. I had lied to Balsan about my origins; now, for the first time, I told someone else the unvarnished truth and though it felt awkward, too revealing, it relieved me of a secret burden I had not realized I carried.

He smiled. "I think you'll do very well. It requires a lot of capital and you'll lose far more than you make at first, but the important thing is that you're happy doing what you love."

No one had ever said such words to me. In Aubazine, the nuns had extolled the need for a life without expectations, as if happiness was not something we created. If I didn't know I loved Boy before, I knew it then, with every fiber of my being. Had he asked me to go to his bed that night, I'd have done so willingly, no matter that the château of Pau was crammed to its eaves with snoring drunkards who might overhear us.

But he did not ask, and I might have worried that he didn't find me attractive or he loved another. If he was irresistible to me, how could he not be to every other woman who crossed his path? Indeed, even Balsan eventually took note of our intimacy, for after Boy departed in his car for Paris, Balsan said, "He's a cad. A mistress in every port. He might be half English by birth but in his groin he's more French than any other man I know."

Had I been more attuned to Balsan's sensibilities, I might have realized that was a warning: don't get entangled with Capel. But he could have hurled lightning and threatened eviction, and nothing would have stopped me. Boy might have a hundred conquests and I might be the latest on his extended list, and still it was, as they say, inevitable.

We were meant for each other.

So I didn't worry that he found me unappealing. I didn't fret that he'd not acted on the communion between us. I knew that in time he would. He must. *We* must.

All I needed to do was free myself.

Still, I hesitated. We celebrated the new year of 1909 in an epic bacchanal at Royallieu, with a masked ball attended by Balsan's friends, including Émilienne and her acquaintances. Only Boy stayed away, having gone to England to see his family. But that wasn't why I delayed. I didn't know the reason myself. Only that I feared the final step, feared plunging into the unknown pool where Adrienne and so many others trod water and hoped for relief.

Surrender had never been part of my plan, especially not to a man.

Émilienne noted the change in me. The house was too crowded for our illicit afternoons, but on the day she left, she whispered in my ear, "I think someone else has taken my place, *ma chérie,*" and when I started to protest, she shushed me. "No need for explanations. Choices, remember? We all must have them."

But those very choices paralyzed me. I couldn't work, wandering my workroom with my hats ready for my scissors and my mind in another place, wondering where Boy was now, what he was doing, if he thought of me. When I envisioned him laughing in a Parisian café with a *cocotte* or strolling along the Seine with one of his many conquests, the sharp pangs I felt bewildered me, until I realized these must be jealousy. It enraged me, that helplessness, the abandon that overcame me; but for once, my anger had no fuel to feed on.

Everything inside me had become kindling for Boy's touch.

HE CAME IN THE SPRING, as the snow melted on the grounds and the chestnuts budded with tight-furled leaves. I heard the bronchial wheeze of his overheated car pulling into the driveway before the château and I threw my scissors aside, racing from my room in my bare feet to hurtle down the staircase. Before he had even stepped into the foyer to unbutton his coat, before he could pass a hand through his mop of windblown hair, I flung myself into his arms.

He kissed me then. A hard, breath-quenching kiss that flattened me against his body, unraveling and rearranging me, ripping out the lining of my tired self to create a new garment of my skin, made of pliant silk without buttonholes or stays.

"I missed you," he whispered. As he let me down, the soles of my feet not feeling the icy chill of the floor, the sound of slow applause reached me.

I whirled around. Balsan stood in the doorway to the library. With a grimace, he raised his hands again and clapped. "Bravo. At last, someone has thawed my petite Coco's heart."

He turned on his heel, going back into the library. He'd been packing for a trip to Argentina, where horse breeding was the rage and he had heard there was excellent stock to be found. When he failed to reemerge, I whispered to Boy, "What do we do now?"

"Tell him the truth. You're coming with me to Paris. I want to finance your shop." As I gaped at him, he added, "Émilienne visited me after she left here. She believes you are destined for success. I believe it, too. I want to be part of it, if you'll let me."

I would have kissed him again, but he led me into the library, where we found Balsan at his desk, a tumbler of cognac at his side. "Drink?" he asked without looking up.

"Étienne, *mon ami*," began Boy, and Balsan glanced up with a droll smile. "Careful, Englishman. In France, friends do not steal their friends' lovers."

"You know I never intended to——," said Boy, but I interrupted him, unwinding my fingers from his to step to Balsan. "Blame me if you must blame someone."

His mouth twitched. "You do not know anything. You're as naive as the day I fetched you out of that hovel in Vichy."

"Perhaps," I said, feeling Boy stiffen behind me. "But this is what I want."

"Do you?" Balsan smiled. "Are you quite certain? Because once you leave here, you cannot think to come back. I'll not be so generous, no matter how much I care for you."

"Yes," I said. "I know."

He lifted his gaze over my head to Boy. "Will you take care of her?"

Though I didn't look around, I knew Boy nodded.

"Then it's settled," said Balsan. "She goes to you."

"Not to me," corrected Boy. "She goes *with* me. There is a difference." Before Balsan could react, I added, "He's going to help me open my shop. I'll not be kept by anyone anymore."

Balsan rolled his eyes, emptying his glass. "Again with the shop! God save us, she's stubborn as a mule." He crossed the library to the tray with his cut-glass decanters. Pouring himself another measure of cognac, he said to Boy, "She'll ruin you if you indulge this fantasy of hers. She'll take every centime you have."

"I'm prepared for it," Boy replied. "You may think her ambition frivolous but I do not. I'm extending her a loan, to be repaid with interest whenever she can."

"Is that so? Well, well." Balsan emptied his glass once more. Though he didn't display it in his speech, I saw he was trembling and felt pity for him, for that shuttered mind I had once believed so open, and his clinging to a world that faded all around him. "A loan with interest," he mocked. "How generous, seeing that it'll take her years, if ever, to repay it."

"We'll see about that." Boy motioned to me. "Come, Coco."

"I won't take anything from here that isn't mine," I told Balsan. "I promise."

"Then you might as well go in the clothes you wear, for nothing else is yours."

"That is why I must go." I returned to Boy's side with as much pride as I could muster.

At the doorway, I looked over my shoulder, though I didn't know what I hoped to see. He sipped his cognac, contemplating something far away. I was about to leave him with only a suitcase filled with my hats and the few clothes I had made; he had rescued me, safeguarded me, yet I felt only vague regret for hurting him. Already this house that had been my home for nearly four years seemed as remote as his distant gaze, a ruined pile of stone that would not remember me after I had gone.

Just as I turned back to Boy, I heard Balsan sigh. "I unlocked her cage, but you, my thieving friend, aim to set her free. Be careful with what you do. Wild things are never tamed."

Boy's answer was to enclose my hand in his and take me away.

ACT TWO
21 RUE CAMBON
1909–1914

"I WANT TO BE PART OF WHAT HAPPENS."

I

Paris.

How can I describe those first months? I had become a resident of that city I had yearned to see all my life. The demolition of the cramped medieval districts initiated under the Second Empire was complete, tangled labyrinths of crooked lanes and tenements gutted to make way for sweeping boulevards lined with imposing ivory-hued apartment buildings, splendid parks, and squares with elaborate fountains.

The noise took weeks for me to grow used to: the blaring of horns on the dashboards of new motorcars interrupting the jangle and clip-clop of hackneys and carriages, the mixture of grease and animal ordure creating an acrid stench that permeated the air. And the people everywhere, strolling the streets and chattering in cafés, catching the cabs from Montmartre to the banks of the Seine, flowing in and out of restaurants, bistros, and theaters. Artists, musicians, dancers, and sculptors; tradesmen, shop owners, and fishmongers—poor, rich, and everyone in between, blurring the lines of distinction in, as Boy put it, "an emancipated world where we'll not be judged by how we were born but by what we become."

Oh, it was dazzling, infusing me with an excitement that stole my sleep. He took me to see the mansion on the avenue d'Ilène in the sixteenth arrondissement where he'd been raised—a fluted excess that had once belonged to the Rouchefauld dynasty and the sight of which left me with a sensation of panic, as I began to understand how different Boy's background and mine truly were. Later, as we dined at Maxim's, he explained that after his mother's death when he was twenty-one, his father had returned to London. An embassy now rented their Paris mansion, as if such changes were commonplace. Boy might not be an aristocrat like Balsan, but his family clearly had almost as much money; indeed, I suspected they might have a good deal more.

Boy also took me to the grandiose glass-hewn shopping emporiums—Printemps, Bon Marché, and the palatial Galeries Lafayette—that sold everything anyone could desire, from furnishings to ready-made garments, cheap stockings, and affordable shoes. It was almost pagan, this surfeit of things one could purchase, and he chuckled as I wandered the tiered floors in a daze, filling my arms with new hat forms to decorate and the clothes I needed to fit into this new world where everything I'd brought with me, save for my hats, made me look like an urchin.

He had business engagements, as well, which he did not take me to, such as society galas and invitations to prestigious clubs. Boy explained that while he didn't give a fig for what people said—indeed, he often went to such events dressed in tweed instead of the requisite black tie—he couldn't afford to offend those with whom he did business or upset sensibilities by showing up with a mistress on his arm, no matter how enchanting she might be.

So he left me behind to roam his stark, masculine apartment off the Champs-Élysées, with its dark crimson painted walls, mahogany accents, and still-life paintings of fowl and sheaves of wheat. From the terrace, I could glimpse the black skeleton of the Tour Eiffel and watch the fashionable amble the boulevards, shopping and partaking of evening aperitifs.

Did I feel lost? Absolutely, like a lamb in the woods. Paris was a wolf waiting to devour the hapless, and I had no preparation to do battle with her, not yet. Instead, I worked feverishly, using a spare room in the back of the apartment to make as many new hats as I could. Boy would often come home late at night to find me crouched over my work, a cigarette dangling in a pillar of ash from my lips, my eyes burning and my fingers bloody with my needle's stigmata.

"We're going to need more space," he would remark, and then he'd take the instruments of my trade away from me and guide me into the bathroom—a marble-and-tile temple to cleanliness—to draw me a hot bath in the claw-footed tub, where I could soak away my exertions.

And once he'd dried me himself with his fluffy white towels and had wrung the excess water from my ropes of hair, he took me to his walnut-paneled bed.

I hesitate even now to speak of it. Such moments, forged of a volcanic passion that I sincerely felt might rupture me from within, are not meant to be shared. Suffice it to say that it was everything I'd read it should be, and much, much more. He had a lean body, his face, throat, and forearms tanned, but the rest of him as white as milk, his musculature defined under his skin—ribs and wrists, hips and ankles, jutting yet soft as he pressed them into mine. He fit me like a key, and he unlocked that glacial core I'd nurtured from the hour my father had ridden away in his cart. As he slid inside me and I arched to meet his thrusts, he whispered, "I love you, Coco. I love you so much"—the breathless litany of every coupling between lovers yet which I still couldn't offer in return until he grasped my face between his hands and, still moving inside me, demanded, with near-desperate urgency, "Say it. Tell me!" and I gasped, "I . . . I love you, too," though it always sounded so false, as though such banality could not begin to encompass the enormity of what I felt.

Later, as he smoked and I lay with my head on his chest, tangling my fingers in the dark matting on his chest, he chuckled. "Balsan was right. You are stubborn," and as I made to pull away, he wrapped his arms tighter about me and murmured, "No, hush. Stay as you are. I don't care if you cannot say it. I know that you do."

Oh, I did. I would have died for him. He was everything to me—my lover, my family, my best friend. I knew almost no one else in Paris, though as time passed some of those I had met with Balsan began to appear. One of the first was Léon de Laborde, as debonair as ever, bringing me tales of Balsan's trip to Argentina and a basket of lemons Balsan sent, for he knew how much I loved to use the rinds on my eyes to ease their puffiness. It was Balsan's token apology, the only way he knew to ask for forgiveness, and I was so happy with Boy, I accepted it without hesitation.

Happy . . .

Yes, I was happy. It was not a comfortable feeling for me. Sometimes, after we made love and he fell asleep, I watched him like a cat, the steady rise and fall of his chest, the exhalation of nicotine-tinged breath, and the occasional mutterings of dreams. Terror would seize me that he'd be taken from me, that our idyll couldn't last, for when had anything I loved remained as it was? Where was it written that I, child of no one, deserved such joy? It only happened at night, this abyss of dread, never during the day. Only in the empty hours between today and yesterday, when I was alone with my sleeping lover and the weight of the past crept upon me like a reproachful ghost.

"I do need more space," I announced one morning, after we break-fasted on the terrace and he dressed for a business meeting. "What about my shop?"

He eyed me in the mirror, adjusting his collar. "We'll have to start looking." He paused. "Balsan has offered his bachelor apartment on the boulevard Malesherbes. He says you can use it for as long as you like until we find a more suitable location."

I stared at him. He shrugged. "He wrote to me at my office. He is repentant. He says the manner in which he left things between us is inex-cusable. He wants to make amends."

That was Balsan to his core: unable to bear a grudge. I disliked that I could, that while I had accepted his lemons, I could not bring myself to accept more of his charity.

"It's not a bad area," Boy went on, sensing my turmoil. "He's also offered to help find an expert milliner to assist you; he mentioned one Lucienne Rabaté, currently employed at the Maison Lewis, but apparently eager for new opportunity."

The Maison Lewis was one of Paris's most prestigious hat salons; Capel had taken me there, and I was amused to discover Monsieur Lewis's prices far exceeded his overwrought styles. Still, a milliner from such an exalted atelier was a boon. She could help me master my craft, and perhaps lure influential customers to sample my hats.

"He said all that, did he?" I lit a cigarette, watching him through the curling smoke.

Boy chuckled. "No, he said more, but that is all you need to hear." As he buttoned up his jacket and reached for his driving cap, I grumbled, "I'll think about it."

He leaned over to kiss my cheek. "Do. And while you're at it, write to Adrienne and ask if she'd still like to help manage the shop. You're too prickly to attend customers."

I wrote to Adrienne that very day. When her reply arrived a week later, stamped from Moulins, I took one look at the first lines and let out a howl that brought Boy running to me.

He caught me about my waist as my legs buckled and the letter fluttered from my fingers.

"My sister Julia," I whispered, burying my face in his neck. "She's dead."

II

It had been a terrible set of circumstances, Adrienne wrote. Sitting on the terrace as the August sun slipped behind the rooftops, I read of how my sister had fallen in love with an officer from the garrison, who met her working at our grandparents' market stall and courted her. Julia—innocent, gullible Julia—became pregnant; and as these matters so often went, the officer promptly requested a transfer and disappeared. Left with the disapproval of our grandparents, Julia packed her belongings and moved in with Louise. Nine months later, she gave birth and then slit her wrists. Adrienne sent word to Royallieu about the funeral, but the house was empty except for the servants, with me in Paris and Balsan in Argentina. Her letter went unanswered, lost in the correspondence awaiting Balsan on his return, if it even arrived.

Adrienne declined to come to Paris. She was now living with her baron in Moulins, another small battle won in her war, and couldn't risk leaving now. But she asked if I might assume responsibility for my nephew, little André, who was with Louise, and suggested I write to my sister Antoinette, who'd left the convent and was now working as we had at the horrid House of Grampayre.

I had not given Antoinette a second thought. My guilt drove me to send urgent word to her. With Boy's help, I also wired a large bank draft to Moulins for André's upkeep, promising that once he reached the proper age, I would see to his education, but not in a convent or institution for foundlings. After a long talk with Boy, I determined that he should attend Eton, the English boarding school Boy recommended and offered to pay for. He sent a letter to the headmaster, whom he knew personally, to ensure André's admittance when the time came.

Julia's death cast a pall over me. I had left her without a word. Haunted by my own callousness, by memories of the times we had shared and my fervent declaration at Aubazine that I would never abandon her, I could not escape the horrible thought that had I only inquired after her, taken her under my wing, she might still be alive.

When Boy found me one evening upon his return from one of his business trips, sobbing on the sofa in the living room, he sat beside me, pulled my head to his shoulder, and whispered, "Coco, you must forgive yourself. You are not to blame. Take Balsan's offer. Open your shop. You cannot bring your sister back. You mustn't die with her."

He took me to Balsan's apartment on Malesherbes. He had phoned ahead; none other than Lucienne Rabaté, the milliner, waited for us. A freckled, red-haired, opinionated woman, she marched before me to inspect the small ground-floor space at street level below Balsan's empty bachelor apartment, sniffing as she toed the dust on the plank-wood floor.

"It's not the Place Vendôme," she said. "But with some nice displays, a rug, and a bell over the door, it will do." She paused, eyeing me. I wasn't sure I liked her; she had the sharp gaze of a lifelong Parisian and an expert in her trade, while I was nobody, really, a novice who made odd hats. "That said, before I accept any offer of employment, I will need to see what you intend to sell. I have a reputation to uphold. I'll not leave my current post to peddle inferior wares."

I had brought four of my hats with me, but before I could remove one from the box, she thrust her hand inside and yanked it out. She held it up to the light filtering through the grimy front window, turning it about, examining it for imperfections.

"Hmm." She held out her hand, returning the hat to me. "Another, if you please."

Once she inspected each of the hats, she pursed her lips. Boy stepped outside to smoke. At length, she turned to me. "Your hats are certainly not like anything in the shops or salons. They are simple, elegant; they could appeal to the right clientele. But it will not be easy. Established milliners, as well as Worth and Paul Poiret, do not welcome competition. Indeed, they both have been at war since Poiret left Worth's employ to open his own atelier. Do you know of them?"

I shook my head, feeling dejected by her harangue.

"No?" She tapped her foot. "Well, mademoiselle, if you're going to launch a hat business, you should. Monsieur Frederick Worth is an Englishman who dresses every woman of importance, including royalty. His gowns are exclusive. No dress is alike; he creates unique apparel for each of his clients. Poiret learned his trade under Worth but now dresses our more defiant ladies in scandalous Oriental-themed ensembles. All their outfits require headpieces; they hire milliners to make these under confidential agreements that protect their designs. Is that what you wish to do?"

"No." I squared my shoulders. "No," I repeated more firmly. "I want to work for myself."

"And your clients, I presume?" She motioned about with disdain. "This location is hardly ideal. Poiret's atelier is near the Opéra; Worth has salons on Place Vendôme and in London. You'll need to find your customers, as they're unlikely to stroll in here on their own."

"Then I will." I'd started to pack my hats into the box when I heard her step to me. I looked up. She held a paper in her hand. "Here is a list of potential clients I can invite, whom I have met through the Maison Lewis. I suggest you look it over carefully, as under the circumstances I must ask that mademoiselle not request a reference. I do not wish for my employer to be made aware that I seek a position elsewhere."

I let out a weak laugh. "And I, madame, wouldn't recognize a single name on that list."

"Indeed." She glanced past the window toward Boy, standing on the curb by his car. "Perhaps Monsieur Capel might."

"He might," I retorted, taking up the box. "But he is not my employer."

I was walking to the door when she said, "Then I believe we are in agreement." I paused, and looked back at her. "I cannot pay much," I told her. "As you say, this will not be easy."

"I have saved my wages," was her dry reply. "And I've never been afraid of hard work."

It seemed we had something in common, after all.

I nodded. "We are in agreement, Madame Rabaté."

LUCIENNE AND I CLEANED the shop of every cobweb, scrubbed the floors, washed the window, and set up a work area in the cramped back room by the staircase leading to the apartment. Boy opened a line of credit for me at his bank for funds to purchase glass displays to show off my hats, a marble-topped counter, a gilded chair and mirror for the wall, and a rug and chiming bell for the door. I wanted an awning with my name, but the building manager forbade it; instead, I had a hand-lettered sign made in block letters for the window: GABRIELLE CHANEL.

A few days before I was due to open the shop, my collection of sample hats perched on felt model heads in tiers on the displays and the window featuring an exclusive creation fashioned by me and Lucienne—an elegant cream hat with a black silk band and single egret feather—Antoinette appeared at the door with her valise.

Taking one look at her, I had to bite back tears. At twenty-two years of age, she was a sparrow of a woman, with our big Chanel eyes and wealth of hair, though hers was a lighter shade than my own, and she had our mother's piquant expression. She looked as if she hadn't eaten in weeks. I took her to the corner café, plying her with ham-filled croissants and hot chocolate as she related the familiar story of enduring years of humiliation as a charity case at the convent in Moulins before she went to work under the tyrannical Madame G.

"That is over now," I assured her. "You shall stay in Balsan's apartment over the shop; there is a nice bedroom and sitting room. You'll work for me, attending to the customers, for I don't think I can do that and design hats at the same time."

The truth was neither could she, or not at first. She was very timid, though she flourished in time under Lucienne's tutelage, while I remained terrified of that little bell above the door, tinkling the arrival of a curious customer. Lucienne had been true to her word and sent out invitations to her list. They all came, well-dressed women in sumptuous outfits with maidservants, perusing my wares as I hid in the back room, refusing to come out. If they had asked me to give them my hats for free, I would have, so apprehensive was I of my reception.

As my business slowly grew, abetted by Lucienne's loyal clients, as well as the arrival of Émilienne and her coterie, who bought everything in sight, Lucienne kept me informed of the cloistered world outside my door.

"Poiret held a ball in his atelier, a masquerade à la Arabian Nights, and stole away ten of Worth's clients, the most influential ones." Lucienne sniffed, her reaction to everything. "He seizes advantage in change. Worth has become outmoded, his designs too confining. Poiret has banned corsets; he offers flowing skirts and harem pants. He's also developed a signature *parfum*, Nuit de Chine, which he gave away at his masquerade. It's a musky horror but all his clients use it. He reaps a fortune. Worth is furious." She paused in emphasis, forcing me to look up from my littered worktable. "He's heard of you, as well, mademoiselle. Several of his clients now wear your hats."

"They do?" I was incredulous.

She nodded. "Something you would be aware of if you ever set foot outside this workroom. Everyone grows curious; they want to know who this Gabrielle Chanel is."

"I . . . I don't like attending customers," I said, haltingly, though we had had this discussion before. At the salons, as she so often informed me, designers personally attended their clients, serving them coffee and cake, catering to their every whim. A woman could easily spend an entire afternoon in an atelier, between her arrival, fitting, and departure; it was how the couturier exerted his stranglehold, compelling them to wear only his designs.

"You'll need to learn to like it," she said. "Or hide your dislike of it. In order to succeed, you must be seen. The customer wants to see the hands that design what she buys."

"But only on her terms," I riposted. "Not even Poiret, for all his influence, is granted entrée to her home or social circle. Once she leaves his atelier, he does not exist."

"Ah, but he is there, nevertheless. On their very person, *sans* corset." Lucienne turned back into the shop as the bell rang. "Consider this," she added, tossing her wisdom at me over her shoulder. "He influences them even when he is absent. That right person, at the right time, with the right approach, can exert more impact than we realize. Do you not wish to do the same?"

I stared after her. I did wish it. More than anything. But to my dismay, running a shop was not as I had imagined. I worked nonstop, filling orders. Lucienne proved a godsend and managed to lure away two Maison Lewis assistants to help with our production, but we clashed over everything— prices, styles, sales methods, displays. I wanted to move as many hats as I could; whenever Émilienne and her friends swarmed us (dear Émilienne, with her relentless cheer), I let them take as much as they could, reasoning they would be seen wearing my hats, and entice others. Already, one of her actress friends had worn a hat of mine onstage and it was commented upon in the widely circulated gazette *Comoedia Illustré*; surely, this type of free advertising would reap rewards.

"Yes," stormed Lucienne. "Indeed, it will! We'll have a mob of more tawdry actresses seeking something for nothing. Are we running a charity? Because last time I checked the account books, you haven't enough to buy supplies, much less pay me or your sister."

We sparred like ruffians, shouting until Antoinette piped up with one of the rondelles from the coffeehouses in Moulins and halted us in our tracks. "'I've lost my poor Coco, Coco my lovable dog,'" she sang out, "'lost him, close to the Trocadéro. You didn't happen to see my Coco?'"

I started to laugh, doubled over as Lucienne pressed a hand to her mouth to stifle her rare giggle before the three of us launched into the chorus: "'Co at the Tro. Who has seen my Coco?'"

One evening as we dined at the Café de Paris, Boy finally asked me how business fared.

"Wonderful," I said. "I'm making lots of money and contacts. It's so easy, all I have to do is oversee the workroom and write checks." I wasn't about to admit that I could have fallen dead asleep with my head in the soup, that my feet were sore with blisters, and my stiff hands felt like claws. Everything had to seem wonderful. Boy seemed to ratchet up success after success with ease; he would never understand how overwhelmed I felt.

"Is it?" He regarded me without a hint of a smile. "Why are you lying to me, Coco? I set up a security on your account at the bank to cover the shop's expenses; I receive the statements. You overdrew on your line of credit again, the fifth time in as many months."

My heart started a rapid thumping that made me queasy. "How is that possible?"

"It tends to happen," he said dryly, "when we spend more than we earn."

"But I—I deposit money every week. They wouldn't give me any if I didn't have it."

He sighed. "They give it to you, my love, because I give it to them. Your deposits do not cover the shop's expenses. They barely cover Madame Rabaté's salary."

"So, you're saying . . . I'm in debt to *you*?"

He met my horrified gaze. I shoved back my chair, staggered from the table in the middle of the crowded restaurant, grabbing my coat and hat and running out. It was pouring rain, one of those autumn tempests that turned the city into a swamp. I started down the street, blinded by the rain and my own furious tears. I didn't hear him coming after me, didn't acknowledge his shouts until he grasped my arm and pulled me around, his drenched hair plastered to his head as he said, "Coco, stop this! Be reasonable. It's only a business."

"Yes, *my* business!" I wrenched my arm from him. "Mine! I don't want to be kept by you or anyone else. I never asked for it. That was never our agreement."

He stood still, rain pooling over his shoulders. "I told you, I would help you if you let me. If you don't want my help, all you have to do is say so."

"Help?" My laughter exploded—ugly and raw, colored by shame and my realization that I had exchanged one gilded cage for another. "You told me once that what we don't earn for ourselves is never ours, that it can always be taken away. Is that what your help means? Will you close my shop whenever you please?"

His own fury, rare to kindle but implacable once lit, darkened his eyes. "You insult me. What's worse, you insult us. You cannot run a business properly? Fine, you don't have to. Hire an accountant. Do what you do best and leave the numbers to those who know how. But don't ever tell me again that I will snatch anything from you. I will not stand for it."

I went limp, suddenly feeling the sodden weight of my clothes, the chill of the rain. I averted my face. "I'm not saying that."

"Yes, you are. I told you, I am not Balsan. What I give you now, you will repay. I know you will. What I want is for you to know it. To *believe* it. It doesn't matter how much I must invest if you'll only trust in your talent and tell me the truth."

I bit down on my quivering lip. "I will repay it. Every last centime."

"So I hope." He gave me a pensive look. "You're the proudest person I know, but remember, you are still only a woman. And though I love you for it, pride will make you suffer."

Only a woman . . . In the end, was this how he saw me? A helpless creature, dependent on his goodwill? It terrified me to even consider it. It was Balsan all over again, only this time I was in love and had no defense against it.

I did not speak as he engulfed me in his arm, leading me back to our motorcar. Upon my arrival at the shop the next day, I summoned my staff and announced, "I'm not here to spend money as if it grows on trees. Henceforth, I must authorize every expense. And," I added, with a glance at Lucienne's satisfied face, "no more free hats."

It was a small step, in light of my profligacy, but hard earned, nevertheless.

Money was freedom. I did not intend to squander freedom again.

III

In the summer of 1911, Boy took me on vacation to the resort of Deauville.

He insisted on it, though I did not want to leave my shop. Through a harsh regimen of fifteen-hour days and many sleepless nights, I had begun to prosper. Not meteorically, but my clientele steadily increased and improved in stature, the courtesans and actresses augmented by a select list of society women who embraced Poiret's modernized dress and found my hats the perfect accompaniment. The grandes dames of the haut monde remained enslaved by Worth and other luxury ateliers that garbed them from head to toe; they eschewed me. But others with less to lose, hostesses welcoming artists and bohemians to their salons, began to exchange my plain white calling card among themselves. During my remorseless weekly reviews of my accounts, I finally saw I'd turned a corner and could repay Boy some of the debt I owed him. Soon, I would no longer need his retainer on my line of credit.

He didn't comment on it, though he must have seen the statements that arrived at his office. I appreciated his discretion, his ability to observe my improvement without gloating over it, and when he suggested it was time to take a holiday, I reluctantly agreed.

Deauville proved to be the balm I needed. Situated on the Normandy coast, before the English Channel, it was full of glamorous restaurants, hotels, casinos, and lengthy promenades. Here, I experienced a relaxation I rarely allowed myself, swimming every day in a daring bathing costume that exposed my arms and shoulders and dining at night in our suite at the Hôtel Normandy, overlooking the pier.

One night, I asked Boy to meet me for dinner in the casino. We had spent several evenings there in the company of his friends—people I'd never met who also lived in Paris, who welcomed him with a familiarity that made me clench my teeth. Among them were long-nosed, beautiful women shimmering with jewels who eyed me from behind languid swishes of their fans. I could practically hear their cruel appraisal of the trades-woman whom Arthur Capel had seen fit to take up with. I was determined to show them who I truly was.

In a boutique in town, I bought a white silk dress that clung to the body, supple and tucked high at the waist, a dress for sultry nights, unlike any I had seen in Paris. Pairing it with a length of pearls that Boy had given me, I sauntered into the casino with my hair swept back into a chignon at the nape of my neck, held by a piqué band; my long throat and arms were tan from the sun, a touch of kohl at my eyes enhanced their luster.

Boy waited at the table. As he saw me approach, he stood with a know-ing smile and drew out my chair. Around us, the haut monde dined on caviar and poached salmon in mint sauce. Champagne by the gallon cooled in buckets of ice. I paused, marking my prey, then leaned to Boy and grazed his cheek with my lips. I heard the rustle of alarm ripple through the dining room, as if the walls had turned to tissue, an urgent susurration as all eyes shifted to watch me sit, not across from Boy as was customary, but directly by his side.

The rest of our table's chairs, as I had ensured, were empty.

After dinner, they gathered in the mirrored salon to greet me. I was at my most charming, exchanging witticisms and bestowing smiles as though I mixed with such company every hour of every day. With that uncanny intuition women have for threats, I was besieged at the end of the evening for my card, along with promises that as soon as they returned to Paris, they would call upon me at my shop.

"So daring," they said, "this bronze color of yours. Do you not fear getting spots from the sun? No? And that dress and pearls—oh, my dear, it's sublime. You say you make hats? Well, I simply must see them. I'm so terribly bored with the usual."

When we returned to our hotel, Boy watched me loosen the knot at my nape and allow my hair to fall. He mused, "You would look exquisite with short hair, I think."

I smiled. "One thing at a time. We mustn't frighten the herd too much at first."

"Frighten them?" he growled, and he stalked across the room to seize me in his arms. "You're a lioness. You'll eat them all alive and still be ravenous for more."

He was right. Those credulous gazelles would not sate a hunger like mine.

But it was a start.

WHEN WE ARRIVED BACK IN PARIS, he said he would drive me to the shop. I was eager to get back to work, to see how many orders had come in during my absence, and get everything ready for the stampede I anticipated. I had no doubt that every one of the women I'd met in Deauville would come.

Boy did not take the route to boulevard Malesherbes, however. Instead, he turned toward the Place Vendôme and the district that sold the finest furs, jewelry, and perfumes, driving down the exclusive rue de Saint-Honoré onto rue Cambon across from the back entrance of the Hôtel Ritz, an eighteenth-century palace converted into a luxury hotel renowned for its exclusivity. He brought the car to a halt before a white building festooned with stucco garlands and cherub heads over its classical block façade.

"What is this?" I asked, bemused. Reaching into his pocket, he handed me a set of keys.

"I signed a lease. The back room and mezzanine are yours. It is time."

With the keys clutched in my hand as he stood behind me grinning, I passed speechless into my new premises. Applause greeted me. Through a haze, I saw my counters and displays with my hats, arranged in black-and-white symmetry to match the decor, with Antoinette, Lucienne, and our assistants, Angèle and Marie-Louise, welcoming me with joy in their eyes.

As I spun about to look back at Boy, he waved from outside and drove away.

THUS DID I INAUGURATE CHANEL MODES. My new address was elite enough to beckon first the rich wives and daughters of the Deauville set, followed by a few countesses and minor princesses. By 1912, I was photographed for the *Comoedia Illustré* modeling my creations and the popular review *Les Modes* declared me "an original artist."

Business was brisk, requiring long hours and constant supervision. Boy and I often just passed each other in our apartment on avenue Gabriel, snatching a kiss, a coffee, a quick tumble in the bed, before we parted for our assignments. He was investing heavily in coal, as rumblings from abroad predicted that a looming conflict with Germany would skyrocket the price of fuel. I focused on my immediate turf, gauging the ongoing feud between Poiret and Worth. After everyone else went home, I would experiment in my workroom with certain styles of blouses, belted jackets, and my favored plain skirts. I had begun to hanker for more than hats. I had room to expand if I desired it, but my lease at rue Cambon prohibited me from selling dresses, as there was already a dressmaker in the building—a sour-breathed crone who liked to poke her nose into my shop to wag her finger and threaten, "If I see a single dress in here, I'll see you evicted."

What to do?

My answer came from Boy again, though this time it was unintentional. He'd gone to England on business, returning with suitcases packed with items he couldn't buy in Paris. Fishermen sweaters in cable-knit wool, cardigans of Scottish tartan in subtle hues, and pullovers in a durable fabric called jersey, which I'd not seen before, utilized by English tailors for school blazers, sporting clothes, and military uniforms, but never for women's apparel.

I tried on one of his pullovers. The fit overwhelmed me, for Boy was much taller, but I loved the way the ingenious knit draped without the need for excess seams, seeming to have a sense of its own of where to adjust and where to hang loose.

Boy was amused. "I bought those for me," he said as he found me padding about the apartment in his pullover, getting a feel for how the fabric held up. "They're for polo games. You're going to make them smell like you, and then I'll be too distracted to play."

I could barely draw a straight line but that didn't stop me from spending many nights at my worktable trying my hand at different looks I could make with jersey. When I showed these rudimentary sketches to Lucienne, she shook her head. "We only just got off our knees with the hats and now you want to add dresses? Absolutely not. Our lease forbids it. Would you have us thrown out?"

Tapping my foot, I pushed the sketches toward her. "They're not dresses. They are jackets, blouses, sweaters, coats, and skirts. Not one dress." I paused, grimacing. "As if any of us needs another frock, with the way those tyrants Poiret and Worth smother us. These are for women like us, everyday women on the streets, made to complement our lifestyle."

Lucienne did not glance at my designs. "Women on the streets can shop in cheap department stores. These will be too expensive to produce. We would need more staff, have to purchase sewing machines. It's too difficult. We cannot possibly compete."

Our sparring had become so routine, none of the staff paid us any mind. Today, however, something different must have heated our tones, for Antoinette approached carefully, scrutinizing each sketch before she ventured, "Why not try? These designs are unique; they go with our hats. I think our customers will like them."

Seeing that my sister almost never offered an opinion, she managed to quell Lucienne, who took in my regard before she said, "I'm not a modiste. Selling clothes is not my expertise."

"Then as you once advised me, you shall have to learn," I said. "We all must learn. I want to grow Chanel Modes. It is the perfect time, with so much attention on our hats, and our client list gaining prestige. No one else is offering this type of fashion. I know it can be a success."

"Not with me," said Lucienne. "It's not why I came to work for you."

"Then you needn't stay," I told her, and I heard Antoinette gasp. "But I *will* do this, with or without you. I'll provide you with an excellent reference, of course," I added, refusing to let sentimentality or fear dissuade me. Boy had said I must believe in myself, and I believed in this new enterprise even more than I had believed in my hats.

Lucienne nodded and turned away. As I looked at my sister, Antoinette asked nervously, "How will we manage without her?"

I collected my sketches. "We'll manage. I always do."

LUCIENNE DEPARTED FOR ANOTHER HAT ATELIER. In time, she would become its director, lauded as Paris's top milliner. I missed her determination and drive—she was one of the few women I'd met who could match my own—but I'd learned enough by now to supervise the workroom myself and I did not miss our quarrels.

I promoted Angèle to head seamstress, or *première*, in charge of hiring *arpètes*, young girls who apprenticed in the workroom doing chores like passing a magnet over the floor to catch stray needles, or steaming fabric. The most talented of these *arpètes* could rise to become a *petite main* or intermediate seamstress, trained in the craft of producing clothes. Though skilled with my needle and scissors, I was by no means a practiced designer. My method of work was to drape fabric directly upon a dummy or preferably a live model—Antoinette, mostly. I sat for hours, a cigarette hanging from my lips as I pinned and stitched my original garment. Then Angèle and her staff transformed my originals into *toiles*, reproducible patterns sewn in muslin to construct samples for display. We purchased electrical sewing machines but much of the work still required hand sewing, with each article fitted to a client's measurements. Antoinette and Angèle would oversee these fittings, while I inspected every item before it went on display, and again, after completion, to ensure it met the client specifications.

Of course, all of this took time: time to import jersey from England; time to decide how to launch my line and decide whether to risk doing it at rue Cambon. The delays gnawed at my patience, for by the end of 1912, Poiret had released simplified apparel that echoed my vision. He couldn't resist adding dolman sleeves, weighting his day coats with embroidery or sable, marring the streamlined image he sought to achieve, but he, too, had sniffed the hint of change in the air and I fretted he would steal my thunder before I had begun.

Frustrated, I sought an outlet beyond my atelier. I redecorated Boy's apartment, repainting the red walls in cream, replacing the Oriental carpets with rugs dyed in earth tones, and the still-life paintings with exquisite Coromandel screens. After this was completed—"It looks like a Bedouin palace," Boy said—I went in pursuit of somewhere else to vent my energy.

The American dancer Isadora Duncan was creating a sensation in Paris with her innovative performances; her philosophy of liberation of the senses through the body appealed to me. I was twenty-nine, I wanted to maintain my slim figure; a couturier, I told myself, must look the part. I didn't care to consider that I was perhaps more motivated by the fact that Boy traveled often and I suspected he might have other lovers. We had never discussed monogamy or marriage; he used costly lambskin prophylactics to avoid my getting pregnant, and as I had never heard so much as a hint of a bastard child in his life, I assumed he did the same with others. But I was too proud to ask. Instead, I teased, "You must meet many pretty women on your trips."

Glancing up from his newspaper, he replied, "Not as pretty as you."

"Me?" I scoffed. "I'm not pretty."

"No," he said, "but I've never met anyone more beautiful."

I decided the occasional dalliance when he was away was less worthy of concern than remaining the most beautiful woman he knew, so I enrolled in lessons from the highly regarded instructor, Élyse Toulemont, known as Caryathis. Every evening I climbed the steep hill to her studio in Montmartre to endure the banging of her cane on the plank floor, which reminded me of les Tantes, and her pinch between my shoulders when I failed to retain a proper stance, which reminded me of the nuns of Aubazine. I was determined to excel, even if I was too old to entertain ballerina ideas.

My fervor for dance amused Boy. In 1913, he bought us tickets to the premiere of the Ballets Russes' *Le Sacre du printemps* with music by the Russian composer Igor Stravinsky.

IV

The newly built Théâtre des Champs-Élysées was crammed to overflowing. The Ballets Russes, overseen by its flamboyant Russian director, Sergei Diaghilev, was already famous, having staged performances such as *L'après-midi d'un faune*, in which Diaghilev's lover Nijinsky scandalized the audience with his orgasmic simulations and astonishing pirouettes. Having never seen the company, I was eager to be here. We had loge placement, the best seats in the house, but I grimaced as I beheld the sea of tiaras, aigrettes, and ostrich feathers below me. Every woman present wore the ubiquitous pigeon silhouette in violet tulle, nectarine silk, and every glaring shade in between, bejeweled fowl mincing on baroque heels down the aisles, easing onto their seats as though their undergarments contained thorns.

"I'd like to dress them in black serge," I muttered, and Boy gave me a cynical smile. I wore black myself, a velvet sheath I'd designed with a collar of silk camellia petals. Sitting among the explosion of pagoda hips and foaming crinoline, I stood out like a raven on a tombstone—though my attire was to be the last thing people commented upon once Diaghilev's ballet began.

A discordant throbbing of bassoon piping initiated the spectacle. The first dancers appeared, writhing in plaited wigs and tunics adorned in Russian peasant motifs, contorting themselves into unfathomable poses as the music twanged. Some of the audience members began to hiss. At my side, Boy leaned forward in excitement, but he was a minority in an auditorium that, with astonishing lack of restraint, descended into catcalls that drowned out the score. By the final act, as Nijinsky appeared in a revealing black-and-white costume to exult in the sacrificial rites of spring, chaos erupted, with the composer himself, a thick-lipped bespectacled man, cowering below us as a society lady harangued him for indecency.

The stampede to leave the theater tumbled us outside. Boy scowled at a monocle-wearing man who elbowed us out of the way as he stalked to his carriage with his disconsolate wife crying out, "It is an abomination!" I had to curb my tongue when another corseted-to-her-teeth matron wailed, "Never in my life has anyone dared make a fool of me until now!" because if she ever bothered to look in her mirror, she would have seen that her dressmaker had done precisely that.

"Diaghilev certainly knows how to make an impression," Boy remarked.

"Yes, I think I should like to meet him someday," I said. "It's been an experience."

Boy shot me a quizzical look. "Did you enjoy it?"

I shrugged. "I did not care for it, personally, but I hardly see the fuss. We should at least appreciate the innovation."

He chuckled. "I thought you might say that."

I remained thoughtful as we returned to our apartment. To me, the furor the ballet roused was another sign that old orders were crumbling and that one person could make a difference.

Perhaps the next person to do it would be me.

I PRESENTED BOY WITH MY IDEA. He went pensive, fingering his mustache. At length, he said, "I suppose you'll need start-up capital?" It was precisely what I longed to hear. No remonstrations that I had only just brought my rue Cambon shop out of debt, no warnings that I ran ahead of myself. I threw myself into his arms, covering him with kisses as he fended me off with halfhearted attempts before he swept me into the bedroom.

"You're like a child," he said later, as I basked in the ache of his ferocious lovemaking and my own near-unbearable anticipation. "You never think of what might go wrong."

I cuddled up beside him. "That's because nothing can go wrong. Not while I have you."

In the summer of 1913, I opened my boutique in Deauville, featuring a collection of summer wear in the very resort where I'd made my first breakthrough. I rented a location on rue Gontaut-Biron in the center of the shopping district—where everyone on vacation strolled and where no one could miss the white awning with my name, GABRIELLE CHANEL, in black letters.

Hiring five local girls who'd apprenticed at dressmaker shops and were fiends with their needles, I left Antoinette and Angèle behind in Paris to run rue Cambon and wrote to Adrienne in Moulins, telling her to visit me. She arrived with her beloved Nexon; she was as beautiful as ever, but dowdily dressed in her old-fashioned black coat, veiled *capote*, and fur-trimmed collar, despite the blazing heat. In fact, that summer proved to be one of the hottest on record. Seeing me about town in my white pleated skirt and open-necked blouse, the pockets of my oversize beige knit jacket stuffed with my calling cards, women of leisure flocked to my boutique in search of relief. I had samples made of unconstructed pullovers modeled on those Boy wore for his polo games, as well as belted jackets, ankle-length skirts that did not require a corset or stays, and simple afternoon dresses made in the jersey I so admired.

I had to field doubtful questions about my fabrics; jersey was almost unknown and knit deemed suitable only for men's undergarments. I did not relish having to guide dubious customers into the fitting area to help them into the samples, snapping my fingers at my assistants to bring me the straw boaters or soft-brimmed hats that completed my ensembles. But once the client felt the rib-expanding release from her previous garb and beheld in the full-length mirror how different she looked, her expression underwent an equally marked alteration.

"And are you sure, mademoiselle, it's not *too* plain?" Baroness Kitty de Rothschild asked as she surveyed herself in one of my midlength jackets and jersey skirts. She had arrived in the shop unexpectedly, alerted by a friend. Her entrance had set my heart to racing, for she was one of the most influential women in France, married to the wealthy Rothschild financier, with innumerable contacts who could make my reputation. "I do love how cool and comfortable this is, but it seems so . . . understated."

I smiled. "Elegance is refusal, madame. We should be the ones who wear our clothes."

She tugged at the sample. "It also doesn't fit."

I stepped behind her to pull the jacket waist back an inch, no more. She was tall and graceful, with a long patrician face, but her breasts were small and her hips broad, so the jacket should hang loose, to disguise her flaws. "We will make everything for you, baroness. What you see on display are samples. The actual garment will be constructed to your measurements."

"So it won't be mine alone?" she persisted. It was the most challenging obstacle I faced. Like others of her ilk, Kitty de Rothschild adhered to the prevailing sentiment that their apparel must be one of a kind, made by a couturier she visited at a private atelier, not one who ran a shop on the busiest thoroughfare in Deauville.

Drawing in a breath, I said, "Each woman is unique by nature. Why must her clothing be, when by the very act of wearing it, she herself makes it so? My clothes are designed so that *you*, baroness, will be seen first."

She went quiet for an interminable moment, while I waited, knowing that if she walked out now, without making a purchase, I would lose the very clientele I desperately sought.

Then, to my relief, she nodded. "Let's see how this theory of yours works in practice. I'll take this ensemble and two of your day dresses in—what do you call that fabric again?"

"Jersey," I said, feeling a sudden light-headedness that made me sway.

"Yes, jersey. Two. I trust you can keep my measurements on file, should I wish to purchase additional items? Fittings can be so tedious." She sighed. "I detest them."

"Of course. Just a moment and I'll send Adrienne in to measure you."

I emerged elated, promising the baroness that her purchases would be ready within the week and then marching into the back room, where my staff labored at long tables equipped with a sewing machine at each end. "Not one extra fitting," I said, wagging my finger. "We have the baroness's measurements. In three days, I expect her to walk out in her new clothes. Am I understood?"

I spent long hours once the shop closed, haranguing my beleaguered seamstresses over a sloppy hem or irregular sleeve, and failed to realize how much of an impact I was making until Adrienne drew me outside to point at passersby.

"Do you see it? Gabrielle, there is the Baroness de Rothschild in your skirt and day jacket. With her is her friend, the diva Cécile Sorel, who was in the shop last week, remember? She's wearing your striped blouse with the blue pullover. And there, and there: Gabrielle, all these women are wearing your clothes!"

I blinked, focusing as if through a haze. Seeing me at the doorway, the women paused, turned to look at me with Adrienne, and then each one inclined her head to me before moving on with perspiring maids in tow, laden with boxes from other stores.

"They . . . they greeted me," I said, stunned. No one greeted those who dressed them in public; even the despotic Poiret had failed to befriend his clients. "They *acknowledged* me."

Adrienne squeezed my hand. "Of course they did. Oh, Gabrielle, it's finally happening. You are a success! They will tell all their friends. They'll come in droves and before you know it, you will be received in the best of society, for how can you not? You're not a man dressing women; you're a woman dressing your own and you're as fashionable as they are—more so, because you teach them." She hugged me, right there in the doorway. "I'm so proud of you. I always knew this day would come. And I'm going to help," she said, drawing back. "Maurice says it's time we moved to Paris so I can do something other than wait for his family to let us marry. I'll work for you in your rue Cambon shop, if you still want me."

I hated tears. I hated to cry. But I couldn't resist as I hauled her into the boutique and clung to her. Then, wiping the streaks from my face as she sniffled, I said, "*Allez!* Enough with this corset. If you want to work for me, you must wear only my style."

THE UNEXPECTED WHIRLWIND of that summer in Deauville spilled over into Paris.

Upon the end of the season, with Adrienne assisting Antoinette at rue Cambon, the same women who promenaded through the resort in my apparel arrived at my shop, disappointed to discover I had no clothes but eager nonetheless for my innovative hats. Within a few months of biting my nails to the quick, I set up displays with my knitwear, seeking advantage in the new vogue for sportsmanship. Ladies now wanted smart jersey skirts and jackets for riding bicycles, pullovers for playing golf or croquet, and flannel coats for excursions in the car. No dresses, I assured the ill-tempered modiste in the building. These were casual separates, nothing she could deem an infringement on her territory, although I had begun to envision gowns that would unbolt the stays suffocating us, enhancing our elegance in our natural forms.

My bank account burgeoned; I pestered Boy about buying out my lease and taking over additional space in the building. I now had more than a hundred society women on my client list, including women of title, courtesy of Kitty de Rothschild, who recommended me to everyone. While I'd not yet been invited to their galas, I had become recognizable enough to earn a caricature in the newspaper *Le Figaro*, which depicted Boy as a centaur, his polo mallet topped with a hat, and me clasping him with a box in my hand bearing my name.

"Look, we are famous," I told Boy, brandishing the cartoon. "And I'm earning more than enough money. It's time to expand."

He frowned. "You should wait. This could all change sooner than you think."

"Change? How? I've been right about everything so far." My tone became adamant. "If you don't want to help me, then I'll do it myself."

"Coco, do you ever look at anything in the newspapers that isn't about you? We could be at war before the year is out. My political connections tell me—"

"Women still need clothes. They can't send their soldiers off to war in the nude."

He rolled his eyes, returning to his papers. "Do what you want. You will anyway."

I should have realized he was so worried that he didn't have the energy to argue. But I was too enthused. Boy was right; I barely read the newspapers. Every moment was dedicated solely to my success. To conquer that ultimate bastion, acceptance in society, seemed to me the zenith of my ambitions. I was resolved to become the first designer to be welcomed into those sequestered circles, where I would dress the lot.

It was November 1913. By the summer of 1914, Europe went up in flames.

ACT THREE
DISCARDING FRILLS
1914–1919

"IF YOU WERE BORN WITHOUT WINGS,
DO NOTHING TO PREVENT THEM
FROM GROWING."

I

I was in Deauville when the telegram arrived—a brief notice from Boy, advising me that he'd been drafted. All summer, the news had been ominous, first with the shocking assassination of Archduke Ferdinand of Austria in Sarajevo. That was followed by Austria's declaration of war on Serbia and a shove of Teutonic aggression by Germany, which declared against Russia and demanded neutrality from France and Britain, neither of which was willing to agree.

I remained in blissful ignorance. The season at Deauville promised to be more lucrative than the previous one, the heat like an anvil. It took every spare hour I had to replenish my shelves with my assistants and Adrienne. Kitty de Rothschild brought her friends—princesses, countesses, and wives of renowned painters, such as Madame Matisse, to ransack my store.

When I tore open the telegram, I froze. I was expecting Boy to join me; in fact, he was late. I had left Paris early to prepare the boutique while he stayed behind to close up the apartment and attend to his business affairs. Now I stood looking at three terse lines:

BEEN CALLED TO ACTION. DON'T CLOSE THE
STORE. LOVE, BOY.

Three lines. Ten words. Stop.

Adrienne leaned over my shoulder. Before she could let out a cry of dismay, I clapped a hand to her wrist and pulled her into the back room.

She was white, quivering. I hissed, "Not a word. We have customers. It can't be too serious or Boy wouldn't have told us to stay open, and everyone here would be talking about it. We must continue attending to business until we know more."

"But Maurice . . . he's in Paris, too. He'll be called to arms!"

"Then he'll let you know in due time, won't he? Now, let's get back out there. The Princess de Saint-Sauver needs her hem adjusted. You know how she hates dangling threads."

Moving like a sleepwalker, Adrienne returned to work. I shoved the telegram into my sweater pocket and followed, keeping a close eye on her as she replied in a monotone to the princess and other clients darted curious glances in her direction.

"Is anything amiss?" asked Kitty de Rothschild as I tallied her purchases and Adrienne desultorily wrote down the acquisitions in a ledger for the workroom.

"She's just heard about our declaration of war," I said, for in truth I was too flustered myself to fabricate a convenient lie on the spot. "She's worried for the Baron of Nexon."

"Oh, is that all?" Kitty shrugged. "So much wind in the grass. It will be over before we return to Paris. Those Germans do like to bully everyone, don't they? They're like boys in a playground."

I laughed, and kissed her on both cheeks. "*Demain*," she said as her maid staggered behind with my white-and-black boxes containing her purchases. "Cécile Sorel is coming again to visit and so is Madame Santos-Dumont, who's dying to see your clothes. *Plus tard!*" She blew me a kiss as she sailed out the door with the princess. Together, they had bought half my inventory.

Adrienne was crying again. I told her to go back to our suite in the hotel. She was no use to me in her current state and I wanted to reconcile the day's profits without her laments.

We would remain open, as Boy had requested. But as I pulled out my account books and hunched over them to count, my hands were trembling.

SO MUCH WIND IN THE GRASS . . .

Kitty de Rothschild's careless pronouncement stayed with me as summer ended, emptying Deauville of its sun-worshipping inhabitants. The war of bullies transformed into a monster intent on devouring us alive.

I did not return to Paris. I saw no point with Boy gone, though Adrienne did, boarding the first train she could with the breathless promise to write once she had any news.

"Call me instead," I told her. "We have a telephone in the hotel, remember?"

Returning to the Hôtel Normandy through the ghostly streets, I wondered at my own reluctance to succumb to anxiety, my seemingly imperturbable calm. Not until I was sipping a rare cognac—I never drank much—and smoking on the balcony, gazing out to the Channel, did I realize that what I felt was not indifference.

I simply refused to consider that anything bad could ever happen to him.

THE MONTHS DRAGGED ON. I learned via another telegram from Boy that he was stationed as a lieutenant with the British division on the Marne. Deauville filled again, this time in panic, when the Germans tromped over Belgium and menaced Paris. They did not enter the city, but the mere threat sent the women racing onto trains to the nearest haven they could find that offered an escape route across the Channel. Once more, I was up to my elbows in work, sending urgent telegrams to Adrienne—she never did master using the telephone—to join me and stop moping over Maurice, who had enlisted with our forces to stop the Germans before we all ended up saluting the kaiser. She refused several times before she finally came. By then, I was selling my designs faster than I could deliver them.

Many of the women were now eager to support the cause as communiqués reported massive casualties at the front, and formed voluntary nursing teams at the hospital.

They needed comfortable attire they could move in all day, sensible clothing that would withstand the wear and tear of labor. Unwittingly, my sportswear had become exactly that, and I dove into the workroom to create special smock-type dresses to fit the requirements. Society matrons who had not so much as pulled on a glove by themselves now rolled up the sleeves of my open-collared shirts and tucked rolls of gauze and morphine vials into my jacket pockets. Once again, every woman in Deauville wore my styles but I took no satisfaction in it. Opportunity had again favored me, but it came at the price of the disintegration of the world I had known. I did not possess the sangfroid to see it as anything but soul wrenching.

Besides, by now what I had refused to consider was fast becoming a possibility. When I heard Royallieu had been occupied and Balsan's prized stables converted into barracks, I had to go into the back room to clutch my stomach and resist the dread churning inside me.

If Balsan's château was not safe, if Paris was not safe, what would happen to Boy?

REASSURING NEWS THAT MAURICE WAS ALIVE eased Adrienne's worries. Living and working with her was a test in forbearance, and as soon as word came that we could return to Paris, I left my Deauville boutique in the hands of a formidable head seamstress and boarded the train with Adrienne.

Paris was a cemetery of waiting, devoid of able-bodied men, with frantic mothers, daughters, and wives checking the daily posters announcing the names of the dead. Business at rue Cambon, however, was better than I expected. Here, too, sensibility in apparel was at a premium, so I installed the same types of merchandise as I had in Deauville, save for the dresses. I spent my days in the shop and my after hours in the Ritz, as Allied officers came to the hotel bar across from my shop bringing news of the front.

The horrors they related stunned me. The losses numbered in the tens of thousands, entire armies crushed under the German heel. Every night when I returned to the apartment on rue Gabriel, my mind reeled with images of Boy blown to shreds in a trench, hanging on barbed wire with his guts spilling out, and other indescribable nightmares. When telegrams arrived, I had to hand them to Antoinette to read instead. God help me, when news came from Moulins that Adrienne's parents, my paternal grandparents, had finally died of decrepitude, I uttered a prayer of thanks under my breath and accompanied her to the train to see to their burial. She left with money from me for flowers and a bank draft for my five-year-old nephew, André, whom I ordered sent to boarding school in England at once. Though he was still too young and we had never met, I wanted him safe from harm.

I did not spare a thought for my long-lost father or my brothers. Too much time had passed for me to pretend we had anything but our shared blood between us.

As long as my nephew and Boy survived, I did not care who perished in their stead.

BOY CAME HOME ON LEAVE in the spring of 1915 after nearly a year of absence—gaunt, weary, but alive. After he slept for nearly two days without waking, he told me that when the war was over, he wanted to write a book about his experiences. He would title it *Reflections on Victory* and removed from his burlap sack tomes by Napoleon, Bismarck, and Sully. He set these battered volumes muddied with dirt from the front on the bed. He had read them as bombs crashed and tear gas flooded the trenches. I started to cry, burying my face in my hands and releasing all the suppressed fear and anxiety for him that I had carried within me.

"Oh, no, not my Coco," he murmured, gathering me in his arms. "Not my brave lioness. I can bear to see anyone cry but you."

He had only had a few weeks before he had to return to duty and he suggested a vacation in Biarritz, the resort near the Spanish border—not far, in fact, from Pau, where we first fell in love. Spain had refused to become embroiled in the war and an unsettling nonchalance cushioned the resort, with aristocrats, black-market entrepreneurs, the bored haut monde, and other wealthy scions seeking diversion as though the suffering of thousands was an unfortunate circumstance.

Boy needed the respite, so I ignored this folly of extravagance in a time of desperation. We danced at the Miramar and the Hôtel du Palais and took drives along the cliffs of Saint-Jean-de-Luz in sleek new automobiles. We picnicked on the beach with our new acquaintances, the sugar-refinery heir, Constant Say, and his acclaimed diva mistress, Marthe Davelli, whose swan's neck, enigmatic dark eyes, and wide mouth bore an uncanny resemblance to my own. She insisted I cut my hair short like hers so we could dress alike and confuse our lovers. I allowed her to trim my locks to shoulder length. When we entered the casino in matching white gowns and ropes of pearls, Boy deliberately kissed her instead before turning to me with an impish grin to say, "Hello. Who might you be?"

It was to be a vacation, nothing more. Marthe became a friend and client, but I never intended our trip to be anything else until she piped up one evening shortly before Boy was due to return to Paris and his war duties, "Why doesn't Coco open a shop in Biarritz? It's going to be *the* place to vacation, once this tedious war is over. Property values are rising faster here than the price of petrol. After her success in Deauville, she's certain to double or triple her clientele."

Boy glanced at me through the fog of smoke drifting over the table. We had drunk too much champagne and I had no head for it. As he escorted me back to our suite in the Miramar, I felt as though I floated in a bubble. He had to help me undress.

As I drifted into drunken slumber, I heard him say, "You know, it's not a bad idea."

My *maison de couture* in Biarritz was to be my pièce de résistance, the resort's first fashion house in the center of town, located on the rue Gardères in the castlelike structure of the Villa Larralde. It faced the casino, en route to the beach promenade—a prime location, certain to attract the wealthiest visitors. In order to satisfy their demand for innovation and style, I had to offer more upscale apparel without sacrificing my code of utility and simplicity. However, with the war in full force, obtaining adequate supplies of fabric was an issue.

"I'll put you in touch with suppliers of Scottish wools," said Boy before he left, having deposited an enormous sum for me to draw upon. "You should also contact Balsan's brothers in Lyons. Their family textile plants are churning out broadcloth in bales for the army. Balsan is always offering to help you. Let this be his contribution to the cause."

He didn't seem to mind that we were seizing advantage from chaos. I voiced doubts about such an undertaking, wondering how I'd manage three shops, much less deliver merchandise as the war raged on. Boy shrugged my concerns aside. "You didn't start the war. Anyone who can seeks profit in it; why shouldn't we? I certainly intend to emerge from this fiasco richer than when I started. Frankly, if we don't, others will—and in fact, already are."

I contacted Balsan, who was willing to send whatever I required and put the family silk stock at my disposal, as well. Through him, I located a manufacturer named Rodier who had developed a raw jersey for sportsmen's underwear. His samples had proved too scratchy, leaving him with a sizeable quantity he could not sell. I requested everything he had and placed an order for more. With the samples he sent, I made frock coats in its natural cream and beige hues, with discreet embroidery on the sleeves and linings of Balsan silk. They sold within hours. Soon thereafter, I received my next order. Rodier had modified the product with cotton, at my suggestion, so it would be more malleable, and dyed it in colors I requested: coral, azure, shades of gray and cream. I presented a new line of dresses, cardigans, and coats, some in the wools Boy had arranged for me, trimming my collars and sleeve cuffs with available pelts like rabbit, squirrel, or skunk (importing fur from Russia or South America was now impossible and locally produced skins bolstered the economy at home). I accessorized these ensembles with new suede and felt hats in various shapes, banded in velvet or broadcloth, with faux-pearl pins.

I could barely keep up with the demand. Orders came from as far as Madrid, as aristocratic Spanish women returned home from Biarritz carrying luggage stuffed with my garb, prompting envious friends to rush my store. I even had a massive order from the Spanish royal family, with the infantas photographed strolling through El Prado in my dresses and coats.

I hired sixty seamstresses and dispatched urgent word to Antoinette to find her replacement for rue Cambon and come to Biarritz as soon as possible. I also wrote to Adrienne, who demurred because Maurice was on leave from the front. I gritted my teeth at his poor timing and searched locally for someone to oversee the workroom.

Enter Madame Deray. She was another Lucienne, a veteran of the craft—imperious, demanding, and indefatigable. We clashed from the moment we met, when she criticized the excessive formlessness of my silhouettes. I hired her on the spot. She, in turn, brought in more help and took charge with an iron fist. She had mouths to feed, a large family of cousins and aunts who had lost men in the war. Her salary was adequate but I promised a raise if she could increase production. She did. She worked harder than I did, mastering the latest sewing machines and supervising the legion of seamstresses who created our clothes even as she personally oversaw each client fitting, often the first to arrive and the last to leave. We never became friends, but I relied on her as I had on none of my other *premières,* for I knew that whenever I needed to depart from Biarritz to attend to my other businesses, I left my *maison* in the best of hands.

Antoinette arrived with a sullen air. When I asked what ailed her, she muttered, "I'm twenty-eight, Gabrielle, and now you want me to manage this salon in a resort that empties in winter. How am I to find a husband? You have Boy. I have no one."

"No one?" I exclaimed, taken aback by her petulance. "You have me. You are my sister. Would you call what we are building here nothing?"

She pouted. "What *you* are building. I am only your employee. I want to marry one day and have a family of my own. Don't you? It is what's expected of us."

"Who expects it?" I flared. "I certainly do not. If you so desire a husband, where else to find him than here in Biarritz, where rich men abound? As for me, I'm married already—to my work."

I turned on my heel and left her, exasperated that even as I worked my fingers to the bone to liberate women from our cloth chains, our minds remained as closed as ever to the possibility that we might deserve more than a husband, children, and growing old cooking sausage.

I left Biarritz at the end of the season to supervise my other shops and prepare a new line of clothes for the spring. Antoinette sulked that she had to stay behind at my insistence; my new establishment needed tending in the off-season, as winter visitors from Spain often arrived.

As I rode the express to Paris in a first-class compartment where I could stretch my legs and review my accounts (my first season in Biarritz had yielded unbelievable profit, thanks to Madame Deray, who priced my dresses at 3,000 francs apiece). I marveled that Antoinette could have thought I'd ever entertain such a notion as marriage. I had never broached the subject with her or anyone else, not even Boy . . .

It is what's expected of us.

It might be expected but I was more unsettled by the fact that now I couldn't stop thinking about it, nor wonder once again, as I had with Balsan, if something was wrong with me that I didn't crave what so many others of my gender did. Why did I not desire the comforts of an established home, of a husband and children running underfoot? Had my own childhood damaged me in some way that I rejected the very things that made women happy?

I was thirty-two years old. By 1916, I had three hundred employees on my payroll and was deemed a rising figure in fashion. America's premier magazines, *Women's Wear Daily* and *Harper's Bazaar,* ran articles heralding my latest skirt length, which daringly allowed a glimpse of ankle and upper calf. Even that bastion of credibility, *Vogue,* had featured my designs and declared me "the designer to watch."

Conformity was the last thing I should ever want.

THE WAR CONTINUED to slaughter men like a thresher scything wheat. Boy returned to Paris on leave, looked fitter than the last time but was cryptic about his duties. I suspected he acted as an intelligence officer for the English, but, as had been established since the start of our relationship, I did not ask.

He was delighted to find me thriving, to read the magazine clippings I showed him, even if thus far no established French fashion publication had given me their stamp of approval. He had finished his book and it would be published in England—again, I didn't inquire as to how or where he'd found the time to write. To celebrate, we went out on the town.

Paris was regaining some of its faded allure. We had grown accustomed to war and while everyone lamented the shortages it caused—the lack of consistent hot water being the worst for me—the bistros and cabarets helped to ease our deprivations, filled with officers on leave from every nation, drinking and romancing gullible girls. Boy and I dined at Maxim's and the Café de Paris; we attended the theater and were even invited to a society dinner by the actress Cécile Sorel, who frequented my shops and had been presented to me by my fearless champion Baroness Rothschild.

It was at this dinner where I met Misia.

HER HOME ON THE RUE DE RIVOLI overlooking the Tuileries was like a tinker's shop—if tinkers collected masses of African masks and primitive statuettes, porcelain bric-a-brac from Russia, gilded English tea tables, antique busts from Italy, and dozens of paintings and sketches by every working and unknown artist in Paris. "Is it all for sale?" Boy whispered to me as we weaved our way through the detritus. He was appalled; his tastes always bordered on the traditionally austere. He had trouble tearing his gaze away from a black marble reproduction of Michelangelo's *David* propped in a corner, festooned with discarded hats, scarves, and coats.

"Here is a portrait Toulouse-Lautrec made of me at the piano," Misia said, pointing at the painting crammed between twenty others hanging in haphazard array on the wall. "I'm an accomplished pianist, taught by Franz Liszt himself. I used to give lessons. I first trained in St. Petersburg, where I was born. Oh, Lautrec was such a divine little man," she went on. "How they made fun of him! As if they could ever have seen the world with half his sensitivity. I was so sorry when he died." And: "This is Renoir. I posed for him. He wanted me to show my breasts and I regret to this day that I declined. No man knew better how to capture the sheen of a woman's skin. Oh, and this is my latest acquisition: Van Gogh. Do you know him? No? He was brilliant. Just look at his palette; he bathed in color. Forget Botticelli and Da Vinci; such rubbish, so antiquated! This man was the soul of divinity. It's a crime that talent often goes hand in hand with insanity." She sighed. "He killed himself. Not only was he as mad as a war widow but he didn't understand the first thing about selling his work. Even if he had, no one knew what to do with it. They couldn't figure out whether to hang his paintings upside down or not."

Sheet music drifted in her wake, her piano heaped with annotated scores by Stravinsky, Ravel, and Debussy, all of whom, Misia airily informed us, she knew and had nurtured personally.

She was a rotund, bustling figure with a pompadour hairstyle that couldn't restrain its natural frizz. Her round, gleaming eyes seemed to gauge everything at once, her exaggerated gestures strewing potpourri cushions from her divans. Her house suffocated me. It smelled of old perfume and dust, damp soil from the jungle of plants in Chinese pots, and too many books, but she proved as fascinating as she was repellent. Her staccato voice rang with authority as she sat her guests at the overcrowded table and between courses of fowl and legumes, pontificated on a variety of topics ranging from music to the outrageous backlash in Paris against Cubist artists.

"Pablo himself told me he almost returned to Catalonia, though he detests it," she proclaimed, jabbing her fork at no one in particular. "I insisted he not let his quarrel with Braque get the best of him or his considerable talent; after all, why should he enlist when Spain has no interest in the war? He must stay here and paint, which is what he does best, and what the world will one day appreciate him for."

Before anyone at the table could respond—there were nine of us, including Cécile; myself and Boy; and Misia's burly Catalan lover, the sculptor and painter, José María Sert, who grunted and guzzled food as if he were at a trough—Misia continued, "Which is why I insisted Pablo decorate the sets for Diaghilev's new season. Poor Diag is beside himself that the Ballets Russes hasn't had a single opening here since the apocalypse that was *Rite of Spring*. He's had a fantastically successful tour in America and Spain, but he needs to return to his roots. Of course," she added, with a tragic clasp of her hands to the very bosom she had refused to show Renoir, "Nijinsky's betrayal was a dagger in his heart. After all those years of nurturing that ingrate's temper and talent, the moment Diag turns his back, the scoundrel absconds to marry the first woman who can turn a blind eye to his penchant for cock."

A thick-haired, gimlet-faced youth next to me giggled. "I wonder how that wedding night went?" and as Misia gave a mock gasp, saying, "Jean Cocteau, honestly!" Sert rumbled, "How else could it go? 'Darling, it seems you're having some trouble down there. Shall I stick my fist up your ass like Diag used to do?'"

As Misia cackled in delight, I felt Boy go rigid at my side. Cécile arched her brow at me, as if to say she had no idea the evening would be so raucous. I wasn't offended. I had heard similar coarseness in my days of friendship with Émilienne and her courtesan friends, but Boy's jaw clenched as Cocteau mimed the aforementioned fist and declared, "Nijinsky will regret it. This new ballet *Parade* that we plan with Diag will turn Paris on its ear. A carnival spoof, with something for everyone, and enough subversion to please the rest of us. And Diag has that exquisite new dancer of his—I forget his name?" He turned to Misia, with an overt lewdness that made Boy glance sharply at him. A homosexual and open about it, too. Boy detested them.

"Who knows?" Misia shrugged. "There have been, and will be, so many men who love Diag. The important thing is, he's willing to try it again. And with Pablo painting the sets, you, dearest Jean, writing the scenario, and Satie composing the score—well, darlings, it simply cannot be anything but extraordinary."

I did not mention that I had seen the catastrophe that was *Rite of Spring*. The conversation, dominated by Misia, turned to politics and whether or not the Americans would see fit to assist us before the entire continent was doomed to eating sauerkraut. Boy said President Wilson would have no choice but to get involved, since Germany had begun to employ submarine attacks and poison gas. In fact, he assured us with a confidence that silenced the table, he had it on excellent authority that Wilson was preparing to legislate a selective draft service that would bring over a million American soldiers to fight in the war.

"We can only hope," blared Misia. "The Germans are detestable. We should build a wall around their country that will keep them inside permanently like hogs."

Speaking of which, her lover Sert had just pushed back his plate, belched without apology, and lit a noxious cigar that was making my eyes water. He leered at me, giving me a lascivious wink.

The evening was a disaster as far as Boy was concerned. He found the company crass and uninformed, wallowing in frivolity while outside their door Europe struggled for survival. But I was intrigued. I had never met such people before, teeming with rebellion and insouciance. They appealed to me; and evidently I appealed to them, or rather to their lead hostess, for as we said good night and I slipped on my skunk-trimmed red velvet coat, Misia looked me up and down and said, "Why, you are bewitching, my dear. Such style. What is your name again?"

I smiled. She probably hadn't heard me say it when we were introduced, or if she had, she'd forgotten it in the heat of her own bombast.

"Coco," I said as Boy stood at my side, his hat clenched in his hand.

"Coco?" She frowned. "Such a silly name for such an exceptional person, as if it were somebody's pet. Are you someone's pet, my dear? I don't see a collar or lead anywhere."

As I struggled for a response, Boy said tersely, "If you don't like Coco, madame, you can call her Gabrielle. Gabrielle Chanel. She owns a millinery shop on rue Cambon."

"A shop," Misia exclaimed. "How delightful! I adore hats. I'll come visit you tomorrow, my dear. We can have lunch together. I want to hear all about you." She planted two wet kisses on my cheeks, saturating me with her sandalwood scent. As my gaze drifted over her shoulder to a teetering pile of books in the corner, she cast a malicious little smile at Boy. "Do let us know when your political book is published, Monsieur Capel. We love to read in this house."

She flounced off in her kimonolike attire. As we descended the stairs into the Tuileries, little Cocteau came running up beside us, clamping a beret to his briar thatch of hair and saying with a lopsided smile, "I'll send you free tickets to our ballet next month. You must come. Diaghilev will want to meet you, mademoiselle." He narrowed his elfin eyes. "Be careful of Misia. She's a back-street abortionist with her friends." He nodded to

Boy, who ignored him. "And don't believe a word she says about books. She's never read one in her life."

"Now that," muttered Boy as Cocteau scampered into the dusk, "I can believe."

I took his hand and squeezed it. It was the first time in our eight years together that I pitied him for his inability to understand that we had just spent an evening with the future.

III

As promised, Misia showed up the next morning at my shop, dressed in a makeshift assemblage that would have been grotesque on anyone else. I sold her three hats, four sweaters, and five skirts; she resisted with every breath, huffing that she was too old for "eccentricities." In fact, she was forty-two, eleven years older than I was, and more voluble than anyone else I had met. She had no restraint. Over lunch at the Ritz, she regaled me with the story of her privileged but lonely childhood. Her mother had died giving birth to her in St. Petersburg—"She'd gone there chasing after my father, who was a sculptor and wanted nothing to do with her"—after which her grandparents in Brussels took charge of her and Liszt gave concerts at their house. Then her philandering father reclaimed her and enrolled her in the Sacré-Coeur boarding school in Paris—"Oh, how I loathed it! Those nuns were all lesbians who watched us when we bathed"—until she fled to teach piano and pose for artists before the first of her two marriages took place.

"My first husband was my Polish cousin, Thadée Natanson. He founded *La Revue blanche,* dedicated to promoting new artists. I met him when Lautrec painted me for a poster for the revue, the dear gnome. Oh, the marriage was a catastrophe! Thadée was awful in bed. Just terrible, so I began an affair with Alfred Edwards, owner of *Le Figaro.* Thadée needed a benefactor for his revue and Alfred agreed on the condition that he divorce me so we could marry. That is how I moved into my home on the rue de Rivoli and where I met Ravel and Enrico Caruso. I used to sing Neapolitan duets with Caruso while Ravel played the piano. Such delight!" She barely paused to take a breath yet she managed to consume her croque-monsieur without any difficulty, and down endless cups of tea, which explained the stains on her teeth.

"Alfred was a boor. A tiger between the sheets, but a boor outside. He slept with everyone. Men or women, he didn't care. I divorced him in '09. I made a stink so he would leave me the house. It was the least he could do, considering I had decorated it and nurtured all the talent that came through its doors. I met Sert five years later. I adore his work. He is going to be very famous. He's done a mural at the Hôtel de Ville and several American millionaires are vying to have him decorate their buildings in New York. I would love to see New York, wouldn't you, my dear? Americans can be so conventional but they do love modern art, and unlike many here, they have the money for it. I keep telling Sert to accept one of their commissions, but he's Catalan, you see, lazy and too vested in his food. He says all people in America eat is white bread, so he refuses to go."

She finally rattled to a halt. "And you? How is it that you run a shop and live with the eligible Monsieur Capel? Come now, don't be shy. You must tell me everything if we're to be friends."

I told her enough to satisfy her, downplaying my success, though she was quick to notice it when I mentioned my shops in Deauville and Biarritz. That same unerring presentiment she had for sniffing out promising artists, she had for money in all its forms; the only thing she reveled in more was failure, because it meant she could pick up the pieces and put it all together again, rendering one in her debt. I had noted this at her house when she was discussing Diaghilev—"A hopeless romantic, too greedy for his own good. He consumes everything: men, chocolates, talent, money. He'd be begging on the streets were it not for me, but I do love him so." I decided it was better to never fall prey to her destructive instincts.

Thus we became friends, but only because she persisted more than I did, visiting me regularly and hauling me off to the flea markets in Saint-Germain-des-Prés, where she'd rummage for hours among junk I wouldn't touch. She was perhaps the only friend of my sex I'd had since Émilienne, with whom I'd lost contact, but I was never sure whether Misia aimed to adore or destroy. A backstreet abortionist with her friends, Cocteau had dubbed her: I never forgot the epithet, though our relationship would become one of the most enduring of my life.

MEANWHILE, THE WAR ENTERED its fourth and most devastating year, with appalling losses suffered on the front as the Allies waited for the American troops to arrive. In Russia, mass anarchy erupted, giving birth to the revolution that resulted in the execution of the tsar and his family, in addition to the murder or penniless exile of hundreds of Russian aristocrats and nobles.

At the debut of Diaghilev's new ballet *Parade*, which featured all the satirical outrageousness one could expect, Misia blew her nose (she had a cold and should have stayed in bed) before drawling through clogged sinuses, "It's appropriate, is it not? A spoof here in Paris and a spoof in Moscow. Only here we dance the parts of fools, and there the fools are shot."

It was the last straw for Boy. We had invited her and Sert for dinner at our apartment before the ballet, where he presented them with a first edition of his published book. It had received acclaim for its insightful meditations on the conflict but Misia had scarcely glanced at it before she started to cajole me into giving her one of our Coromandel screens, infuriating Boy.

"She has no room for it," I assured him as we entered the theater. "She collects everything. You saw her house. If she could fit a stuffed rhinoceros in the parlor, she would."

But he detested Misia, and after the ballet, he went home, leaving me to attend the celebratory dinner for the Ballets Russes, where I met portly Diaghilev in his Russian sable hat and wool coat with lavish Slavic motifs. He was drunk, fondling one of his male dancers, but he smiled and told me we must have dinner sometime, for Misia had told him "what a treasure" I was. I was also introduced to the composer Stravinsky, whose thinning blond hair and myopic gaze stirred something tender in me; and to the artist responsible for the ballet's Cubist sets, Pablo Picasso, who disconcerted me with his intense stare and tangible air of virility. He was already involved with one of Diaghilev's lead ballerinas, Olga Khokhlova, whom he would marry, but he struck me as a man possessed of a voracious appetite for everything and everyone.

When I returned to the apartment on rue Gabriel long after midnight, it was empty. Boy had left a note on the entry table. He'd been unexpectedly called to England.

Crushing the note in my hand, I took up a pair of scissors and went into the bathroom. Before the mirror, with deliberate defiance that incinerated the tears behind my eyes, I cut my shoulder-length hair to just below my chin—a final act of nonconformity before reality set in.

IV

I sensed the calamity before it materialized.

As the war shuddered into 1918, its bloody finale sending thousands more to their graves, I bought out my lease at 21 rue Cambon, evicted the troublesome modiste, and began to seek additional space in the nearby six-story building at number 31.

I also repaid every centime of my debt to Boy with interest, including the 300,000 francs he had put up for my *maison* in Biarritz. I saw him whenever his new duties as a liaison officer brought him to Paris; he had been with me, in fact, during the presentation of my spring collection at rue Cambon, on the very day of the Germans' final rally of bombing outside the city. The shattering of windows sent everyone racing for cover across the Place Vendôme to the basements of the Ritz, which were equipped with a fully stocked bar, gas masks, and Hermès sleeping bags. In the following days, I reaped a surge of sales in raw silk pajamas, as the women required more coverage than nightgowns to pass their evenings underground.

But Boy was preoccupied and distant. When I ventured to ask what troubled him, expecting him to cite his concern over this latest thrust against Germany, he replied quietly, "I'm afraid of losing you," striking unease in my heart. Why would he fear such a thing, after the world had exploded and we managed to not only survive, but also, as he intended, become richer than when we started? Then I began to notice small items missing from our apartment: a bottle of the aftershave he favored, a robe, a few books, his nail clippers. Nothing substantial, certainly nothing I could use to accuse him of betrayal.

"He's found someone else," Misia deduced, not without a certain gloating. "He has aristocratic pretensions. Everyone knows it. He'll never marry a tradeswoman, no matter how successful or famous you are, because it's not respectable."

It was one of her carelessly wounding pronouncements and I shot a glare at her. "I never intended for us to be respectable. And if Sert might one day see fit to marry you, a woman twice divorced, I don't see why Boy shouldn't marry me."

She shrugged. She was immune to insults, much as she doled them out. "I know of a fabulous apartment on the avenue de Tokio, across from the Trocadéro and overlooking the Seine. An acquaintance of mine has abandoned it without finishing out his lease. It's simply stunning, and you can move in whenever you want. Tomorrow, if you like."

"I don't want another apartment," I said, but I let her take me to see it anyway. It was indeed stunning, with walls of mirrors, a black lacquered ceiling, and silk-papered walls, despite the pervasive smell of cocoa in the air—"Opium," explained Misia. "My acquaintance was an aficionado. He left because he couldn't obtain it in Paris anymore"—and the enormous statue of Buddha posed in the entryway. I signed the lease, pocketing the keys without any intention of moving in. I told Misia as much and she patted my hand. "Of course not, darling, but it's good to have the option nevertheless."

Her words reminded me of Émilienne—*Choices, remember? We all must have them*—and the very next time Boy appeared, unannounced, as was his habit these days, I confronted him.

"What is the matter?" I said, standing with my hand on my hip and my cigarette smoldering as he went wearily to his closet, avoiding my eyes. "Is it my hair? Do you not like it? You told me you thought I'd look exquisite with short hair." When he failed to reply, I charged on, terrified of what he was refusing to say. "Or is it Misia? I know you don't like her or her friends, but they've brought me clients between them, and you really don't need to see them—"

"Coco." He turned to me. I froze, feeling my cigarette singe my fingers. "I'm getting married."

I must have looked as if he had hit me on the head with one of his polo mallets. He didn't attempt to justify it, only continued in that emotionless tone: "Her name is Diana Lyster Wyndham, daughter of Lord Ribblesdale. I met her in Arras when I visited the front; she was working with the Red Cross. She lost her husband and brother in the war. Our families approve."

That simple. He had met her on the front. Their families approved. I tried to bring my cigarette to my lips but it scattered in ash over the front of my pajamas. Affecting an ironic smile, though my heart was breaking apart, I said, "Why is it, I wonder, that these ladies of the aristocracy always have three names? Do you think if I used my full name, Gabrielle Bonheur Chanel, I'd be even more successful than I already am?"

He regarded me helplessly, making me want to fly across the room and gouge his cheeks with my nails. "She's very nice, Coco. I think . . . you would like her."

"I'm sure I would. Perhaps I can design her wedding gown. I've never done one before. But no"—I flipped my cigarette butt into a Lalique ashtray, thinking as I did that hurling the ashtray at him would do the job perfectly—"that would be awkward. And she no doubt wants an English designer for her dress, to do her patriotic duty, as apparently you have done."

I turned and went into the living room. I was quivering, digging my fingers into my palms as I heard him follow me. "Nothing needs to change," he said. "It's not about us. I'll still be stationed in Paris most of the time as part of my assignment, and we can—"

"It's a good thing I rented an apartment, don't you think?" I spun to him so fast that he took a faltering step back. "I'll move out as soon as I can."

"That's not necessary. I always intended for this apartment to be yours."

"No." I moved away from him to the sofa, where I fumbled with my cigarette case. "I think it is necessary. Imperative, in fact." I could hear myself speaking but it sounded like another woman's voice—an icy woman with acrid smoke in her lungs, who had no stake in this life we had built together. "I wouldn't have it any other way."

His sigh was disconsolate. "You see? This is what I feared. I will lose you."

"You should have thought about that before you became engaged to the aristocratic lady with three names," I retorted. I made myself sit, curling my legs under me and yanking a nearby shawl over them. All of a sudden, I was freezing, as though I would never feel warmth again.

He returned to the bedroom. A few moments later, he emerged with his leather travel valise, shouldering his coat. I didn't move a muscle, watching him turn to the door to walk out, for all I knew, forever. Then he paused. "I never meant to hurt you," he said.

I remained coiled on the sofa in silence as he pulled open the door and left.

It took all of my strength to rise, pad into the bedroom on my numb bare feet, and fling open his closet door. As I stared at his racks of trousers, the shirts and folded sweaters he had left, as if he'd departed for one of his extended trips, I thought of fetching my scissors again, only this time I'd savage everything he owned. When he eventually came back—for he would come back, though I didn't know when—he would find my disdain had shredded his clothes.

Instead, I found myself reaching for a faded beige pullover almost hidden under the others, the one I'd first tried on when he brought it from England, its soft drape enveloping me with possibilities. I brought it to my face tentatively, with shaking hands. It smelled faintly of him, of his sweat from playing polo and a trace of his lemon-scented aftershave.

But it smelled more like me.

Cradling it in my arms, I stumbled to the bed and lay down, closing my eyes. This is the last time I will cry over him, I told myself. The very last time I let him or any other man surprise or confound me. Never again. Never, I swore, as long as I lived.

I did not sleep. Nor, to my surprise, did I cry.

There were not enough tears to fill the chasm inside me.

V

I moved into my new apartment as German resistance to the Allied juggernaut crumbled and the kaiser sued for a humiliating armistice. All of Paris took to the streets, cracking champagne bottles over the Pont Neuf, dancing on tabletops, and honking horns as they roared ten to a car down the Champs-Élysées. Later, there would be sober reflection, as news of the final death toll reached over two million in France alone, not to mention countless others in the Allied forces. The northeastern part of the country lay ravaged, and Germany left, contained, yet seething.

I saw and heard it all as if I dwelled under glass. I had brought to the apartment only my clothes, toiletries, and Coromandel screens. Everything else, I left behind. Misia clucked and fussed over me. She wanted me to employ live-in servants to look after me: "I'll give you my butler, Joseph, and his wife, Marie; they have a lovely little girl, Suzanne. Sert wants to bring a family he's known since childhood from Catalonia to serve us and we don't need two butlers and two maids in the house."

I declined. I was at the atelier most of the time and all I required was a day maid to keep things in order. I didn't want potential spies of Misia's poking around in my affairs. Instead, she brought me two hideous statues of blackamoors on marble plinths to decorate my entryway. I hated them but curbed my tongue, though I longed to ask her what was the point of getting rid of that monstrous Buddha if she was going to clutter up my apartment with objets d'art that resembled something from a rummage sale?

Frankly, she could have brought me that stuffed rhinoceros I always teased her about and I wouldn't have cared. It took all the strength I had to set up my bedroom and living space so that I could abide living there, and attend to my work at the atelier, which I was moving to my new building at 31 rue Cambon.

"In with the new and out with the old," Misia was fond of declaring as the war ground to a halt. The peace conferences summoned diplomats, generals, and ambassadors to Paris, along with their mistresses, daughters, and wives—all of whom had heard about my shop and crowded there to gossip, flaunt their men's achievements and insignias, and buy everything I had to sell.

The glamorous life resumed, though without its prior staid opulence. Those days were gone forever, blown apart with the lives of so many young men. Now, a frenetic gaiety overtook us, a joie de vivre that preceded the scintillating percussion of jazz. Hordes of ambitious writers, artists, and musicians who had survived the war became enraptured with Paris, and sought to make their names in the city that never slept.

It was a time to prosper, particularly for me. My daring silhouettes matched the times. Women could no longer abide confinement. After tending the putrid wounds of soldiers, serving gruel, driving ambulances and streetcars, they sought freedom in self-expression and attire. I began to present my collections on actual models, the dummies banished to storage. My clothes had never looked right on dummies anyway; they required a woman to embody them. My live models showed clients how my dresses draped from the shoulders, cut with extra length to eliminate folds between the buttocks; how my coats were layered to flow with the stride, and how my hats complemented the new bobbed hairstyle that, like everything else, was a result of the war, long tresses being ill-suited to disinfecting bedpans.

Everyone wanted a Chanel creation, from my lounge pajamas to my cardigans and twinsets, my coats and blouses with matching linings. My tea gowns of jet-beaded Chantilly lace and black velvet capes trimmed with ostrich were the height of style; I woke up one morning to discover I had become truly famous, the principal *couturière* for fashion-forward women. That bastion of fashion Paul Poiret had returned to his atelier having spent the war designing soldier uniforms. He reverted to his prodigal style, offering leopard-trimmed coats and gowns with epaulettes, but his fame was fading. He failed to adjust to the fast-paced world around him, bursting with vitality and disregard for everything that carried a hint of the old guard. I had other competitors, too, such as the dressmaker Madeleine Vionnet, whose exquisite bias-cut evening wear modeled on Grecian sheaths were works of art but inordinately expensive, reserved for the highest echelons of society. I respected her craft, and in time would translate it for my own collections, but we kept an implicit distance from each other, not poaching on our respective clientele, two women intent on conquest without stepping on each other's hem.

Instead, my clothes bridged the exclusive and the commonplace. I often told my clients that women believed luxury was the opposite of poverty, when in fact it was the opposite of vulgarity. "Simplicity," I said, "is true elegance. A woman is closest to being naked when she is well dressed. Her clothing should be seen only after she herself is."

They flocked to my call, so that it appeared I did not work at all, when in truth I worked harder than ever to maintain the illusion that success was effortless. A woman who toiled was still déclassé. It would take several years of the war's aftermath to truly challenge the restrictions that prevented us from making a living as anything other than seamstresses, actresses, or whores.

But I no longer minded the caustic whispers of "She's a tradeswoman, you know." The tradeswoman they flattered in my salon and denigrated behind my back now commanded more influence and had more wealth than the majority of those I dressed—and we all knew it.

OLD FRIENDS RETURNED in the wake of my separation from Boy. Among the first was Balsan, who had enlisted and narrowly escaped death. He looked haggard but said he was fine; he brought Émilienne with him. Her era, too, was over, that of the grand courtesans enshrined in Dumas's popular novel and Verdi's opera. She'd married and divorced one of Balsan's jockeys, and engaged in torrid affairs, still a lady about town but florid now, with her forty-nine years showing. She was as affectionate as ever, embracing me in her fleshy arms and whispering, "*Mon coeur,* how thin you are. He left you a rag, that foolish Englishman."

I didn't like hearing about him. I didn't want to know. He was in France, attending the peace talks; I heard his name mentioned often, if never by me. I didn't even heed the news of his wedding. Within the month, Misia took glee in informing me that his wife, Diana, was pregnant.

Again, I refrained from comment. I behaved before all as if he no longer existed.

Balsan sensed my resolve and did not say a word, bringing me a bouquet of yellow roses he said he'd cut in the gardens of Royallieu. I introduced him to Misia and Sert, to Cocteau, Picasso, and Diaghilev. They adored his bonhomie, his gargantuan capacity for women and drink, the casual way he carried his stupendous wealth (his textile-driven family, like me, had amassed a fortune from the war). He invested in Diaghilev's latest ballet and prompted me to do the same. He bought a few of Picasso's paintings; when he heard that Stravinsky wanted to send for his wife and daughter from the chaos of Russia, he cajoled me into helping him set up a fund.

I found it painful that the man I had never loved could be so readily accepted into the bohemian world where I moved, while the man I adored was considered an intransigent outsider.

I consoled myself that it was over. Much as I loved Boy, much as I suffered in the solitude of the night, he was someone I must consign to the past.

How wrong I was.

VI

The end began with the defection of Antoinette.

It was 1919, the first year when we were no longer at war. The spring and summer had been hectic, as I shuttled between my shops in Paris, Deauville, and Biarritz. I barely had time to see friends, prompting Misia to threaten to disown me. Business came first, and it was all I could do to keep up. I was preparing to launch my first official collection of evening wear. In order to find some measure of peace, away from Misia's insistent telephone calls and unannounced appearances, I rented a villa in the hills of Saint-Cloud outside Paris, where the fresh air and gardens, and an efficient anonymous staff, could tend to my frayed nerves.

In truth, I also made the decision to rent the villa in order to escape any chance of running into Boy after we collided unexpectedly in a restaurant. He accosted me as I emerged from the powder room even as his pretty, pregnant wife sat at his table with their English friends. Seizing me by my arm, he yanked me into a corner, his breath rank with liquor as he hissed, "Will you avoid me forever? I thought this was a passing fancy of yours and by now we could go back to being who we were."

I took an icy glance at his hand, not speaking until he removed it. He did not look at all well. He had gained more weight than I was used to seeing on his spare frame; his skin was mottled and eyes bloodshot. There was an air of dissipation about him, a loss of that confidence that had attracted me to him, and I said firmly, so he could not fail to understand, "Who we were no longer exists. You are married. You have a child on the way. My passing fancy, as you call it, was that you might come to your senses. You did not."

"Coco, please." His voice ruptured. As he gazed at me in anguish, I thought he might actually start to weep. "Don't do this. I love you. I will always love you. I had to marry for my family, because it is what's expected of me. If I had known I would end up losing you, I never would have done it. I swear I would have married you instead."

I hadn't believed it could get any worse. I had taken cold comfort in the fact that as much as it hurt, the sharp hook of it was behind me. I had my work, my friends; I had my life. But as he uttered those words, I remembered him telling me pride would make me suffer and I longed to shriek that had he only bothered to ask, just once, I might have said yes. I might have married him and borne his children.

Instead, laughter escaped me—a cruel mockery that drained the flush from his skin. "You think I ever cared about being your wife? You think I want to be your property, your possession, beholden to hunting parties and decorating the manor while you gallivant about? It is better this way. This way, we had something beautiful that no one can take from me, not even you. Go back to what is expected. I don't love you anymore."

I pushed past him and stalked away, grabbing my fur wrap off the chair as Misia and Cocteau, with whom I'd been dining, flung money onto the table to cover the check, and hurried after me. As I stormed from the restaurant, I passed his wife at her table. She gave me a pitying look that only enraged me more. She clearly knew who I was.

"The nerve of the man!" Misia declared while I signaled for my car. "I saw him follow you when you went to the toilet. He wants you back, doesn't he?"

Cocteau murmured, "Misia, stop it. Can't you see she's upset?"

"Of course she's upset! *He* upset her. Coco, darling, come. Let us—"

I whirled to her as my chauffeur halted my car at the curb. "Leave me alone," I said in a dead-calm voice. She blanched. "All of you, just leave me alone, damn you."

I rented the villa shortly thereafter. Misia implored my forgiveness—a rarity for her, which only proved how much she loved me, or so Cocteau said when he came to visit. It was that afternoon, as we drank coffee on my veranda, that he told Misia's secret. "She's ruthless and treacherous, never more so than when she thinks you're hers, but I know she's disconsolate at your estrangement. And she's not well herself. She hasn't been for years."

"Not well?" I snorted. "I know she has some aches and pains, but it's entirely her fault. She eats too much. She and Sert both—they live like elephants."

Cocteau tittered, always game for a bit of degradation at someone else's expense. "It's not the meals that will kill her." He leaned to me. "She's a lotus eater, has been ever since her days as Lautrec's muse. He introduced her to it. He used it to ease the pain in his legs."

I had heard the expression before. "She takes laudanum?" I said in disbelief. I'd never seen Misia act intoxicated, though I couldn't be sure. It wasn't as if I was versed in the signs.

He nodded, clearly delighted we now shared a secret *entre nous*. "Laudanum, if that's all there is, which there always is. Opium or morphine when she can get it. The war has helped. They used barrels of the stuff to ease the pain when they had to amputate. Now, it's practically free on the black market. She only does it at home or when she has to attend a function she detests; she was on it the night you met her at her house. Couldn't you tell?" He rolled his eyes, as if I had fallen out of a pear tree in the middle of Paris. "Coco, don't be so naive. It's quite common; all the artists and writers use it. How do you think Misia's beloved Pablo came up with those horrendous sets for Diaghilev?"

"Have you . . . ?" I asked, though I already knew the answer.

"On occasion, yes, when the mood suits. But I'm careful. You have to respect the lotus. She's not a lady you want to invite too often." He laughed. "Just like Misia!"

I didn't probe further. I had thought he was the only one I could abide, for at least he had shown some sensitivity after my encounter with Boy, but after that afternoon, I didn't want to see him, Misia, or anyone else if I could avoid it. I was sorry for her. Any addiction except to work terrified me, but I had too much to contend with. Hundreds of people depended on me for their salaries, and so I imposed a punishing schedule, pushing everything and everyone aside, even as I kept hearing over again in my mind, *Pride will make you suffer.*

Now I stood in the salon of rue Cambon after a grueling trip from Biarritz, confronted by forlorn Adrienne and my sister Antoinette, who defiantly informed me she was engaged to marry Oscar Fleming.

"Who?" I had to search my memory. "Oh, is he that Canadian airman? But you've only known each other a few months. Honestly, Antoinette. Do you even know where Canada is?"

"He loves me." She squared her jaw in an unsettling reflection of my own. "He wants me to be his wife and move with him to Ontario. He says he comes from an excellent family, and if I want, I can open a salon there to sell your clothes."

I threw my coat aside, and searched my crammed travel bag for my cigarettes. Lighting one with my new Cartier gold lighter, an extravagance I'd permitted myself while in Biarritz, I exhaled smoke in her face, making her cough. "You're insane. How many of these foreign airmen and soldiers have proposed to silly French girls since the war ended? I'll wager your Mr. Fleming has a dozen like you all over this city, packing up their trousseaus to move to Ontario, wherever that may be."

Antoinette took a step back out of the cloud of smoke and derision I blew in her direction. "Well, I'm going to marry him whether you approve or not. Just because you're miserable because Boy didn't marry you doesn't mean the rest of us must be miserable, too."

She ran upstairs, leaving me alone with Adrienne. She started to say, "Gabrielle, she's thirty. This might be her last chance for a husband and children. Don't you think she deserves—"

I cut her off with an impatient flick of my hand, stubbing my cigarette out on the sole of my shoe. "Don't you start. If she wants to go to Ontario to be a stranger's wife, fine. Let her go." I glanced at her as she lowered her eyes. "Oh, for pity's sake, Adrienne, stop looking as if the world were coming to an end. We already had one war and survived it. And put some ashtrays in here." I tossed the butt onto the pristine counter. "Women can smoke in public now. Where are our clients supposed to extinguish their cigarettes? On my hats?"

Tromping downstairs to the main workroom—my new establishment on rue Cambon had several floors where I could design and show my collections—I scolded my *premières* Angèle and Madame Aubert for taking so long with the samples for my evening wear.

"Must I do everything?" I said, hauling down the bolts of Lyons white satin and gesturing brusquely to the model in her undergarments. "You. Come over here. And stand still. It seems that if I want this collection to debut before next Christmas, I'll have to sew it myself."

That night, my chauffeur drove me back to my neglected apartment in the avenue de Tokio, as I was too tired to return to Saint-Cloud. An autumn chill was in the air. As I searched my multiple bags for my keys, regretting having turned down Misia's offer of a live-in butler, I heard excited yapping nearby. It must be one of the neighbors walking her pets. It was the latest accessory, fluffy toy dogs that women carried about like muffs—"to keep fleas off," Misia smirked. I missed her. I missed her caustic wit and irreverence. I must telephone her later, to catch up, make a reservation for us to have lunch at the Ritz. I could use a laugh.

The barking came closer. All of a sudden, as I extracted my keys, I felt wet noses sniffing my ankles and spun about to find Boy behind me, holding the straining leashes of two terriers with bristly white-brown fur and vivid button eyes, leaping up at me and ruining my stockings.

I stood with my keys dangling, afraid to move. He looked much better, his face pale but composed, his thick black hair and mustache shining with pomade, his green eyes clear.

"What . . . what do you want?" I said.

"They're for you. Pita and Poppée. I thought that since you don't love me anymore and choose to live alone, you need the company."

"What?" I turned away, inserting my key into the portal lock. "Did your wife not like them? I thought English ladies with three names adored dogs."

"Coco," he said. The way he uttered my name, with such tenderness, without reproaching or imploring, as he used to when we were in bed and he'd take my face between his hands and force me to admit what I could not, made me whisper, "It's impossible." I reached blindly for the leashes as the dogs pranced ahead of me to nudge at the door.

He stood still. I fumbled with the key and managed to shove the door open with my foot. The dogs bounded into the entryway, immediately drawn to Misia's blackamoors.

"Maybe they'll pee on them," he said. He was directly behind me now, his mouth at my ear. As I choked back a sudden burst of laughter, he engulfed me in his arms.

After that, I had no words. What was there to say?

I could not escape him, after all.

VII

Boy was miserable. With our habitual tacit consent, he didn't tell me as much, but it was evident in the way he melted against me afterward and fell fast asleep, in the slightly flaccid musculature of his body that betrayed he'd not been playing polo. I lay awake most of that night, holding him. By the morning, I had accepted this was how it must be. There would be challenges, times when I would regret my decision, when he returned to London and his family to spend months apart from me. I would hate and curse him then, rail at my own foolishness, but I would endure. I had no alternative, unless I banished him from my life again and that I could not do. I had tried and failed. And it did feel as if nothing had changed, not as far as we were concerned.

I was still the only woman he had ever loved.

MISIA GLEANED IT AT ONCE, as soon as I sat at the table in the Ritz where she waited. She took one look at me and said, "So, you did it. You took him back. I knew you would."

I braced for her avalanche of warnings that he'd destroy my peace of mind. I was prepared to inform her, as I would anyone else who dared ask, that it was none of her business. To my relief, she went on in a surprisingly mild tone, "How could you not, with him mooning after you like a lovesick suitor, and you, frankly, impossible to be around without him?" She wagged her teaspoon at me. "No, no. Don't tell me you weren't. It was obvious. You hated us because we weren't him. Cocteau told me how awful you looked when he went to see you at that villa of yours—and I'll not even mention how upset I was that you saw fit to invite that ferret and not me. He said you looked like a ghost."

I wondered if he'd also mentioned what he divulged about her. Somehow, I doubted it.

"But no matter," she said, with the finality of a judge rendering a verdict. "You already look like yourself again, and that's all that matters. If he makes you happy, I am happy." She paused, eyeing me from under the brim of her hat—one of mine, which she'd ruined by adding a sprout of silk sunflowers, as though she were advertising one of Van Gogh's paintings. "You do know I want only for you to be happy, darling? I simply couldn't bear it if you thought I was in any way responsible for your misery."

"Yes." I reached across the table and took her plump hand in mine. "I know. I'm sorry for what happened. It was wrong of me to treat you that way." An apology from me, I thought. Wonders never ceased. Boy certainly did have a salubrious effect on my temper.

She smiled, appeased. "What did he do to win you back? Send roses by the dozens, furs and expensive jewelry? No, it couldn't possibly be jewels. You never care much about that. Well, what was it? Tell me everything."

"Actually," I said, lighting a cigarette and gesturing to the waiter. "He gave me dogs."

She stared at me, openmouthed.

"Pita and Poppée. They're adorable."

"They're not . . . ?"

"No, they're not faux muffs. But I regret to say, they did urinate on your statues."

She howled in laughter—a huge, belly-rumbling explosion of mirth that had us doubled over the table as the prim and proper dames of the Ritz glared at us.

"Dogs," she gasped, wiping tears from her eyes. "Who could have thought it would be so easy to win the impervious Coco Chanel?"

BOY SPENT TIME WITH ME at Saint-Cloud. I delayed the debut of my evening wear collection; the silk had proved so problematic, I decided to order a jersey-silk blend instead, along with crêpe de chine, to see if these might work better. Until the new fabric was woven and delivered, I had a few days off to bask in Boy's company.

We slept until noon, ate breakfast on the terrace, played tennis, and took long drives in his new car—a fast, convertible Bugatti in bright blue, which we raced through the hills into Paris. We stopped to eat at bistros and walked hand in hand along the Seine, thus spreading the word, without ever stating it, that we were back together and did not care who knew it.

Did I spare a thought for his wife back in England, nursing his newborn child? I did not, save to pity her for a fleeting instance as she had pitied me that night in the restaurant. She might be everything a man should want in a wife, but she had not won Boy's heart. Though he would probably never divorce her, she was his wife in name alone, the mother of his children.

In a malicious moment of mischief, I suggested that we send her a package with my latest skirts and sweaters, which were made of Scottish wool and perfect for winter nights in manors.

He gazed at me from over his newspaper, sitting in his robe on a wicker chair on the terrace. "You are an imp, Coco. She will never accept them."

"Why not? I'm the best designer in Paris, according to the most recent issue of *Vogue*."

"She won't," he said, "because I already tried. I ordered your entire summer line from Biarritz for her. She would not even look at it. She gave the clothes to her sister."

"Did she?" I was impressed. I could admire her spirit and liked that she saw me as a threat. It meant I had nothing to worry about, for she did not threaten me anymore, not in the least.

BOY SERVED AS A WITNESS at Antoinette's wedding to her Canadian in October. I made her gown out of the silk I didn't use for my collection, defeating its quarrelsome tendency to droop with appliqués of lace. Antoinette was delirious; she thought she had my blessing. She did not. I thought her officer sullen and his claim of an excellent family a fabrication, but who was I to protest? She was adamant, and nothing anyone said or did could change this. Moreover, to my exasperation, she had the full support of Adrienne, who still pined for respectability with Nexon and filtered my sister's improbable dreams through her own. They connived to see Antoinette wed, and I was too content with Boy to let it bother me.

We saw Antoinette off on a steam liner to Canada with her new husband and seventeen trunks. Before she boarded the ship, my sister clung to me and wept, promising to write once she arrived and determined the best site to set up Chanel Modes, Ontario.

"Yes, yes," I said, dabbing her tears. "Be safe. I hear there are bears in Canada."

I did not think I would see her again. It was unlikely I would visit. As for the shop she wanted to open, it seemed to me an unlikely prospect, as well. Her husband did not seem like the type of man who would allow his wife to work outside the home.

Adrienne walked around like a mourner afterward. I was certain that when she went home to poor Maurice at night, she harassed him mercilessly about their eternal stalemate. If Nexon hadn't been ready to capitulate before, I told Boy, he'd certainly find himself hard-pressed now, after my younger sister had gone and married before Adrienne.

It was December. As snow veiled Paris, Boy returned to England for a brief visit. I was back in the atelier, wrestling with my evening wear collection. I'd hoped to present it at a special spring fête on February 5, my established date for debuts, and invite my most prestigious clientele, including Baroness Rothschild and Cécile Sorel, who'd been after me daily to let them see my samples before I showed them to the public. I finally relented, allowing each of them to try on one of the four gowns I'd prepared. Kitty swooned and begged me to let her buy hers on the spot. I refused. I wasn't satisfied, but assured her she would have first choice once I was.

On December 20, three days before Christmas Eve, Boy was due to return to Saint-Cloud. Misia had dragged me all over Paris that day to buy coral to make Chinese Christmas trees—a thing I had never heard of and assumed must be exceedingly vulgar. "But they'll match the decor in your apartment," she bleated. "Everything there is styled à la Orient."

She was right, of course. My Paris apartment needed an overhaul, though I'd come to appreciate the odd black lacquer ceiling and mirrors, and was considering a similar motif for the staircase between the private workroom and salon at my rue Cambon atelier.

I left her at her house on rue de Rivoli, insisting I had to get back to the villa, as Boy was expecting me. She harrumphed. She wanted us to spend the holidays with her and Sert, a catastrophe I was avoiding at all costs. Once again, she pressed her beleaguered butler and his family on me. "The Catalans are arriving in the New Year; Jojo is set on it. Would you have me turn out my own servants into the streets after years of loyalty?"

As usual, her crisis became mine. I nodded hastily, kissing her on the cheek. "Yes, yes. In the New Year, they can come work for me. I'll need their help when I redecorate the Tokio apartment. *Joyeux Noël*, dearest Misia!" I called out as I raced down the stairs to my car and bundled up in the freezing backseat under my mink shawl.

I couldn't wait to see Boy.

"SHE'S PREGNANT AGAIN." We reclined in the vast living room before the fireplace, nursing cognacs, and enfolded in each other. "She told me when I arrived."

"It must be an immaculate conception," I muttered. "You've barely been there at all." Disgust writhed in me. Was the woman a sheep, to conceive at the first spurt of semen? I didn't dwell on the inevitable fact that Boy had had something to do with it. Proper English ladies with three names didn't take lovers, or at least none that I had heard of, and with me, at least, he still used his lambskin prophylactics.

"What will you do?" I finally asked as he twined my short curls between his fingers.

He sighed. "She insists that we spend the New Year in Cannes. She says winters in England are too harsh and she and our daughter, Anne, need a respite."

More likely, she feels the need to wreck our plans, I almost said. We'd been invited by Balsan to his party at Royallieu to celebrate the start of a new decade.

"That means I won't see you until 1920," I quipped.

Boy kissed the tip of my nose. "We can still spend Christmas together. I told her I had to stay in Paris for business, so she will celebrate the holiday with her family. I'll go to London afterward to fetch her and take her to Cannes. It's a nine-hour drive in the Bugatti from here to there, so I'll come here as much as I can. Diana wants her sisters, my sister Bertha, and Bertha's mother-in-law to join us; in fact, Bertha and Lady Michelham are already in Cannes, staying at the Grand Hôtel. That's too many women in one house for my taste. I'll need a respite. Often."

Here it was, one of those times I had dreaded: my submission to the wife's caprices.

I made myself smile. "Then it's settled. When will you go?"

"Tomorrow, I suppose. Early. That way, I drive to Cannes, visit with Bertha, find the house, and return the day after to see your—what did you call it?"

"Chinese Christmas tree." I elbowed his ribs. "Misia thinks it'll look perfect in my Oriental-themed apartment."

"Along with her stuffed rhinoceros and blackamoors." He cupped my chin. "I, on the other hand," he breathed, lowering his lips to mine, "will give you my Christmas gift now . . ."

He left at dawn, as lavender-tinged clouds crept across the icy sky and I huddled under the down coverlet, languid with sleep and too much cognac, our dogs snoring at my feet.

"Tomorrow," he whispered, ruffling my hair. "Wait for me."

VIII

An urgent ringing of the doorbell sent Pita and Poppée lunging from the bed, barking and racing from the bedroom. I was groggy from the cognacs I'd imbibed after having waited all day to hear from Boy. I finally checked the telephone to discover that the bad weather must have shut down the line. Now, I fumbled for my slippers but couldn't find them. Voices echoed in the villa's foyer as I padded into the corridor.

The dogs' frenzied barking ceased. The lights had been turned on below, making me blink as I descended the stairs. Balsan was standing in the foyer, his coat and hat speckled with snow. He spoke in a low voice to the villa's butler, who had answered the door. With him was his friend Léon de Laborde, crouched by my dogs, soothing them. I should have put on a robe, I thought, raking my hands through my tousled hair as I stood facing them from the bottom steps in my pajamas and bare feet.

"It's a bit late for carousing," I said, my voice hoarse from smoking. "Even if it is Christmas. Could you find no better place to sleep it off?"

Laborde lifted his eyes. Something in his gaze chilled me. Balsan stepped forth, removing his hat. He was ashen. "Coco, there's been an accident." He paused. I didn't speak. "Boy . . . a tire of his car blew out on the road. His sister tried to call here."

"Yes, the phone," I said haltingly, without moving a muscle. "It's not working."

"They called Misia instead. She called me. She would have come herself, only . . ."

Because she was drugged, I thought. She couldn't.

"Coco." Balsan took another step to me. I had to resist the impulse to fling up my hands and ward him off like a superstitious peasant. If I didn't hear it, it wasn't true. It was still in my head, a nightmare I could evade as soon as I made myself wake up. "The car overturned," he said. "The injuries Boy sustained are serious."

Behind him, Laborde whispered, "Tell her the truth, Étienne. She already knows."

Balsan met my stare. "There was a fire." His voice broke. "I'm so sorry, Coco."

I nodded. Without a word, I went back upstairs, the dogs following me, sensing my distress. They leaped onto the bed and lowered their heads between their paws, watching me as I went through my bureau, packing items of clothing I didn't even look at into my travel bag.

When I returned downstairs, Balsan had taken off his coat and was leaning against Laborde. He saw me, and said haltingly, "Your butler went to make tea. Let's sit down and—"

"No." My voice was eerily calm. "I must go there. Now. Will you take me?"

As Balsan hesitated, Laborde said, "Use my car. I'll stay here with her dogs." He looked at me. "Anything you need, Coco. I mean it. Anything, just send word."

I nodded, wanting to thank him but somehow unable to say the words. The butler returned to help me to the car, putting my bag in the trunk while I sidled onto the seat next to Balsan. "Can you drive?" I asked, for I could smell alcohol on him. Misia must have tracked him down at one of the artist garrets or one of the late-night clubs he frequented. I had thought him already at Royallieu, preparing for his party . . .

Then I realized I ruminated on things that didn't matter—anything except what did.

"I can drive." He started the engine, then reached toward me as if to take my hand.

"Don't," I whispered. If I felt one touch, one hint of compassion or sorrow, I'd fall apart. And I couldn't do that, not yet.

Shifting the gear stick, Balsan drove down the hill.

I BARELY SAID A WORD during the twelve-hour drive to Cannes. We arrived in the evening, pulling up at the Grand Hôtel where Boy's sister and her mother-in-law were staying. Balsan was gray with fatigue, as I refused to make a single stop. The hotel was full, the manager informed us in the unctuous tone of a lifelong caterer to other people's whims; the British had come en masse to celebrate the holidays, the first since the war had ended, and every hotel and casino in Cannes was overbooked.

"Do you know who she is?" Balsan yelled. I finally let myself graze his sleeve. "It's fine, I'll sleep anywhere, on the floor in the lobby if need be. Don't shout."

After the manager rang her suite, Bertha came downstairs. Her resemblance to Boy in the green of her eyes and her dark hair choked me. I had met her before, briefly, when I lived with her brother and she visited Paris. She had married into the aristocracy, her father-in-law an infirm lord who died a week after her wedding. Her marriage to his heir guaranteed her a fortune. As she made to embrace me, her eyes bruised from crying, I wanted to push her away, thinking the death of her father-in-law had been a harbinger of doom for Boy.

Bertha wept into my shoulder, disconsolate. When she finally managed to gain control of herself, I said, "I want to see him," and she brought a trembling hand to her chest.

"You can't. He . . . the coffin, it's already been sealed at the morgue."

I gazed at her as if she had uttered an obscenity. "Sealed?"

"Yes." She shuddered, fighting back tears. "Gabrielle, he was burned beyond recognition. You wouldn't have wanted to see him, not like that. He wouldn't have wanted it. When he left us the day before, he was so eager to return to Paris, to be with you. He . . . he loved you so."

He had been driving home. To Paris. To me.

I began to scream. I could hear it, startling the desk clerks and manager, the passing curious guests. But when I focused on Bertha, I saw the scream was only in my head. I felt Balsan cup my elbow. "Coco, you must rest. You can't do anything more," and I found myself allowing him and Bertha to accompany me to her suite.

THE NEXT MORNING, CHRISTMAS DAY, I told Bertha I wanted to go to the site of the accident. Her mother-in-law, Lady Michelham—one of those very proper ladies with three or four very proper names—made a moue of distaste; she was already dressed from head to foot in black.

"How morbid. There is nothing to see except the car. We've made arrangements to have it hauled away, as it's unsightly for travelers to encounter. The funeral is to be held in Paris," she went on. "According to his testament, which Bertha witnessed, he wanted to be buried in the cemetery of Montmartre, a request we assume can be honored, as he was titled a knight of your Légion d'honneur for his contributions during the war."

She imparted this news as if it were an item in a society column, in the voice of someone chastising an interloper for spilling wine on her tablecloth. No, not just any interloper: me. She did not welcome my unexpected intrusion in her family's time of grief, my spending the night awake on a chaise lounge in her suite, smoking incessantly, without saying a word. I must have seemed unnatural, as baseborn as she supposed—the quintessential mistress, unable to recognize her proper place, which was nowhere near here. I could count myself fortunate that Boy had not yet gone to fetch his wife and daughter from London. Had they been here, I had no doubt his mother-in-law would have refused to grant me entry.

Ignoring her, I said to Bertha, "Balsan is exhausted. Can you lend me your car?"

She nodded, but when I went to the lobby, clad in my dark navy blue coat and hat, I found Balsan waiting. I knew it was futile to convince him otherwise. The firm set of his jaw assured me he would walk to the site if necessary.

Boy had not made it far, only an hour or so from Cannes. The road veered around a sharp curve; a kilometer stone near the site bore an angry smear of bright blue paint.

His beautiful automobile, the splendid Bugatti we'd sped around Paris in, was tilted on its side, a carbonized ruin, tires melted into the underside, its spokes twisted and blackened, sticking outward like imploring fingers.

Bertha's chauffeur halted a short distance away. Balsan waited with the driver as I walked alone to the wreckage. My heels crunched over the charred ground. With the trembling grope of the newly blind, I reached out to touch the ruptured opening near the crushed side door, where they must have broken through to retrieve his body.

It was so quiet. So still. Not a single bird chirped in the nearby poplars; not a sough of wind rustled my skirt. It was as though the entire world held its breath, to allow me this moment as I stood before the unexpected annihilation of my existence and the loss of the only man I'd ever known whose life had been too magnificent, too intense, to be constrained by banal time.

He had been thirty-eight, just two years older than me.

I wished I had died with him.

Turning from the car, I staggered to the kilometer stone, gouged by the violence. I sat, buried my face in my hands, and let the frozen pit inside me melt, turn molten, submerging me in a wail of fury as hot and pitiless as the fire that had consumed him.

I sat there for an eternity. I might never have left had Balsan not finally moved to me, gathered me in his arms, and whispered, "Come, Coco. Let me take you home."

ACT FOUR

NO. 5

1920–1929

"EITHER I DIE, AS WELL, OR I FINISH
WHAT WE STARTED."

I

Balsan had wanted to take me home. But in the months following Boy's death, there was no such place. I left the villa in Saint-Cloud; closed up my apartment on avenue de Tokio and sold it, purchasing a slate-roofed house with the fanciful name of Bel Respiro in the western Parisian suburb of Garches—walled and gated, surrounded by gardens. Misia's former servants came to work for me. Joseph Leclerc, his wife, Marie, and their daughter, Suzanne, had been serving in the home of an avowed eccentric, but they must have found me even more of a challenge.

After ordering my entire bedroom swathed in black, the color that wipes out everything else, I could not spend a single night there and called for Joseph to save me from this tomb and make up a bed for me in another room. I barely ate, though Marie sought to entice me with a variety of native Catalan dishes—hearty meat potages that I pushed away after three bites. In the atelier, my staff whispered that mademoiselle was looking frail, wasting away before their very eyes, while Adrienne tiptoed around me as though I might explode.

She had good reason. I became a tyrant, the first to arrive at work, watching the clock with my foot tapping as everyone else bustled in, re-minding them we had set hours of work at Chanel Modes and I'd not tolerate slacking. I knew how someone's grief could become another's profit, for had I not spun gold from the chaff of war? And as I watched them, demanding unswerving fulfillment to the terms of their employment, nitpicking every detail in the workroom, so did I watch my accounts, until Madame Aubert, one of my most trusted and efficient *premières*, informed me that if I suspected thievery, she would hand in her notice. I took her threat under advisement. I could not afford to lose her. My staff at rue Cambon now consisted of over a hundred seamstresses, as well as numerous *habilleuses*, who assisted in the dressing rooms, and *vendeuses*, my sales personnel on the floor. Despite the advice that clients preferred a designer's service, I would only personally see to an elite few.

And the clients still came—business was as heartless as death. A few ventured to tell me, "You mustn't let this horrible thing overcome you. You must take care of yourself."

This horrible thing.

This was what Boy's death meant to them: an unfortunate circumstance, like the war or the epidemic of Spanish flu already killing thousands, something to be acknowledged and regretted, but never given proper due. In a flash of rage, as Adrienne tallied the clients' purchases and I clenched a pen I longed to stick in their eyes, I began to scrawl on a pad of paper: *Capel and Coco, Coco and Capel, Capel and Coco . . .*

C and C. In time, I would revert the positions, interlocked but facing outward, independent yet together. Always. It would become my emblem. It was how I would honor him.

Of my private clientele, only Kitty de Rothschild showed true sympathy. Sweeping into the atelier with tears in her eyes, she tossed propriety aside to hug me and say, "Oh, I was beside myself when I heard! My poor Coco, you must be devastated. I remember how he looked at you, as if you were everything he ever wanted to see. He loved you as few do. Remember that later, even if you cannot remember it now. What you had with him, many wished was theirs."

I never forgot her kindness, which dissolved for a moment our disparate places in society, where even now they did not accept me as an equal.

She also gave me comfort, though I did not say it at the time. For she had spoken a truth no other would dare admit: Boy and I had been envied because we were everything to each other.

Work sustained me, even if I found myself biting back tears as I bent over a swath of fabric or yanked out the cuff on a troublesome sleeve. I still had clothes to design, produce, and sell, even if I decided to set aside for the time my aborted attempt at formal evening wear.

But once my day was done, in my house alone with my servants, I succumbed to despair. Sleep eluded me. I paced all night, the specter of my bed waiting. There were times in those terrible months when I felt I could not endure life without him, everything turning as black as that room I would not enter. I called my decorator, ordered my mourning room turned into a pink satin boudoir. Even then, I drowned awake in carnation sheets.

My beloved Pita and Poppée were the only creatures who kept me sane; they still needed walks, affection, to cuddle at night. They clung to me like mute children who recognize a terrible blow has been sustained, making such a fuss in the morning when I dressed for work that I started taking them with me to the shop. I glared at Madame Aubert when she informed me that she and Adrienne had spent the previous day picking stray fur off the displays.

"You can leave any time you wish. But my dogs stay."

They were Boy's final gift to me, the only thing I had left of him that still breathed. I would have fired the entire staff before I relinquished them.

I DID NOT ATTEND HIS FUNERAL, though many important dignitaries and friends did. Later, I heard his wife had not been there, either, so shocked by his death she almost miscarried his second child. When his will was read in January, I received a terse letter from his London attorney. Boy had bequeathed me the sum of £40,000—the entire price of my Biarritz establishment, which I had reimbursed him for with interest. Accompanying the letter was a small package from Bertha; when I finally forced myself to open it, I found Boy's wristwatch, still marking perfect time.

That day, I did not get out of bed.

TIME PASSED BUT IT DID NOT HEAL MY WOUNDS, contrary to the cliché. It excavated and deepened my grief, making hollow niches in my heart where memories perpetually burned.

But it did pass, bringing me some shallow relief. Misia had been pleading with me to go out, see friends, attend the theater and the ballet. She trudged every week to my atelier, hauling me to the Ritz for lunch. On those nights when she telephoned while I was still at work—I began to stay past midnight, avoiding the desolation of my house—to ask me to join her and Sert, I demurred, citing the long drive home. Finally, she suggested I either remodel the vacant apartment above my atelier or rent a suite at the Ritz so we could see each other more.

Both ideas sounded reasonable. Neither appealed, but I did it anyway, bringing in a designer to see to the apartment and taking a two-room suite in the Hôtel Ritz where I could gaze out to the Place Vendôme and watch late-night lovers stroll.

"You look like death," Misia pronounced when she came to fetch me for a gala at the mansion of the Comte de Graumont and his wife, who was a client of mine. We were, in effect, crashing the party, as the American saying went. The only invitation to this notorious spring party, where the Graumonts wore flamboyant costumes and allowed the haut monde and avant-garde to intermingle, was for Sert, who had painted the gala sets. Misia was outraged to learn I'd been excluded. "You dress the countess! How dare they ignore you?" and upon declaring she wouldn't go if I did not accompany them, she managed to drag me out of my self-imposed exile for a night of revelry I was not looking forward to.

"I'm not sleeping well," I told her.

"Not well? My darling, you aren't sleeping at all! You could sell those bags under your eyes in your shop. This cannot go on. I refuse to let you die, too."

Sert guffawed. I sat sandwiched between them in the car. "Tosh means it," he said, using his nickname for her. "If she has to, she'll force-feed you pâté and camp at the foot of your bed."

I loathed the gala. I was in no mood for blaring saxophones, cheek-to-cheek dancing, or gossipy innuendo, but Graumont expressed his delight that we'd come uninvited and offered me a commission to design the costumes for his next event. When Sert and Misia saw me back to the Ritz, she opened the beaded bag in which she seemed to carry an endless supply of everything and thrust a small blue bottle at me. "Ten drops before bed. You'll sleep like a baby. Don't let me hear you say again that you are not. You will eat, work, and rest. Or I *will* move in with you."

I didn't know if it was her alarming threat or the night itself, for I'd felt so alone at the party, stranded among delirium, but as I climbed the stairs to my suite, hearing Pita and Poppée barking behind the door at my arrival, her little bottle weighted my hand.

I left it on my bedside table, took the dogs for a walk, and returned. I had eaten sparingly from the canapés at the party but I wasn't hungry. I wasn't tired, either. Or rather, I was beyond fatigue. I dwelled in eternal exhaustion, in a haze of the fragmented past and terror of the future.

You have to respect the lotus. She's not a lady you want to invite too often . . .

Unscrewing the bottle cap with its glass syringe, I dripped ten drops of the mud-colored, bitter liquid on my tongue. Then, as I faced the dogs already lolling on the bed, asleep in that untroubled manner of animals, I took five drops more.

I did not think. I did not question it.

Misia was right. For the first time since losing Boy, I slept like a baby.

II

They're asking if we have any perfume." Adrienne had come upstairs to the apartment where I was overseeing the recent changes by my decorator. I had to approve new furnishings, search for objets d'art and other items to make it a place where I could stay. It was the first time I'd had a blank canvas, not a fully furnished residence. This would be my special abode, my refuge from the demands of work and life, and I barely paid heed as she repeated, "The Americans, they're buying up everything we have, but they want to know why we don't sell perfumes."

I grimaced, flipping through swatches of wallpaper. "Because we're not a souvenir kiosk. There are a hundred shops in Paris, selling a thousand horrid scents the Americans will adore. Send them there." As I heard her turn away, I added, "Don't give them accounts. They must pay for what they take. Unless they have a permanent address in Paris, no credit. We can't bill them when they return to wherever they came from. Understood?"

"Yes, Gabrielle." She left me, down in the mouth as she tended to be these days, no closer to marrying Nexon than she'd ever been and consequently miserable because of it.

I lit a cigarette, paced to the apartment's newly enlarged windows. It was cozy in here, not much larger than my suite at the Ritz. Whether or not I could sleep here was another question. As I thought this, I glanced at my purse on one of the gilded Empire-style chairs that the designer had left for me to try.

No. I turned back around. Not during the day and never at work.

Misia's elixir had become my talisman. I had finally begun to sleep regularly, not as restfully as I had before Boy's death, but better than I had since. I was also starting to rely on it too much, the first initial fifteen drops becoming twenty, then twenty-five, numbing me until I floated in a dreamless cave. I awoke parched, groggy for hours afterward, so that eventually I'd adjusted my schedule, arriving at the atelier at noon—no doubt, to my staff's relief.

I chuckled to myself as I thought of the Americans, downstairs in my shop looting the shelves. They had inundated Paris since the war; everywhere I turned, I heard their grating, nasal language or mutilated attempts to speak French. They colonized every district—the Latin Quarter, Montmartre, Saint-Germain—consuming endless plates of steak and *pommes frites*, throwing dollars around as if they grew them in fields. Money, money, money. They had an endless supply, the boom in construction, in automobile industries, in steel and railroads and everything else they could exploit turning their vast country into a bottomless gold mine. Remembering that Boy had often said America was a whore willing to do anything for a buck, I gave a harsh laugh. It suited me like pearls. They were making my already lucrative establishments and reputation impossible to ignore.

They're asking if we have any perfume . . .

I snorted, stubbed out my cigarette, and called my dogs, who trotted from the other rooms. Perfume. As if they could ever recognize a decent scent. They probably thought the eau de toilette sold in the local pharmacies was perfume!

Nevertheless, as I went downstairs to see how much profit the Americans had made me today, the idea lingered.

A *parfum* by Chanel. Now, wouldn't that be something?

"I'M THINKING OF DEVELOPING A PERFUME," I said a few weeks later at one of Misia and Jojo's dinners. I'd started visiting again for informal gatherings, where the usual suspects—Cocteau; Picasso; his wife, Olga; and a revolving host of others—sat around drinking and debating art. We had become a close circle, linked by the artery of defiance running through Paris, its blood the color of paint, clay, and ink, or, in my case, blue, cream, and coral. Evenings at the Serts' were never heavy, never too mysterious; the most immediate concerns after promulgating the value of art and how it would transform the world were how to pay the rent, the latest nightclub to sneak into, who bedded whom, and which new cocktail to imbibe.

I enjoyed the informality of it. I wanted everything light, hedonistic, forgettable. The less I had to dwell on, the less I remembered Boy. He was always there, of course, lurking in the corners of my heart, but I had begun to see him less, to cease turning about with a gasp on a crowded street or in a restaurant, catching a glimpse of a tall, dark-haired figure who stopped my breath. There were days now when I barely cried. I had reached the stage where his memory had been absorbed, soaked inside my skin like indelible dye—a part of me I would never forget. But I was still haunted by his fading smell on the one pullover of his I'd kept and the last set of sheets we'd slept in, which remained unwashed—that subtle aroma of soap and leather, of his musk licked by lemons, now becoming a ghost I tried in vain to summon.

Scent. Here it was again. Why did I suddenly find myself pursuing something so elusive?

"A perfume?" piped up Cocteau. "L'eau de Coco!" Then, when he saw my disgusted moue, he smirked. "No, you're right. Too tropical. What would you call it?"

He was always interested in what I had to say. He had a magpie mind. He'd begun to explore the radical analytical theories of Freud alongside the melancholic poetry of Rimbaud. Though he sharpened his social teeth at Misia's knee, I'd grown fond of him, for of all those who attended the Serts', Cocteau was one of the few who had more than a passing interest in fashion.

"I don't know yet," I said. "It's only an idea."

"Poiret sold perfumes, didn't he?" said Cocteau. "Nuit de Chine, Lucreze Borgia, and several others. I remember hearing about a grand party he gave to launch the first one. I don't think he ever made money on his perfumes, but it became de rigueur for his clients to wear them."

"Yes, they smelled . . ." I shuddered. His perfumes had been ghastly but I didn't care to say it aloud, not when Poiret faced his final decay, most of his clientele having abandoned his atelier. A few powdered matrons of the gilded past still adhered to his adage that the more luxuriously one dressed, the wealthier one appeared, but the younger generation, the daughters and granddaughters of his matrons, had absconded to me.

"Perfume does have a low margin of profitability," I said, "and so much competition, too. Maybe it's not a good idea."

Whether it was or not was of no concern to Misia, judging by her yawn. "Well, don't get too involved in a new project, darling, because you must design my dress for my wedding. And you're coming with us on our honeymoon to Italy, isn't she, Jojo?"

I started, turned to look at Sert where he reclined on the sofa beside me, puffing on his cigarillo. He was a fat little gnome, furry everywhere, coarse black matting even on the tops of his paint-spattered hands yet as bald as an egg on top. I had come to adore him. He embodied his native soil—earthy and unpretentious, surprisingly erudite but without the compulsion to prove it. And very patient. He had to be, living with Misia.

"So, you finally asked her," I said. Misia had been after him for months to make their union official—not, I suspected, because she cared about the formality. Rather, Boy's death had so shaken her that it compelled her to review her own situation and realize that unlike me, who earned my own income, she could be left without an insurance policy, such as a will or an amicable divorce settlement. Sert made money on his commissions and the American millionaire Rockefeller had extended an open invitation for him to come work in New York.

"She wore me down," Sert replied affably. "My Tosh won't take no for an answer, never could." He gave me a sly smile. "You must know that by now. Best start packing for Venice."

"But when is the wedding? I've not heard anything about it until now," exclaimed Cocteau. No one else in the room was paying the news notice; Picasso was deep in talk with another of the Ballets Russes dancers, his wife, Olga, to my amusement, perched as close to him as she could get without crawling into his lap. Her virile Pablo had a wandering eye.

"I was going to invite you, too," said Misia. "To the wedding, that is. Not to Italy."

Cocteau pouted. "I'm small. I can fit in a suitcase," but Misia had already fixed her stare on me. "We'll wed in June and leave for Italy soon thereafter. Does that suit, darling?"

The thought of having to fit her for a gown was enough to make me want to plead incompetence. Sert knew it, too. He grinned from ear to ear, revealing tobacco-stained teeth. "June would be impossible," I said, trying to sound apologetic instead of relieved. "I'm scheduled to go to Biarritz. I must attend to my *maison;* it has been too long since I visited and Marthe Davelli wants to meet me there. I'm staying through July."

Misia scowled. She soured at any mention of my other friends. "You didn't tell me."

"It hadn't come up. I am sorry, Misia. But I can still design your dress."

"No, no." She flicked her wrist, jangling her numerous bracelets. "We'll wait."

"Wait?" I glanced again at Sert.

"Until you're ready," he explained. He leaned over to whisper, "She should marry you instead. I'm not important if you're not there." He didn't say it with rancor. As I laughed and reached for my cigarettes, he arched his brow and sat back in smug contentment.

The next day, I rang up Marthe to confirm that I would be in Biarritz by the end of the month.

III

My establishment in Biarritz was my own personal gold mine, so that my *première*, Madame Deray, greeted me with a rare smile and escorted me through the immaculate salon into the workrooms where my sports-and-leisure wear were produced in expensive fabrics for the resort's discerning clientele.

I fussed over this or that; ordered minimal changes to confirm my authority, but the rest of the time I spent with Marthe Davelli, who had first spurred me to open the Biarritz *maison*. She expressed dramatic sorrow over Boy and proceeded to plunge me into a whirlwind of beach mornings and late lunches, evening dinners with gambling, followed by champagne-and-jazz-soaked parties in the nightclubs and her casino suite that lasted until dawn.

She had left Constant Say, whose sugar fortune crumbled in the wake of the war. Her career as an acclaimed soprano was at its height, and in Say's absence, she consoled herself with various lovers. The latest, she told me, was an exiled Romanov.

It was hardly remarkable. The Russian revolution that murdered the last tsar had prompted the exodus of anyone with the slightest trace of aristocratic lineage. Stateless princes, princesses, archduchesses, and archdukes, along with their assorted servants, fled the vengeful motherland with whatever they could carry, which, in most cases, was nothing at all.

Marthe introduced me to her lover at one of her parties. "Darling, I present Grand Duke Dmitri Pavlovich, son of Grand Duke Paul Alexandrovich and cousin of Tsar Nicholas II."

Though it was unnecessary to cite his credentials, he was worth the effort. One could say many critical things about the Romanov dynasty, but they had always bred magnificent men. This particular specimen bowing to kiss my hand—"*Enchanté*, mademoiselle"—personified every romantic notion of what a prince should be. Tall and stork thin, he had light chestnut hair slicked with brilliantine on his shapely head, a sculpted aquiline nose, and a full mouth. His deep-set eyes of a mercurial amber hue lingered on me until I wondered if he expected a curtsy.

Marthe said, "Dmitri, be a love and bring Coco a fresh drink. Her glass is empty," and he took my champagne flute from my hand, grazing my fingers with his. He had beautiful hands, tapered and white, hands whose most onerous duty until the fall of his world had been to adjust a decorative saber at his waist before a ceremonial procession.

"Isn't he divine?" whispered Marthe as I watched his broad-shouldered stride across the room to the bar. With a jolt, I realized I felt . . . something. Nothing overpowering, certainly, nothing like what I felt when I first met Boy, but something nevertheless—a faint stirring that compelled me to smile and say, "He certainly is. Fatally attractive."

"He's been dying to meet you. Since I mentioned your name, you are all he has asked about. Did you know he helped murder Rasputin? If you find the attraction is mutual, you must take him. He's far too expensive for me."

I INVITED HIM TO MY BED. There is no other way to put it. He didn't leave my side the rest of the night, reciting a mournful litany of his sufferings, from the hour he killed the tsarina's mystic to his exile to Siberia and escape after the war to Italy, Spain, and eventually France, where he met Marthe through his aunt, Grand Duchess Marie Pavlovna, a fellow exile residing in Paris. While I found his story tedious—I had little pity for aristocrats—his apparent interest went beyond the social, as he made clear toward the end of the night when the debauchery of the party reached its height and I prepared to make my exit.

"May I call upon you tomorrow, Mademoiselle Chanel?" he breathed, with an antiquated reserve that almost made me chuckle. Around us, drunken and opium-sotted couples were gyrating; Marthe herself was shrieking with laughter as two muscular black men from the band hoisted her on their shoulders while playing their trombones.

"Why wait?" Reaching into my evening bag, I gave him the extra key to my suite. "Number twenty-five. Bring champagne." I strode out before he could respond, never expecting to see him again. It was an impetuous act. I reasoned a man like him, born to the rigidity of a slaughtered past, would find me too crass, too modern, for his refined taste.

An hour later, a knock came at the door. He did not use the key. Nevertheless, when I opened it, dressed in my robe, my dogs barking until I shushed them, he entered carrying a bottle of Bollinger. He set it upon my dressing table and turned with a flush in his cheeks.

"Expensive," I remarked, glancing at the bottle. "I trust you charged it to my room?" Again, I did not wait for a reply. I stood, staring at him, as he lifted his long hands and, with a slight tremble, began to unbutton his dark gray suit that had seen better days.

He could not do it; his trembling became so pronounced it drove me to him. "Allow me," I said, and I divested him of his jacket and shirt so that he stood bare chested before me, not as darkly muscular as Boy but rather ethereal in his narrow, marble purity.

"You are beautiful," I said, and I paused. Now that he was here, I was starting to regret my impulsiveness. It had been little more than a year since Boy's death. My skin suddenly recoiled at the thought of another man's touch.

He didn't allow me to voice my doubts. Coming at me suddenly, he seized me in arms that were, despite their thinness, astonishingly strong, his mouth on mine with an ardor that rivaled the most lurid kiss in my favorite novels. I might have laughed at the absurdity of it—me, the bereaved mistress of a dead man, acting the slut with an impoverished Russian duke who would no doubt fleece me of everything he could—but again, I felt that stir inside me and it was more powerful now, more insistent, my deprived senses responding with animal need.

He was murmuring against my throat in Russian, unintelligible words I found surprisingly erotic. I closed my eyes and let him take me to the bed.

For once, I refused to think.

This time, I wanted only to feel something that meant nothing.

DMITRI BECAME MY LOVER. Back in Paris, I installed him in my house in Garches. Joseph and Marie did not blink twice when I announced that my guest would be living in one of the spare bedrooms for an undetermined time. Appearances must be kept, though he came to my bed every night and met me after work to dine, attend the theater, and visit the Serts.

Misia was flabbergasted at first, the only time before, or since, I actually saw her struggle for an appropriate response. When she finally did after dinner, as Jojo regaled Dmitri with tales about his art commissions, she dragged me into the parlor to hiss, "Do you love him?"

I laughed. "Don't be ridiculous."

"Then why? He's rather young. How old is he, exactly?"

"Thirty." I held up a hand, anticipating her next outburst. "I'm perfectly aware that's eight years younger than me and that he is penniless. I don't care. He's what I need right now."

"What you *need*? Have you considered the scandal? He's royalty— many believe that if the monarchy is ever restored in Russia, he is the rightful heir." She suddenly paused, her eyes narrowing. "Or is that your plan? Society will have to receive you if you are with him. Although he has nothing but the clothes on his back, which you no doubt paid for, every blue-blooded matron in Paris will kill to receive him. It's all the rage, inviting exiled Russians to tea."

"When did I ever care about that?" Behind me, I heard Dmitri's slow, careful laugh as Sert let out one of his bawdy quips. "I'm with him because he amuses me. What the blue-blooded matrons do or say is inconsequential."

Misia harrumphed. "I'm sure that's what you want everyone to believe. But it's me you're talking to, darling; I know how you hunger for acceptance, and how better to achieve it than to be seen with a dashing Romanov on your arm?"

"Think whatever you like. He is a lover, nothing more. And," I added, "he's coming with me to your wedding and to Italy, too. His sister the Grand Duchess Marie is in Venice, vacationing with our friend Diaghilev. He wants me to meet her."

I walked away, preempting her protest. Misia was perceptive, but she had sniffed out the wrong clue. During our time in Biarritz, I had found myself telling Dmitri about how I'd established my clothing business (without mentioning Boy or Balsan) and of my idea about developing my own signature perfume. I knew the Romanovs had been mad for scents, as they were for everything that reeked of luxury, and he mentioned that the French perfumery house Rallet, which established itself in Moscow under Romanov patronage, had created the Tsarina Alexandra's favorite *parfum.*

"Such an exquisite scent," Dmitri had said wistfully, his eyes growing distant as they always did when he recalled the past. "I can still smell it now: a mixture of rose, jasmine, and something indefinable that made everyone stop. Alexandra wouldn't let anyone else wear it. Ernest Beaux originally designed the formula for Rallet to release during the jubilee celebrations, but it proved too costly for anyone but her."

"Do you have a sample or know where this Beaux is?" I asked eagerly.

Dmitri sighed. "The perfume must be lost, like everything else. Beaux enlisted during the war; I don't know where he is now. Perhaps in Grasse? Rallet owns fields there. My sister Marie might know."

Grasse was famous, a swath in southern France where such distinguished houses as Coty and Guerlain grew special hybrids for their scents. I wanted to go there at once, to track down this mysterious Beaux, but Misia's upcoming wedding derailed my plan. No sooner had I decided to extend my time away than she telephoned to inform me that she and Sert would wed in August and she expected me back in Paris by then.

Fitting her gown in less than a month was a torment; combative and resistant to anything less than the traditional, in the end we settled for the usual lace-and-silk affair. The wedding was a simple celebration, however, and as August thickened over Paris, we embarked on a monthlong yacht tour of Italy.

IV

Italy enchanted me. I had never been abroad and was swept up in the crumbling mosaic grandeur and serpentine waterways of Venice, where we stayed on the Lido, its stony beach washed by the turquoise lagoon.

Sert proved an ideal travel companion. Bursting with exuberant knowledge, he took us to see the plundered Byzantine horses in San Marco, the wealth of Titians and other paintings in the museums, and yanked us down twisted byways to find hidden restaurants that served roasted sparrows wrapped in prosciutto. He was indefatigable, to the point that he exhausted us and Misia declared, "Enough with dead masters!" and hauled me off to antiques shops that yielded gilded masks, painted icons, and incense-suffused relics.

I was happier than I had been since losing Boy. I thought of him often, not with the suffocating sadness that had accompanied his memory until now, but with a yearning that he could have been there with me, to share my fascination with this sinking city known as La Serenissima. I ceased to rely as much on Misia's elixir, the lapping of water instead rocking me to sleep without the need to numb my senses. My penchant for gondolier-inspired loose trousers that reached above the ankles, nautical pullovers, and cork-soled sandals spawned an international trend.

But Dmitri became a stone about my neck. He walked around with a mournful air, as if the beauty around him only reminded him of the beauty he had lost. I soon grew tired of his moods and nightly cough, exacerbated by the damp, as well as his increasing penchant for heavy drinking and unimaginative lovemaking.

Sensing my impatience, Misia dug in the knife. "I heard he was madly in love with his own cousin, Felix Yusupov, who connived with him to kill Rasputin. He even made his way to London after the revolution to reunite with Felix, but they had a falling-out because Felix was bragging to everyone that he helped bring down the tsar. Dmitri accused him of threatening his own hopes of being restored to the throne." She paused at my deliberate lack of reaction. "I trust you're taking precautions. These men who go with other men, well . . . they can give one the most horrendous ailments. Having to take mercury cures for the clap would put a significant damper on your schedule."

I rolled my eyes. I didn't tell her that by now Dmitri's sole enthusiasm was for vodka. The only time he perked up was when we went to meet his sister and Diaghilev for lunch in a palazzo on the Grand Canal. Grand Duchess Marie was staying as the guest of an illustrious Italian aristocrat's wife, for much like their counterparts in Paris, the Italian nobility found entertaining a displaced Russian princess irresistible, regardless of the expense.

Diaghilev was delighted to see us. I had not spent time with him outside of the parties held for the Ballets Russes, when he'd been invariably intoxicated and preoccupied with his latest dancer du jour. I saw his genuine but wary affection for Misia, who did not try, as she usually did, to dominate the conversation when he griped about his financial setbacks in attempting to mount a revival of Stravinsky's *Rite of Spring*. The composer had moved to Switzerland to recover from a bout of typhoid but remained dogged by ill fortune: "He has his family with him now, but his wife, Katya, has consumption and he's barely eking out a living," Diaghilev said. "I want to bring him back to Paris and reintroduce his genius to the world. The times have changed. I'm certain we'd have great success together."

If he was looking for support from Misia, he didn't receive it. She went as quiet as a tomb, intent now on securing her own future. Diag's keen interest took me aback. Peering through his monocle, he bombarded me with questions about my shops, and my hopes of developing a perfume. Portly and double chinned, with an enormous head that seemed to sit directly upon his massive frame and a streak of dramatic white in his ebony hair, he dressed flamboyantly but with style, his crimson velvet jacket bristling with embroidery, his great hands peppered with rings, and a black pearl affixed to his damask cravat.

"So Russian," he declared, turning effusively to the grand duchess. "Isn't it, Your Highness? The French may have refined perfume for the modern age but we knew best how to wear it. Remember how everyone scented themselves with a different perfume for the ballet in Moscow—men and women alike, so that the entire house seethed like a summer garden? Ah, it was magnificent, like plunging into Aphrodite's temple. One could perish of olfactory lust."

Grand Duchess Marie smiled. She was another superlative example of Romanov breeding, with her thick-lashed eyes and symmetrical features, her pampered complexion untouched by the sun, while I, on the other hand, had taken to sunbathing and was as brown as an Indian. I also noticed her slim hands were chafed and her cuticles ragged, like those of a seamstress.

She saw me glance at them as she poured tea. With a gracious incline of her head, she said, "You must come visit me when you return to Paris. I've opened a small atelier myself, called Kitmir, where I do specialized embroidery and beading; Madame Vionnet has hired me to decorate some of her gowns. Perhaps I could be of assistance to you, as well."

If Vionnet had hired her, her work must be excellent. It impressed me, too, that unlike her brother, with his laments and drinking binges, Marie Pavlovna had rolled up her sleeves. "We must make our own way now," she added, when I assured her I would certainly visit. "The past is dead. We must learn to adapt to everyday concerns."

I wanted to ask her if she knew anything about the tsarina's perfume, but it was Dmitri, roused from his torpor, who said, "I told Coco about Alexandra's special scent. She's very intrigued by it and wants to know if we have the formula or know where Ernest Beaux is."

Marie's reply was to lead me through the cavernous palazzo to her bedroom. Opening a drawer in her bureau, she removed a tiny bottle of diamond-shaped glass. "This is Rallet number one. Those savages looted our palaces and stole whatever they could, including Alexandra's stores of perfume. It may be the only sample left."

With reverential caution, I uncapped the bottle and raised it to my nostrils. The fragrance immediately sank through me—a complex alchemy of flowers, with a hint of something deeper that evoked opulent privilege, the premier status of an empress: cultured, luxurious, and very expensive. Though not quite what I had hoped for, its tone conveying the slight fustiness of older women, it was still undoubtedly unique.

"Try it," urged Marie. "I don't ever use it. It was never mine."

Dabbing a few drops on my wrist, I waited. When I lifted my hand to my nose once more, I gasped. There it was: the very essence I sought without understanding what it was, a hidden scent as disquieting as it was unexpected—the secret allure of feminine ardor, spent upon crisp white sheets.

Marie's face softened as I gazed at her, mesmerized. "Ernest Beaux is indeed in Grasse, in the village of La Bocca. He still works for Rallet but maintains his own laboratory to make custom scents. If anyone still knows the formula for Alexandra's perfume, he does."

"I . . . I must see him," I said.

"Yes, I thought you might." She turned to her desk. "I'll write a letter of introduction."

FROM VENICE TO FLORENCE AND PISA, and then on to Rome. Before the torrid ruins of the Colosseum, Sert threw out his arms and proclaimed it Rome's unburied skeleton. "Architecture is the bones of a city. Everything is bone structure. A painting, a sculpture, even us: a face without bones cannot last. You," he added, pinching my cheek, "will look pretty even when dead."

Overwhelmed by everything I had experienced, I was also weary of Misia and suitcases, longing to return to work, to start my journey to Grasse and the quest for my perfume. By now, I was determined: Marie Pavlovna had given me her sample, insisting it was but a memento, and she carried within her the scent of her tsarina.

In return, I promised to visit her in Paris and help her expand her own business with commissions from my atelier. She would help me create gowns to rival Vionnet's, for now I was past the mutual distance I had thus far maintained with my rival. To launch a perfume, I needed the clothes to go with it—clothes with Russian flair, evoking bygone splendor.

Upon our return to France in the autumn of 1921, Dmitri no longer infatuated me.

I had set my sights upon a different obsession.

V

The year ended with tragic news.

My younger sister, Antoinette, whose impulsive marriage to Oscar Fleming had resulted in predictable disaster, had met an Argentinian and fled with him to Buenos Aires. She became pregnant, and like Julia before her, her lover promptly deserted her. Left penniless in a foreign land, she had sent me an urgent missive through a kind stranger who took her in, but it arrived too late. Antoinette had fallen victim to the catastrophic Spanish flu.

Sitting alone in my room after telling my servants not to disturb me, I wept for her. I recalled my flippancy when she announced her intent to marry, my impatience with her willingness to conform to whoever came her way, my certainty that we'd never see each other again. Now she was gone. I was the sole daughter left of my parents' ill-fated union. Once I recovered from the news, I wrote to Louise in Moulins to see if she knew where my lost brothers, Alphonse and Lucien, were. Louise returned word that both were alive. Alphonse was a veteran of the war; with the subsidy paid by the government, he had opened a *tabac* shop. He was married, with three children. Lucien was an itinerant vendor like our father, sowing in his wake a series of unhappy mistresses before he, too, married and settled down, as much as any Chanel man could.

In memory of Antoinette and Julia, I arranged to send my brothers monthly payments to augment their earnings. I also wrote to my nephew André at his school in England and had him brought to Paris to share a long weekend with me. The notion of family terrified me, for I would never have chosen the circle into which I was born, but I wanted to see my nephew.

He surprised me when he arrived, with his subdued resemblance to my sister Julia, but also graced with the angular cheekbones and long-lashed dreamy eyes of the Chanel men, reminding me with a jolt of my father. He was almost ten years old, and remarkably thin of build like me. As he entered my boutique on rue Cambon, he looked about with a discerning expression at my displays. As I swept down the staircase to greet him, my scissors hung on a ribbon from my neck, needles and stray threads stuck to my jacket, and my dogs capering at my heels, he held out his hand.

I paused. Then, with a smile, I clasped it. He shook my hand as though he was meeting an important stranger, standing very erect. "Mademoiselle Chanel," he said in excellent French, his diction clipped, with the nuance of an English boarding institution, "I am very pleased to make your acquaintance." He did not even look down at Pita and Poppée, who were engaged in a thorough inspection of his lace-up boots.

Around us, my staff made a collective cooing sound, hands at their chests in that way women will do when impressed by a child's manners, no matter whose he might be.

"Yes." I winked at him. "But I trust we will soon be more than acquaintances. You must call me Tante Coco. Mademoiselle Chanel makes me sound like a schoolteacher, and I should think you've had quite enough of those for a while."

A flush crept into his pallid cheeks. "Tante Coco," he repeated, evidently taken aback by my candor. Then his face suddenly twisted, as if he was holding back an inopportune hiccup. Instead, though he tried his best to control it, a wet little cough came out, which he immediately tried to smother by covering his mouth.

"Are you sick?" I exclaimed. "Did you catch cold on the boat?"

"No, no," he replied, but he coughed again, harder this time, sending Adrienne racing into the back room for a glass of water. "It's nothing, just a tiresome cough I always have." He sounded embarrassed, as if he suffered from a harelip or other gross inconvenience. "I'm not allowed to play cricket because of it. My headmaster says it's my French lungs."

He took the glass Adrienne extended to him. As he sipped, I gauged him carefully. He was very slender. It hadn't struck me as unusual because I could still remember how gangly my siblings and I had been at his age—all jutting knees, ankles and elbows like pegs, as though we lacked flesh for our bones. We had in fact lacked it, but André should not. I had placed him in the most expensive school at Boy's recommendation. If anything, considering the cost of his board and tuition, my nephew should be rosy and plump.

"Sit here." I guided him to a nearby chair. He drank all the water but declined more. His cough had abated but I didn't like how it left him breathless, blue veins visible under his temples. "Are you tired? You had a long trip. Shall we go home and rest awhile?"

"I . . ." He hesitated, reaching down to pet my dogs as they sat beside him with adoring expressions. I had the sense that he wasn't used to voicing preferences, so I urged, "What would you like to do? It's your holiday. We can go wherever you like."

This time, his blush was definitely one of timidity. "I should like to see your atelier, if that isn't an imposition? I hear you are very famous."

"Is she ever!" declared Adrienne. "The most famous designer in Paris!" She gave him a wide smile. "And I am your great-aunt, so you must call me Tante Adrienne."

"I have two aunts?" He looked at us in awe. I saw my dead sisters then in his eyes, our lost childhood, and that haunted sensation that we did not belong anywhere.

"You do." I took him by the hand. "Let me show you how famous your aunt is."

He went wide-eyed as I gave him a tour of my premises, from the ground-floor boutique to my second-floor salon where clients had their fittings and I presented my collections; up past the apartment on the third floor to the workroom with its fabric-strewn tables and dummies on which garments were fashioned, overlaid by the clatter of sewing machines and my seamstresses' chatter.

I showed him my *toiles* in muslin to create my clothes and the alterations of a dress that his arrival had interrupted. "This is for a baroness. She needs it next week, but I have to fix it because she lost weight after her last fitting and . . . Well, this is how I work. As you can see, I might be famous but it's not very glamorous."

"Oh, it is." He appeared utterly fascinated. "It's like nothing I have ever seen."

"Then you must come work for me when you finish your education," I declared, and the moment I spoke, I realized I meant it. I had not thought he would affect me as he did. While he was my sister's son, I'd never felt any maternal sentiments, yet as he wandered the workroom, asking polite questions that my seamstresses were delighted to oblige, I watched him through a haze in my eyes that I did not realize was caused by tears until Adrienne pressed a handkerchief into my palm.

"Careful," she murmured. "Your heart is showing."

I scowled, dabbing my eyes. "Does he look frail to you? He is too thin, isn't he?"

She nodded. "Yes. I hate to say it, but that cough of his; I don't like the sound of it."

"I'm going to take him to a specialist. French lungs, indeed. If that school has been neglecting him, they are going to hear from me. With what I pay them, they can damn well light a fire in his room every night to offset the foul English damp."

I made the appointment with the best physician in Paris; while he had

André take off his shirt, exposing his painfully narrow chest, I hid my tumult, fearing a diagnosis of tuberculosis. "A mild weakness in his bronchial tubes," the doctor declared. "He needs to stay warm. If possible, he should reside in a dry climate."

It was not possible; André had his schooling to complete, but I sent him back at the end of his visit with a satchel full of herbal remedies and telephoned the headmaster to demand regular monitoring of his health. Before he left, I took him to the Ritz for afternoon high tea; I thought it the quintessential English experience, but he laughed and said they never served such delicious croissants or éclairs at Eton. His hearty appetite reassured me, so I queried him about his studies. He was not poorly treated, and he expressed genuine enjoyment with his school. Only his delicate health gave him the sense of being different, in the way he interacted with the other boys and the restrictions it placed on him.

"Well, you'll have to find other ways to prove yourself," I said. "You must be the best student, read everything you can to strengthen your mind. Education is the most important thing you can possess; without it, you're just another ox under the yoke."

He tilted his head, mulling this over. At length, he nodded with that preternatural maturity which made me think that despite his physical impediment and uncanny resemblance to my brothers, André would grow up to be a fine young man, unfettered by the wanderlust that had wreaked such havoc on the Chanel men's lives.

"I like to read. And I don't ever want to be an ox." He smiled. Then, without warning, he stood, came around the table, and to my surprise, embraced me. He did not speak. He just held me tight, his little body like a splinter against me, until I said softly, "They're going to think we're lovers," and I bit my lip, cursing my own ineptness with children.

He replied, "That's because I love you, Tante Coco. You smell like Paris."

With Antoinette's death, I finally felt like the orphan I had so vehemently denied being as a girl. I vowed André would never experience the same. He would never know the desolation my sisters and I had endured, because he had me.

A FEW WEEKS AFTER ANDRÉ LEFT and before I embarked on my trip to Grasse in the summer of 1922, I left my atelier early and made my way to the Hôtel Continental on the rue Castiglione, a short walk from rue Cambon. From the lobby, I had word sent upstairs. A half hour later, Diaghilev arrived, rumpled and emanating the sour tang of cigarettes and drink. He blinked in confusion before his vodka-soaked brain recognized me, and he stammered, "Mademoiselle Chanel, no one told me it was you." He was obviously flustered, the dandified overlord of the Ballets Russes exposed as a paunchy, intemperate man.

I handed him a sealed envelope. He was bewildered until I explained, "I've thought a lot about what you said in Venice about Stravinsky and launching a new performance of his *Rite*. I am in complete agreement as to his genius; I was at the first performance of the *Rite* in 1913. You will find there sufficient funds to bring him to Paris and begin production. Tell him the *couturière* Coco Chanel offers him and his family my home of Bel Respiro until he can find an appropriate residence elsewhere. But I would request one condition."

He gaped at me, the envelope in hand.

"No one is to know," I said. "I hope you will oblige."

I smiled as I walked away, fully aware that the first thing he'd do after ripping open the envelope to find my check for 300,000 francs would be to race to the nearest telephone to tell Misia. Much as I loved her, it was time she learned that I was not beholden to her anymore.

Stravinsky arrived the following week, leaving his two daughters behind in Switzerland with his wife so they could finish out the term in the convent school where he had enrolled them. He was gaunt, pared to mere flesh and bone, his thick lips quivering as he thanked me repeatedly and offered to put Katya to work in the house to repay my generosity.

"Nonsense," I said. "I have plenty of help. When she arrives, she must rest." I led him up to the room where he would stay, after having shown him the Steinway piano I had installed in the living room for his use. As we passed Dmitri in the hall, Stravinsky edged around the glaring Romanov and almost wept when he beheld the spacious suite I had prepared for him.

"Is he your new lover?" Dmitri spat out with more passion than he had displayed in months. "That bespectacled wreck who stinks of gratitude and penury?"

I eyed him, refusing to dignify his question with an answer. He was looking rather a wreck himself, his vodka consumption having reached alarming heights. "I'm going to lock up the liquor if you don't take a bath this instant and put on a fresh shirt," I finally said. "We leave for Biarritz tomorrow and I'll not have you looking like a stray dog. Be at the Ritz by nine. I'm going to stay there for the time being."

Our affair was in its final throes, of that there was no question.

But I still needed him for this final task.

WE DROVE FIRST TO BIARRITZ in my Rolls, where I checked on my *maison* to find that business had begun to falter, the migrations of the rich having sent them flocking to Cannes and Monte Carlo instead. Taking the winding roads through Toulouse to Nîmes, Dmitri and I stopped in Marseilles and went on to Cannes, where I scouted a location for a new establishment. We then went on to the village of La Bocca in Grasse. It took us a few days to find Beaux's laboratory, tucked among endless fields of roses, jasmine, and fragrant lavender—an oasis of calm in a serene, extremely prosperous region that had been the beating heart of the French perfume industry since the seventeenth century. Once we found him, his employers at the House of Rallet refused us access until I showed them the letter of introduction from the Grand Duchess and Dmitri presented himself in person for an afternoon tea at their château.

The presence of a living Romanov, as I suspected, mobilized the powers that be at Rallet, who protected their perfumers as much as they did their perfume secrets. After two days of dallying in Grasse's bucolic splendor, we received word that Beaux could meet with us for an hour.

Ernest Beaux was a fastidious man close to me in age, with an appropriately dignified nose and clad in a medicinal smock. He was reluctant to listen to the reason for my trip until I removed the tiny bottle of Rallet number one from my pocket. Speechless, he turned the bottle over in his hands. "I never thought I'd see this again," he uttered. "I thought it was lost forever."

"That would have been a great pity," I said. "It's a magnificent scent. But," I added, "it doesn't last. It fades too quickly. I would need you to—"

"Fades?" He gazed at me in astonishment. "You have *tried* it?"

"Of course." I refrained from lighting a cigarette, sensing he would not appreciate smoke in his pristine environment. "I had to test its quality. Now I understand why the tsarina set such store by it and kept a surplus. It has no power. After two hours, it vanishes."

"That was my intent. Her Imperial Majesty desired a scent that would last only as long as her engagements required. She did not wish to go to bed smelling of it."

I doubted that. The undertone I had detected was unabashedly sensual, and everyone knew how much Alexandra had adored her husband, Nicholas.

"Well, I need it to last longer," I said, and when he started to protest that it was impossible, I interrupted. "I don't care about expense. I realize a perfume like this does not come cheap. In fact, I want it to be as expensive as possible, for that is the only way to assure its exclusivity. But it also must be worth its price in value. I would need certain notes enhanced, to linger after the initial bouquet fades. My perfume must mimic nature not by exaggeration but rather by emphasizing the naturalness within it—it must distinguish and individualize, be unforgettable on every woman who wears it. Above all, it must last."

Despite his apparent skepticism, I saw his eyes widen. He could tell that I'd been studying the complex art of perfume; indeed, I'd done little else in the months since my return from Italy, heaps of books on the subject littering my apartment on rue Cambon. I understood and respected the painstaking science behind it.

"I was thinking you could add more powdery notes," I suggested, "iris root, perhaps, and synthetic aldehydes to strengthen its resilience. Do not be afraid to experiment."

I paused, waiting. After a moment's hesitation, he leaned to a writing pad before him and began to scrawl in an illegible hand. Then he sighed again. "I really don't know, mademoiselle. I respect your vision, but this type of endeavor has not been done before, let alone sold by a couture house. Moreover, I cannot reproduce the tsarina's special perfume as formulated under the terms of my contract with Rallet. It belongs to them."

I leaned over to him, placing both my hands on the table between us. "I'm not asking you to reproduce it. I don't want my clients smelling like a dead empress." As he sucked in a shocked breath, I said, "I'm prepared to pay extremely well if you undertake this project. Dmitri—" I glanced about, but he was gone, had wandered off somewhere, an infuriating tendency he had of late. "The grand duke has assured me you're the most skilled perfumer in the world. I merely want you to adapt parts of the original formula in order to devise an entirely new fragrance. I leave it up to you as to how you achieve it."

I had finally snared him; I saw it at once. He was as much a visionary as he claimed I was. Competition in his industry was fierce, a slew of new fragrances appearing as the trend gained momentum, and Ernest Beaux could not repress his love for the special scent he had created for Alexandra. Moreover, I had already delved into his circumstances. He was not Rallet's chief perfumer, and I offered him a once-in-a-lifetime opportunity. He also knew, as I did, that intellectual property rights did not include perfume formulas. His lie about the company owning the formula for Rallet number one had merely been to test my knowledge.

"How long do I have?" he asked at length.

I considered. "As long as it might take. I can rent a villa nearby and wait."

"It could take longer than mademoiselle thinks," he warned. "These distillations are delicate; the synthesis doesn't happen overnight."

"I'm aware of it." I took out my checkbook and wrote an amount, tearing out the draft and slipping it across the table to him. "Will that be enough to start?"

He exhaled, stunned. "My employers will be most grateful for the—"

"No, no." I smiled. "Your employers need not know. I am hiring you, Monsieur Beaux, not Rallet and Company. This transaction must remain between us."

As he nodded and pocketed my check, I reached out my hand. He paused, confused, then, when he understood, tentatively took my hand and shook it. I kept my grip firm. "It's a pleasure to do business with you, Monsieur Beaux."

As I turned to the door of his office, he said, "That remains to be seen, mademoiselle. I've not given you anything of substance yet."

"Oh, but you will," I told him. "I have no doubt."

I HAD GROWN DISINTERESTED in Dmitri as a lover but the idle months we spent in the villa I rented, where we swam, went shopping in local boutiques, and took evening walks with Pita and Poppée, became some of the most idyllic I would remember.

Dmitri reverted to his sensitive self, attentive during the day and energetic in bed at night; the exposure to sea and sun toughened his demeanor and he drank less.

One evening, he whispered to me, "I know this must end. I do not love you and you don't love me. But I want to tell you now, before we say goodbye, how grateful I am for your kindness. I will never forget it. I was lost before I met you, but now I have the strength to go out into the world and make something of myself, as Marie has done. You have been so generous to her, too; I know you already commissioned her for your gowns. Coco, you saved our lives."

I averted my gaze, discomfited by this sudden flood of emotion. "You make me sound like Joan of Arc. You also helped me, as has your sister. It's not as if I gave something for nothing." I chuckled, looking back to him. "You should know by now, I never do."

He arched his brow. "You do far more for others than you care to admit."

BEAUX HAD PREPARED ELEVEN SAMPLES, aligned in anonymous glass bottles with plain labels attached, featuring only numbers. I hadn't eaten or smoked all day; my nose had to be as clear as possible. I did not want to make a mistake.

One by one, Beaux uncapped each sample, starting in reverse. I inhaled deeply, waited, and if the scent showed promise, dripped it on a piece of paper and waved it in the air of that hermetic room. Dmitri waited outside; I went to him with each sample. He shook his head. "No, that's not it." I knew he sought the elusive scent of his childhood; returning to the room, I rejected numbers eleven through six.

Beaux handed me sample number five. It was my talismanic numeral, which I had seen reproduced in the star motifs and river-stone mosaics of Aubazine. As I prepared to smell, I heard the abbess as if she stood beside me in her robes:

Wind, earth, fire, water, and, most important of all, spirit. Everything we see around us contains these five elements. Five is the most sacred number in the firmament.

Then I inhaled.

It took only an instant. I felt it move through me, resurrecting memories of starched linens piled high in cupboards at Aubazine and of the lye soap I still used, of the cool forest of Compiègne I had ridden through with Balsan, and of Émilienne's rare freshness. And then, with a shudder that brought my hand to my face to hide my sudden tears, the tantalizing hint of warm skin flushed with lust—the smell of me, when Boy had filled my entire being.

"This is it," I whispered. "This is the one."

Beaux said anxiously, "Mademoiselle, there are four others. That one, it's not . . ." His brow furrowed in consternation. "It's a mistake. I added too much jasmine. I almost didn't include this sample because it would be the most expensive of the batch to produce, but I liked its effect so much . . . I didn't think you'd choose it."

"This is it." I dabbed a few drops on my wrist, let it sit for a moment before I brought it again to my nostrils. "I don't need to smell anything else. This is my perfume, Number 5 by Chanel."

"It'll cost a fortune. It's almost as costly to make as Rallet number one."

Of course it was. How could it not be?

"I need one hundred bottles," I said. "I'll telephone you with the rest of my order."

I dabbed more of the flawless scent on my throat and wrists, wrote him another substantial check, and drifted out in a haze to Dmitri. I inclined to him, tendering my neck.

He sighed. "Now, you smell like a Romanov."

I LEFT DMITRI IN BIARRITZ with a fond farewell and sufficient money to ensure he indeed made something of himself—a goal that apparently entailed meeting an heiress. Before I departed, he handed me an azure velvet box containing a rope of exquisite pearls with an antique gold and diamond boule.

"How did you . . . ?" I let my question linger. We both knew he had no resources with which to have bought me such an extravagance, unless of course he had done so with my money.

"They were my aunt's, one of the few things I was able to take with me when I was exiled. I've had them stored in a vault in the casino all this time." He grimaced. "Marthe Davelli wanted me to give them to her, but our relationship hardly warranted Romanov pearls."

"Neither does ours. These are an heirloom. You must give them to your sister."

"Marie doesn't want them. She knows I am giving them to you and she approves."

He had not been the ideal lover, but his gesture, like his sister's before him, touched me deeply. "I can never wear them in public," I teased, putting the velvet box into my bag. "Someone will slit my throat to steal them."

"Then hide them among fake ones," he replied, unwittingly seeding an idea. "No one will be able to tell which pearls are real and which are not, the same as the way you hide yourself."

Thus did I return to Paris with my Romanov pearls and a hundred samples of my perfume in square-cut glass bottles that echoed the smaller test samples. I loved the simplicity of the design. Together with Misia, who simply had to have a hand in the packaging, I designed an elegant diamond-shaped stopper that reflected the Place Vendôme, along with a white box with black piping. It complemented the seal on the bottleneck with my C within a circle and my new reversed CC logo branded on the lid. I gave the perfume away as gifts to my most loyal clients, ordering my sales force to vaporize the salon with the scent every afternoon when clients came. My live mannequins—I now had over fifty models on whom I created my designs and presented my collections—were to wear the perfume at all times, even when outside the atelier.

I did no other advertising, allowing the clients to spread word among themselves. "Mademoiselle," they asked, "that exquisite *parfum*. I must tell you, when I wore it to the Opéra the other night my friends buzzed around me, demanding to know where I had bought it."

"My perfume?" I feigned astonishment. "But it was my gift to you and a few others, a token of my esteem. I discovered it while on summer holiday at this tiny perfumery in Provence. I do not even recall the store's name. Your friends actually liked it?"

"Mademoiselle, they *adored* it. You simply must bring more to sell!"

Chanel No. 5 proved an instant success. When Beaux sent word that production could begin, I ordered a large supply for my shops in Paris, Deauville, and Biarritz, where it sold out in a matter of weeks. I desperately needed more to offer with my upcoming winter collection inspired by the glamour of Russia and my new working relationship with Marie Pavlovna.

Taking advantage of her workshop's extraordinary skills, I designed the roubachka, a peasant blouse made in black crêpe de chine. I also had astrakhan-trimmed coats in silk velvet and quilted charmeuse with matching linings; black, red, and gold tabard dresses with square necklines, flared embroidered cuffs, and low-slung waists; and waterfall gowns beaded in lignite jet. For more traditional day wear, I offered pale gray cape suits fringed in squirrel pelt and lined in foulard; chenille-knitted sweaters and Scottish tricot accessorized with silk-scarf bandeaux for the new short "shingle" hairstyle, as well as cloche hats adorned with faux-jewel pins. My button-strap low-heeled shoes and drop-waist skirts that reached daringly to midcalf caused an uproar. They ushered in the silhouette dubbed as *la garçonne* in Paris—based on the scandalous novel by Victor Margueritte— and as the flapper in London and New York.

My Russian collection garnered me international acclaim. Orders came in from the moment I presented it, my salon filled to overflowing. Needing more salespeople, I supplemented my staff with several Russian princesses and countesses who were eager to work after having sold their jewels to keep a roof over their heads. By the end of 1922, I had two thousand employees working for me in my three establishments.

I entreated Beaux to increase production of No. 5, as we couldn't satisfy the demand. His inability to keep up would lead me to new business entanglements that I would live to regret.

VI

Scandal of my own awaited me upon my return to Bel Respiro in Garches.

Diaghilev's second premiere of Stravinsky's *Rite of Spring*, which I financed, had been a triumph, and the Ballets Russes booked subsequent engagements in Germany and Spain. While the composer traveled with the company, his wife and two frail daughters (the entire family seemed destined for an early grave) came from Switzerland to my house and were there by the time I arrived home from Biarritz. Stravinsky returned soon after to waylay me in the living room and declare his undying love for me.

At first, I was flattered, if taken aback. "But your wife is upstairs," I said. In fact, I could hear her coughing where we stood—a lung-heaving hack that filtered through the floorboards.

"She knows," he said. "To whom, if not her, would I confide such a great thing as this?"

God save me. Having left one impecunious Russian lover behind, I wasn't prepared to entertain another. He seemed almost feverish, clasping my hands as Marie, my housekeeper, entered with a tray of tea and cakes, setting it on the table without any indication she'd heard anything. Her discretion was exemplary, matching that of her husband, my butler Joseph, but I feared Stravinsky's would not be—as he proved when I withdrew my hands and demurred, "I fear it's impossible. I'm not . . . I do not feel the same way." His long, forlorn face tightened as I added, "Oh, I'm very fond of you and in awe of your extraordinary talent, but that's as far as it can go. You are married. I am not."

"You've loved other men who were married," he burst out, though I could not determine whether he spoke in anger or sorrow. Regardless, I did not appreciate his allusion to Boy. Then he sighed. "But I see everything I've been told is true. Your heart is taken by another."

The melodrama of the moment might have elicited a dismissive laugh from me had his words not frozen me where I stood. "Everything you've been told?" I repeated.

He wrenched a crumpled yellow paper from his pocket. "I was warned. But I thought the Romanov could not hold your affections for long, not when he has so little to offer an accomplished woman like yourself."

"May I see?" Taking the paper from him—a telegram, sent to Spain from Paris—I read:

COCO IS A LITTLE SEAMSTRESS WHO PREFERS
GRAND DUKES TO ARTISTS.

I crunched the paper in my fist. I didn't need to ask who had wired it to him, at considerable expense. Misia was the culprit, her petty revenge for my financing of Diaghilev, which usurped her place. Stravinsky must have confided his fascination for me to her, and she had sought to ruin our perceived affair, although, in fact, it existed only in his imagination.

Stravinsky blanched. "I've offended you. It is inexcusable. I will depart at once."

"No." The chill in my tone brought him to a halt. "The woman who sent this is the one whose behavior is inexcusable. I'll not hear of you leaving." I forced out a laugh that scraped my throat. "Now, let us have tea, and discuss your future as friends, yes?"

I persuaded him to stay and concentrate on the upcoming engagements he had with the Ballets Russes, emphasizing his wife's precarious health and his daughters' need for stability. Even as he nodded helplessly and implored my forgiveness, I decided my course.

I would not banish Misia from my life, much as I wanted to. She only did what was in her nature; wherever she loved, she scorched. I would simply need to ensure that her destructive tendencies did not upend my existence any further.

Friends we would remain, but only on my terms.

IN EARLY 1923, I approached my fortieth birthday. I took excellent care of myself, keeping up my dance lessons and refraining from overindulgences. Everyone always told me I looked half my age; what was my secret? Their flattery had seeped into me, soothing the thin doubtful child I had been and the brash young woman who had sung her heart out at La Rotunde, even if I could see the passage of time leaving its subtle mark upon me. I abetted my illusion of youthfulness by framing my elfin features with my short stylish hair, using only the faintest traces of mascara to enhance my great black eyes and never appearing in public without my signature red lipstick. In defiance of the norm, I was bronze from sunbathing, a habit I had picked up in Italy and which prompted every client of mine to lather themselves in coconut oil on the beaches from the Côte d'Azur to Deauville.

Still, forty years was a milestone I was determined to celebrate not with coy evasions but rather in the bold style for which I had become famous. Moving out of Bel Respiro, I leased the spacious Hôtel de Lauzan in the Faubourg Saint-Honoré—an estate built in 1719 with a garden that stretched down to avenue Gabriel, where Boy and I had spent our happiest years. Perhaps I had not escaped my father's urge to wander, or maybe I grew weary of the weight of memories that my homes seemed to accumulate. I had become accustomed to a peripatetic existence and welcomed the change, furnishing my new residence with my sandalwood Coromandel screens, Venetian mirrors, and antique statues bought in Italy. I added crystal-ball lamps with parchment shades and Louis XIV sofas in beige.

Here, I became a hostess in my own right. Friends came in droves—Picasso, Cocteau, Diaghilev, and Vera Bate, a charming redheaded divorcée with numerous social connections who'd met me in my atelier and urged me to open a boutique in London. My biggest orders still came from America, where my clothes matched that fast-paced world, but I gained fame in England, as well, and Vera was one of my staunchest advocates. A fixture on the elite British circuit, she was also perennially short of funds, so I hired her to wear my designs and attract potential clients in her circle.

"That little writer of yours, Cocteau," Vera now remarked, "he needs a cure."

My friends were gathered in my living room for cocktails before attending a performance of the Ballets Russes, whose costumes I had designed. A Bessie Smith recording played on my brand-new Brunswick phonograph, imported from America, as Vera and I sat at my mirrored bar on the raised stools that gave me an imperious view of the assembly.

I sipped my drink. "He's merely exuberant. He wrote the libretto for the play tonight. He always gets nervous before premieres." At that moment, Cocteau was perched atop one of my sofas, gesticulating, his hair tangled about his animated face as Misia, who had begrudgingly joined my soirees after she realized she'd otherwise be left bored at home, urged him on.

"Oh, I think he's more than exuberant," said Vera. "Haven't you noticed he's flown with cocaine? He and that other gaunt fellow—what's his name again?"

"Raymond Radiguet. He's also a writer."

"Another one?" Vera sighed, toying with the bugle beads of her gown, one of my creations. "Well, he and his friend Radiguet were holed up in one of the powder rooms upstairs, snorting it. I believe they smoked opium, too. The entire upper floor reeks of it."

I smiled through my teeth. I had warned Cocteau about not indulging his vices in my house but he was desperately infatuated with handsome, dissolute Radiguet, whose sexually explicit novel *The Devil in the Flesh* had catapulted him to fame. "It's all the rage among these writers and artists," I said, with feigned nonchalance. "They mean no harm."

She shrugged. "Perhaps. But don't you get tired of their bombast and poverty, all crowded together in Montparnasse? It's so passé. You should broaden your social horizons. None of these people can properly wear your clothes, much less afford them. And you have a birthday coming up in August; you cannot mean to spend it like this, among scribblers and addicts? Forty years should be done up in style."

"Actually, I plan to throw a party in Monte Carlo, on a yacht." As her expression turned avid, for Vera loved extravagance, though like those she denigrated she could hardly afford it, I went on, "Though how I'll fit all my scribblers and addicts onboard remains to be seen."

"A yacht!" she exclaimed. "I know the perfect one! And there's a perfect English lord to go with it, who asked me all sorts of questions about you when I was in London. He's——"

Cocteau's febrile voice interrupted her: "Coco, darling, are you coming?" Someone had coaxed him off the sofa and the guests were gathering to depart for the theater. As I slipped from the stool to reach for my black embroidered wrap, Vera said, "He really is divine. You must meet him. He'll be in Monte Carlo this very summer, in fact."

"Oh?" With a glazed smile, I waved Vera to my car, telling her I would join her in a minute. As Misia struggled into her too-snug coat, I pulled her aside. "I need the address of the best rehabilitation facility you know," I hissed, even as I didn't fail to note the irony that I sought the assistance of another addict. But Misia had never shown Cocteau's level of excess, though I wondered if she perhaps abetted it. My rising social influence had eclipsed hers, and as she demonstrated with Stravinsky, she was nothing if not envious. She was perfectly capable of giving Cocteau the drugs in order to lure him from my side.

Misia went still. "Oh, no. Have you been using too much . . . ?"

"Not for me. For Cocteau." I hauled her coat over her shoulders, tucking her bobbed hair over the collar (she had cut her hair short like mine, though it did not suit her). "That lover of his, Radiguet, is intolerable, and you know how easily influenced Jean is. He needs our help before he ends up in the gutter."

As I'd hoped, the words "our help" were music to her ear. "I'll telephone you tomorrow," she said eagerly. "The poor dear, now that you mention it, he hasn't been looking at all well." As I turned to follow the others to the waiting cars, Misia added spitefully, "You must be so pleased with yourself. So celebrated everywhere, the toast of the society columns, the most acclaimed *couturière* in Paris, and now, muse to every starving artist. No one even remembers that it was *I*, darling, who first taught you to appreciate modern art. Perhaps it won't be too long before you welcome one of them into your empty bed, as well?"

I glowered. She always managed to find one raw nerve.

After I slid into the backseat of my Rolls and rapped on the glass partition to alert my chauffeur that he could drive, Vera gave me a tart look. "Misia Sert certainly seems to know a great deal about too many things, doesn't she?" she said, betraying that she had overheard.

"Entirely," I replied. "This Englishman you mentioned, I'd like to hear more about him."

VII

I ran myself ragged up until the last minute before I departed for Monte Carlo and my fortieth birthday celebration. First, I met with the owner of Galeries Lafayette to ask him to carry my perfume in the hope a slew of new orders would incite Ernest Beaux to increase production. But the Galeries' owner told me a "nose" like Beaux could never produce sufficient quantities for a department store. He telephoned Pierre Wertheimer, co-owner of France's largest fragrance and cosmetics company, Parfumeries Bourjois. When Wertheimer expressed interest in helping me, I had to make a quick trip to Longchamp, the very racetrack where I first met Boy, to discuss our arrangement. Before I went, I called Balsan to ask his advice; he knew everyone in the business world and he warned me to be careful. Pierre and his brother Paul were aggressive entrepreneurs who had amassed an empire with ruthless disdain for those they did business with because, according to Balsan, they were Jews.

I didn't care if they were but I was taken aback when the stocky Pierre told me, between shouts while watching his Thoroughbreds race, that I needed to incorporate if I wanted to make and distribute my perfume through his company.

"We can do it for you," he said, "but you'll need to sign a contract."

I detested contracts. Recalling how Boy had admonished me to focus on what I did best and leave those things I did not to the experts, I replied, "Fine. But I'll not surrender a stake in my fashion house nor allow you to sell inferior products under my name. I'm satisfied with ten percent of the capital. For the rest, I don't want to have to answer to anyone. And Beaux will develop my perfumes until I say otherwise."

Wertheimer agreed. Upon my return to Paris with a draft contract, I plunged into the finishing touches for my latest collection, which included sheath dresses in silk and wool crepe that camouflaged the waist, bust, and hips, overlaid with beaded appliqués. I'd even begun a new venture into faux jewelry. Dmitri's idea had served me in good stead; I'd set up my own workshops to manufacture necklaces, pendants, and brooches with oversize glass stones in rich Byzantine and Renaissance designs, as well as multicolored strands of pearls. I wore my creations myself to great effect, even donning one black pearl earring and one white, layering my wrists with enamel-and-mosaic cuffs or gold-coin bracelets, which highlighted the seemingly shapeless cut of my clothes.

Now here I was on the eve of my fortieth birthday, dressed in a black sheath gown (I was the only woman allowed to wear black tonight; I'd made it a stipulation in my invitation), on a rented yacht in Monte Carlo strung with lights and listening to the music of a full orchestra. Everyone who knew me attended, plus quite a few who wanted to. I planned to relax in Monaco's playground for the rich under a harvest moon that to me augured luck for the coming year, both in my couture and *parfum* ventures.

Vera had told me that the Englishman who'd asked her about me was known as Bendor to his friends. To everyone else, he was Hugh Richard Arthur Grosvenor, second Duke of Westminster, one of the richest men in the world. I had seen his famous yacht, the *Silver Cloud,* entering the harbor, a titan of a ship, fully lit and gleaming, dwarfing every other vessel around it, including the one for my party. To me, it seemed vulgar ostentation, more like a floating hotel—and replete, I was certain, with the requisite staff of butlers, chambermaids, and other hirelings.

"He wants us to come onboard later," Vera said as I dressed for the party, "for aperitifs."

I chuckled. "We'll see." I had no intention of obliging. His Grace Lord Bendor was in no position to offer me an aperitif or anything else at this time, for he was in the process of unloading a troublesome second wife. His acrimonious divorce had made front-page news, with his wife declaring to all and sundry that he had been rabidly unfaithful, which she cited as the reason she'd failed to provide him with his coveted male heir. His previous marriage had also ended in divorce, after that wife gave him a son who died tragically at the age of four, and two daughters, who under England's barbaric inheritance laws could not claim his estate.

"He's looking for a new wife as soon as his divorce is final," Vera explained. "Unfortunately, most women he meets bore him to tears. He isn't what you might think. He prefers working and self-made people. He claims the aristocracy remind him of stuffed boar heads, and he should know. He has plenty of both around him."

Be that as it may, I wasn't looking for a husband. It was the furthest thing from my mind. Misia, with her unerring talent for snooping, also regaled me with contradictory and less savory tales about Bendor as soon as I revealed Vera's plan.

"He's a horrible snob. He hates working people, unless they work for him. He's also monstrously prejudiced. He despises Jews, homosexuals, and socialists. He has declared they will be the ruin of Europe's economy."

"Homosexuals?" I was amused. "How can they possibly ruin the economy? Jewelry and cosmetics, perhaps; they always want us to wear too much of both. But money? Most homosexuals we know are as poor as rats. Just look at our Cocteau."

Poor Jean was not at my party. I had convinced him to enter a sanatorium specializing in opiate addiction. He agreed when I also told him I would pay and his friend Radiguet could join him. Radiguet refused but Cocteau went, because if he didn't wean himself off the drug there was no hope for his future with Radiguet, as they were both likely to perish of an overdose.

Turning my gaze from Bendor's leviathan yacht, I watched my guests chatter, gyrate to the latest dances—the Charleston, with its pigeon-toed gait and goose-wing gestures was all the rage—and toss my rented glasses overboard with an abandon they'd never have shown if they were paying for it.

When Vera spied me at the railing, she excused herself and sidled through the crowd. Her curves were accentuated by one of my scarlet evening dresses, with ropes of my fashionable new pearls about her throat and a silk camellia pinned in her curled red hair.

"Well?" she asked. "Are you going to accept Bendor's invitation? He telephoned our suite after you left. He's very keen on meeting you."

"Yes," I said, reaching into my tassel bag for my cigarettes. Her friend, a tall man with a sleek demeanor whom I did not recognize, kept staring at me. Something about the intensity of his stare made me uncomfortable. Turning away, I lit a cigarette and said to Vera, "Why is your duke so keen, I wonder? Have you been filling his ears with lurid tales about me?"

"Only of your charming person. He already knows how wildly successful you are and that you're currently unattached—"

"I'm always unattached," I cut in, with a smile. "I've never been attached—unless it's to my work, and that attachment is permanent. I might as well wear a Chanel wedding band."

"Yes, yes." She waved her hand to dispel my smoke; Vera was one of the few people I knew who abhorred cigarettes. "He knows that, too. He admires it. I told you, he prefers self-made people, and you're one of the most famous self-made women in the—"

"Dmitri!" I swept from her to greet my grand duke, who had just arrived. He looked marvelous, healthy and tan from his long idyll in Biarritz, wearing impeccable white tails and silver-and-onyx cuffs. "I have missed you," I breathed, kissing him on the lips as he gazed at me, bemused, before he gave a knowing smile.

"Who are you trying to avoid?"

"Everyone." I linked my arm in his, bringing him to Vera. "Have you met Grand Duke Dmitri Pavlovich?"

Vera simpered; to Dmitri's mirth, she dipped a curtsy that revealed her rouged knees. "*Enchanté*, Your Highness."

"Careful," I whispered as I then guided him away, past the staring blue-eyed stranger. "All she thinks about is hunting men, the richer and more titled the better."

"I'm hardly either these days," he said, "but that could soon change." He lowered his voice. "I've met an American, a real-estate heiress. I'm thinking of proposing to her."

"Do you love her?" I said, in wry amusement.

"Do I need to?" he replied, with equally wry indifference.

We laughed. Our affair might have ended, but I still found him irresistible, and especially now that I did not have to maintain him.

"Who is your English lady friend trying to hunt for you?" he asked as we drank champagne. My wide-eyed friends kept coming by to introduce themselves, agog that an actual living Romanov was in our midst.

"The Duke of Westminster."

"Really?" Dmitri's eyes widened. "He's terribly rich."

"So I'm told. He wants me to visit him later on that beast in the harbor. But I don't think I will, now that you're here."

"Why not? I would like to see his beast. I hear it's a marvel. He could reside on it all year if he chose—not that he would, with all his estates."

I paused, a hand on my hip. "You want to see his yacht?"

He shrugged. "What's the harm? Besides, if I go with you, your virtue will be secure. I don't think the English duke would violate you with a Russian prince onboard."

"Honestly, Dmitri, if you're thinking of asking him for a loan . . ."

"I wouldn't dream of it." He bowed with an elegance that made the women dancing the Charleston behind us stumble. "But," he said, with a wink, "you might get one for me."

WE WENT AFTER MIDNIGHT, as my party reached a crescendo and those few guests not drunk enough to notice my absence would not have minded if they did. Bendor sent a motorboat to bring us to his yacht; I had to tie a scarf about my head to protect my hair, arriving upon the *Silver Cloud* looking, as Dmitri teased, "like a Russian lady in a wind-torn babushka."

Bendor waited for us on deck—a tall, slightly florid man with a broad brow, slicked dark blond hair parted in the middle, cherubic lips that were almost sultry, and pale blue eyes. He wore rumpled white linen trousers, an open-necked shirt that showed a hint of bronzed throat, and a navy blue sailor's blazer I coveted on the spot. He was elegant, but not overly so, masculine without overt coarseness. To my surprise, I found him attractive—a fact, I realized, that would not come as a surprise to him. Being who he was, he no doubt found himself attractive to a good many women.

Vera kissed him on both cheeks in the French manner, bringing a blush to his face. "Mademoiselle," he said, turning to me. "I'm honored you agreed to meet me."

"Oh, no," I said carelessly, "I'm assured the honor is all mine."

As he gave us a tour of his yacht, which proved even more impressive on the inside, with old master paintings covering the portholes and furnishings fit for a great hall, he spoke in a clipped, low voice about how he loved to sail more than anything else. While a hired Gypsy band strummed mandolins outside the polished mahogany stateroom, he treated us to more champagne and caviar. I was becoming quite drunk. Dmitri kept smiling, fending off Vera's attentions as he observed my flirtation with Bendor. I flipped open my cigarette case only to exclaim that I'd forgotten my lighter, obliging him to light my cigarette for me. I asked him endless questions about the yacht so he could explain it all to me, though I couldn't have cared less about special engines or navigation systems.

I didn't know why I acted as I did, only that it amused me to see if I could fluster him and determine if his intent was purely one of conquest or a genuine desire to discover who I was. By the night's end, I remained undecided. He inquired about my business, nodding in somber approval as I detailed my latest ventures, the champagne having loosened my usually reticent tongue. He did not touch me once until I felt his fingertips on my arm as he assisted me to the motorboat that would take us back to shore. He behaved with consummate propriety, which only intrigued me the more. Before I stepped down into the motorboat, he said haltingly, as if I might refuse, "I own a home in Deauville, mademoiselle, where I understand one of your boutiques is located. I would be delighted if you'd allow me to see you the next time I'm there."

I handed him my card. "Do telephone me."

He was not exactly smiling as I boarded the motorboat, but the steadiness in his gaze assured me that I had not heard the last of him.

After saying good night to Dmitri, Vera and I made our way to the Hôtel de Paris, where we were staying. She talked breathlessly of how gorgeous the grand duke was, how sublime, causing me to hide my smile, for she was blithely unaware that her bank account, or lack thereof, was not sufficient to win Dmitri's attention. Then she suddenly said as I unlocked my suite door, "And Bendor was very taken with you, I could tell."

"You could?" I pushed the door open. "Surely, he invites many people to his yacht and house in Deauville. It's not as if it was unique to me or—"

I came to a halt as Vera gasped behind me. Enormous vases of white roses and floating camellias were set on every available surface.

Stunned by the display, I couldn't move. Vera wriggled past me and lunged at the nearest vase, seizing the white card propped against it.

"'Mademoiselle,'" she read aloud. "'The honor was indeed all mine.'" She laughed uproariously, with that abandon some Englishwomen have. "See? He is smitten! Oh, Coco, look at this; how much proof do you need? Please tell me you're not going to make the man beg."

"No," I said, closing the door. "Not beg. But I will make him wait."

VIII

Bendor dubbed his English estate "St. Pancras Station"—a humorous motto for a huge and appropriately Gothic pile straddling acres of hunting land in Cheshire. Eaton Hall, as it was more properly known, even had a suit of medieval armor poised on the landing of its grand staircase, which I greeted every morning when I floated downstairs with his favorite dachshunds dashing in between my feet, eager for whatever activity he had in store.

I had finally given in to his persistent wooing. He emptied entire gardens of flowers and sent them to my home; he hid insanely expensive jewelry—diamond and ruby bracelets, aquamarine brooches set in platinum, more pearls than I could ever wear in a lifetime—inside boxes of rare orchids. Once, he even dispatched a batch of fresh salmon via airplane from his castle in Scotland. They were still writhing in a tub of water when they arrived.

"How long are you going to make him wait?" Vera implored. "The more you ignore him, the more he wants you."

"Precisely," I said, but by 1925, I had kept him at bay long enough. He was not dissuaded by my cool demeanor when he came to Paris to view my collection for the l'Exposition Internationale des Arts Décoratifs et Industriels Modernes. There, I debuted a collarless braided cardigan suit, as well as crepella pleated dresses, tweed topcoats, and masculine-cut sailor jackets inspired by the one I'd first seen on him. He took me out to dinner, accepting my chaste good-night kiss when his chauffeur drove me home. He visited my jewelry workshops, which had begun to yield a significant profit, and sniffed the latest perfume developed by Beaux for my new corporation, Parfums Chanel. I invited him to my soirees, where he met the Serts; Diaghilev and his new twenty-year-old paramour, the Ukrainian dancer Serge Lifar; and my dear Cocteau, who emerged from his cure only to suffer the devastating loss of Radiguet to typhoid. I paid for the funeral, of course.

These informal gatherings at my home proved disastrous. Bendor was too English, too aristocratic, to appreciate our racy repartee. Like Boy before him, he did not find humor in Jojo Sert's lewd jokes and flatulence; he eyed Lifar's lithe beauty with open suspicion and ignored Misia's forbidding appraisal. When Cocteau griped that he might have to hunt down a rich woman, for he didn't want to turn forty and be known as *la pauvre* Madame Cocteau, Bendor finally spoke. His command of French was that of every upper-crust Englishman, schooled in the formality but not the nuance, and to everyone's horror, he said, "If you're low on funds, monsieur, I could hire you to write a history of my dogs."

I saw at once that he did not mean to be rude. Later, after everyone left, he said to me with sincere puzzlement, "Everyone looked as if I'd suggested he clean out my kennels. Our hounds are famous for their breeding; a history of them would sell very well, I should think."

He failed to fit in with my circle in Paris, so after several unaccepted invitations to visit England, I relented and braved the stomach-churning voyage across the Channel.

I had never been to England. I thought it a quaint country—unbelievably verdant and all too damp. The smoke-darkened huddle of London could not compare with Paris's expansive boulevards, lively cafés, or elegant nightlife; it seemed to me the English preferred to congregate in their ubiquitous pubs to partake of indigestible cuisine.

But Bendor's stately town house near Grosvenor Square was well appointed and here he invited Vera and her cadre of illustrious English society ladies for tea. They all begged me to open a London establishment. I also summoned my nephew André from his boarding school to spend a weekend with us touring the sights. I was impressed by André's excellent manners, his unfailing correctness in addressing Bendor as "Your Grace," though Bendor told him several times he needn't be so formal.

In London, I also succumbed to Bendor's amorous advances. To my amusement, he'd timidly taken my hand after late-night drinks in his parlor and made a mumbled declaration that he had never met a woman like me, and would I mind terribly if he kissed me?

"I would mind if you did not," I replied, and his subsequent kiss, while not exactly electrifying, was interesting enough for me to permit him further exploration. He turned out to be a capable lover, tender and considerate, if not overly inventive. In sum, I found him satisfactory. He had more money than me, which, after Dmitri, was refreshing; and despite Vera's assertions, he did not act as if he was in any hurry to marry again with his divorce still pending. Most important, he showed a genuine interest in me that was both flattering and reassuring. I sensed potential here, more so than I had since Boy's death. I could not say I was in love, but then again, I did not expect to be. I had come to understand that the passion I experienced with Boy came along only once in a lifetime, if we were lucky.

Still, I could not help but marvel as he gave me a tour of his country estate, where entire villages in France might have fit with ease. Bendor's wealth exceeded any I had seen before. Only royalty or American tycoons could indulge like this, with stables spanning entire city blocks, ornamental gardens the size of hamlets, halls with vaulted ceilings that had seen kings dine, along with hundreds of unoccupied rooms whose linens were changed regardless of the expense.

Misia (who else?) had warned me that life in English manors was stultifying, arranged around an unvaried schedule of riding, hunting, and high tea, followed by cigars in the library for the gentlemen and conversation in the parlor for the ladies. Bendor eschewed this stereotype. His staff operated like clockwork, but there were no set hours for anything, for he relished spontaneity.

One morning after we slept in and he got up to dress, I laughed as I watched him put on his shoes.

"What?" He gave me a perplexed look. My sudden bursts of amusement often came at his expense, as he had learned by now. "What have I done wrong this time?"

"Your shoes have holes," I pointed out. "How long have you had them?"

He frowned, looking at the soles. "I have no idea."

"No idea? Well, they must be ten years old at least. Have you ever considered getting the soles replaced, or perhaps buying new ones?"

"I like these. My socks are thick enough. And I have plenty of those; my butler has a standing order to buy a dozen new pairs every week."

"Every week!" I threw off the sheet and padded naked to the door. When I reached for the latch, I paused, glancing slyly over my shoulder at him. "I must see this. Where is the room where you keep your socks? Your butler couldn't possibly fit that many in a bureau."

"Actually," he replied mildly, "I believe my butler replaces them. Every time a new set arrives, he distributes the older ones among the staff; it's more economical that way." He began tying his shoelaces. When I did not speak, he said without looking up, "If you're going to go out there like Lady Godiva to search for my socks, please don't wait for me. I'd rather you enjoyed the scandal entirely on your own."

He had a wit when he cared to use it. It, too, reminded me of Boy, and endeared him to me. I also liked some of his friends—the actual ones, not the hundreds of people who knew him and claimed to be. One in particular became a friend of mine: Sir Winston Churchill, a short, portly man with a severely receding hairline and noticeable raspy lisp, who was nonetheless one of the most eloquent, intelligent persons I had ever met.

He was a guest at Eaton Hall one weekend for a foxhunt. I'd never witnessed this quintessential English tradition and was taken aback by its ritual, the gathering in smart red riding coats and white jodhpurs, the delegation of seniority as to who would ride where, the ceremonial release of the terrified fox from its cage, and the almost reverential unleashing of the hounds. It seemed to me ridiculous. After all, it was a given that the fox would be tracked and killed, but everyone rode off in a clamor of excitement, as though it was their first time. Only Churchill, stuffed uncomfortably into his riding costume, muttered to me in perfect French, *"Mon brave,* now you will see how foolish we English can be when we've nothing better to do."

That day, I missed the slaughter; my horse ducked a branch halfway into the hunt and tumbled me from the saddle; I cut my lip and twisted my ankle. Bendor was far ahead—when it came to hunting, I could have been mauled by wolves and he wouldn't have noticed—but Churchill, perspiring and bouncing on his enormous black horse, pulled to a halt to assist me. As I leaned on his shoulder, grimacing at the pain and my own clumsiness, he said, "Just as well. I had no interest chasing after a defenseless animal. Now, we can pass our afternoon instead icing that ankle and talking. I'd like to hear all about the famous Mademoiselle Chanel."

He was the only one who called me that. To everyone else, I was Coco, mademoiselle, or simply Chanel, but Winston Churchill never assumed familiarity until it was earned. I thought I could easily have become his lover, had he asked, no matter that he was married, as homely as a frog, and still grieving over his beloved eldest daughter's recent death.

"Oh, it was dreadful," he said, as I rested on the red sofa in the library, an ice pack on my swollen ankle and ointment dabbed on my lip. He reclined in one of the armchairs and smoked a cigar. "Devastating, in truth. We were here for a weekend of tennis with Bendor when we received an urgent call from our governess. Marigold had had a cold, but we'd been assured she was on the mend. By the time we arrived, our darling girl was dying." He paused, his eyes misting. "Have you ever lost someone you loved more than yourself, mademoiselle, something so precious, so irreplaceable, you'd have given your life to save theirs?"

"Yes," I said, fighting back sudden tears. "I did, once."

He smiled sadly. "I rather thought you had. Nothing is the same afterward, is it? We carry on, as indeed we must, but we are never who we were."

He must have known about Boy and me. Our affair had hardly been secret, and Churchill, like Bendor, was familiar with the scandals of his privileged circle, of which Boy's widow was a member. Yet he did not mention Boy's name or allude to the fact that he was aware of whom I spoke. He was too much the gentleman for that.

We spoke of many things. A career politician and currently chancellor of the exchequer, he had served in Cuba, India, the Sudan, and Egypt, and led a battalion on the Western Front. "I hope never to see such horrors again," he said. "Sometimes, it is not enough to do our best, but rather to do what is required. And fighting Germany was required, though it cost us thousands of our best young men."

He told me he loved pigs, making me laugh. "Dogs look up to us. Cats look down on us. Pigs treat us as equals." He said he was attracted to those who never let obstacles impede them.

"I have the sense you are one of those people, mademoiselle. You have fearlessness in your eyes," he said, and I sensed an unspoken sadness in him, an invisible burden that weighed on him. "My mother had it, and she was American. Are you quite sure you're only French?"

I assured him I was, and in that long afternoon as we waited for the hunters to return, I shared with him, as I had not shared with anyone since Boy, the full tale of my ambitions to overcome that forgotten girl from Aubazine. I had the sense as I spoke that everything I told him would stay between us, that for him, a confidence was sacred.

After I finished, he nodded, contemplative. "Attitude is a little thing that makes a big difference," he said at length. "I admire you. You have learned to rise with the wind, rather than fight it. Too many people struggle to become what is expected of them, when, as we both know, what is expected of us is rarely what we desire."

When Bendor eventually arrived, chagrined by my absence, Churchill rose and waddled out, patting Bendor's arm as he said, "She's quite a prize, your mademoiselle. See that you act accordingly."

"Coco," I said, and Churchill paused at the door. "Call me Coco," I told him.

He smiled, inclining his head. "Coco it is."

Bendor tugged at his lip. "I say, did that scoundrel just charm you out of my arms?"

"Almost," I replied. "You're fortunate that he is married and you are not."

BENDOR'S DIVORCE BECAME FINAL THAT YEAR. His liaison with me had made the news, naturally; before I even set foot on English soil, the papers were calling me the next Duchess of Westminster. Bendor seemed nonplussed. I, on the other hand, disconcertedly found myself wondering what it might be like to settle down with him.

In those weeks we spent together, traveling from Eaton Hall to his castle in Caithness in the Scottish Highlands, I realized I could enjoy a life like his—freed of the harassment of work and the foibles of my celebrity, exchanging couture and perfume for titled dignity and insular comfort. It frightened me, my sudden hankering for commitment, after having rejected the notion for so long. I had never wanted it before, not even with Boy, or at least not until he married someone else. Was that what concerned me, that if Bendor did not propose to me, he would find another woman? Did I want to merely dally with him, knowing that in time I would be passed over for one of the proper ladies of means with three names and a readily available womb?

This turmoil only led to more disquieting questions. I had never become pregnant, though there had been opportunity. In Venice, Misia had maliciously remarked she hoped I took precautions. In truth, I did not. Boy had, with his prophylactics, but we'd had our accidents when his condoms leaked or broke; and since him, I never thought of it. I told myself that I had trained my body—I believed the mind capable of it— and had not become pregnant because I did not want it. Dmitri and I had been reckless and I could count myself fortunate; with Bendor, we had an unspoken but implied agreement: he either used a condom or pulled out before his seed spilled, as Balsan had done before him.

Now I began to fret. I neared my forty-first birthday; if I was capable of it, I should become a mother soon. Yet even as I considered it, something recoiled inside me. I had André, whom I treated as if he were my child, and he lived far away at school, his day-to-day existence overseen by others. I knew, all too well, how it felt to lack parents and grow up far from a place to call home. I did my best to ensure André's upkeep but I could hardly deem such attentions maternal. I behaved like what I was—a conscientious yet distant aunt.

To be a true mother meant sacrificing my needs. Far more pressing than the physical challenges of pregnancy, in itself daunting enough, was I prepared to give up the life I had fought so hard to achieve? I knew that I was not, that I would resent it, perhaps in time even blame the child for it. Again, that specter of my youth rose to haunt me:

What was wrong with me?

I did not confide my concerns to Bendor. I simply ended our sojourn with the announcement that I had to return to Paris to attend to my atelier, which I had neglected for too long.

He accompanied me to London to embark on my voyage home. "Don't forget," he said, standing there awkwardly in his long overcoat and hat. "We're taking a cruise this summer on my yacht to the Riviera. You promised you would find the time."

I smiled, nodding. "I won't forget. And I'll see you in Paris soon?"

"Naturally." With a tug on his hat, he returned to his car. No kiss good-bye, no public display of affection; reporters lurked everywhere.

On the train back to Paris, I felt relieved. It struck me in the moment that for me, Paris had become home, with all its memories and tragedies. Paris was where I belonged.

I doubted the next Duchess of Westminster would enjoy such liberty.

IX

Nineteen twenty-six became known as the year of my little black dress. I presented it in my spring collection after having debated it for months. Black was now a staple in my evening collections, but well into the new century, to wear black in daytime was deemed suitable only for school uniforms, mourning, or nuns. I decided to take the risk anyway, spending months on a new silhouette—a sheath of Moroccan crepe with slim sleeves, their cuffs embroidered in zigzag gold thread, the neckline square, and a simple skirt reaching to just below the knee, with inverted V pleating to accentuate the dropped waist. I accessorized the dress with a cloche hat in banded satin, its soft brim almost hiding the eyes and dubbed a "tea strainer," along with black pearls and gloves. Stockings were, of course, required; I believed in wearing stockings at all times.

My black dress caused a sensation, if not the one I'd initially hoped for. As my models paraded up and down the floor of my salon, carrying the numbered placards for each ensemble, the silence was palpable. From my perch above my staircase, which I had had mirrored so I could observe the presentation without being seen, I spied shock, dismay, even disapproval on my clients' faces and the majority of the attending fashion journalists. I had gone far before, but never as far as this.

"They hate it," Adrienne said as we reviewed the paltry orders. "It's too excessive. No one wants to wear black in the day, Gabrielle. I told you, it was too great a risk."

My *première* Madame Aubert was more sanguine. "Let's wait and see," she advised when I pondered whether to retire the idea. "It's too early to tell. We've had reactions like this before, and our customers always come around."

"Not like this." I nervously lit a cigarette. "I haven't heard such a silence since the war."

"Wait," said Madame Aubert.

The next week, every major fashion gazette in France panned my black day dress. But American *Vogue* declared it "a frock every woman will wear" and predicted that by breaking with tradition, I had made fashion accessible to those who could afford it. "Chanel's little black dress," *Vogue* reported, "will become standard for the masses, much like Ford's motorcars."

Orders started trickling in, slowly at first, then faster, as my more daring clients—including my beloved Kitty de Rothschild—read the article in *Vogue* and came in to be fitted, walking out in my black dress, cloche hat, gloves, and pearls. "Women have always thought of every color except its absence," I said when *Vogue* interviewed me. "Nothing is more difficult than making a black dress, but when you dress a woman in black, she is the only one you see."

Like No. 5 before it, my little black dress became one of my biggest sellers, cementing my reputation. A telegram came from the Hollywood studio of Metro-Goldwyn-Mayer, offering me a lavish salary to travel to Los Angeles to dress the stars. It was such an exorbitant sum, nearly a million dollars, that Adrienne was dumbfounded.

Madame Aubert smiled. "See? To the brave, the kingdom, mademoiselle."

"You are going to accept?" Misia asked breathlessly. "If so, I'm going with you." She hankered for America. She had seen all she wanted of Europe and, in her inimitable manner, was bored with it. More to the point, she had discovered Sert was being unfaithful with one of his art students—an exiled Russian princess, no less—and while she did her best to ignore it, her disillusionment with their marriage caused her to cling to me. "You could become a star yourself," she said. "Think of the press coverage, the contacts: you'll conquer them like Columbus. They'll erect statues in your name."

"Statues?" I rolled my eyes. "How vulgar."

Instead, I returned word that I was far too busy to go to Los Angeles and took the season off to embark on my cruise with Bendor.

X

"What am I supposed to be looking at?" I inched my sunglasses farther down my nose and peered over the tinted lenses as Bendor told our driver to pull the car to a halt.

We had spent the season sailing around the Mediterranean, stopping in whatever ports caught his fancy, which, to my discomfort, were very few. He liked being surrounded by aquamarine sea and endless horizon whenever possible—and though I never admitted it aloud, I found sailing a crushing bore.

When we finally docked in Monte Carlo, my legs were wobbly and I was consistently nauseous. I couldn't bear the thought of returning to the yacht and cited a dinner of bad clams as my excuse to remain on dry land for a spell. In response, Bendor promptly drove me by car up the steep pine-forested hills to this odd but lovely summit near the village of Roquebrune, with breathtaking views of the Bay of Monaco on one side and the Italian border on the other, the snow-dusted foothills of the Alps rearing behind us.

"The property, of course," he said, unlocking an iron gate and leading me into a grove of ancient olive trees that shaded acres of land, with a commodious but outdated villa and two guesthouses. As Bendor took me around the property, pointing out this and that, I began to sense a definite purpose in him and halted in the villa's marble entry.

"What are we doing here?" I demanded.

"Doing?" he echoed. "Why, nothing, Coco. I'm merely showing you this house." He paused. "Why? Do you like it?"

I pursed my lips. As I reached for my cigarette case in the pocket of my loose linen trousers, he said, "No smoking inside. The owners don't like it."

"Owners?" I had noticed signs of habitation, of course; the entire house was a rococo-inspired nightmare. "So, why are we here? Are you planning on renting it?"

"No." He set his hands on his hips, looking around. "I'm planning on buying it. For you."

I stared at him, my mouth agape. He chuckled. "Ah, I see I've managed the impossible at last: I've rendered Coco Chanel speechless."

As I started to say that I certainly did not need a property here, in the middle of nowhere, as beautiful as it might be, and if I ever did, I could buy it myself, I heard Boy's voice in my head: *Pride will make you suffer.* I bit back my retort. I allowed him to continue the tour, and when we returned hours later to his car, I smiled as he lit my much-needed cigarette and said, "Many of my friends are buying properties here, as the popular resorts have become so crowded. I know of a local architect named Robert Streitz, who renovated a villa nearby. I've invited him to cocktails on the yacht next week, if you don't mind?"

"Why would I mind?" I replied. "It's your yacht and your house."

He suddenly reached over to take my hand. The gesture was so abrupt and unusual for him (his reticence in public was a running joke between us) that I froze.

"For *us*, Coco. The house is for us. I want it to be our special place, our retreat from the world. We need a refuge, something that is ours. Don't think I haven't noticed how restless you get when we are at sea," he added.

"You need company about you. Well, if we have a house here, you can entertain. And I'll still have plenty of room to myself."

It wasn't a proposal of marriage, but I saw a gravity in his expression that I could not make light of. While I also did not fail to think of how rich men often put up their lovers in style, I kissed him on the lips.

"Fine, I agree. But if it's to be our house, you must let me pay for it."

THE OWNERS SOLD THE PROPERTY to me for 1.8 million francs, more than I had paid for anything in my life. When we met with the architect Streitz, I liked him immediately; he was diffident and young, only twenty-eight, but he came highly recommended and, as his portfolio demonstrated, had the talent to back it up. He was willing to oversee the demolition of the main property and redesign it to my specifications, which included terracing the lower hillside to make space for a swimming pool. "I want the best materials," I informed him. "White stucco walls, local hand-baked tiles, and a grand staircase." As Streitz made these annotations, he glanced at me. "Does mademoiselle have a certain type of staircase in mind?"

Bendor lounged nearby on the deck, admiring the view. He'd done his part; he had introduced me to the property and the concept of sharing a house together, far from the exigencies of our lives. The details he now left to me. Still, I hesitated for a moment, looking toward him as the architect waited. "Give me your pen," I told Streitz, and when he did, I took his pad of paper and wrote on it. I slid the pad back to him.

"This must stay strictly between us," I said. "If you say a word of it to anyone, I will dismiss you at once and make sure you never work again. Do I make myself clear?"

"Mademoiselle, you are a client. I am bound to confidentiality, like a lawyer or a doctor."

I laughed to dispel the tension. "I hope not like a lawyer. I never trust them."

After Streitz left, Bendor looked over at me. "Everything went as you hoped?"

"Yes." I closed my eyes, enjoying the sway of the yacht in the harbor as the sun caressed my skin. "I think it will be a lovely house."

I did not tell him that I had sent Streitz on a confidential pilgrimage to my forsaken past, to the mountains of my childhood and the convent of Aubazine, where a certain stone staircase with all its embedded symbolism and mystery had been my passage from the life I had to the one awaiting me. I wanted that staircase for my new home, re-created in every detail—an unspoken tribute to the industrious nuns who had unknowingly prepared me for my future.

"I've heard a legend that Mary Magdalene took rest in the chapel near here after she fled the Holy Land upon Christ's crucifixion," I said at length. "The chapel is called La Pausa. What do you think if we call the house that?"

Bendor gave a lazy chuckle. "Restful pause. Yes, I think I like it very much, Coco."

I sighed. "Me, too."

I TRAVELED TO AND FROM PARIS on the express Blue Train, taking time between my collections to supervise the construction. Streitz had visited the convent and told me the Reverend Mother, now aged and infirm, still remembered me, which touched my heart. He had made detailed sketches of the staircase based on his photographs, which I approved.

"I want the steps to look aged," I told him. "Everything except the furnishings should look lived in. The house must not appear like a hideaway for the nouveaux riches. It must look as if it has stood here all along, blended in with its surroundings. No central heat; I detest it. Instead, put fireplaces in every room. And the gardens: I want more olive trees, lavender, roses, and iris. Nothing manicured or showy; everything should look natural."

It would take a year before the villa was finished in 1929 and it cost me a fortune. But when it was done, La Pausa was everything I'd envisioned—a serene estate, smaller than many of its neighbors, but all the more intimate because of it, decorated in my preferred neutral palette of cream, coral, and beige, with a large tiled bathroom separating Bendor's suite and my own, and seven ample guest rooms for our friends. The central stone staircase dominated the entryway with its artificially aged treads—austere and entrancing, the subject of much speculation.

I believed that here, at long last, I could settle in with Bendor.

Instead, fate decided to set me on a different course.

XI

I t was Misia, as usual, who brought me the news.

We were at La Pausa, where I had brought her to spend the summer of 1929 with me, far from Paris and the torment of her collapsing marriage to Sert. His affair with the Russian princess, which had begun as another in a series of infidelities Misia tolerated and at times even encouraged, had turned serious, she told me in tears over lunch at the Ritz. He had asked for a divorce. Her anguished paroxysms so disturbed me, as did her opiate-induced pallor and general dishevelment, that I bundled her up and ordered her to go to La Pausa at once, assuring her that I'd meet her there as soon as I could and sending word to my resident staff to receive her.

When Bendor telephoned to say he was delayed due to some business affair, I scarcely paid heed, telling him I would be at La Pausa. As always, the fresh pine-scented air and silence restored me. I slept, as was my habit, until noon, and then went to take a dip in the pool.

Misia accosted me as I toweled myself dry, barely getting my robe on before she slapped a newspaper on the glass table between us, making the ashtray shudder.

"He's seeing someone else."

"He is?" I did not glance at the paper. "Well, that's good news, isn't it? Now he might not want a divorce, especially if he plans to go through lovers like he does paint."

She scowled. "Not Jojo. Your duke. Bendor. He's been seen escorting a proper lady with three names. Isn't that what you call them?"

For a moment, I found it impossible to move. She stood before me in a shapeless dress, a ragged straw hat on her head, her avid flushed face seemingly recovered from her tragedy. I abruptly regretted having invited her; she was due to join Bendor and me on the *Silver Cloud* when he arrived and already I envisioned the mayhem that would ensue. Misia was never content unless someone else was miserable.

Tossing my towel aside, I picked up the paper, not caring that my hands were still wet and smeared the ink. After I read the item in the society column she had circled, I dropped the paper back onto the table with indifference, even as I felt a chasm crack open inside me.

"It's nothing. It doesn't even warrant a headline. He was escorting this whoever she is to a social engagement, which is ordinary enough—"

"Her name is Loelia Mary Ponsonby, daughter of Lord Sisonby," interjected Misia, "and he escorted her to a dinner attended by King George himself. I would not call that ordinary."

"To him, it is," I snapped, and then, when I saw the excitement on her face, I made myself add, somewhat defensively, "We are not exclusive. If he wants to escort this Loelia Mary Ponsonby, or whomever else he cares to, to dinner, he is free to do so."

Misia gave me one of her penetrating looks. I despised how well she could read me, as if I were a book she had perused many times. "Coco, darling. I know how much you hoped he might marry you. Why go through the expense of all this homemaking"—she flung out her arms, encompassing my estate—"if not to become his wife?"

I stared at her, horrified by her uncanny ability to voice what I myself would never openly admit. She went on, relentless as only she could be, when she sensed capitulation within her grasp. "Don't think we haven't all noticed. Before he and Diag left for Venice, Lifar commented that you were so secretive these days, he hardly knew what to ask you. 'When Coco gets quiet,' I told him, 'it means she's planning something.' What else could it be but the capture of your English prince?"

"You—you know nothing," I whispered. Seizing the towel and newspaper, I stormed back to the house, flinging over my shoulder as I did, "Lunch will be served in an hour. Do take a swim or a bath, darling. You *reek* of intrigue."

By the time I reached my cream-and-coral suite upstairs, I could barely draw a full breath. The newspaper was bunched in my fist, the damp paper shredding as I again read the item, which was in truth nothing, really, only five or six lines announcing that His Grace the Duke of Westminster had been seen escorting Lady Ponsonby to—

With a guttural cry, I flung the paper across the room. As it thumped upon my dressing table, upending hairbrushes and vials of creams and unguents, I could hear my own breathing, labored, almost panting. I clutched my towel to my chest, my clammy bathing suit clinging to my skin under my robe.

In the large Venetian mirror above my dressing table, I caught my reflection—a hunched figure, distorted somehow in the glass. Casting aside the towel, I moved toward it slowly, as if my reflection might flee or dissolve. When I was close enough to take a full, unflattering view, I shut my eyes, inhaled deeply, and then forced myself to look.

How many times had I gazed into a mirror? Thousands? Tens of thousands? It was the timeless ritual of every woman as we clasped earrings or necklaces and adjusted an errant curl, applied eyeliner, a last-minute touch of powder or a spritz of perfume. I had seen my face every day for most of my life; I thought I knew it as intimately as I knew anything. But the woman I now beheld seemed different, every one of my forty-six years showing, from the lines of tension bracketing my mouth to the visible webs at the corners of my eyes.

I recalled a novel I had once read, in which an aging courtesan ordered all of the mirrors in her house broken because she could not abide the sight of her impending decrepitude. I had thought it ludicrous, a self-indulgent vanity, for age is the price we pay for longevity and there is no shame in it. I had never considered myself so beautiful in any event that I would ever turn away from a mirror—and I did not do so now. I gazed intently, reaching up to touch the curve under my chin, the slight loss of tautness below my cheeks. Spreading my arms wide, I examined the toned skin of my lean arms, and then posed, like a mannequin in my salon, extending my legs this way and that, tightening slim muscles I strived to maintain with dance classes, swimming, and a frenetic lifestyle. I turned to look at my behind, snug and small, not plump, in my bathing costume, and the etched blades of my shoulders.

No, I was not a girl anymore. No longer the gamine creature who'd entranced Balsan and enraptured Boy. I was a mature woman—incredibly wealthy and successful, with the world at my feet, surrounded by everything I could possibly desire, and more, if I cared to take it.

Yet as my questing hands lowered to my flaccid abdomen, where more than any other place my age showed, I felt the hollow within like a palpable vacancy.

Did nothing else matter if I failed to accomplish the one feat that defined women? Was my lack of a husband and child to become the seed of my discontent, as it was with my aunt Adrienne, bound to Nexon but without the ring or child in the nursery to show for her resolve?

With trembling fingers, I reached for my cigarettes. Lighting one, I took up the rumpled newspaper once more. I tried to find reassurance in its banality, a pompous announcement without any pomp, but the words turned unintelligible and I let the paper slip from my hand.

Crushing out my cigarette, I stepped over the newspaper strewn on the floor and padded to my bathroom for a hot shower before lunch.

Though I could not yet admit it, I sensed my affair with Bendor was fast approaching its finale.

OUR TIME ON THE YACHT proved as uncomfortable as I supposed it would be. While Misia alternated between woeful sighs and ruminations over her future without Sert, I evaded Bendor with an efficiency I myself did not recognize until he cornered me in our stateroom after we'd seen Misia tottering off to hers, drunk on champagne, and he said brusquely, for him, "May I ask what in hell is the matter? You've barely said three words to me since we left Monte Carlo."

"Really?" I turned to him, and as I did, I found myself longing to find something in his appearance to displease me, a new hint of silver in his receding hairline, an overt wrinkle or sagging under his chin. "Misia is here. She's a full-time occupation, as you have seen."

"Yes, and we have plenty of staff to attend to her." He squared his shoulders. "Coco, what is it? You are not telling me something. I do not like it."

"No," I heard myself laugh. "I didn't like it, either, when I first heard. So, as you English are fond of saying, there we have it."

He went still. "Ah. I believe I know what this is about."

"I'm sure you do." I moved to the bedside table. "Where are my cigarettes? Oh, no. I must have left them up on deck." As I started to move past him, he said, "You know it cannot be helped," and I halted. Much as I wanted to resist, it all came flooding back like the recollection of some terrible illness: the memory of Boy, telling me it was expected of him.

"Not helped?" Incredulity sharpened my voice. "Did I miss something in the news item about her holding a pistol to your head?"

"Coco." He sighed, rummaging in his pockets to draw out his cigarette case. I snatched it from him. "Did you honestly think we were going to . . . ?" The note of mournful regret in his unfinished question went through me, as keen as a scalpel. He lowered his eyes. "If I ever gave you cause for it, I must apologize. You are the most engaging woman I have ever known. I would not wish to cause you any pain. Yet surely you realize how impossible it is. We are from different worlds. You would not be happy in mine, and I . . . well, I do not understand yours."

"Of course." I managed to extricate a cigarette from his case, even smile as I bent to his proffered lighter. "I'm fully aware of how incompatible we are." I smiled, though it felt like a rictus on my face. "I still would have liked to be told in person."

"I haven't told you because nothing has been decided yet."

"But it might." I blew out smoke, thinking his lady with three names probably didn't smoke, or at least not as much as I did. It made me want to laugh aloud at the absurdity of it, my own foolishness, blown back in my face. How could I have imagined he would find me worthy of the title of duchess? What was worse, how could I have imagined I desired it?

His next words, however, cut to the quick. "Not might. It *must*. I must marry again and have a son. You always knew that. If I do not, my entire estate will pass to a cousin I've scarcely met. I can make provisions for my daughters, but only a son can protect my fortune, my name. It is my duty; it must come before my happiness. You do not understand," he added, gazing at me with pitiful sorrow, "because you do not have this burden to carry. You have only your shops. You are free."

I could not believe it. I could not fathom how I had let this happen, how I had willingly set myself up for this devastation. Despite the constant assertions that I was free to do as I pleased, everyone seemed to forget that my heart was not made of stone. I was not as resilient as they believed. Though I did not love Bendor as I had Boy, I feared the impact would prove harder to bear this time because I was not young anymore. It was not only infuriating but also deeply humiliating.

"I do . . . love you," he went on, tripping over his tongue. "But even if it were possible, we have not—you cannot . . ."

I went to him swiftly, rising on my toes to kiss his mouth and silence him. He looked like a miserable child, forlorn because he must relinquish his toys. It will not last, I wanted to whisper; unlike Boy, your love will pass. It was always transient. Only I had tried to make it permanent, laboring under the delusion that it was something we both wanted.

Instead, all I said was, "Once it is settled, you will let me know?"

He nodded. "I would want you to meet her."

I forced myself to shrug. "Naturally, darling. I'll have to approve her wardrobe," and I left the stateroom to clamber up the steps to the deck, fighting back a horrifying surge of despair as I pretended to search for my missing cigarette case.

It was in my pocket. It had been there the entire time.

But I would have flung myself overboard before I let him see me cry.

THREE DAYS LATER, an urgent telegram arrived from Venice.

Diaghilev was dying.

WE WENT IN HASTE to the Hotel Des Bains, on the Lido; as we took the staircase to Diaghilev's suite, I seized Misia's arm. "No histrionics," I whispered. "The last thing he needs is to see you falling apart at his bedside."

The room was in chaos, room service trays scattered on the floor along with suitcases bursting with unpacked clothes. Serge Lifar, Diaghilev's lithe dark-haired Ukrainian lover, came to me.

"Coco," he murmured, his deep brown eyes circled by shadows, "I fear it is very serious. His rheumatism . . . he refused to take his medicines. He collapsed, and . . ." Serge choked back a sudden sob. "Oh, dear God, what will we do without him?"

I took his hand, holding it tight. "No tears, yes? He must see us happy. A lift to his spirit can do wonders for his constitution."

But as Lifar led me to the bed where Misia already sat, crumpled like sodden tissue, one look at Diaghilev's wasted frame told me it was too late. I'd not witnessed the death of anyone I had loved since my mother. I could now be grateful I'd been spared the sight as Diaghilev struggled to open his eyes, his gaze wavering, already poised on a distant threshold until he recognized us and murmured, "Coco. Misia. How charming of you to join us."

I heard faint humor in his remark, which caused Misia to clutch her hand to her mouth. Grief—a bane she'd always evaded—engulfed her. I could feel her every loss rack her as I stood with my hands on her shoulders, her abandonment by her parents, her divorces, the realization that she was about to lose this man whom she had championed and savaged on a whim. Turning to press her face into my skirt, she wept with heart-wrenching abandon.

"Surely it's not as terrible as all that," Diag said weakly, but as his gaze met mine, I saw that he knew it was, and he acknowledged my awareness without a word.

"We'll stay with you," I told him, and he smiled, closing his eyes again.

"Yes," he sighed. "I would like that."

HE DIED TWO DAYS LATER, slipping away in the early morning hours as the turquoise sea lapped the floating city, and Lifar, his last love, held his hand. There was, as usual, not enough in the Ballets Russes' coffers to cover the expense. I took charge. His body was in such a terrible state from his neglected disease that we could not transport him back to Paris. He must be interred on the island of San Michele, Venice's sole cemetery, and I ensured it would be done in style, with a white gondola bearing his coffin and us sailing behind in a flotilla of black ones.

I sent word to Bendor, who had moored his yacht outside Venice, but he did not appear at the appointed hour. The hotel's manager had expressed concern; Diag's demise had left him with an outstanding bill and worries that a death on the premises would affect business adversely. I paid the bill and arranged for the removal of the corpse at dawn, before the hotel guests woke.

Misia resembled a specter as we watched the coffin lowered into its grave. "He'll be so alone here," she moaned. "So far from Paris, from everything and everyone he loved."

"He loved Venice, too," I said. "Besides, he's not here anymore."

We had an unexpected moment of drama when Lifar, overcome by the enormity of his loss, gave a howl and made as if to throw himself upon the coffin. We held him back as he cried and cast despairing looks about him, as though he couldn't believe it was not some horrible joke and Diaghilev would come strolling out from behind the tombstones at any moment. I almost expected it myself. As we ferried back to the city, I kept looking over my shoulder for a glimpse of his portly figure in his astrakhan and pearled cravat, waving good-bye.

"Someone has to send word to Igor," I said, and Misia blew into her handkerchief. "He'll be devastated. He loved Diag like a brother."

Stravinsky would indeed be that, I thought, as would Cocteau, Picasso, his dancers, and everyone else who had the great fortune to participate in his whimsical, extravagant, tradition-shattering sensations. None of us would ever see the likes of him again.

In this life, there could be only one Sergei Diaghilev.

His death affected me more than I realized, but I had to bury my own sorrow to care for Misia, who indeed appeared to fall apart at the seams, bereft in a world without her Jojo or beloved Diag, without a place where she reigned supreme as a muse.

Cutting short the trip with Bendor, in late August I returned with Misia to my home on Faubourg Saint-Honoré in Paris. I installed her in one of the guest suites so she and Cocteau, also residing in my house, could commiserate. They no doubt shared their opiates, too, but I gave them leeway under the circumstances, returning to my atelier and never-ending work.

Vera Bate, recently engaged to the Italian officer and champion equestrian Alberto Lombardi, came to visit. I had put her in charge of overseeing the upcoming opening of my London boutique; she told me that once she did, she would see to her replacement, as Lombardi wished to return to Italy upon their marriage. In turn, I shared news of Dmitri, who had proposed to his American heiress, and of my aunt Adrienne. Her baron's cantankerous father, who had most opposed her liaison with his son, was dying; upon his death, the family had finally granted Nexon permission to take Adrienne for his wife.

"So, we're all settling down," Vera said as we sat at my bar and my friends lolled on the sofas, drinking and talking. "Except you, Coco dearest. You seem determined to remain like the sphinx—enigmatic, gorgeous, and eternally by yourself."

I smiled. "We need someone to pay for these parties. If I married and stopped working, what on earth would everyone do?"

"Ah," she said, and I glanced at her, more piercingly than I should have, for she added, "I was wondering what happened with Bendor. I saw him in London; he was with Lord Sisonby's daughter but he did not look happy. He asked me if you were coming to London for the boutique's inauguration. I said I had no idea." She paused. "I trust I did the right thing?"

"Yes, of course," I replied, even as the glitter of my party faded around me. "My schedule is as insane as ever. In any event, Bendor and I are in perfect accord. There was never any question of marriage, if that is what you think. Men do not understand me. They say, 'You needn't worry anymore; you don't have to do anything because I will take care of you.' But what they really mean is, 'You don't have to do anything except be there for me.'" I forced out a brittle laugh, seeing her startled look. "It is not my plan. I never want to weigh more heavily on a man than a bird."

Before she could respond, I went forth in my pearls and black crêpe de chine to swipe a champagne flute off the table before Cocteau, once again in the throes of opium, knocked it onto the carpet. I exchanged a few words with Picasso's wife, Olga, who wore one of my latest beige jersey dresses and two-toned shoes, but seemed careworn from her roving painter's infidelities.

On the stroke of two, I went upstairs. I never said good night these days; by now, everyone was accustomed to my departure. They would stay until they were either too drunk to leave and my butler Joseph escorted them to rooms prepared for them, or would drift off to one of the many late-night cabarets for more divertissements.

While I went to bed with my loyal dogs at my side, the weight of my solitude hung like an anchor upon me nevertheless.

ACT FIVE

NOT THE TIME FOR FASHION

1929–1945

"I AM NOT VAIN ENOUGH TO PRETEND
TO KNOW TODAY WHAT TOMORROW
IS GOING TO BE."

I

On October 29, 1929, the American stock market crashed. The fallout was epic, demolishing entire fortunes in seconds, with reports of tycoons and their wives throwing themselves out of windows rather than face sudden destitution. Within the year, the ripples of America's Depression reached us; I experienced an alarming reduction in orders from abroad as clients scurried for what would be a long hibernation from spending.

Bendor had warned me. We remained friends; he had proposed to Lady Ponsonby, and naturally, she accepted. In between the wedding plans, he brought his fiancée to Paris for tea with me (she was as pretty, bland, and blue blooded as I'd imagined) and told me that his battalion of fiscal analysts foresaw disaster overseas. I took initial precautions to safeguard my business, cutting back on new hires and paring back the number of dresses I presented. But nothing could prepare me for what ensued. The horn of plenty that had brought the Americans and the British in droves to my boutiques dried up. Even the much-vaunted opening of my store in London was subdued. Once again, I found myself adjusting to austerity.

Lavish beading and ornamentation were no longer appropriate (or cost effective) for such lean times. My little black dress alone had a resurgence—perhaps, I commented dryly, because it suited the new decade's funereal tone. For my London debut, I designed cotton-blend ensembles at reduced prices, paring down my evening wear to a few selections in piqué, organdy, and lace, with flared hems and tailored silk-velvet jackets, while expanding my line of separates in printed fabric for women on a budget. I also introduced supple suits in an exclusive new silk-and-wool shantung cloth woven for me, and shoulder-strap handbags in quilted leather.

Despite the agonized end of *les années folles,* I welcomed this enforced return to simplicity. I had always adhered to the adage that less is more, and never wavered before a challenge. Moreover, unlike other designers who saw their customer base shrivel in the wake of the crash, I still had my talisman, my *parfum* No. 5, which remained astonishingly popular, as women everywhere forwent other indulgences for the comforting allure of my scent.

Nevertheless, the steady decline in my business began to trouble me. My boutiques in Deauville, Cannes, and Biarritz suffered as the gush of rich vacationers slowed to a trickle. Moreover, after years of unrivaled supremacy, new designers were appearing on the scene, including the Italian Elsa Schiaparelli, whose bathing suits and skiwear earned her acclaim. I found her style derivative, even as her prominence alarmed me. I knew I required a new venture to bolster my success. During a summer reprieve at La Pausa, Dmitri arrived with an offer that seemed the perfect opportunity.

His American heiress had survived the crisis that decimated so many of her privileged friends. Her family had invested in the motion picture industry, Dmitri explained, and now one of the lions of that business, Samuel Goldwyn, was making another play for my magic touch.

"He's eager to bring you to Los Angeles. He's willing to offer you carte blanche and a considerable salary to dress his most bankable stars," said Dmitri as we lounged by the pool, Misia nearby in her straw hat and enormous sunglasses, nursing a martini. "He'll be here in the Côte d'Azur next week on vacation. Why don't you let me introduce you?"

At any other time, I would have declined. I had no interest in traveling to that brash nation where so many were suffering, nor, in truth, had I ever.

Unlike most of my friends, including Misia, the faux glamour of Holly-wood held no appeal for me. Still, I wondered at my hesitation. My clothing had always sold extremely well in the United States, as had my perfume. I might never have visited, but my name must be legendary if one of the richest moguls there was so determined to hire me. Even as I began to frown, think-ing it really was not the time, Misia bleated, "Coco, what could be the harm? He is obviously very interested. It's the second time he has asked."

Dmitri gave me a laconic smile. He was looking as polished as only a Romanov with a secure bank account and a rich wife could, so much so that I contemplated enticing him to my bed just to see if I still could.

"Second time?" he said. "So, Goldwyn has offered before?"

"Yes. He sent me an offer . . . oh, maybe two or three years ago. The salary was indeed considerable," I added. "You might even say extraor-dinary."

His eyes narrowed. "Well. Then you must accept his invitation."

"Not accept." I stood, stretching my arms over my head as I stepped past Dmitri with deliberate seductiveness. "But I will see him," I said before I plunged into my pool.

GOLDWYN WAS SHORT, sweaty, and stank of cigar. I arranged a lun-cheon at La Pausa, nothing too elaborate, easy fare with good wine and my friends. For some inexplicable reason, I felt as though I needed their protection. That feeling only increased as the mogul in his awful Hawaiian print shirt and shapeless slacks appraised my house as if he was tallying up its worth. Then he ordered the manicured blond wife at his side to the buffet and rattled on in staccato English that I barely understood, for while I spoke the language somewhat, I was hardly fluent.

"See here, Miss Chanel. What I propose is a once-in-a-lifetime oppor-tunity for you to dress my most lucrative stars: Swanson, Garbo, Colbert, Norma Talmadge, Ina Claire—they'll wear only your clothes, made by you for their films and in their private lives, as well. You will make a fortune!

No other designer has ever had such a chance. Every picture screen in the United States and abroad will be your—uh, what do you call it again?"

"Atelier," I said, with a slight smile.

"Ate-what?"

"Salon, if you prefer. A glass of wine, Mr. Goldwyn?"

"No. Never touch the stuff. Gives me gas." He guffawed; I winced, expecting the obligatory belch to follow. I recalled how Sert had refused to go to America because they only ate white bread. Apparently, they also rarely drank wine. Of course, Sert had reconsidered. Misia had told me, sniffling, that he'd finally accepted Rockefeller's commission to paint a mural in one of his New York skyscrapers. There might not be much money these days, but evidently America still had plenty to squander, judging by Goldwyn's enthusiastic harangue.

"So, what do you say? That Russian, Erté, came to Hollywood to design my sets and loved it. He took a contract for a year. I gave him a house. I can do the same for you."

"I have a house," I demurred. God save me, he reminded me of those hucksters from the marketplaces of my childhood, setting out soiled playing cards on upended crates to lure the gullible. "And I couldn't possibly go for a year. My business is here."

He peered at me, openmouthed.

"In France," I explained, reaching for my cigarettes. "My atelier is in Paris. I couldn't leave it for an entire year."

"Don't you have people who work for you?" he asked in genuine bafflement.

"Yes, but I still design and oversee the production of every article of clothing. That is why you want to hire me, yes?" I flicked my lighter. "Because of my talent?"

"Yes, yes, of course," he said, but I saw at once that it wasn't. "Your talent, yes," he went on, quickening his pace, like a train gathering speed over a bumpy track. "Fine, so you can't be away a year. You can come by invitation to dress my stars and then we'll see."

"Your stars," I said, giving him another smile. "You say they will wear my designs in your films and in their private lives? Forgive me, Mr. Gold-wyn, but I have been around the theater; actresses are an opinionated breed. Surely you cannot oblige them to wear Chanel all the time?"

"They'll do whatever I say," he blared, making Dmitri and the others at the table jump. "I pay them. I *made* them. If they don't do as I say when I say it, they're out. Finished."

"I see." I widened my smile, for I did see. All too well. And he apparently saw it, too, for he dug into his roast chicken, muttering between mouthfuls, "My offer stands at a million dollars. Upon contract. You can come and see what my pictures have to offer, and if you like it, well, then we both sign on the dotted line. Agreed?"

The silence that fell was so absolute that I clearly heard Misia's sudden gasp. Dmitri arched a brow at me. It was indeed, as I had said, extraordinary. I would be a fool to refuse. Still, I could not bring myself to say yes, despite Goldwyn's puffed chest and Misia's imploring eyes, until Goldwyn added, "I'll pay your expenses—the trip, accommodations, everything. You can even bring a companion, if you like, a secretary or an assistant designer. I suppose you have people like that on your staff?"

Misia was about to leap from her chair. Shooting a warning glare at her, I stubbed out my cigarette and took up my glass of wine. "By invitation only? And if I agree, you grant me full control over my designs? If I don't like it, I am free to go?"

"Yes, yes, but you're going to love it," he beamed. "Everyone loves Hollywood."

I was not convinced, but as I nodded and Misia laughed aloud for the first time in months, I thought it would certainly be an adventure, if nothing else.

BEFORE I LEFT FOR AMERICA, I helped organize, after nearly thirty years of waiting, Adrienne's wedding to Nexon. My youngest aunt was radiant in the white organza and silk bias-cut gown I designed for her, her baron now paunchy but otherwise distinguished as they exchanged their vows. I had to marvel at their commitment; Nexon might have done what Boy and Bendor had, marrying for convenience and maintaining Adrienne on the side, but he had remained faithful through it all, a man more in love than any other I had known.

Afterward, Adrienne came to me and said, "I want to stop working. I'll give you plenty of time, delay, even, until you return from America, but Nexon would like us to live at his family château, and . . ." She did not elaborate further, but I understood. Though she and I were the same age, she still wanted to try to have a child.

"Of course," I said. "Don't trouble yourself another moment about it. Go. Be his baroness. You've earned it."

"But what will you do?"

"Hire someone else. Countess Hélène de Leusse has been inquiring about a position. She knows all our clients. You might train her before you go, if you don't mind?"

Adrienne nodded, though she looked crestfallen until I leaned to her and kissed her cheek. "You can always return. You must know that by now. When I said I would replace you, I did not mean anyone can fill your shoes."

She brightened. "Thank you, Gabrielle." She was so relieved that I didn't have the heart to tell her I thought she would indeed be back. Though she had lived for the day when she would be Nexon's wife, she had found independence in my success. She wouldn't be able to stay away for long, not unless she miraculously became pregnant, which was highly unlikely at her age.

Still, I felt an unusual sentimentality as I watched her and Nexon dance at their wedding reception. Though far past the initial glow of infatuation, there was no mistaking the love in their eyes. To my surprise, Balsan, who'd traveled to Paris from Royallieu for the wedding along with his own new fiancée, asked me to dance. I found myself again in his arms after so many years, his expression as sardonic as ever, though he was weathered now, with an unseemly gut that pressed against my stomach.

"You need to do something about that," I said as he swept me around in the waltz. "You'll give your horses a hernia if you keep eating so much."

"Ah, yes. The sedate comforts of age: good food, old friends, boring sex—" He smiled. He had that same devil-may-care air, and it made me laugh despite myself. "But you, Coco, you remain untouched by time. No compromise for you, is there?"

"I have no idea what you mean. I, too, am growing old."

"Not like the rest of us." His smile faded. Gentleness came over his face and almost made me falter in our steps. "Do you still miss Boy?"

Only he would have dared. No one else. And I would only have ever allowed it from him. "Every day," I whispered.

He held me closer. "That is good. You loved and were loved. It is all we can ask from this life. Some people never have it."

I departed the reception early, citing the need to get home to start packing. In truth, I couldn't get away fast enough, dashing to my Rolls as if the hotel was on fire.

Only as my chauffeur pulled into the driveway of my home on Faubourg Saint-Honoré did I realize that what I felt was more than sorrow. It was the intangible melancholy of the end of an era. Adrienne had shared my first longings to become more than I was; she had encouraged me, even after I became Balsan's mistress. Balsan had provided refuge, setting me unwittingly on the path to my future by introducing me to Boy. Now, Boy was dead; both Adrienne and Balsan had found spouses with whom to share the rest of their lives, while I remained alone.

The house door opened. Misia came trudging out, with Cocteau, fresh from another month in rehabilitation, scampering after her. "Coco!" he cried out, exasperated. "Tell her she cannot take that hideous straw hat of hers to California. They'll think she's your governess!"

I laughed, stepping from the car.

How could I ever think I'd be alone when I had so many orphans in my life?

II

I thought being trapped on an ocean liner with Misia would be a purgatory. Even at La Pausa, with all the extra room, the house often felt too small with her in it, strewing her belongings wherever they happened to fall, chattering ceaselessly about everything and nothing, silence being anathema to her, not the great solace it was for me. I also fretted about leaving my dogs, Pita and Poppée, who were old now, almost thirteen, plagued by arthritis and bad teeth, but as devoted to me as I was to them. Joseph had convinced me a long voyage would not be good for them; he'd take excellent care of them, he assured me, as did Cocteau, who, while sullen that Misia and I were leaving without him (another worry of mine, as he was still fragile), promised my dogs would be with him at all times.

Yet once we boarded the SS *Europa* on March 1, 1931, with the Atlantic around us and nothing to do but stroll the decks, dine, read, and gossip, I discovered an experience much like the one I'd shared in Moulins with Adrienne—intimate time with a friend, during which I could relax and forget my obligations.

Misia reveled in the novelty, and we found ourselves giggling as we sat on deck under an awning, drinks in hand, as I told her about Bendor's visit with his fiancée to my house.

"You should have seen her expression. She looked as if I might eat her alive. Bendor made some excuse and left us alone, the coward! If I'd said I disapproved, I rather think he'd have informed her the wedding was off."

"But you didn't." Misia gave me a pointed look from over her sunglasses. "You wanted him to marry her because that way, he couldn't marry you."

I shrugged, sipping my cocktail. "She reminded me of that custard the British love—all cream and sugar, without any spice. I arranged myself like a queen on my chaise lounge, wearing as much of my jewelry as I could," I said as Misia snorted. "Pita and Poppée were on the chairs, so she had to perch on a stool at my feet. I didn't say a word. Finally, she blurted out that her papa had given her one of my necklaces for Christmas and she loved it. Can you believe it? I made her describe the necklace to me."

"And . . . ?" said Misia, her teeth showing. "Was it yours?"

"Oh, yes. But I told her it couldn't possibly be, because I would never allow anything so vulgar to carry my name. She was mortified. After that, our conversation was over. Later, Bendor called me to say she had found me very much what she expected."

Misia cackled. "She thought you were a monster!"

"Naturally." I gazed out to the ocean. "But she'll never forget me, either."

Misia turned pensive. When I did not speak, she said, "Do you regret it? You could have been his wife. He was in love with you; I believe he still is. A man only brings his fiancée to his mistress for approval when he wants her to tell him she's unsuitable."

I contemplated this. Had Bendor truly hoped I would crush his resolve by declaring Loelia Ponsonby as insipid as pudding? It had occurred to me at the time; I had known within minutes of meeting her that she would either bore him to distraction or lead him on a merry dance to his grave so she could enjoy life as his widow. I could have ruined his illusions, or even retained him as a lover after the wedding. But I had not. I told him she was lovely and let them proceed to their nuptials.

"No," I finally said. "I don't regret it. God knows, I want love. But the moment I must choose between a man and my dresses, I choose my dresses. He would have insisted that I stop working and I could never do that. There have been other duchesses of Westminster, but there can only be one Coco Chanel."

Misia reached over, squeezing my hand. "Everyone admires you for it. Me most of all. Look at me, thrice divorced, without much to my name. I am almost sixty. Who will ever love me again?"

"I love you," I said, and I realized that I did. She was my one constant. As infuriating as she could be, she knew me better than anyone else, and in her own inimitable way, was unfailingly honest with me, even when I did not appreciate it.

"Yes, well. Pity we're not lesbians," she rejoined, and as I chuckled, she added, "Besides, if it's any consolation, you did the right thing. Bendor is not the gallant knight he seems. Did you read the papers before we left? No? Well, he gave his new duchess a fine wedding present. He told the king that his own brother-in-law William Lygon, Earl of Beauchamp, is a homosexual, and ruined the man's reputation. It was a disgrace. Lygon was obliged to relinquish his political duties by the king's order and his wife petitioned for a divorce."

I stared at her, aghast. "There was nothing in the newspapers about that!"

She gave a mischievous smile. "Wasn't there? Then I must have heard it somewhere. He is quite the barbarian, your Bendor. He has also given several speeches in Parliament about how Jewish greed brought about the collapse of the stock market in America, and if Europe doesn't do something to stop them, we're headed for the same. He is not someone you want to be associated with; he'd alienate all your friends. In time, you would despise him for it."

Her pronouncement unsettled me. For all her apparent self-involvement, Misia had always cultivated an ear for scandal, so I did not doubt her report. Moreover, I had heard Bendor make disparaging remarks about Jews; but then, so many in his circle did. And like Boy, he nursed a paranoiac distaste for homosexuals, but again it was so common among men of his class, I had scarcely paid it any mind. Besides, when he met my eclectic mix of friends, many of whom were Jewish or queer or both, he had seemed amenable enough, even if he had suggested, albeit innocently, that Cocteau write about his dogs.

I shuddered, the air turning chill, the ocean whipped into froth by a rising wind. A shadow came over me. Turning to Misia, I said, "Let's go inside and nap until dinner. I'm tired."

"Yes," she sighed. "So am I."

III

New York was a bewildering fury, a multitude of impossibly tall buildings raking the sky and thousands of people scurrying below them; hundreds of flashing signs and an endless barrage of car horns and shouting, a deafening cacophony that made me want to cover my ears and hide.

It did not help that I disembarked with a cold that had me feverish and sneezing, the first time in years I could recall being ill. Misia fed me hot soup while I sweated out the fever in our hotel suite, even as hordes of reporters besieged the lobby in hopes of catching a glimpse of me.

Once I felt sufficiently recovered, I donned one of my red jersey dresses with white cuffs and rounded collar, and invited the reporters to my room, hiding my astonishment at their eagerness to interview me. All they wanted to know was what I planned to do in Hollywood.

"I have not brought my scissors," I told them, "I'm simply going to see what the studio can offer. It's by invitation, without commitment." By the next morning, the papers were reporting all sorts of erroneous declarations attributed to me, including the remark, Misia read aloud, that "long hair would be back in style" and I found "men who wore scent disgusting." The papers also predicted I would find Hollywood a challenge, given my preferred method of work, during which I designed a dress, saw it to the workroom, and rarely touched it again. Mr. Goldwyn's film stars, noted the *New York Times*, would demand more personalized attention from Chanel.

"I don't doubt it," I grumbled.

The subsequent twenty-hour train ride to California was a claustrophobic misery made more so by glimpses of tar-shack towns and vagabonds at every stop, the visible poverty reminding me so much of my childhood that I pulled the blinds shut. The accompanying reporters continued to barrage me, as if I might disclose some master plan to drape every actress in sight in tweed and jersey.

Los Angeles was so . . . *bright*. I had no other description for it. Although it was only late March, the sprawling metropolis seemed ablaze under its merciless sun, so white and vast it was like a movie set itself. Everything in America seemed oversized to me—the buildings and cars, the numbers of people, the bewildering array of products in storefronts. Los Angeles epitomized this excess, snarling with traffic, the endless beaches full of hopefuls and has-beens, with the bold Hollywoodland sign overseeing the city like a deity.

It had been less than two weeks and I missed Paris already. My cold had not fully abated. I wanted to hole up with Misia in the immense suite in the Chateau Marmont that Goldwyn had reserved for me but I was obliged to attend an ostentatious reception, where I sat, sniffling at his side, as he presented an assortment of his talent. I was surprised by how small boned these famous sirens of the screen were in their slinky lamé, practically curtsying as they gushed, "Oh, Miss Chanel, you are absolutely my favorite designer!" It was obvious they'd never worn a thing of mine in their lives. I might have started laughing at the rehearsed ridiculousness of it all had I not been trying to keep from sneezing. I was only amused when I met Greta Garbo, whose sad eyes and surprisingly big feet caught my attention, as did her whisper, "I would be nowhere without your raincoat and hat, mademoiselle," alluding to my rain gear for women. I was supposed to dress her for her next film.

The following day, I toured Goldwyn's cavernous soundstages, glaringly illuminated by banks of overhead lights. I was impressed. How could

I not be? He had made millions by peddling fantasies. But I was not impressed enough to believe this was where I belonged. In fact, as the days passed and I found myself obliged to read horrid scripts to get a sense of the characters for whom I would design, I began to feel something I had not experienced since my earliest days: insecurity.

I knew my clothes worked. Thousands of women could not be wrong. But could I translate my vision of restraint for a medium that thrived on exaggeration, where artificial grandeur replaced reality? I had built my career on comfort and style; even as my couture became inordinately expensive, I firmly believed that fashion did not succeed until women on the streets adopted it. Now I was expected to produce designs that must not only remain relevant during the two years it took to complete filming but also exalt the very stars who wore them, women reared on plumage and sequins, who reveled in excess and unattainable ideals.

It was the most perplexing dilemma I'd faced; from the beginning, I had the disquieting sense that I would fail.

But Goldwyn insisted, introducing me to everyone, and the flattery proved overwhelming. Here, I was indeed a legend. I signed for a year, pocketing the million-dollar fee on the condition that I could do the required work in Paris and send my designs to fitters in Hollywood for completion.

With the designs for my first film approved, I hauled Misia back to New York. There, I again submitted to the onslaught of reporters and meetings with editors who covered my work.

Vogue escorted me on a tour of New York's fashion district. In the upscale department stores on Fifth Avenue, I discovered my perfume No. 5 selling at such a brisk rate they could barely keep it in stock. My suspicion was aroused. The Wertheimer brothers, with whom I had signed a contract for 10 percent of the proceeds, were obviously making a killing off my name. I decided to consult a lawyer when I returned to Paris. The Wertheimers could not expect me to be satisfied with a meager percentage of what was obviously a fortune in sales.

I was also fascinated, and appalled, by the burgeoning trade in ready-to-wear. In a discount department store called S. Klein on Union Square, while Misia yawned and tapped her foot, I watched women browse through apparel hung on plain racks, trying on the dresses in barren dressing rooms under signs warning that shoplifters would be arrested. To my disbelief, some of the clothing was marked down to under a dollar! The turnover, my escort from *Vogue* explained, was merciless. If an item failed to sell in two months, it was sold at a base rate to make room for new merchandise—of which there was an endless supply. Mass production in assorted sizes by large sweatshops had replaced the time-consuming process of samples followed by fittings. Finally stepping to a rack, I forced myself to sift through it. Within minutes, with a shudder I located one of my own designs in basic cotton, almost identical, right down to the white piqué cuffs.

"This is mine," I exclaimed. "I showed this very dress last year in London."

The escort grimaced. "Manufacturers send spies to couture shows, pretending to be reporters. They sketch everything they see. The clothes are then reproduced in cheap fabrics with modifications like zippers. See? That dress has a zipper up its side, which I am sure was not part of your original design."

It wasn't, and I found the novelty as horrifying as it was clever. For five dollars and a zipper, whoever bought this would be wearing Chanel, if not by label, then by association.

I was staring at the future. I recognized it at once, with the same jolt of insight that had propelled me to open my first shop. The Depression had spawned many changes and I could not afford to ignore this one. Ready-to-wear was how the majority of women would soon buy their clothes, and I embarked on my trip home in April 1931 with a new goal.

Hollywood had not suited me and, frankly, neither had America, but it reinforced my long-held belief that to resist progress was to risk extinction.

OTHER UNPLEASANT SURPRISES awaited me in Paris.

The first and most devastating was the loss of both my Pita and

Poppée. Both had become increasingly feeble, Joseph informed me, but they had waited patiently for my return before succumbing within days of each other. I wept as I had not since Boy, feeling his death all over again. I had my dogs cremated and their ashes sealed in white boxes, which I kept in a cabinet. For days afterward, I could barely speak or venture outside, until Bendor telephoned to invite me to London and I sobbed over the line to him. He promised to buy me a Great Dane puppy from the next litter that a friend of his bred. It was typical of him to think I could simply replace what had been lost with something new, but at least he didn't chide me for being ridiculous, as Misia did when she found me crying.

The next surprise cut deep. The Italian Schiaparelli had had such resounding success that she dared to open a shop near mine on the Place Vendôme. After hovering at the edge of distinction, she seized inspiration from the Spanish surrealist painter Salvador Dalí, featuring ludicrous trompe l'oeil designs on sweaters and shockingly pink gowns printed with lobster motifs, as if women were food platters.

I laughed when I saw the coverage of her new collection in the 1932 issue of *Vogue,* albeit through my teeth. "It's an exercise in how to make women look foolish," I declared, even as I seethed that while the magazine fawned over Schiaparelli's irreverent style, they relegated me to a sidebar with the comment that I had revolutionized Hollywood by putting Ina Claire in white silk pajamas. An editorial in *The New Yorker* declared, "Chanel wants a lady to look like a lady, but Hollywood wants a lady to look like two ladies," lauding me as a designer of principle in an amoral environment. Still, the overall message remained clear:

I had failed to make an impression.

Adding salt to the wound, the pictures I designed for flopped. The fashion gazettes of Paris delighted in reporting how Chanel could not guarantee box-office gold. In a fit of rage, I fled to Bendor's London townhome at his invitation. I had been right to assume my work was not meant for film but the confirmation proved bitter. Though I was a million dollars richer, it marked the first major failure of my career.

"Hollywood wouldn't know elegance if it spat on them," I cried, striding about with my drink in hand as Bendor eyed me from his armchair. His marriage had already faltered; his young bride found his lifestyle intolerable and refused to join him on his endless yacht excursions or hunting expeditions, so he eagerly welcomed me. He would have taken me to bed, too, had I not been in such a state.

"I've had to cut my prices nearly in half because of this damn Depression. And those Wertheimers——," I cried, stabbing my cigarette in the air, "they rob me blind! My perfume is earning millions in America alone, and they refuse to renegotiate our contract with my lawyer."

He drawled, "What did you expect, Coco? Jews rob everyone blind." He stood, then moved to the bar to refill my drink, which I gulped down. As he chipped more ice, he added, "You should never have signed a deal with them. The Jews are a menace."

I paused. Misia's assessment of him had been accurate, it seemed, but his stance still took me aback. "They did get my perfume into the department stores," I found myself saying, in sudden contrition. "Number Five is distributed across America. Without their contacts, I would never——"

"They are not responsible for your success," he interrupted. "You created the perfume and they profit by it. Jews always do that. They never do any work; they merely find the easiest way to drain money from others, like leeches. Let me recommend you to another lawyer for advice here in London. You need to sever your contract with them before it's too late."

I paused, my glass half lifted to my lips. A sudden chill went through me, reminding me of what I had felt that afternoon on the *Europa* with Misia. "Whatever do you mean?"

"Haven't you been paying attention? Adolf Hitler is about to be appointed chancellor in Germany. He has an agenda to deal with the Marxist threat and the Jews who bolster it." Bendor returned to his chair and the table beside it, heaped with books. He withdrew a volume. "This is his treatise, *Mein Kampf*. You should read it. It is brilliant; he writes of the Jewish conspiracy to gain world leadership, abetted by America. Germany's woes are the Weimar Republic, Jews, and social democrats, as well as the bloody Marxists. He will abolish them all if he can."

I was aghast. "The Germans nearly destroyed us the last time. Would you advocate their resurgence, after everything they did?"

"We need a strong Europe," was his terse reply. "Germany is part of it. Hitler does not want war with us. He simply wants to rebuild his country for those who deserve it."

I forced out a shrug, setting down my untouched drink. "What do I know of politics? I'm only a designer. But there is something you could do for me," I went on, recalling my disturbing experiences in New York. "I want to do something unprecedented—an exclusive presentation of one-of-a-kind designs that garment manufacturers can copy under my license. I can present it here, in your home, and invite everyone we know. That ought to give Schiaparelli a run for her money. She can't afford to give away her ludicrously expensive designs for free."

He smiled. "You know I'm always willing to help you." Setting the book aside, he came to me. "And that other lawyer I mentioned, you will meet with him? I think you should. A time of change is coming. You cannot allow Jews to steal your life's work."

I nodded. "I'll see him after the presentation. Why not?"

Evading his amorous advances, I excused myself, saying I needed to rest. As I went upstairs to my guest suite, I heard Misia in my head: *"He is not someone you want to be associated with . . ."*

I was relieved now that he had never proposed. Yet in my fervor to retain my grip on fame, I did not pause to mark the darkness about to envelop us.

IV

My prêt-à-porter collection helped reestablish my reputation. I earned significant fees from the licensing to manufacturers, and as I had predicted, Schiaparelli was vociferous in her criticism of me, calling my decision to allow copies of my work made "a betrayal of couture." When asked about my reasons by the *Daily Mail*, I replied, "Clothes are made to be worn and discarded. You cannot protect what is already dead."

Nevertheless, my clientele continued to dwindle; I had to cut my workforce from nearly four thousand to three thousand, and economize in my choice of fabrics.

Abandoning my *garçonne* silhouette that epitomized the 1920s, I presented a dazzling new collection for the 1933 spring season, emphasizing the feminine in white day dresses of cotton-silk and chiffon with gossamer sleeves, floppy bows at the waist or rhinestone-studded ribbons crisscrossing shoulders and backs, as well as unisex trousers and a camellia motif on black suits. *Vogue* applauded my innovation, but more and more fickle women absconded to Schiaparelli and her partnership with Dalí. In return, I expanded my perfume empire with new fragrances: No. 22, Glamour, and Gardenia. None proved as profitable as No. 5—none could be—and my battle with the Wertheimers turned acrimonious as I fought them with everything at my disposal, including paying a retainer to Bendor's lawyer to advise mine in France, seeking any means I could to break the contract I had signed so carelessly years before.

Pierre Wertheimer eventually came to see me at my atelier. He arrived with his briefcase in hand, alone and portly in his bowler hat and overcoat, his expression mournful but steadfast.

"My brother Paul and I have discussed this at length and agree to increase your share by five percent. We do not want legal trouble between us. It does not serve our mutual interests."

"That is unacceptable," I said. "My name is on the bottle and that warrants a far bigger share in the profits. Lest you forget, I hired you, monsieur, not the other way around."

"Yes, you hired us to *distribute* it, mademoiselle." He smiled. "We have done what we promised, as stated in the contract." He tapped the document, as if to draw my attention to it. "You cannot now decide to renegotiate terms because the perfume is more successful than you envisioned. It is successful precisely because of our hard work."

"But I am the one who created it." I leaned to him, taking momentary satisfaction in his visible discomfort. "My name gives the perfume prestige, so a raise of a mere five percent is a crime. You are taking millions in profit to line your own pockets."

He sat quietly for a moment, regarding me, before he sighed, leafed through the contract to a page toward the back. He motioned that I should read it. When I refused, he said, "This clause binds you to our contract for its duration. Is that your signature below?"

"You know that it is," I said. "I wish now that I never signed it."

"Then all I can say is that I am sorry, mademoiselle, but this is business and you did sign a binding contract. Personal feelings are not a factor."

"Not a factor?" I echoed, and I felt my self-control disintegrate, so that I gripped the edge of my desk until my fingers hurt. "It most certainly is a factor. *My* feelings are everything."

"Perhaps in how you choose to run your boutiques," he replied, turning even calmer as he watched my outrage increase. "But not in how we run

Bourjois. If that were the case, we'd never make a profit on anything we—"

"You conniving crook," I hissed, cutting him off. "How dare you sit there and tell me that my feelings mean nothing? Your company reaps a fortune off my name! I will not stand for it." I stabbed my hand at him. "Your contract is invalid; I signed it without realizing what I was doing. You will give me my fair share or I will see you in court."

His expression hardened. "Insulting me will not avail you, mademoiselle. With all due respect, I find such words beneath you." He came to his feet, leaving the contract on the desk. "You may consult with your lawyer Chambrun or whomever else you like. It will not change a legal contract. And," he said, "I now feel compelled to warn you that as majority shareholders in Les Parfums Chanel, we have the right to protect ourselves."

"Protect yourselves?" I was shuddering with fury, so much so that I almost leaped around the desk to yell in his face. "Are you *threatening* me?"

"I merely warn you, as I have said. If you persist in bringing suit against us, we can remove you from the board of directors."

It was too much. Flinging my hand across the desk, I swept his contract and several other items from its surface, tumbling paper and pens and bric-a-brac to the carpet as I brandished a letter opener and shouted, "Do so and you will regret it. You have my word!"

He inclined his head, taking up his case and hat. "Perhaps," he said, and he turned on his heel to depart, though he was a brave man indeed to show his back, for I was within seconds of plunging the letter opener into it.

Instead, he left me panting at my desk like a cornered animal. I grabbed up the phone to call my lawyer René. "Sue them! I want the contract voided. Take them to court, file as many legal injunctions as you think necessary. I never want to do business with them again."

He could not do it. Instead, René telephoned me a week later to say that the Wertheimers had indeed removed me from the board as president and filed a countersuit against me for defamation, which now required months of wrangling to overturn. I vowed that I would take my revenge. Come what may, I would disentangle myself from Pierre Wertheimer if it was the last thing I did. No one owned me; I had built my wealth with my own hands, overcoming poverty and other obstacles through sheer force of will. I refused to be held hostage because of some careless oversight. Deep within, I recognized my own irrationality. Years before, Balsan had warned me to be careful, but I'd ignored his advice, signing my perfume contract in haste. This was my fault; but my fear of being exploited, and the bitter seed of Hollywood, as well as my faltering business and fervent anger that my hard work filled someone else's bank account overwhelmed me. All I could see, all I could think, was that the Wertheimers were thieves.

They had become my enemy.

It was under this noxious cloud of acrimony that I met Paul Iribe. Bendor introduced him, though he was already familiar to me by reputation—a Basque caricaturist, he had illustrated Poiret's fashion catalogs until his second marriage to an heiress allowed him to expand into interior design. Bendor was a fan of his magazine *Le Témoin*, which Iribe had founded before the war but now languished, out of print.

"You should help him relaunch it," Bendor suggested. "He has a brand-new concept for it and you keep saying you need a new venture. Why not this? I predict it'll be very popular."

He knew exactly how to hook me, Bendor did; and so I agreed to meet Iribe at his new shop on the Faubourg Saint-Honoré, not far from my residence.

The man who came to greet me was thickset and short as Jojo Sert, if less sallow in his complexion—hardly handsome by any measure, though his dark eyes were piercing behind his wire-rim glasses, and he exuded an extraordinary charisma that he knew how to wield.

His designs were exquisite, in particular his jewelry, which I lingered over in his display cases, entranced by its baroque style. "They are commissions for the International Guild of Diamond Merchants," he explained. "If you like, I will recommend you to them, made-moi-selle." He enunciated every syllable in a modulated tone that made me think he had gone to some pains to disguise the fact that Catalan, not French, was his native tongue.

"Whatever for?" I said. "As beautiful as these are, who can possibly afford gems now?" Yet even as I spoke, I found myself considering his offer, urged by his next pronouncement: "With the name of Chanel on the pieces, who could afford *not* to afford them?"

I nodded, thinking it would come to nothing. He was clearly being flirtatious, promising whatever he could to press his agenda. He proceeded to show me illustrations for his new proposed edition of *Le Témoin*, along with sample text. I winced as I read it; I should have guessed, given that Bendor was a fan. Iribe's rhetoric was fervently nationalistic, promulgating an anti-Marxist view with a strong dose of anti-Semitic hatred. I was not offended, but I wasn't charmed, either. I told him I must think on it, wondering why he needed me to fund his magazine when he had a wife with money. Then, as I turned to leave, he himself answered my unvoiced question. "I'd like to see you again, mademoiselle. In private."

Startled by his directness, I turned to him. It had been so long since a man had been that forward—there was no mistaking his intent—that I had a mind to refuse, just to see how he would react. Instead, as his eyes locked on mine, without evasion or apology, I found myself teasing, "Aren't you married?"

"Yes. Does it matter?"

"It might—to your wife."

He shrugged. "It might." He stared at me with an insolence that was almost amusing. "The important thing is, does it matter to you? Because I assure you, it has never mattered to me."

I had to stifle my laughter. What a cad! But an interesting one, nevertheless. I had always had a fondness—or, as some might say, a weakness—for men who went after what they wanted without fanfare. At my age especially, it was refreshing.

"Let's see about this commission with the guild first, yes?" I replied, and I sailed from his shop, feeling his gaze boring into me through his display windows.

THE COMMISSION CAME two weeks later. The guild was overjoyed by my offer and I set myself to designing pieces for a charity benefit. I would be paid for my work, though not through the sale of any pieces, which were promotional. I recruited Misia to assist me, for she needed something to occupy her time. All she had done since our return to Paris was rattle about her apartment or mine. We took astronomy as our inspiration, scavenging books for ideas. In November, we presented the collection at my home, displayed on wax mannequins in police-guarded vitrines. Thousands queued outside to gawk at the lopsided diamond stars echoing the secret mosaics of Aubazine; the comet-shaped necklace with shower-spray clasp; yellow-gold bracelets and crescent moon barrettes; solar brooches in saffron-hued gems; and cascading tiaras.

Every major newspaper and magazine reported on the exhibit, skyrocketing the price of De Beers stock. My name was again on everyone's lips. Ingeniously, I had designed the jewelry to mimic my clothes, separates that could be taken apart: the tiaras turned into bracelets, eardrops to brooches, the star-shaped pendants as buckles for shoes or belts. To enhance the prestige of the event, I gave several interviews declaring that "the point of jewelry isn't to make a woman look rich but to adorn her, which is not the same thing" and "diamonds offer the best value in the smallest package"—a slogan De Beers used to advantage in their advertising.

That evening after everyone left, I invited Paul Iribe to my bed. He proved energetic, rousing a fire I had not felt in years. No one save Boy had done what he did with his fingers and tongue, and he was not satisfied until I was, highlighting the fact that for all our rapport, Bendor and I had not been compatible under the sheets.

Iribe was not so accommodating outside the sheets, however. Despite his gluttony for luxury in all its forms, he despised my home. "You turned it into a museum for the diamond collection and that is how it should remain. So many rooms; so much waste. It's preposterous, a mausoleum. Do you want to be entombed there among your Chinese screens?"

At the time, we were staying in my suite at the Ritz, as I had emptied my living space for the jewelry show. Once he mentioned it, I realized I had ceased to feel at ease there since my return to Paris and the death of my beloved dogs. My butler Joseph's wife, Marie, had also died recently, leaving him a forlorn widower. As with my other homes before it, unwelcome memories had begun to tarnish Faubourg Saint-Honoré.

"If we lived here," Iribe said, gazing at me from where he stood at the suite windows overlooking the Place Vendôme, "we'd be more comfortable. There is no past here, no tokens of former lovers to taunt me. Here, I could even think of marrying you."

"Marry me?" With an uneasy laugh, I disguised my surprise. "You're already married."

"I'll divorce her." He stared at me. "I don't love her. I never have. I want you. And unlike Bendor or your other Englishman, I don't care about lineage or children."

It was cruel: *he* was cruel. Remorseless, in fact, especially in his zeal to see France restored to national pride. In his latest issue of *Le Témoin*, he had depicted me as the face of our iconic symbol, la Marianne, lying at the feet of a gravedigger ready to bury France—the gravedigger being our embattled prime minister. I now saw he was sincere in this proposal, as well, opening doors inside me that had remained bolted since the end of my affair with Bendor.

"Or don't you want to get married?" he said. "If you don't, I won't ask again."

A valid question—even if, as usual, I had no easy answer. In August 1933, I had turned fifty. Did I intend to remain like this for the rest of my life, careening from liaison to liaison until men ceased to notice me? Until now, I had accepted this as my fate: to be wedded to my work and my friends. Iribe was hardly the man I envisioned for a husband; he was as unlike Boy or Bendor as any man could be—common born and uncouth, feral in his ambitions, and scathingly dismissive of what other people thought of him.

Still, I did not want to grow old alone or, God forbid, chained to Misia. Children were out of the question, and in any event, I had my nephew André, who had completed his education and now worked overseeing one of my mills. He and his lovely Dutch wife had even had a daughter, naming her Gabrielle in my honor. Adrienne, too, had settled at the Nexon château in Limoges. Although she had not managed to get pregnant, she was content, a happy wife and aunt to her husband's nephews and nieces. To finally have a companion, a husband with whom to share my waning years—how much time did I have before that door, too, closed on me forever?

"You'll marry me if we move here to the Ritz? I hardly call that romantic."

"Maybe not." He stalked to the bed, ripping off his lounge robe to expose his hirsute body. He was erect, his manhood hard as he grasped it in his fist and said, "I want to fuck you every night, Coco, and help you conquer every day. I am ugly and greedy—but you like me and I like you, very much. Why shouldn't we marry? Together, there's nothing we cannot do."

Not romantic, no, but I was hardly of an age anymore for such posturing, and I began to laugh as he flung himself onto the bed, pressing himself against me and murmuring, his voice rough as ardor took over, "Say yes. Say yes and make me the happiest man in France."

"I . . . I don't know," I gasped, his fingers stroking me. "I'll think about it . . ."

I had said the same words when I told him I would consider financing his magazine and in the end, I had written him a check. As he now played me until I was shuddering and bucking my hips, I realized I would probably agree this time, too.

He was right. Why shouldn't I grasp whatever happiness came my way?

"MARRY HIM?" MISIA REGARDED ME, appalled, at breakfast in the Ritz dining room. Outside, a cold February snow, the first of 1934, drifted over the city. "Are you insane? He is monstrous, an opportunist! That magazine of his spews nothing but garbage. He goes through women and money like wine. He will bleed you dry. Everyone says so."

"Everyone being you, most of all," I retorted. "I'm starting to wonder if it's truly me you're so concerned for. First, it was Boy, whom you thought a snob, then Bendor was a bigot, and now Iribe is a monster. Perhaps you just want me to yourself, seeing as your own three marriages have failed."

She quavered, "That's . . . a horrid thing to say. I want you to be happy, but Iribe is—"

I cut her off. "I'll not hear another word. He has petitioned his wife for a divorce; he's coming with me to La Pausa to plan our wedding. I'm moving out of Faubourg Saint-Honoré to live here. I gave Joseph notice, as I have no need for a butler anymore. I'll use my apartment at rue Cambon to store my clothes and possessions."

"You let Joseph go . . . ?" Misia turned white. "Coco, he has served you for years! Please, think of what you're doing—" She stopped abruptly, but this time, not because of me. Everyone in the dining room had turned in their chairs to stare, perplexed, toward the sound of distant thunder—a cacophony of shouts and tromping feet that within seconds had the maître d' hurrying toward us to recommend that we remain inside.

"Why?" I demanded. "What is the matter?"

"A demonstration," he said. "There are thousands of them marching to the place de la Concorde. The police warn that it is not safe to leave the hotel. We're locking the doors."

"Honestly!" I huffed, and I dragged Misia to my suite on the top floor, from which we could look across the place. Alarm swept through me. Gusts of tear gas floated over raised, clenched fists as mounted police rammed into the crowd of bellowing young men in berets, carrying banners with slogans and sharpened sticks.

Beside me, Misia whispered, "Who are they?"

"I don't know." As I watched the clash build to a furious struggle, with some of the men lunging at the police to yank them from their saddles, while others fled with faces bloodied, coughing and stumbling from the tear gas. "Come." I drew Misia away from the window. "We'll wait here. I have to telephone the shop to make sure everyone is safe. And Paul will be here as soon as he can; he'll tell us what this uproar is about."

I called the store. They had shut the doors and sent the workforce home, although my manager, Hélène de Leusse, told me our workers had not shown up this morning. "They went to the demonstration against the government. They marched on the Chamber of Deputies and the Élysée

Palace demanding the resignation of everyone. The unemployment and depression—" She gasped as I heard muffled chanting coming through the line from the streets outside the shop. "God save us, mademoiselle, it's like the Bolshevik revolution. They want to bring everything down!"

"Go up to my apartment," I ordered. "Lock every door and window, pull the shutters, and stay there until it's over. Do not go outside. Just stay there and I'll come to you as soon as I can."

I wanted to go now, dreading the thought of violence, the inevitable smashing of windows and looting, and as I turned to Misia, she must have seen it, for she moaned, "Don't leave me alone. You cannot go out there. It's a mob!"

"I won't," I reassured her. I poured two stiff vodkas, which she fortified with her habitual blue drops. I refused to take any. I had almost weaned myself from it, as Iribe loathed my dependence on it for sleep. Clenching my jaw, I smoked an endless succession of cigarettes instead, seated on the sofa with Misia nodding off as the riot outside went on for hours.

Iribe arrived at dusk, drenched in sweat despite the cold. The riot had been crushed but it was the worst seen in Paris since the 1871 Paris Commune. The newspapers would report over two thousand injuries and seventeen deaths. Our prime minister now struggled for compromise before the 1936 elections; Iribe sneered, and his next magazine called for the defeat of the republican government.

Paris was in shambles. Though my shop was spared damage, others reported looting and burning everywhere. I wanted to leave for La Pausa. Exacerbating my discontent was Iribe's decision to delay our wedding plans. His wife had resisted his petition for divorce and he had his agenda to further, his nationalist propaganda in *Le Témoin* having gained a wide audience in the wake of the discord. He was illustrating and publishing a monthly edition, under my patronage, I noted sourly; but I had my own demons to battle, mainly Elsa Schiaparelli, whose latest collection had earned her the cover of *Vogue*. Enraged, I called the editor, demanding equal treatment for my most recent collection, which featured bias-cut gowns and embroidered cloaks. "I offer style, not circus costumes," I shouted over the telephone. "You're rewarding her for setting us all back a hundred years!"

Vogue's response was to refuse me further coverage until I cooled my temper. In a fit of frustration, I left Iribe behind and took Misia to La Pausa, where Lifar and several others joined us. There, amid my olive groves, with the vista of the coast below my windows, I tried to let go of my discontent, my growing fear that I was becoming what I dreaded more than anything else—irrelevant.

Such was my blindness that I did not allow any newspapers or political discussions inside the house. I did not want to see or know that while I sought retreat, time was running out.

V

I greeted 1935 with renewed resolve.

Schiaparelli debuted a new military look of regimental suits with peplums and more of her outrageous squashed *capotes*. The magazines went into ecstasies; I wanted to shriek when I read that the American divorcée Wallis Simpson, whose scandalous liaison with the Prince of Wales rocked the British monarchy, had visited Schiaparelli's atelier for a fitting. My *premières* urged me to bow to the taste of the times by incorporating an element of surrealism in my designs. I refused. During my summer at La Pausa, I had seen my beach pajamas everywhere on the Riviera. I was not finished yet, and set myself to presenting half-sleeve bolero jackets in velvet with overlapping V-necked collars; tucked-waist tweed suits with double rows of buttons, crisp frilled blouses, and my signature two-tone pumps.

My latest collection proved a success. British *Vogue* abased itself and offered to send a photographer to La Pausa to take pictures of me; I left Paris early to prepare the villa. Iribe said he would join me later, once he had seen to his latest magazine. Our relationship had cooled, given his obsession with everything political, but I reasoned once he was at La Pausa with me, away from work, we could discuss our future. I was beginning to regret my precipitous agreement to marry him. Not only was I uncertain of whether we loved each other, but I had my doubts that either of us was even capable of sustaining an actual marriage. I was still willing to try, but first I must be reassured that he shared my vision of a life together, one that was not subject to more pressing, outside engagements.

La Pausa was glorious that year, the irises and roses blooming in profusion, so that their delicate scent tinged everything in the house. The photographer employed by *Vogue* was a Russian baron who had fled the motherland; he told me that his father had once refused to salute the kaiser because he considered the German a mere upstart compared with his own exalted lineage. I mentioned that I was friends with Dmitri Pavlovich, who was currently speaking at rallies in France against the German chancellor. Misia then regaled him with tales of her own fabulous, if mostly fabricated, ancestry, her shameless flirting making him smile.

Iribe telephoned that he would take the overnight express from Paris. We picked him up at the station in Cannes; during the drive to the villa, I noticed he looked paler than usual and unsteady on his feet when we arrived. "I'm just tired and hungry," he grumbled, waving off my concern. "Let me rest and tomorrow we'll play tennis. You put that new court in, right?"

"Yes." I gave him a wary smile. He really did not look well. "But it can wait. Our guests are arriving in a few days. Take all the rest you need."

He ate a little and went upstairs to the suite that had been Bendor's. He did not come down for our informal dinner, so I took him a tray. I found him fast asleep, but still sweating, though the room located at the rear of the house was cool. Tucking the sheets about him, I left one of the windows ajar to let in the breeze from the sea and retired. If he wasn't improved tomorrow, I would insist that he see a doctor.

The next morning, he seemed like himself. We shared breakfast on the terrace, where he went on at length about his political preoccupations, and then we went to play tennis. I wasn't skilled at the game and he soon had me perspiring and chasing after the ball as he whacked it hard across the net. Finally, breathless and aggravated that I was spending the morning running rather than actually playing, I snarled, "Can you at least try to not humiliate me?"

He paused, wiping sweat from his brow with a towel, peering at me from over his damp glasses. "Humiliate you . . . ?" he echoed, and then, as I stood there watching in confusion, the blood drained from his face. He swayed. The racket he held dropped from his hand. "I feel faint," he whispered. All of a sudden, he collapsed to his knees, clutching his arm. Crying out, I bolted around the net; by the time I reached him, he was prone on the court, groaning. "A doctor," he said through colorless, pinched lips. "My heart . . ."

Screaming toward the house, I cradled him in my arms as he gave a spasm and then, to my wail of horror, went still.

Misia and the servants raced from the villa. We bundled him in the car and drove at breakneck speed to the clinic in Cannes, but by the time we arrived, it was too late.

At fifty-two years of age, the same age as me, the man I had planned to marry was dead.

"COCO, DARLING, you must eat something. You cannot go on like this." Misia spoke from the doorway of my bedroom; without looking up, I said, "Leave me alone. I'm not hungry."

"But you must eat." I heard the clack of her heels cross the threshold. "It's been four days. It wasn't your fault. He had a coronary. It happens. He was ill and he—"

I whirled around. I had not seen myself since his death, but I could imagine the sight I presented, the disheveled shock of it reflected in Misia's recoil. "Shut up," I hissed. "You *wanted* him dead. You hated him! You've hated every man I ever loved. Go away. I don't want you here. I never want to see you again."

"Oh, Coco," she said, and the tremulous pity in her voice, in her open hands as she reached out to me, dislodged the cold stone inside my chest, the ember of my hope and illusions charred to ash. Once again, someone I loved had deserted me; once more, I was left stranded, struggling to absorb the unexpected blow. Only this time, I felt as though I had no strength to withstand it. I did not fail to recognize the irony that only days before Iribe's arrival, I had doubted our commitment. It gnawed a wound in my broken heart, a splinter of guilt driving home my lifelong fear that I was not worthy of love. Grabbing the nearest object, which happened to be a half-empty glass of water, I threw it at Misia. She ducked in time, the glass shattering against the wall behind her.

"*Go away!*" I shrieked.

She bolted from the room, but she did not leave. She sent up Lifar, who had arrived as planned for a visit and found me grieving. "Coco," he said, coming toward me without any fear, his beautiful features drawn with worry. "You cannot do this. Misia is just trying to help. She is distraught for you. Please, let us do something to comfort you."

"There is nothing anyone can do," I whispered. Seeing him brought back the vivid reminder of his own wretched agony on the day Diaghilev had died. I clapped my hands to my mouth and started to sob, my legs giving way as he caught me in his arms. "No one can do anything," I heard myself say through choking breaths. "No one. He left me alone. They always leave. Why? Why does nobody stay?"

He cradled me against his broad chest. I didn't see or hear anyone else in the room until he whispered, "We must fetch the doctor. She is hysterical. She needs a sedative . . ."

THE SYRINGE PRICKED MY ARM; a cool pulse turned to warmth as the injection shot into my veins. The doctor from Cannes, who had overseen Iribe's corpse, smiled at me. "There, now. This will help you sleep. You must not take it so to heart, mademoiselle. You're making yourself ill, and your friends are very anxious for you. Rest now. Tomorrow, you'll feel better."

It was easing, the terrible pain. Disappearing into vaporous nothingness. I sighed. Oblivion.

It was all I wanted now.

VI

I did not recover. I knew I never would recover, not this time. Every loss—every death, every abandonment, every betrayal from the time I'd been a child—was unearthed, stripped of its layers of lies and myth. Exposed.

It showed in my face; it calcified in my heart.

I was not the same woman when I returned to Paris in the autumn of that year. I had dictated my latest collection over the telephone to my *premières* without caring if it made an impact, though it did, for my work always thrived on misfortune, and my sleeveless azure lamé evening gown caused a sensation. My staff noticed the change in me at once. The deference they showed me, the caution; it was palpable. I wasn't as I had been after Boy, lost in a rage of smoke. Now, cruelty became my defense, a shield to deflect anything that did not serve my purpose, which was to survive, no matter what.

God, or whatever pitiless deity ruled our fates, had forsaken me.

I would never forsake myself.

MY BATTLE WITH SCHIAPARELLI played out before the eager press. Those final years before the cataclysm sped past were nothing but an escapist return to foibles, with hemlines dropping and everything festooned in beads and feathers. Nights whirled away at champagne-drenched parties held under Chinese lanterns, on floors fitted with tiny springs to add buoyancy to the dance. I attacked Schiaparelli with everything in my arsenal. While she became ever more extravagant and superficial, her black gloves spiked with red satin fingernails, her blue leggings showing under flounced dresses, I cleaved to elegance, though I did succumb to the rage for shoulder pads and pale satin luxury. I denounced her in interviews as a futurist with nothing to say of the future, an optical illusion. She retorted, "Chanel launched the sailor sweater and short skirt, but I took her sweater, changed the line, and *voilà*—Chanel is finished!" Colleagues took sides; *Time* magazine put Schiaparelli on its cover and pronounced her "the new genius in fashion." *Harper's Bazaar* proclaimed, "Chanel remains the quintessence of restraint in an unrestrained world." Magazines delighted in our rivalry because it sold copies. They were not engaged in a life-or-death struggle for their reputation, as I was.

At the annual lavish costume party held by the Comte de Graumont, Schiaparelli showed up in an aquarium-print sari and a wig piled to pompadour heights, speckled with amphibious-looking gewgaws. I had never seen her up close before, marking her long face and bovine eyes; on her arm was none other than the mustachioed Spanish artist Salvador Dalí, along with his scowling Russian-born wife, Gala.

I wore white silk from head to toe. Bronzed from my recent time on the Riviera, my hair coiled in loose waves and pearls dangling from my throat, I sallied forth to introduce myself. Schiap, as her friends called her, seemed bemused; Dalí expressed himself "honored beyond words"— which was just as well, for I smiled at Schiap and said, "Shall we prove we needn't quarrel in public?" and invited her to dance. She was delighted, exhibitionist that she was. The Graumonts' balls were notorious for a liberal mingling of sexes, with men dressed as Marie Antoinette and women as Hitler, complete with his block-square mustache. Schiap threw herself into my challenge with abandon as I guided her around the crowded dance floor, closer and closer to the candles stuck in wax at the corners. Her glazed smile was directed outward, away from my face, to the crowd mesmerized by our pas de deux.

Flame seared her hem. I gasped and leaped away. The delighted guests swarmed her with bottles of soda water and sprayed until her gown was a sopping wreckage, assuring she did not go up in a blaze. As she glared at me through now-crooked false eyelashes, mascara streaking her face, I murmured so only she could hear, "Now you will remember that a little goes a long way."

A caw of high laughter erupted, turning everyone toward the tables. There, clutching the side of a chair as he cackled uproariously, with malicious glee, was Salvador Dalí.

I winked at him.

IN THE SPRING OF 1936, France elected a new left-wing coalition, the Popular Front. Our new socialist premier was Jewish, prompting the dailies to blare: "France under the Jew!"

Since Iribe's death, I had closed my ears to politics. I heard (as everyone did) and read in newspapers (as many did not) of Hitler's stranglehold on Germany, his tirades at the podium denouncing Marxism and the malign Jewish plague overtaking Europe, but I put it out of my mind.

But not for long. The unrest soon struck home. That spring, the working class held the largest strike ever seen, hoisting their petards and marching in the streets. The infection spread; one morning I crossed the Place Vendôme to my shop to find my entry barred, my seamstresses and saleswomen blocking the door as cameras flashed. They refused to let me pass, chanting some slogan that rang in my ears as the reporters turned their attention on me. Fleeing back to the Ritz, I telephoned my lawyer in a rage, threatening to sack the entire lot.

René advised caution. As he had with the Wertheimer fiasco, he suggested moderation, a meeting with my workers to hear their complaints.

"Meeting?" I cried. "I'll close my atelier first. I had to work like a mule for everything I own. I will not give them what they have not earned."

I might as well have shouted to the wind. After several days of the strike, our new premier signed an agreement granting the working class everything I had predicted. The people took their victory to the streets. Seething at being locked out of my own shop, I dismissed three hundred of my staff. I would have fired more had René not advised me to relent, lest my business suffer irreparable damage. Other designers who had refused to conform to the law had found themselves coming to work to deserted ateliers.

I did relent, because I had no choice. But my harsh rule, which had ensured my success for over thirty years, grew harsher. Everyone who worked for me now knew that a single infraction, a single instance of tardiness or sloppy work, would show them the curb.

They had their benefits. In return, I would exact a heavy price.

NINETEEN THIRTY-SEVEN CAREENED INTO 1938.

La Pausa became my haven, my nightly injections of the sedative Sedol my refuge. My insomnia returned worse than ever, until I couldn't sleep without a dose. Misia took furtive trips with me to Switzerland, where we could buy drugs without prescriptions. I refused to concede that I was dependent, even after seeing the terrifying results of addiction when Jojo Sert's young mistress perished of advanced tuberculosis and an enslavement to morphine.

Growing fear over the economic instability incited the rich to export their assets, costing the Banque de France millions and the Popular Front its power. In Spain, the brutal civil war sent thousands of refugees across the border; in England, King Edward abdicated to marry Wallis Simpson. I sent a gift to the royal couple and a consoling letter to Churchill, inviting him to La Pausa, as he had helped draft the abdication speech and was heartbroken.

During his visit to La Pausa that final summer, Churchill was beset by what he called his Black Dog—a pervasive melancholy from which he found relief only when he turned to his writing or watercolor painting. He spent the weeks at my villa working on both, while his wife and I attended to his comfort and shook our heads over the Simpson affair that had turned England upside down. Before he left, Churchill advised, "You must prepare to leave Europe at a moment's notice, Coco. I fear war is upon us."

Like the rest of the world, I did not heed his warning.

VII

How did we let the cataclysm happen? It was quite simple, really. Like everything unexpected, it crept through the back door while no one but Churchill was watching.

The spring season of 1939 saw Schiaparelli and me again in a full duel, her collection dominated by sulfuric yellow and plum purple gowns embroidered with the silhouettes of faces and cellophane butterflies, topped by monumental grosgrain hats. I countered her with camellia-print dresses, Gypsy-inspired evening wear in the defiant tricolor of the French flag, as well as expanded prêt-à-porter pieces that included truncated pressed-pleat jackets over ruffled blouses and tweed slacks, all in additional sizes for petite women—a first among my peers.

In September, Hitler invaded Poland; we sat, stunned, listening to the news over the wireless at La Pausa, Misia letting out a howl of despair for her native land. General mobilization began against Germany. Soon thereafter, upon my return to the Ritz, I received a telegram from my nephew André, who was living in Lembeye, near the Pyrenees, in a house I had bought him after his chronic bronchial issues took a turn for the worse. Despite his medical condition, France had called him to service. He entrusted his wife, Katharina, and daughter to me.

With his telegram in hand, I turned to Misia. "I think I should close the atelier." I had not articulated the thought until this moment, yet as soon as I spoke, I realized that deep down the decision had been building all along, ever since the strike had forced me to concede to my workers. I had enough money. I had saved far more than I spent, my frugality ingrained in me since childhood, and I had the sense that now was the right time to retire. It would be a difficult adjustment, no doubt; one I might find cause to regret, but with the terrible news all around me, it would also be a sensational gesture of solidarity with my country as we braced for conflict. Once again, war tendered me an opportunity. Only this time, rather than profiteering, I would walk away with my head high, unfettered by a struggle that suddenly felt pointless.

"You would do that?" Misia regarded me through hollow eyes. I'd expected an incredulous burst of laughter. After all these years, how could I even entertain the idea, much less feel at peace with it? But her desolate expression and subsequent silence only reflected what I felt. She did not protest as she might have on any other occasion. While we had been through one war and survived it, this time both of us knew it would be different. Hitler's savage reprisal on Poland and pitiless advance across Europe signaled a darker twist to German aggression. Cornered after the first great war by Allied powers and a treaty that had brought Germany to its collective knees, they would now wreak their vengeance.

"It is not the time for fashion," I said. "After this, none of us can make dresses again."

Did I know what was coming? I believed I did. But I was the only designer in Paris who proceeded to gather my staff and inform them of my decision. My atelier at rue Cambon, as well as my shops in Biarritz, Deauville, and Cannes, would close indefinitely; I would continue to sell my perfume and jewelry but nothing else. For that purpose, I would retain a small staff; the rest were to leave by the end of the week. Outraged, convinced I was punishing them for their defiance during the strike, my workers appealed to the labor board. Lucien Lelong, president of the Chambre

Syndicale, which oversaw the fashion industry in Paris, took me to lunch to convince me to keep my shop open, citing that as during the First World War, we would be required to hold charity shows and fashion auctions, perhaps even design uniforms for the military.

I snorted. "I doubt the swastika will make a suitable accessory."

Perhaps something else motivated me, something unvoiced—a bitter disillusionment with everything in my life. Iribe's unexpected death and my rivalry with Schiaparelli, the advent of another war that would compel me to adapt as the world fell into chaos; perhaps it had all finally sapped me of my relentless drive.

At night, alone in the Ritz, I smoked and looked out to the Place Vendôme and the streets beyond, the lights blacked out in case of air raids. Though the Germans had recently swept into Denmark and Norway, life still went on around me, my friend Lifar still dancing at the Ballets Russes, the cabarets, bars, and restaurants still thriving. I had shuttered my atelier but Paris remained open, exuberant, even though everyone of status was losing male servants and relatives to the draft, bundling up their children to dispatch them to safety in the country, storing valuables in safes before taking residence in easily vacated hotels. Our memory of the last war permeated our existence. Only now, our haunted déjà vu had a quality of exhaustion about it, a resigned wait for the inevitable. Most of my intimates, such as Cocteau and Misia, declared they would never abandon Paris. After all, the Germans had not invaded the city before. I shared their sentiment, even if it increasingly began to sound more like desperation than defiance.

Nevertheless, I doubted. Had I made an impulsive error in closing my atelier? Was I the first to surrender in a conflict that had thus far yet to take its toll?

Only time would tell, I thought, turning back to my suite. I took the low staircase leading to my garret bedroom, as austere as a nun's cell; I had paid the hotel to install it so I could have a quiet place to rest, with nothing near me save Boy's ticking watch, which I faithfully wound every day. Nestled within crisp white sheets, I let my mind drift backward in time, to my youth in Moulins, Vichy, and Royallieu, reliving my frenetic yearning to escape, those first awkward hats, the disappointments and compromises, until I reached the hour when Boy took my hand.

He was still here with me, tangible, his dark green eyes warm, his thick hair tousled as he leaned over me, a satyr of musk, to whisper, "Remember, Coco, you are only a woman . . ."

For the first time in years, I slept without my sedative.

A SIMULTANEOUS KNOCKING at my suite door and the insistent ringing of my telephone jolted me awake. Stumbling down the stairs, I grappled for the phone receiver; it was Misia on the other end, babbling frantically: "They're coming into Paris, Coco! The Germans—they are invading. You must come to the house at once. Jojo is here with me. We'll hide and—"

"Misia," I said, cutting her off, for she had telephoned me several times in the past few weeks with similar dire predictions, "I must call you back. Someone's at the door."

The Ritz's maître d'hôtel waited on my threshold; with an apologetic incline of his head, he relayed the terrifying news as if he was informing me about a temporary shortage of hot water. "Mademoiselle, I fear I must inform you that our defenses have crumbled. The wireless reports that German panzer divisions crossed the Ardennes and are marching upon the city; we are in imminent danger of air strikes by their Luftwaffe. The metro is closing down. Herr Elminger has advised me to inform all residents that while we plan to remain open and will do our best to accommodate, we cannot guarantee anyone's safety."

I knew the Ritz's longtime director was serving in the army; his deputy director, Herr Elminger, was a Swiss citizen who had employed his native land's much-vaunted neutrality to keep the 150-room hotel, a bastion of Paris, running as smoothly as possible. If he advised what amounted to an evacuation, then the situation must warrant it. Misia, it seemed, had not been exaggerating this time.

"How long do we have?" I asked, thinking of my shop across the place

Vendôme, of my apartment now crammed with my objets d'art since vacating my residence on Faubourg Saint-Honoré—my priceless statues and antiques, my gowns and the other detritus of my wandering life. I couldn't take any of it with me, and as I thought of leaving it behind, risking everything I owned to the marauding Germans, I experienced a viselike tightening in my chest.

"Not long," he replied. "Personally, I would suggest sooner rather than later, mademoiselle. Many of our residents are leaving now. The roads out of the city are reportedly already very crowded."

"Yes, of course." I paused, trying to get my bearings. "I wish to pay my bill in advance to hold my suite for two months, in case this . . . all turns out differently. Will that be agreeable?"

He nodded. "We will do whatever we can, unless the Nazis make reservations."

I almost laughed at his droll remark. "And I'll need a chauffeur," I said, "if you can possibly find one. I can pay whatever is required. Also, please send up a chambermaid to help me pack my suitcases."

As he nodded once more and departed, I turned in a daze back to my suite. For a paralyzing moment, I had no idea what to do next. I stood barefoot in my pajamas, clenching and unclenching my hands, as bewildered as the day I had arrived before the gates of Aubazine.

When the flustered chambermaid arrived, I set her to packing my traveling trunks. Wrapping Boy's watch in a handkerchief, I slipped it into my coat pocket and left my suite to push through the frantic crowd of fleeing guests on the staircases, hastening down the narrow passage connecting the hotel's bar and back entrance to rue Cambon.

In the distance, the disconsolate wail of the air-raid siren on the Eiffel Tower shattered the June air. Outside the shop, the street remained eerily deserted, as though it was just another morning with people still indoors, brewing coffee as they blinked away the excesses of the night. Inside my shop, I found Hélène and my loyal *première*, Madame Aubert—the only two of my staff I had retained—coiffed, dressed in uniform black, and standing at attention behind the counters. They looked up at me with stupefied expressions, much as I imagined I must have looked in my suite, until I barked: "What are you doing here, waiting like fools for customers? Have you not heard? The Germans are upon us. Quick, we must close the shop. Those bottles of perfume and the jewelry"—I stabbed my hand at the vitrines—"bring them up to my apartment."

Leaving them, I took the staircase to the third floor, grappling for my keys and unlocking the mirrored double doors. They opened onto a scene suspended in time—and the sight of it, like a serene oasis in the midst of the growing clangor in my head, brought me to a pause.

Slowly, as though I might disturb a fragile spell, I moved down the entryway lined with my Coromandel screens, their lacquered surfaces festooned with women in wind-flung kimonos astride herons, the wraithlike clouds floating above soaring volcanoes beckoning me to linger and admire a world untouched by time. Misia's two blackamoors, which I had not been able to part with, seemed to welcome me deeper within, the clack of my heels silenced by the thick beige carpet as I glanced toward the looking-glass kaleidoscope of my salon. I turned in the opposite direction, through my vaulted dining room into my sitting room, where more of my concealing screens—the most exquisite and antique, inherited from Boy—glimmered in a patina of scarlet and gold, like flame against the neutral-colored furnishings and floor-to-ceiling shelves lined with my leather-bound books.

Powdery light drifted through the windows. At my rolltop desk, I went still, my gaze drifting from the small gilt-frame painting of a lion propped above the desk, downward to my tortoiseshell fan with its embedded opalescent mother-of-pearl stars, set carelessly next to a stack of my embossed cream stationery.

As I let myself caress the fan, I was overwhelmed by how tenuous, how unbelievably fickle, life could be. Would I see these precious objects again? When, if ever, would I return to this place which had for so long sustained me?

"Mademoiselle?"

Turning about with a stifled gasp, I saw Hélène and Lucie at the threshold with armfuls of my perfume and jewelry stashed in boxes. "Where should we put these?"

My voice, when it came, was hoarse. "Under the dining room table. Pull the blinds and curtains when you're done. You must both leave. There's nothing left to do here."

Lucie went; Hélène hovered in the doorway, uncertain. "Will you stay?" she whispered.

I shook my head, returning my gaze to my fan. "No. There's nothing left for me, either," and I stood with my back to her, waiting until I heard her retreat. Only then did I remove Boy's watch from my pocket to tuck it back inside one of the desk drawers. I allowed myself a single moment, one crumbling instance of weakness, to grieve for what was lost before I, too, left rue Cambon, locking the doors and racing back to the Ritz to make my escape.

I did not look back.

VIII

The driver that the maître d'hôtel located for me went by the name of Larcher and demanded a criminally exorbitant fee. He refused to take my Rolls, arguing that it would only call attention to us. I had to leave my car behind in the Ritz garage and clamber into his rattling Cadillac with its grease-stained seats, already loaded with his own things. The clamor to leave Paris had taken on a frantic air, with even the most privileged bartering for whatever means of transport they could. Given the circumstances, I could not afford to quibble. Ordering the concierge to stencil my name onto my trunks and store them in the hotel, I left with one suitcase, hoping my other belongings would not end up in some Nazi fräulein's closet.

I had not thought in advance of where to go and debated whether to seek refuge with Adrienne. I decided against it, thinking her home would be too crowded. I elected to travel south to La Pausa instead, until I determined what came next.

We braved the congested roads, inching along among carts piled with belongings and aged relatives, packed buses and private cars wedged between mule-drawn wagons and thousands of people with children in tow, trudging by the roads or heaped on bicycles, wincing every time an airplane droned overhead. It was not long before I realized I'd never make it.

That was just as well. Three days into my journey, word came that Italy had joined Germany and was bombing the Riviera in retaliation for a British air strike on Turin. Behind me, Paris was receiving incendiary strikes on its outskirts, prompting more terrified residents to leave everything behind and flee on foot. I could not have turned back even if I had wanted to.

"We'll go to Corbère," I told Larcher, after paying more for petrol from a roadside government profiteer than I would have for diamonds. "My nephew has a house there."

Corbère was near Pau, close to the Pyrenees on the Spanish border. It was rumored that Franco had struck a pact with Hitler. Perhaps there would be no trouble there.

Banished memories of the past returned to torment me. I had not been out in the world with so little since my youth, and I clutched my suitcase and handbag to me like weapons. As the situation grew more dire, people would turn savage. I saw plenty of evidence of this as we drove. Under a drenching rain, those who had been bludgeoned and robbed sat with faces in their bloodied hands as their children and wives stood by helplessly, ransacked luggage at their feet.

Finally, after days of taking muddy back roads to avoid the chaos, we reached Pau, where an afternoon downpour lifted to admit rain-speckled sunshine. I thought of staying awhile but resisted the temptation, pressing onward to the village of Lembeye. By now, I was traveling blind. I had no idea if Paris had fallen, if the Germans had overrun the city or burned it to the ground; if those of us who had escaped would find ourselves trapped, forced into desperate gambits to get across the border into Switzerland or Spain.

By the time we reached Corbère and my nephew's red-tiled home, I was nearly dead from exhaustion. André's Dutch wife, Katharina, rushed out with my niece as I staggered from the mud-spattered car, every inch of me aching from the long drive. Katharina enveloped me in her embrace as she whispered, "Gabrielle, thank God. We thought something terrible might have happened; the news from Paris . . . it's terrifying."

I had not heard any news but could now assume the worst. Murmuring that I was tired but otherwise fine, I turned to my nine-year-old niece. She had grown since I had last seen her several years ago, when André and Katharina came to visit and I took them out for tea at the Ritz. I recalled a sturdy fair-haired toddler who stuffed her mouth with éclairs until Katharina scolded that she'd get a tummy ache, which indeed she had. Now, she regarded me solemnly, with her mother's blue eyes and André's piquant face, reminding me with a jolt of how my sister Antoinette had looked at her age. I found myself blinking back unexpected tears.

"Tipsy," I said softly, using her childhood nickname. "Do you remember me?"

She nodded. "You're Auntie Coco, the lady with the pearls. When we went to Paris to visit, you gave me éclairs."

I smiled despite my overwhelming fatigue. "Yes, I'm Auntie Coco. But this time *sans* the pearls or éclairs, I'm afraid." I held out my hand to Tipsy as Larcher unloaded my suitcase and bag. "Will you help me inside?"

Without a word, she took my hand and led me into the cozy château.

I SLEPT FOR TWELVE HOURS STRAIGHT. When I finally woke and bathed—the water ran off me black with soot—I went downstairs to the kitchen to sit with Katharina, Tipsy close by my side with her somber expression as we listened to a static-filled broadcast over the wireless that confirmed Paris's surrender to the Germans. They had entered the city in a monstrous parade of their indomitable panzer tanks, marching down the Champs-Élysées as silent crowds gathered to watch—all those who'd failed to get out in time or had been forced to turn back when the roads were blocked by Nazi soldiers. On the Arc de Triomphe and the Eiffel Tower, they hoisted their red flag with the black swastika; Hitler had announced he would arrive to make his tour of the city and decide its fate. Our defeated, craven government defected to Vichy, France's southern capital, where I'd first tried my luck at fame. Already they abased themselves to avoid reprisal, offering to abolish the French Republic and institute a cooperative division between occupied areas and the southern portion of France.

I could not hold back my grief anymore. It came pouring out of me, a gut-wrenching torrent of sobs as I sat with tears sliding down my face and whispered, through choking breaths, "Not a fight. Not one. No one even lifted a finger to stop them."

Katharina started to reach for me, but Tipsy hugged me first, wrapping her thin arms around my neck. "Don't cry, Auntie Coco. Don't be sad. Paris is not dead."

Unable to speak against her bony chest, finally, after days of keeping it pent up inside, I let myself *feel*. Misia and Cocteau; my apartment with my possessions; my shop—they were all still there, as far as I knew.

Paris was not dead. But in my heart, nothing would ever be the same again.

THE WIRELESS WENT OUT on occasion or broadcast only a crackling nothingness that sounded more ominous than any news could be but we eventually learned that Hitler had decided to spare Paris. Instead, he would make the city a prized possession of his Third Reich. Triumphant German-paid announcers took to the air to proclaim that the Nazis were our friends and we need not fear friends—"unless of course you're a Jew or a Communist," I remarked to Katharina. "Then you'd better hide in the cellar." I had started to revert to my former self, gaining resolve as the seclusion of Corbère worked its pastoral magic on me. Despite everything, I was still alive.

Unfortunately, Katharina received word through a contact in the village that the Germans had captured and imprisoned thousands of our soldiers. We feared André might be among them, though we had no way of establishing his whereabouts. Katharina rummaged under the floorboards for a tin filled with money, which brought an unwitting chuckle to my lips, reminding me of my tin in Moulins. Together, we went to the village to pay the contact for more information; he worked in the rural telegraph office and promised to try, but I knew almost at once that he would fail.

"We need to be in Paris to make a proper inquiry," I told Katharina as we returned to the house along the winding path, wildflowers flattening under our feet, the mountains rearing in the distance with nature's majestic indifference. "Maybe I should go there and find out myself."

She gave me a startled look. "You only just left Paris, and the wireless says the Germans are not advancing farther. They may leave us alone here."

"Yes, but André isn't safe, not if he's a prisoner. Someone needs to find him and you have Tipsy. You must stay here. I, on the other hand," I said, with a careless shrug, "have nothing to worry about save myself."

She was not convinced, but over the next few days, as Tipsy enticed me to play ball with her and plait daisies in our hair, I formulated a plan. It was rudimentary and risky, as any movement now would be, but I was still somebody, I explained to Katharina, and not suspect in any way. "I'm a famous designer. I paid for my suite at the Ritz in advance. I can return anytime I want. I know everyone; the Germans wouldn't touch me."

She bit her lip, looking down at her work-chafed hands. Though I had always provided André with ample money for his expenses, he and his wife had elected to live simply, their home rustic and tidy, their needs few. She had more than enough to get her through the next months, while I did not. I had fled Paris with a few articles of clothing and not much else. Indeed, I was down to the last precious drops of my sedative, my syringes and supply of injectable Sedol still packed in my trunks at the Ritz. I wasn't sleeping well; I could barely look in the mirror, stunned by my haggard appearance, my dark-rimmed eyes and gaunt cheeks, my sallow skin and seamed lips, which my one red lipstick and powder compact could not erase. I was seeing myself as I had that horrible night in Vichy when Balsan found me—a woman growing old before her time, only I was not young anymore.

"I am almost fifty-eight, too old to be a refugee," I went on, reaching over to clasp Katharina's hand. "I'm not meant for all this. I must go back. André needs me."

At length, she nodded. "But you must not compromise yourself. Promise me. André wouldn't want it. If it's not safe, if you fear any harm, you must come back."

"Of course," I assured her. I refrained from voicing my belief that coming back might prove even more difficult than my exodus had been. Once I returned to Paris, I could not hope to go unnoticed. Even the Germans—especially high-ranking officers—would know who I was.

"You must be very careful," said Katharina. "These rumors we keep hearing about the Jews . . . They say already in Poland, they're herding them into ghettos like cattle."

"I'm not a Jew. You mustn't worry. I'll find André and bring him home. What else is Auntie Coco good for these days, eh, if not to be a spy?"

Prophetic words, though I did not realize it. Still, as I kissed her good night on the cheek and climbed the stairs to my bedroom to pack, I was more frightened than I would ever admit.

For the first time in my life, Paris had become a place I feared.

TAKING LARCHER, who had eaten his fill of goat cheese and ham, and drunk the one tavern in the village dry, I made my way to Vichy. The ramshackle government holed up in the city was supposedly cooperating with Hitler's new order and many of Paris's displaced elite had sought refuge there, their access to deluxe havens in the Riviera cut off by the bombing.

We were down to petrol fumes by the time we reached Vichy. I was amazed by the utter indifference I encountered—the bistros and restaurants bursting with customers, the fashionable strolling as always down the boulevards. The women, I noted, wore stylish huge hats that were the latest trend, but looked as overblown to me as they had been in 1910. I found accommodation in the garret of a gendarme boardinghouse after plying my name everywhere. Alas, every hotel room was booked, I was told. After taking a tepid bath in a lime-streaked tub, I put on my best jersey ensemble, applied my makeup, and went to the spa restaurant to dine.

I had barely sipped my consommé when a voice cried out, "Coco! Coco, darling, is that really you?" A pretty brunette in a slim tweed skirt and fitted jacket hurried over to me. She smiled with exaggerated relief. "It *is* you. Oh, isn't it marvelous to find a familiar face!"

It took me a moment to identify hers: Marie-Louise Bousquet, one of the many socialites who religiously attended the Graumonts' costume balls. She noticed my hesitation, for she pouted, waving her hand over her person. "Have you forgotten me? I am one of your devoted customers. Look—this is one of your outfits."

"Naturally I remember you," I said, rising to kiss her on the cheeks, though in truth I barely did. "Please, won't you join me? Whatever are you doing in Vichy?"

Out came the familiar tale, no doubt shared by thousands. She had left Paris upon the Nazi invasion with whatever she could carry, but now, "I'm so terribly bored. It really is ghastly here. So *provincial*. They're not at all concerned about anything; indeed, I'm told there is nothing to be concerned about."

"Yes." I glanced at a nearby couple, toasting with champagne and laughing. "I did notice it's like high season here."

My tart remark was overheard; the man at the table swerved in his chair to me and glared. "What do you mean by that?" he demanded.

"I meant," I said, "that people seem very cheerful."

Marie-Louise wasn't a skilled socialite for nothing. Turning a brilliant smile to the scowling man, she purred, "Do you know who this is, monsieur? She is Coco Chanel."

He grunted. He clearly didn't know or care who I was, but his wife, at his side, did, for she nervously touched his shoulder, directing an apologetic look at me as she murmured, "Don't be rude, dear. She is quite famous."

"Is she?" The man turned back to his table. "When? She looks a hundred years old."

My hand clenched my fork. Marie-Louise waved aside the remark, saying to me, "I was hoping you were planning to return to Paris. Tell me you are. I am simply desperate. The Graumonts are still there; so are many of our friends. I'm told it's perfectly safe for us."

I did not fail to detect the emphasis she placed on "us." She meant anyone with the means and status to weather the tiresome setbacks of occupation.

"The Germans don't hate us," she went on. "They love France. They're living at the Ritz, attending the theater and the Opéra, dining out; they have money and they're spending it, just like old times. *Très joli!*" As she laughed with as much élan as the couple at the table, I resisted the sour twist in my gut. "Will you come with me?" she asked. "A woman traveling alone these days is hardly safe, but two of us . . ." She paused. "You have a driver, I suppose?"

I nodded. "But no petrol. We barely made it here."

"I know a government official who can sell us a ration of petrol!" she declared, clapping her hands in delight. Then she winced, looking about. "Everyone wants gasoline these days," she said in a hushed voice. "It's the new contraband. That, and meat."

"A ration won't get us there," I mused, "but it's certainly a start . . ."

It was decided. Marie-Louise would travel with me. We'd leave tomorrow at dawn, to try and avoid any crowding on the road. Although, I mused, as I looked about the restaurant, none of these Vichy fools appeared in any hurry to go anywhere.

The next morning, while Larcher loaded up the car—Marie-Louise's claim of having left with nothing resulted in two suitcases packed to their seams with wrinkled couture—I took a short walk to smoke my last cigarette (another scarcity I was starting to resent). Pausing near a crumbling Roman-era wall, I saw a boy in ragged shorts perched at its end. Something about his hungry gaze and pinched cheeks, his birdlike ankles and wrists, clutched at my heart. Time paused and rolled back: I saw myself and my sisters, in hand-me-down dresses with the hems turned out, scampering through graveyards. I started to approach; all of a sudden, he glanced up at me, gasping as if in startled surprise, and toppled from the wall.

He hit the stony ground before I reached him, emitting a loud cry of pain. As I knelt beside him, footsteps ran up behind me and an anxious voice said, "He's my son!" I looked up to see a pregnant woman in a soiled housecoat, her belly jutting out before her. The boy was moaning, cradling his arm. Turning back to him, I said, "We should not move him. Fetch a doctor. His arm; I think he may have broken it."

"A doctor!" she exclaimed, as the boy lifted plaintive eyes. "How can we afford it?"

Unclasping my handbag, slung on my arm, I removed a crinkled hundred-franc note from my wallet. I was down to my last surplus of cash, too, but couldn't let the boy suffer. I knew hunger and pain; I had felt its fangs in this very city in my youth. As I started to smile at the boy, extending the note, his expression shifted. With astonishing alacrity, he seized the note from my hand, leaped to his feet, and raced off as fast as his skinny little legs could carry him.

Still on my haunches, I sighed, returning my gaze to his mother. She snorted. "Thank you, madame whoever you are. Now, my son and I can eat tonight."

She waddled off, yelling for her truant collaborator. Rising and shaking the dust from my trousers, I started to laugh. In my sorrow over the disaster that had befallen France, I had let a pair of common thieves trick me.

It would not be the last time.

IX

Sandbag barricades barred our entry at the Porte d'Orléans, along with German soldiers holding rifles. Larcher remarked, "This is where our journey ends, mesdemoiselles."

Marie-Louise was already scrambling out to lug her suitcases from the trunk; taking a fistful of francs from my purse, I pressed them into Larcher's palm. "Thank you. I'll be at the Ritz if you need anything." I meant it; I would never have gotten as far as I had without him.

"Good luck." Pocketing the francs, he assisted me to unload my suitcase. He stood at the side of the car in his soiled shirt and trousers, reeking of sweat, as Marie-Louise, a suitcase in each hand and an eager smile on her face despite her dishevelment, piped up, "Ready, Coco?"

"Make sure you have your passport ready," advised Larcher as I passed a hand through my tangled hair and looked uncertainly to the Nazi sentries, who were checking documents one by one before admitting a steady queue of returning refugees. "And don't answer anything more than they ask you." He hawked up a gob of spit. "Fucking Germans. This is the last thing I expected to see, Krauts lording it over us in our own city."

As I joined Marie-Louise in the line, I heard the sputtering wreck of a car we'd taken across France drive off. It occurred to me as I stood under the blazing August sun that I had no idea where Larcher had come from or where he now headed. We had been strangers, tossed together out of panicked necessity, who would probably never cross paths again.

It took over two hours to reach the entry point; the sullen, pimple-faced German youth who reviewed our documentation gave Marie-Louise a frankly lascivious appraisal, which she encouraged with a coy simper, and me a cursory look. Our passports were in order; he waved us through even as I heard a ruckus of protest behind us and half-looked around to see two black-clad thugs with short-muzzled guns detaining an elderly couple sad-dled with bags, roughly herding them into a cordoned-off area.

"Don't look," hissed Marie-Louise. "They're probably Jewish. Those men are Gestapo."

I quickly averted my eyes and kept walking, my stomach in knots. It was one thing to hear of the Nazis' policy, quite another to see it in action. That couple looked as if they were about to faint. They were far too old to pose any threat.

"Where are they taking them?" I asked once we had proceeded far enough from the checkpoint to avoid being overheard. Around us, pedes-trians milled—the habitual assortment of Parisians going about their daily business, though there was a definite edge in the air, a tremor of fear riding everyone. No one made eye contact, did not even glance in our direction, as though two rumpled women carrying suitcases down the street was a daily occurrence.

Marie-Louise shrugged. "Who knows? It's not our problem, is it?"

I supposed she was right. Certainly, I had more pressing issues, princi-pal among them how to reach the Ritz and my suite.

"I can't walk all the way," I said, stopping to catch my breath and letting my suitcase fall as I set a hand to the painful cramp in my side. "I need a taxi."

Marie-Louise paused, looking to the boulevard. There were some vehi-cles, but far fewer than usual. "We could try the metro. It must be running again by now."

I gave her an exasperated look. Did I honestly appear as if I could survive the metro in my state? Stepping to the curb before she could protest, I lifted my hand with another wad of francs visible; within moments, a car stopped. A young man in a beret with a cigarette hanging from his mouth reached across to roll down the passenger window. "Ride, ladies?"

"Yes, please." Even as Marie-Louise gaped in amazement, I pulled open the rear door, flung my suitcase into the backseat and left the door open for her, while I took the passenger side. She squeezed between our luggage; she had scarcely adjusted herself before the car took off, the man saying as he entered the stream of traffic, "Are you French?"

"We are." I eyed the blue pack of Gauloises peeping from his shirt pocket. He noticed, retrieved the pack and a box of matches, and handed them to me. "The Germans are giving them out free, like candy," he told me as I lit one and sighed, sitting back as the smoke filled my lungs. He then treated us to a summary of the events we had missed as he drove toward the 1st arrondissement, where the Ritz was located. Nothing he told us helped ease my apprehension.

"The Germans are everywhere. They've taken over *Parlement*, the Chamber of Deputies, and the Senate in the Luxembourg Gardens. All the major hotels are requisitioned for their use—the Ritz, the Majestic, the George V, and the Raphael, as well as most of the better mansions. We have gas and electricity, for the most part, and our police force remains on duty, but they took down all our flags and replaced them with theirs. Make no mistake: Paris is German now." He puffed on his cigarette, his eyes darkening. "They're like locusts. They must have planned it in advance. They took us over so fast, before we knew it we were watching thousands of them marching in, followed by more tanks and armored cars than you can imagine."

I closed my eyes, inhaled an acrid breath. I could imagine it, but I did not want to, though as we reached the Place Vendôme and the stately Ritz rose into view, I could not avoid the sight of their horrid flag over the sandbagged entry or the sentries with swastika armbands guarding the stairway inside.

Marie-Louise tapped my shoulder. "Coco, are you sure you want to stay here? If they've taken over the hotel . . . maybe you should come with me to stay with my friends?"

"No. I'll be fine." I forced a smile. As the young man jumped out to help me with my suitcase, I turned to Marie-Louise. "Ring me later, yes? I'll be in my suite."

She arched a skeptical brow; she seemed quite sure I would not be in my suite, and it only hardened my resolve. Getting out of the car, I took my suitcase. As I started to turn away to walk to the hotel, the young man said, "Are you *the* Coco Chanel?"

I paused, looking askance at him. "I am."

He doffed his beret. "An honor, mademoiselle. My mother always talked about you, about how fashionable you were, how forward thinking. She loved your clothes, though she could never afford them. And your *parfum*. I bought her a bottle on sale in Galeries Lafayette. She wore a little every day until her death. She said nothing lasts like Number Five, not even love."

Impulsively, I leaned to him, kissing his cheek. He smelled of sweat and tobacco, of youth's unquenchable optimism. As he flushed, I whispered, "Your mother was right."

"YOU NEED AN *AUSWEIS*," repeated the German sentry, barring my passage into the hotel. "A permit," he added, in mangled French. Behind him in the lobby, I could see officers in uniforms and a few civilians; straining to catch sight of someone I knew, the sentry started to wave me back when all of a sudden, the maître d'hôtel who had come to advise me of the Germans' arrival glanced in my direction. He went still, his impervious brow creasing.

For a terrifying moment, I thought he would ignore me, until he stepped to the entrance to say, "This is an esteemed guest of ours, Mademoiselle Coco Chanel. Please, let her pass."

The German, who could not have been more than twenty, if he was a day, squared his shoulders belligerently. "She doesn't have a permit. She must see the *Kommandant* first."

"Dirty as I am?" I retorted, even as the maître d' inclined his head and said, "Yes, I shall see to it, I promise." He reached for my suitcase. I was drenched in perspiration, filthy, and exhausted from my days of travel. My knees almost buckled as I stepped past the sentry, unable to avoid dropping my gaze to the pistol lodged in a holster at his belt. I feared he would detain me, remembering the elderly couple at the Porte d'Orléans; but he appeared uncertain and the maître d' took advantage of his hesitation to cup my elbow and propel me into the hotel.

"Dear God," I muttered as he led me toward the reception area. "Are they all like that?"

He nodded. "Everything we do requires an *Ausweis*. I will see to it, mademoiselle, have no concerns on that account. You are, as always, welcome here. Your trunks are as you left them; I put them in storage. Shall I send them to your room?" He was busying himself at the desk, selecting a key. When he handed it to me, it was not for my suite. He met my perplexed stare. "Mademoiselle's suite has been taken, I'm afraid, though they did not make reservations. I had your furnishings removed to your apartment above your shop. I can offer you a smaller room on the third floor on our rue Cambon side, near your atelier, if that is agreeable?"

"Yes, of course. Thank you." I did not care. A room, an attic: as long as it had a bathroom and running water, it would do. He rang the bell. A bellhop appeared to escort me. "Your trunks will be sent up momentarily," the maître d' said. "Have a lovely stay at the Hôtel Ritz, mademoiselle."

He spoke as he always did, with a smooth inflection that marked him as an expert in catered efficiency, but I saw his gaze flicker past me toward the German officers, and I read his unspoken cue. Better to make myself scarce while I still could.

It was a tiny room compared with my spacious suite, but it had a firm bed, the famous built-in closet that the Ritz's founder had insisted on for all his guests, and a tiled connecting bathroom. Pulling off my soiled attire, I luxuriated in a steamy bath before taking a long nap. After I woke, I rang for tea from room service, and enveloped in a plush white robe, telephoned Misia to tell her I was back. It rang several times before she answered. When she did, she sounded out of breath and the static on the line was so terrible, I could barely hear her.

"I'm in Paris," I shouted into the receiver. "At the Ritz."

"The Ritz?" Static fractured her next words, but not her outraged intent. "Why . . . it's full of Nazis . . . you must . . . Jojo and me . . . Insist!"

I retorted, "What difference does it make where I stay? Every hotel is occupied."

The last thing I wanted was to live with her and Jojo in that overcrowded house on rue de Rivoli, enduring their constant bickering and gargantuan hunger. Jojo had returned to Misia after his mistress's death, but I doubted their reunion would last and would rather not contend with the consequences. Besides, I needed to be at the heart of things if I hoped to find out about André; judging by the insignia-bedecked German officials I had glimpsed in the lobby, the Ritz was that heart.

"It's unpatriotic," Misia fumed. "They are invaders! You must come here with us."

Fearing the telephone line might be tapped I said curtly, "I'm settled here. I paid in advance and need to attend to my shop. I'll see you in a few days," and I hung up.

Irate as always at Misia's unwillingness to heed reason even in the worst of times, I tackled my trunks. Nothing had been touched; my syringes and sedative vials were still stored in the hidden compartment under my folded lingerie, just as I had left them. I selected one of my discreet black evening gowns and a rope of pearls, as happy as a child to have my things with me. I must make an impression, and how better than to appear as I always did, impeccably elegant.

Tonight, I would dine in full view so that Paris would know I was home.

THE HOTEL RESTAURANT was as full as ever, though this time not with its usual coterie of wealthy guests, impecunious writers sleeping with bored aristocratic wives, or querulous longtime residents. Oh, there were still a few I recognized and smiled at graciously as I was led to my table: the rich American heiress and divorcée Laura Mae Corrigan, who'd occupied a suite here for several years; the French film actress and sometime client of mine, Arletty; and several other well-groomed women with companions. But I saw far more Germans in tailored suits or white tie, hair slicked with brilliantine and wingtip shoes polished to such a luster they could have doubled as mirrors, their rubicund faces matching the satisfied triumph in their eyes.

"Will mademoiselle be dining alone?" inquired the waiter as he filled my glass with water and set before me the gilt-edged menu with the night's offerings.

I nodded, unfolding the crisp napkin with its monogrammed *R* and setting it into my lap as I covertly surveyed the room. How so much could have changed in so little time astounded me, and yet it all *appeared* the same: the soft strains of a violin lilting in the background, the clink of fine glass-ware and silver on porcelain plates, the weaving between the white-draped tables of black-clad waiters bearing trays of delicacies. I saw oysters served on bassinets of ice; bloody shanks of steak smothered in spiced *pommes frites* and legumes; lobsters, crab, and other *fruits de mer*—all the many renowned gourmet dishes that had made the Ritz's restaurant one of Paris's most exclusive places to dine.

I ordered a shrimp cocktail and onion soup. I had eaten very sparingly during my journey, subsisting on candy bars and rotten oranges we managed to find along the way, so that my gown hung on me as though I had shrunk. But now my appetite had deserted me. I kept hearing Misia's denunciations in my head—*"It's unpatriotic! They are invaders!"*—and began to doubt my decision to remain here. Perhaps it would be better, or at least wiser, to pack up and move to rue de Rivoli. I would be miserable, no doubt, but at least no one could accuse me of ignoring our nation's plight by hobnobbing with the Nazi horde.

It was then I realized someone was watching me.

At first, it was a curious sensation, a subtle prickling along the nape of my neck. I ignored it, focusing on my meal and even engaging in brief pleasantries with Arletty, who wore too much makeup, as usual, as if the cameras were always rolling, and was half drunk on champagne. She introduced me to her "escort," as she called him, though he was clearly a German officer—a stark-boned young man who practically clicked his heels as he bowed over my hand with absurd gallantry, kissing my fingers and declaring it was a privilege to meet the incomparable Chanel.

"Your shop," he told me, "has proved a source of great distraction and inspiration to my fellow soldiers. Everyone wants to bring home to his wife or sister in Germany a token of the grandeur of Paris, and no token is more esteemed than Chanel Number Five."

I must have looked startled, as indeed I was, for Arletty giggled. "Darling, did you not know your boutique has reopened? Life must return to normal and your staff is making a fortune in sales. You should look in tomorrow. Your perfume is a smashing success."

"I will," I said, smiling as they said good night. I glanced over my shoulder as they went to another table where a corpulent, sweaty man— another Nazi and a hefty one, at that—was gobbling his food while a feminine-looking youth stood by attentively with a serviette.

"That is Reichsmarschall Hermann Göring," said a low voice at my back. "He is the führer's second-in-command, general of the Luftwaffe air squadron."

Swerving in my seat, I found myself looking into a pair of piercing ice-blue eyes.

He was undoubtedly attractive, I noticed that at once, and though he bent over my chair, also quite tall. He had the long limbs of an equestrian; his navy blue suit with a hint of red silk handkerchief in the pocket to match his tie, his dark blond hair gleaming with pomade, his thin lips, aquiline nose, and angular cheekbones reminded me with a start of both Bendor's aristocratic pride and Boy's bold appeal.

I stared hard at him. He took a step back, saying in perfect French, "Allow me to introduce myself. I am Baron Hans Gunther von Dincklage. My friends call me Spatz; it means 'sparrow' in German. And I believe you are . . . ?"

"I think you know who I am," I said, more sharply than I should have.

Not a day back in Paris and already I had a German hovering over me—a handsome one, yes, and one who appeared to be some years younger than myself, as well, but a German nevertheless.

"Of course." He set a hand to his chest, his index finger encircled by a silver ring. "I know who you are. I have known for quite some time, in fact. You see, we have met before."

"We have?" I studied him. "I don't think so, monsieur. I would remember."

I was starting to turn back to my plate when he said, "It was years ago in Monte Carlo; you wore black like you do tonight, and pearls. I didn't approach you because you seemed rather taken at the time with a certain Russian archduke."

I froze. Then, without betraying my sudden fear, I turned back to him. He was smiling. In a sudden rush of memory, I saw him standing on the yacht I had rented for my fortieth birthday, a sleek man who followed me with his eyes. He had been talking to Vera Bate.

"Ah." His smile widened. "I see you remember now."

"You were at my party. The night I met—" I stopped myself just in time. I should not advertise my relationship with Bendor. While he had been a vocal supporter of Hitler in the past, he was still British and therefore might be considered a potential enemy of the Third Reich.

"I was." He glanced at the empty chair opposite me. "May I join you?"

How could I refuse? I was in a room filled with Germans, a few seats from one of Hitler's foremost lackeys.

I nodded. He sat. The waiter hurried over. Spatz ordered a bottle of wine—a very expensive one. While we waited for it to be uncorked and aired, he said offhandedly, "May I ask why you are in Paris? I had understood you closed your atelier and left."

I curled a hand at my chin, affecting nonchalance. Was I under suspicion already? I told myself to remain calm. I had done nothing.

"I reside in Paris, here at the Ritz, in fact. My shop is now open again for business. Can I not attend to my affairs without being questioned?"

"Naturally." Taking the bottle from the waiter, he poured wine into my empty glass. He sniffed the aroma before tasting. "Ah, yes. Splendid. No one makes wine like the French."

"You don't have wine in Germany?" I replied tartly, and again, I winced inwardly at my tone. At this rate, I would end up arrested before the night was done.

"We do, but"—he leaned to me with a boyish smile that crinkled the corners of his eyes—"it's not very good. Too fruity. Besides," he added, reclining back in his chair, "I have spent far fewer years there than here. As an attaché to the German embassy on the rue de Lille, I have lived in Paris off and on since 1928. I am not a full-blooded German; my mother was English, you see, and I am from Hannover originally. I even once played polo in Deauville." He paused, his pale eyes assessing me. "I believe you are familiar with the game?"

"I am," I said. I didn't know whether to excuse myself and bolt or indulge him. He intrigued me, if only because he seemed to know more about me than I had expected.

"I am now in service to our foreign minister, Ribbentrop, who is charged by our führer to oversee various affairs of importance in Paris," he explained, though I had not asked. "I've been assigned to the textile division of our military administration. Textiles are your trade, as well, yes?"

"You know I am a designer. So, yes, you could say that." The wine went straight to my head, as I hadn't had a drink in weeks. I found myself wanting to flirt with him. It was inexplicable, the impulse, and as Misia would have said, inexcusable. He was one of *them*, the invader. Yet something about him drew me; there was a hint of wry humor in his manner, an almost overt tone of ridicule, not directed toward me but at the absurd situation we found ourselves in, with the world askew all around us.

"You must be well connected," I finally remarked. I was reaching into my beaded handbag for my cigarette case. As soon as I looked up, he had his lighter extended. It was a Cartier like mine. He lit my cigarette, smiling as I eyed him. "Do you know a lot of important people?" I said. I was probing, testing him, and he knew it. I could see the knowledge dancing in his eyes, mischievous and curious, ready to play. A man of evident sophistication who had moved in society circles, he was familiar with the ploy.

Inclining again to me, he whispered, "I know Reichsmarschall Göring is a morphine addict and the Ritz manager had to install a huge new tub in his suite because he believes long baths in scalding water can relieve his vice."

I repressed a gasp. Looking over my shoulder to the fat Luftwaffe commander, Dincklage added, still in that hushed tone, as if he was imparting a state secret, "But that won't cure his addiction to diamonds or ladies' dresses, as Madame Corrigan has so conveniently discovered. He took over her suite, you see, evicting her, so she now must pay her rent by selling him certain pieces of her priceless collection, which he likes to wear along with purple tulle and silk organza while dancing the waltz with his boys."

I had to bow my head, pressing my knuckles to my mouth to curb my laughter. Spatz leaned back again, his smile blasé. "Probably not very important in the scheme of things," he said, taking up his wineglass. "But rather amusing nevertheless, wouldn't you agree?"

I did. For the first time since the Nazis had swarmed in, I could reduce their fearsome darkness to the ludicrous image of Göring flouncing around his suite in a gown and Laura Mae Corrigan's tiara.

"We are human," Spatz added, uncannily reading my thoughts. "For the moment, we hold power. But"—he shrugged—"who's to say for how long? Those of us caught in the middle, mademoiselle . . . well, as history has shown, we must find the easiest way to survive."

I found myself nodding. "Yes, we must. I certainly intend to."

He made a complacent sound in the back of his throat, a seductive hum of agreement. "I thought you might. So. I have told you a secret. Now, it is your turn to tell me one. Such as, why are you in Paris? I promise it will remain strictly *entre nous*. I am a man of honor. My word means everything to me." His voice turned serious. "I would also like to offer my assistance, if I can. I have a feeling you are searching for something."

"Do you?" I lit another cigarette. "Well, I am indeed searching for *someone*: my nephew, to be precise. And if we are to be friends, the first thing you should do is call me Coco."

X

Spatz was not staying at the Ritz. In his nonchalant manner that made
everything he said sound less significant than it was, he told me he had an
apartment on rue Pergolèse—a trophy obtained from a recent affair with a
"very attractive and rich Parisian hostess who," he added, with a sly wink,
"is not one hundred percent Aryan." His lover had felt compelled to leave
Paris with her complacent husband, entrusting their apartment to his care.

He was far more experienced in wielding his charm than any man had
a right to be, and I sensed that while his interest in me was genuine, as was
his offer to assist, he had more than one purpose in mind. He had made
that clear toward the end of the evening, after he insisted on paying my bill
and escorted me into the reception area, where the officers and their various
companions mingled, smoked, and drank crème de menthe aperitifs.

"Shall I call on you tomorrow after I have made my inquiries?" he
asked as we lit our after-meal cigarettes. I resisted scowling at the sight of
Arletty draped on a chaise lounge by a window, gazing adoringly at her
young officer as he regaled her with some tale. I saw other women likewise
engaged, perfumed hands lightly grazing uniformed arms, demure glances
through mascara-laced lashes promising enticement. As Arletty herself

had said, apparently life must indeed return to normal—if welcoming the Nazis as guests could ever be called normal.

"No, I'm busy tomorrow," I said. "I have my shop to see to and then I want to visit some friends." I gave him one of my dazzling, noncommittal smiles to ease my rebuff. I had enjoyed our time together more than I was willing to admit, but I had no intention of granting him further leeway until he delivered on his promise to look into André's situation. "You have my room number and that of my shop," I added, "in case you find out anything. You can telephone me."

"But you are not otherwise engaged for the evening?" he persisted, again in that informal manner that indicated he was not dissuaded in the least.

I paused before stubbing out my cigarette in a nearby ashtray. "Who can say what tomorrow may bring?" I held out my hand. If he leaned over to kiss my fingertips or held my hand in his, I resolved that I would accept whatever information he might ferret out of his superiors, but that would be it. I would not be seduced simply because a well-connected attaché sought to add me to his no doubt already impressive roster of conquests.

To my disconcertion, he shook my hand once before letting go. "Good night, Coco," he said, and he turned to depart, leaving me standing there, feeling somewhat bemused.

He had surprised me. That rarely happened anymore.

I SLEPT BETTER THAN I HAD since the occupation, buoyed on a light injection of my Sedol. I had relied on increasingly smaller doses of my liquid laudanum while away. When I awoke refreshed and without the cloudy bewilderment I'd grown accustomed to, I realized that I must wean myself from my dependency. Thinking of Göring submerged in his scalding baths added impetus: I had no idea if obtaining my sedative would be possible in the occupied city and did not want to end up resorting to black-market profiteers.

As luck would have it, after I dressed, the telephone rang. I did not answer immediately; I thought it might be Spatz, pressing his advantage. If so, he could leave a message with reception, for I doubted he could have discovered anything in so short a span of time. The phone stopped ringing but then clamored again, until I picked it up and Misia burst out, "Darling, I'm wondering if you have any of our blue drops?"

She sounded breathless again, almost frantic. I understood. She had not left Paris; secluded in the house with Jojo and his taunting humor, watching the Germans roll in, she had resorted to dosing herself around the clock and now suffered severe withdrawal.

"Yes, I'll bring some by this afternoon," I told her, gritting my teeth. Now, I had no choice but to exercise self-control, for she would prove voracious once she determined I could provide her with the coveted drug.

"Oh, thank God." She sighed. "I am desperate. Jojo is just not taking any of this seriously. He wants to invite them to our home—here, in our living room! He says we need the money. They've declared Picasso and other artists degenerates, but they'll buy any paintings on the side. He thinks he can earn commissions if we—"

I interrupted her. "Yes, yes. We can talk about it later. I need to get to the shop."

She went silent. Then she said, in audible disbelief, "The shop? I thought you had closed it. You're not planning on selling your clothes to these savages, are you?"

"Misia." I tempered my voice, worried about surveillance on the line. "They ordered all the businesses to reopen. Everything: the stores, the cinemas and theaters, the publishing houses and couture salons. Lucien Lelong, Madame Grès, Balenciaga, and other designers are preparing collections even as we speak. I simply cannot—"

"Schiaparelli isn't! She went to America. So has Mainbocher. Vionnet closed her atelier, as well, and Molyneux is in London." She took a heaving breath before she added, "Coco, it would be a scandal. A national disgrace. None of them is as famous as you are. And how on earth do you even know those other designers are working? You only returned yesterday."

I went silent. The line crackled and hissed. Spatz had told me about the foreign minister's command that all businesses in Paris must resume regular operations, except the newspapers and the wireless, which were now subject to censored oversight.

"You would not dare indulge . . . ," Misia began. Then she thought better of delivering additional condemnation, knowing that as I refused to answer, I might hang up. "Fine," she said, "do whatever you want. You always do, no matter what I say."

"It's just my perfume," I said. "That is all. My staff had to open. They are selling Number Five and my other fragrances, nothing else. My atelier will remain closed."

"Oh." She went quiet for a moment. "Well. I suppose it can't be helped."

"No, it can't. Misia, I really do have to go. I'll see you soon. Please, don't worry. I am fine, honestly. I just have to do this. André, he . . . he is—" All of a sudden, my voice broke. Before I started confessing things that must never be said over a telephone, I put down the receiver and ended our call.

Going to my trunk, I took out three syringes and vials. I'd help her as much as I could under the circumstances but, I thought as I walked out the door, I must help myself first.

HÉLÈNE AND MADAME AUBERT were delighted to see me once I reassured them I understood they had to open the shop. We were doing a brisk business; German soldiers on leave stood outside my ground-floor boutique, queuing up to purchase my fragrances. I entered through the back door; Hélène showed me the empty stores, saying, "They're buying up even the display bottles, mademoiselle. They want your logo to show back home, to prove they were here. They're not at all rude, but we simply can't keep the perfumes in stock. We had to hire back five of our employees to deal with the demand. It has been like this every day. We're down to our last hundred bottles or so. By tomorrow or the next day, we'll be completely sold out."

Checking the account tallies, I saw she was right. I lifted my eyes to her. "What about the bottles we put upstairs in my apartment?"

"Gone," she said. "I'm sorry, but we had no other option."

"No, no. They want perfume and we've been ordered to sell it. It cannot be helped," I said, echoing Misia. "Let me call Pierre Wertheimer. He will just have to increase our standing order from the distributor. After all the grief he put me through, it's the least he can do."

Madame Aubert said, "We already tried. Monsieur Wertheimer is not available."

I frowned. "Why not?"

"He's not in France. He and his brother left for New York. When we called the distributor, we were told that Bourjois and its affiliates have been entrusted to their cousin, Raymond Bollack. He refused to take our calls. He will only speak to you."

"Fine." I grabbed my account books and went to the staircase. "I'll phone him from my apartment. Sell whatever we have left in stock and I'll get us more."

I spent the remainder of the afternoon wrangling over the telephone with Raymond Bollack, the newly appointed overseer of my Parfums Chanel subsidiary. He was obstinate, as only someone of the Wertheimer blood could be. He drove me into a frenzy, citing the higher costs of transportation and other obstacles implemented by the Germans in order to exact an additional percentage for increasing a supply of my perfume. I ended up shouting at him as I paced my living room, dragging the telephone wire behind me until I almost yanked it from the wall. I had to concede, there was no way around it, but I emerged from my argument with him determined once again to escape the stranglehold of my eighteen-year partnership with the Wertheimers. Court injunctions and lawsuits had failed; I no longer held a position on the board of my own company, after paying a ransom in legal fees. How long was I expected to tolerate it?

Echoes of my harangue must have been overheard downstairs, for when I went back down to the boutique, now crammed with Germans, Madame Aubert gave me an arch look.

"He's impossible," I spat out. "I'll be back tomorrow." And I stormed out to get a taxi to rue de Rivoli, my anger such that had it not been early evening, with me out in public, I would have dosed myself right there in the backseat with a syringe.

TIME SPENT WITH MISIA relieved some of my frustration. Jojo was in his habitual sarcastic mood, quipping that the Germans would finally make him like the taste of bratwurst. After taking an injection in the bedroom, with me helping to hold the syringe, as her hands were trembling, a much-calmer Misia told me that Cocteau and his lover, the actor Jean Marais, had fled to the Côte d'Azur to seek the hospitality of the writer Colette and her Jewish husband.

"They went to Colette?" I snorted. "Why on earth would they do that? She never liked our sort. Didn't she tell you she was horrified that I was considering marrying Iribe?"

"Oh, yes, she did." Misia's expression turned avid. Bored out of her skin with being cooped up indoors, she was eager for her favorite pastime, gossip, and wasted no time in giving me the details of our wayward playwright's latest plight. "Of course, once she saw our Jean *et* Jean going through opium like it was their last day on earth and drinking her out of everything but seawater, Colette told them they had to leave. She was terrified their antics would draw the attention of a Nazi spy and her husband would be arrested."

"I don't understand. Why would she worry? The Germans are not occupying the south."

Misia glanced at Jojo, who was snoring on the couch after having imbibed an entire bottle of cheap table wine and eaten a plate of disgusting tripe. "There are rumors the Vichy government will do whatever they are told," she said, turning back to me. "Otto Abetz, the Reich's ambassador, hates Jews. Everyone knows he shares Hitler's paranoia of them."

Interesting. It never ceased to amaze me how even in alleged isolation, Misia somehow managed to keep apprised of the wider world. It was also, I thought, rather chilling to hear the Nazi policy declared aloud, considering that they were right outside our door.

"And Lifar?" I said, changing the subject. "I haven't told him yet that I'm back. Is he still dancing?"

"He never stopped." She grimaced. "He even welcomed Hitler personally when the führer came here to visit. He gave him a tour of the Opéra. According to Lifar, Hitler took quite a liking to him. He claims no one has handled him like that since Diag."

"Yes, well," I chuckled, "he's always been vain. He thinks he's so beautiful, no one can resist."

Misia gave a smug smile. "Still, it could be true; they say Hitler is an odd duck. In any event, Lifar has made himself a target. He should be careful. Not everyone in Paris is as eager as him to welcome the Germans." She paused, regarding me with discomfiting purpose. "And you, my dear, what are your plans? Have you impressed a Nazi or two yourself?"

"Please." I rolled my eyes but she saw right through me, as she invariably did. "Who is he?" she demanded. "Please tell me it's some high-ranking pig like Göring."

"Göring?" I burst out laughing. "Let me tell you about the feared Reichsmarschall . . ."

My story about Göring's eccentricities made her cackle so much that I thought she had forgotten her prior inquisition. Yet as I prepared to leave before curfew—the Germans had set it for nine P.M. and no one wanted to be caught in the street—she helped me into my coat and said, "You must be careful, whatever it is you're doing. Helping your nephew is admirable, but when this is over, there will be repercussions. Lifar's boasting has proved it. The Free French are watching and you don't want to be trapped by your own actions when we kick these swine out."

I nodded, kissing her. "I'm as innocent as a nun these days," I teased, but as I went down to the curb to hail a taxi, her warning stayed with me, gnawing in the back of my mind.

Perhaps it would be safest to pretend I had never met Spatz von Dincklage.

IN THE NEXT WEEKS, as September crawled through sluggish heat into October, I busied myself in my boutique and attended informal gatherings at the Serts'. Lifar came to see me, as slender and bronzed as ever, overjoyed to have me back, kissing me effusively and regaling me with lurid tales of various encounters with German officers who brought their French mistresses or stodgy wives to see him dance but came backstage afterward to fondle him "like a whore."

"Well, you are," I chided, and he laughed.

"How can I help it? They are all so blond and muscular, so Aryan. I tell you," he said, inclining to my ear with his lascivious grin, "we must persuade Cocteau to return. The pickings in Paris this year are so very *ripe!*"

It was all talk, only perhaps in Lifar's case, rather more than that. He had been invited to tour the Ballets Russes in Berlin—an announcement that brought an immediate glower to Misia's face. "You wouldn't dare. Would you flaunt yourself before Hitler himself?"

"I already have," Lifar smirked. "That is why he invited me."

Marie-Louise, who had joined our soirees, mentioned she was hosting lunches where "pleasant" French-speaking Germans, such as Propaganda Director Heller, came to partake of her black-market goods, hear poets, and enjoy dance recitals by Caryathis.

"Didn't you once take lessons from her?" she said to me as I sat at the piano playing one of my old ballads from my days in Moulins. "She was telling us just the other day about how dedicated you were. You wanted to be a professional dancer, or so she claims."

I scoffed. "I never wanted to be a dancer. And how is Élyse even performing at her age? She must be at least seventy by now. I can't imagine it's a pretty sight."

"Actually," said Marie-Louise, "I believe she's almost the same age as you, Coco dear."

I glared at her. Sharing a trip across France with her had been enough of an ordeal; must I endure her stupidity here, too? But she then went on to mention she'd heard the Germans planned to release most of the three hundred thousand French prisoners of war they had interred in camps, now that hostilities were suspended due to our armistice with the Vichy government, and I queried her for as much information as I could.

"Who's in charge of the releases?" I asked. "Where are they being sent?"

She made a moue of surprise. "I have no idea. Why are you so interested?"

"No reason," I said as Misia shot me a look. "I was merely curious, is all."

Later, Misia warned me: "Marie-Louise and her ilk are up to their eyeballs in Nazi friends. You cannot trust her. She'd inform on her own mother for a steak."

Frustrated, I returned to the Ritz that night, debating whether to phone Spatz. I had not heard from him save for one call to my shop to tell me he was still looking into the matter we had discussed. He had made no attempt to see me, which proved more upsetting than I expected, rousing the specter of my vanishing youth. I had learned he was forty-five, almost thirteen years younger than me. I told myself it was better if he stayed at arm's length. After all, British mother or not, diplomatic attaché or otherwise, he was still one of them, and I heard enough gossip from the Serts to know that besides being indiscreet, some of my friends were downright reckless. Yes, we were at another power's mercy, but Arletty had made herself the scandal of Paris for her liaison with her Nazi lover, and those clamoring for resistance had branded Lifar for death. Not that they seemed to mind—Lifar often joked that if he ever went to the scaffold, he wanted to wear a white wig like Marie Antoinette—but as Misia had said, there would be repercussions if the tide of war began to turn against the Germans.

Still, I could not help but feel both insulted and secretly ashamed that Spatz had not persisted in luring me to his bed.

Had I finally lost my appeal?

SEVERAL WEEKS LATER, after another long day at the shop, I entered the Ritz's lobby to find Spatz waiting.

He stood at once from his chair, his hat in his hands, dressed in a gray suit that brought out the pale blue of his eyes, his dark gold hair tousled about his face, without any pomade. The sight of him brought me to a standstill. My pulses leaped.

I did not welcome the sensation at all.

As I made to sweep past him, he said quietly, "I have news."

I paused, glancing coldly at him. "You know my room number. Wait ten minutes."

Once I reached my room, I locked my door with trembling hands and went at once to the bathroom mirror. I looked much as I would have expected—bruised shadows under my eyes, my lips chewed from shouting over the phone at my suppliers. The fatigue and discomfort of living as I did, in this little room without enough air or light, was etched upon me.

Taking up my preferred shade of red lipstick, I applied only enough to rectify my pallor, rubbing a little into my cheeks and running a brush through my hair, grimacing at the white of my roots. I needed to dye my hair again, which meant scouring the decimated department stores or appealing to horrid Marie-Louise to find me the right color on the black market. I was about to spray on perfume when the knock came at the door. I set down the bottle. He would smell it on me and I did not want to seem overeager.

Letting Spatz into my room fractured something inside me—a hidden shell I had not realized I held so close. I crossed my arms as he loomed in the doorway, appearing larger than he was, and if possible, more hesitant than me.

"Well?" I said, keeping my voice level. "You said you had news."

He nodded, turning the rim of his hat in his fingers. "Your nephew André Palasse is not among those scheduled to be released; I don't know why. The reason is beyond my security clearance. There are things I don't get to see, motives no one explains to me."

"Dear God." I turned blindly to my purse, tossed on my dressing table, fumbling for my cigarettes. I lit one, looked up through the smoke to see him still standing there, only inches over the threshold with the door behind him, as though he feared taking another step.

"I think I can still help," he said. "I have a boyhood friend, Captain Theodore Momm. He's been made *Rittmeister*, in charge of mobilizing the French textile industry to serve the war effort. I could ask him to—"

In my anguish, I suddenly ceased to care if he tried to seduce me or pulled out a gun. "Why don't you say what you truly mean?" I turned to him. "It's not my war effort; I never wanted any of this. You and your people—you brought this mess upon the rest of us, and now my nephew could die in one of your filthy camps because of it."

I knew I should not be saying it; I should be submissive, thank him for his time, and ask him to leave, but in that instant, caution was the last thing I felt. My anxiety over André, the toll of a life turned into a shadow of itself, the humiliations I had to endure to keep hold of a shred of my former existence—it all erupted to the surface, in a hot surge I could no longer contain.

"I hate it." I stepped toward him. "It is beneath contempt. That pig Göring, evicting women from their suites and stealing jewels for centimes; and Abetz with his dirty propaganda, defacing our monuments. Trust us, you say. We are your friends. What kind of friendship is this, what kind of war? You invade our city and country and make us cry 'Heil Hitler' to your ugly red flag? It is absurd. A degrading spectacle. I loathe all of it."

I was so close I could have struck him across the face. I almost did, thinking the cigarette between my fingers would make a nice scorch mark across his handsome cheek, but he disarmed me with four softly spoken words: "I share your sentiments."

I made a disgusted sound. "No, you don't. This is all you Germans have yearned for since the last war, to see us cowering under your heel. You are all doing exactly as your führer tells you, never mind that he's a madman."

He met my eyes. "Are you finished?"

I went still, not moving, not speaking, until my cigarette burned my hand and I had to reach to the ashtray by my bedside to crush it out. As I did, smearing ash on my fingers, I realized I had probably just signed my arrest warrant. I had insulted Hitler. If the reports I heard at the Serts' held any truth, people were disappearing for less.

Spatz said, "I regret that I have upset you; it was not my intent. I may still be of some help with your nephew's circumstances, but it will prove more difficult than I thought. You know how to reach me should you change your mind." He started to turn away, his hand on the door latch, when I said, "Wait."

My voice brought him to a halt. If his presence had goaded me into revealing myself, I would force him to do the same. "Am I in danger?" When he did not answer, I added, "I'm not asking you to tell me what you think I should hear. As you said when we met, I have a feeling you are after something. Did you target me to ascertain my sympathies? Am I now on a list?"

He gave a humorless chuckle. "This is not a parlor game we play, mademoiselle. These lists you cite are weapons, devised to destroy lives. But, at least for the moment, if everyone who spoke against the war was arrested—well, you can imagine how empty Paris would be. Many do not agree with Hitler, including far more Germans than you think. They see what is brewing and, unlike him, they carry the lessons of the past in their bones."

"Do you agree?" I asked, defiant, though I was beginning to regret my outburst.

"I was a soldier during the last war," he said quietly. "I saw how much suffering was caused. I do not want to see it happen again."

"So, are you with or against them?"

He held up his hand. "I cannot say anything more, except that for now, as far as I am aware, you are not on any list, though you must never doubt you are in danger. Everyone is."

I wanted to believe him. I found no deception on his face, no telltale hint of subterfuge, and still I hesitated. I realized, to my horror, how far I had gone. I had said things I could never take back, things that could get me killed.

"I insulted you," I said, haltingly. "I . . . I regret it."

"No, you don't." His smile emerged, that boyish grin that crinkled the edges of his eyes and evoked devastating reminders of the men I had lost. "You are a strong woman. I admire you for it. I thank you for this interlude; I will never forget it."

He turned once more to the door. I stopped him this time by moving forward to touch his sleeve. He did not move for a moment. Then he tilted his face toward mine. "Are you sure?"

I gave a soft laugh. "No. But when has that ever stopped me before?"

LATER, AS HE SLEPT among disheveled sheets, his broad chest with its matting of blond hair rising and falling with his steady breaths, I rose and tiptoed to my purse. Lighting a cigarette, I padded naked to the window of my room overlooking rue Cambon.

My shop across the way stood shuttered, the brisk night wind biting into the white awning over the doorway. I watched the awning flutter, the bold black letters spelling my name folding upon themselves and blurring, becoming indecipherable, much like the world around me.

Glancing at Spatz as he mumbled in his sleep, I smoked and thought of the men who had marked my life: my father with his wine-soaked joy and betrayal; Balsan with his horses and indifference; and Boy, the one with whom I compared all others. But as I tried to summon him, I found I could barely recall the hue of his eyes, the tenor of his hands. Somehow, without realizing it, he had been lost in the long silence that had replaced our love.

Extinguishing my cigarette, I inched back into bed. Spatz enfolded me in his arms, clutching me close, burrowing his face against the nape of my neck, his body large and warm.

I closed my eyes. I had not taken my sedative. I did not want him to see it.

It was time to forget.

XI

Winter roared in, the coldest any of us could remember. The wind had frigid fangs, the air like cut-glass slivers. Icy sleet and snow shrouded Paris, and fuel shortages of every type became endemic, as were frequent losses of electricity and an overall scarcity of food. We heard rumors of people scavenging in garbage piles for anything edible; of brothels flourishing as many women (and men) sought whatever means they could to fight off the starvation overtaking the city despite German-distributed ration cards. Bread, eggs, wine, and meat became more precious than gold. Demand for black-market items soared. Marie-Louise and her cadre brought choice cuts of lamb, beef, and ham to the Serts, part of their illicit trade with farmers outside the city, who gouged Parisians in exchange for items like cigarettes, of which the Germans seemed to have a limitless supply.

In December, I let Spatz introduce me to his contact, Theodore Momm. The *Rittmeister* was a senior officer in the regime holding sway over Paris—an unctuous man like so many of his ilk. I was surprised to find he was also a champion horse breeder who had met Balsan years before and expressed himself "charmed" to assist me. Of course, he said, my name preceded me; he hoped perhaps at some later time I might be willing to return the favor. What could I say? I replied that of course I was at his disposal, though I took pains to emphasize the fact that I was not prepared to reopen my couture salon, as many of my fellow designers had, presenting their collections to the rapacious mistresses of German officers and coarse wives of black-market racketeers.

Momm gave a disconsolate, if unconvincing, sigh. "Yes, it is all most unfortunate, isn't it, but what can we do? We have no choice when you think about it. We must bend to the times as best we are able. None of us wants to end up like your nephew."

I left his office unsure as to whether he had issued a veiled threat, until Spatz assured me that like so many others, Momm only safeguarded his own interest. "If Momm is ever questioned as to why he seeks the release of a prisoner not on the approved roster," he explained when we returned to the Ritz, "he can claim he did it at the behest of Coco Chanel herself, who has in turn expressed her willingness to cooperate."

"Not by designing dresses for them," I retorted. "There are certain lines I will not cross. They can buy all the perfume they want, and my jewelry, too—though I hear they loot enough of the real stuff as it is—but never my dresses."

Spatz chuckled, divesting himself of his clothes and beckoning me to bed. I went to him with a scowl, thinking, as I had since our initial encounter, that I should end this affair before it went beyond my control. He was ostensibly helping me, but as circumspect as I tried to be, I was still a Frenchwoman consorting with a German, as foolhardy as Arletty, and no doubt as talked about behind my back.

Only his touch eased my doubts. He was keen to build my ardor, sensitive to the fact that menopause had made intercourse painful at times, using other skills instead to rouse a desire that sloughed away the layers of loss and fear. For the briefest instant, I felt young again. Who would know that after he left for his apartment or whatever dealings he had outside, I worried and paced, smoking cigarette after cigarette until I had to take a dose of my sedative?

Only me, and I had become an expert at disguising the truth, even from myself.

MY NEPHEW WAS IMPRISONED in a stalag in Germany, Momm told me when I returned to his office several weeks later. This time, all my protestations of pride went by the wayside; if Momm had suggested I design gowns for the führer's mistress, I would have readily agreed. Momm also took delight in explaining how he was incurring considerable risks for my sake.

"These matters are quite complicated, requiring much time and tact to negotiate, as well as significant bribes and paperwork," he said. "It is never easy to obtain a prisoner of war's release. I need a compelling reason to secure your nephew's, given that the approved roster does not include him. I would not wish to be questioned by Berlin for stepping outside my purview."

"But surely it must be some administrative error. André has committed no crime."

"He's an enemy soldier. That is sufficient." Momm sat behind his impressive desk heaped with important-looking documents, his thinning hair greased back from his brow, his spectacles perched on his nose as he assessed me with a bureaucrat's polite indifference. I felt a chill. I had the sensation he would as soon report me to the Gestapo as help me, and my hands trembled as I lit a cigarette, thinking of a plausible excuse he could use.

"What if you tell them André can work for you?" I suddenly said. "You are overseeing the textile industry for the war effort; you must need experienced managers for your mills. You can say he trained in my atelier, overseeing fabric production for my dresses. I do—or I did at one time— create my own cloth, and André was a valued employee of mine."

"Interesting," said Momm. I feigned nonchalance as I waited for the rest of his reply. "I can always use able men," he added at length. "It is capable women who are at a premium."

I smiled to disguise my shock. Was this rat actually *propositioning* me? "You cannot mean to say that I should run a mill, monsieur. I would not be suitable in the slightest."

His slippery smile widened until I saw a hint of nicotine-stained teeth. "Millwork was not what I had in mind." He let his innuendo linger. I was about to inform him that he was grossly mistaken if he thought I would do whatever he implied when he added, "I will keep you informed, mademoiselle. I am certain we can reach a mutually beneficial arrangement. I would ask, however, that in the future you allow me to contact you, yes?"

It was not a request, and I knew it. With a terse nod, I thanked him for his time, then almost ran out the door. That evening when Spatz came to see me, I related my meeting with Momm, my voice shuddering in anger.

"Does he actually think I would—that I am so desperate to . . . the gall of the man! As if I'd ever stoop to his level!" Even as I ranted, I did not fail to acknowledge the irony of it, that I could be so irate at the thought that someone would expect sexual favors of me to advance my goals. Was that not precisely what I had done with Spatz?

He sighed, unknotting his tie. "It's not what you think. Momm telephoned me after you left. He says he can of course petition to employ André in a mill, but they are holding your nephew for a reason, and if we insist too much, they might execute him. They have killed hundreds of prisoners already. You should know, Momm was not raised in Germany. He spent his formative years in Belgium, and while he now serves the Reich, he must tread cautiously, as they may suspect his ultimate allegiance."

"Do they suspect yours?" I said sharply. "Because it seems to me, with everyone around us engaged in some type of subterfuge, someone should be able to bring my nephew home."

He regarded me pensively. "Why is this so important to you? We are at war, with thousands detained or dying every day. You told me André grew up in England; you have only seen him on a few occasions, such as holidays or vacations. Why risk your safety for his sake when you should be focused only on saving yourself?"

I bit my lip, looking down at the cigarette in my fingers. I did not have a ready answer, and it took me aback that I had to think of one. The easiest reply was that André was my family; but I had other relatives, my own brothers, in fact, whose allowances I had cut off without a qualm after closing my atelier, saying I had no funds to spare. It was a lie. I had plenty of money, even if it was limited because bank assets were frozen and

I could only draw on what my shop yielded. No, it was more than the fact that André shared my blood. In an intangible way, he personified all that was good in my life. He had become my redemption now that everything else I cared about was suspended.

"He is my sister's son," I finally said. "Why should I need more reason than that?"

"You don't." Spatz sat beside me on the bed. "But you must realize that by now Berlin is aware that you refuse to reopen your couture salon, though every other designer in Paris has. Your refusal sends a powerful message. Why should they help you, if you choose not to help them?"

I could not look at him. "What am I supposed to do?"

He did not speak. Drawing on my cigarette, I turned to face him. "Well? What is it? You work for them, you must know something. Tell me what it is. Do they want me to make dresses? Fine, I'll make dresses. I'll present a collection in red and black to match their flag."

"Careful, Coco. Never promise what you are not prepared to concede. Momm will take advantage of it. He does think you are desperate, and no, it is not that. Enchanting as you are, he is not interested in humiliating you. He knows you are in my bed—"

"No," I cut in. "You are in *my* bed. There is a difference."

He nodded. "True." He met my stare. "I'm not sure what they want, but they must want something. Perhaps they themselves do not know yet. If you keep pressing the issue, in time we will hear. They hold your nephew. They must have a price."

I gritted my teeth, coming to my feet. "Then whatever their price is, I will pay it." Without turning to him, I said, "I am very tired. I wish to be alone."

He did not protest, gathering his hat and discarded tie, his attaché briefcase with its encoded locks, and moving to the door. He half-turned to glance at me over his shoulder.

"You should know that Marshal Pétain of the Vichy government has agreed to cooperate fully with Berlin. Momm told me that all Jews and other designated undesirables residing in the occupied areas and Vichygoverned France must report to their local prefecture of police. Upon de-naturalization, they will most likely be deported. New laws are also in effect, prohibiting Jews from owning or engaging in any business. I only tell you this because it might be worth exploring whether these changes can benefit you."

With those unsettling words, he left, closing the door behind him.

I stood immobile, my nerves clamoring, craving my drug—a quick jab of the needle in my vein, followed by a descent into dreamless oblivion, if only for a few hours.

But I already knew the escape I sought might never be mine again.

XII

I telephoned Misia. Lunch at the Ritz was out of the question. The staff enforced by day the German mandate that prohibited civilians from mingling with military personnel in the hotel, even if they turned lax at night. The restaurant was a Nazi domain.

We agreed instead to meet in the Tuileries.

Someone had told Misia about Spatz—I did not know whom, but suspected Marie-Louise—and though I had braced myself for her denunciation, all Misia offered was a mordant, "It appears taking a Nazi lover is all the rage these days. For once, rather than setting the trend, darling, you merely follow it."

Her sour acquiescence took me by surprise, and I found myself anxious as we sat in a café near the hulking palace of the Louvre, now emptied of its precious artworks by desperate curators, who tried to hide them in secret storage before the Nazis plundered the museum. Misia and I had not been out in public together since the occupation had begun. Lighting a cigarette, I peered over the top of my sunglasses at the few pedestrians moving past the window toward the place de la Concorde, their gazes averted, swathed in scarves, hats, and gloves, shapeless figures with downcast faces.

Misia said dryly, "You needn't be so apprehensive. Many things may have changed, but two women of a certain age meeting for coffee hardly warrants suspicion."

"You call this coffee?" I winced, looking at the dregs floating in my cup.

"Well," she said, "there is that. Nothing tastes like it used to, not even those smoked hams Jojo consumes by the pound."

She looked drawn and, I noticed, thinner than she had in years. "Are you not eating?"

"Oh, I am." She toyed with her cup. "Just not as much as he is. The man is an animal. Nothing intrudes on his appetites."

Uncomfortable silence fell. As I extinguished my cigarette and immediately lit another, Misia said, "I was curious that you called. We seem to have made a habit of seeing each other only at our little gatherings at the house. Is something troubling you?"

I nodded, looking around again. Then I felt her hand under the table, gripping my knee through the folds of my mink coat. "Stop that. You're acting like a spy." She leaned back in her chair. "Now, tell me what's wrong. Is your lover starting to bore you?"

Her tone, while light, carried a hidden barb. I started to say she had no business judging me, not when she and Jojo dined daily on contraband hams, but I curbed my tongue. As usual, she had aimed uncannily close to the mark.

"Boring is not the description I would use," I said, and proceeded to tell her in a low voice about Momm's enigmatic game and Spatz's suggestion. When I was done, she lifted her hand to tug at her lower lip. "What do you think he meant?" she asked.

"At first, I wasn't sure myself." I tried to sound unperturbed. "But then I called René de Chambrun and he told me that, yes, under the new law I can indeed institute legal proceedings to regain control of Parfums Chanel, as the Wertheimers are . . ."

"Yes, we know what they are. So, is their cousin Bollack also . . . ?"

I nodded. "I believe so."

Her brow arched. "Well, there you have it. You have wanted to regain control of your perfume for years. Here is your chance. You can have them ousted quite easily." Her voice was emotionless, as though she stated an irrefutable fact. But I discerned the unvoiced judgment in her eyes, and it enraged me.

"Are you saying you think I would do this to them because they are—" I had to stop myself, lowering my voice to an indignant whisper. "They have been stealing from me for years. Pierre himself told me it was business— and he was right. This is about business, *my* business. Whether or not they are Jewish has nothing to do with it."

She met my stare. "Doesn't it? Have you ever stopped to consider that perhaps *I* am one?"

I went still. All of a sudden, a chill went through me, even as I scoffed, "Misia, please. You are Catholic. Everyone knows it."

She did not take her gaze from me. "You'd be surprised. Not by me, but by how many of our friends are; you don't know because you never bothered to ask." Suddenly, she smiled. "But of course, I know you'd never willingly use that against anyone—though I must admit, you've given a rather good imitation of it in the past. Your time with Bendor, and then Iribe; it does leave an impression. The Germans must know you funded Iribe's *Le Témoin*. Perhaps you should show them a copy when you sue for the return of your perfume company."

I glared at her. "How can you say such things to me, especially now?"

She chuckled. "If not now, when? You and so many others behave as if the war were an inconvenience. You pretend none of this exists. Ignorance, it seems, is your best revenge."

"That is dreadful. You make me sound like Marie-Louise!"

"Yes. It is dreadful. Even our little Jean has come back with his tail between his legs, meek as a mouse yet full of ideas for a new play to entertain them, with Lifar dancing the lead." Misia shifted her gaze to the window. "It's to be expected, I suppose. No one wants to end up in a camp."

"Misia." I impatiently tapped ash from my cigarette onto the floor. "You are not helping. André is already in a camp. If I take control of my perfume company by using the new laws, do you think it will establish my willingness to cooperate?"

She returned her regard to me. "It certainly couldn't hurt," she said, and drank from her cup. For the first time in as long as I had known her, I could not interpret her expression.

"But you think it's wrong? You think it will make me look as if I'm taking advantage?"

"Since when did what I think matter? You will do what you want. You always have your reasons and they always seem good enough for you at the time."

"But it does matter." My voice thickened. God help me, I was close to tears.

"Why?" Her question hit me like a punch in the stomach. She leaned to me, her frizzy hair sprouting in undyed batches from beneath her knit cap, her jowls red veined and loose, her eyes slightly glazed, indicating she had imbibed some of our blue drops before she left the house. "Are you asking me as a friend or because you want me to tell you it's acceptable to denounce Jews?"

Her words seemed to ring out in the sudden hush between us. I did not dare glance anywhere, as though the Gestapo might fall upon us at any moment. I couldn't speak, couldn't move as she went on. "Do you think my permission matters? Do you think what I say or do makes any difference? I could not spare Lily de Rothschild. She and Baroness Kitty were clients of yours; you know they are married to the wealthiest men in France yet because the Rothschilds are Jewish, they had to flee. Lily stayed after her husband went to England; we heard the Gestapo arrested her after she tried to cross into Paris on a forged permit. I went to testify on her behalf at the police, told them she was coming to see me. They deported her to a work camp. She is not Jewish, but it did not protect her. You are as blind as ever, Coco. Nothing we do can protect any of us, because *they* know no one is willing to stop them."

"I . . . I did not know about Lily," I said, appalled. "I hadn't heard."

She sniffed. "You won't hear much when you're at the Ritz with one of them in your bed." She interrupted my protest. "I don't care if he's playing three ends to the middle, he's still officially one of them. I warned you, Coco. I told you to be careful, that there will be repercussions. You, Lifar, and Arletty, you never listen, yet now you dare ask for *advice*? What do you expect me to say?"

I was trembling so much that I dropped my cigarette. Grinding it under my heel, I had started to rise when she reached out, grasping my gloved hand. "Do it," she said, "and you will regret it. Maybe not immediately, maybe not for some time, but one day, you will. Look around you—this cannot last. Even if we do nothing to stop them, the British will. America must join the fight eventually, as they did before. This war will end, leaving us to pick up the pieces. You'd best be sure you are not one of those pieces."

"He is my nephew." I wrenched my hand from her. "I will not leave him to rot in some godforsaken camp. He has a wife, a child. He has done nothing wrong!"

She guffawed in disbelief. "Coco the invincible rides to the rescue. You failed to save Boy, so now you must save André. Is that your plan?"

"Damn you, Misia," I whispered. "Damn you to hell." I snatched my purse from the table, rattling the cups in their saucers.

"I'm already in hell," I heard her say softly. "We all are," but I did not pause as I strode from the café into the icy spring sunlight.

If I had been undecided before, I thought as I marched through the Tuileries Garden, now I was determined. I had told Spatz I was ready to pay whatever price it took.

I intended to keep my word.

I CALLED RENÉ, telling him to commence proceedings against the Wertheimers. I was pure French, without a drop of undesirable blood in my veins; they had stolen my company from me and profiteered from my perfume for too long. It was high time I took them to task.

Spatz applauded my decision over dinner at the Ritz. "It's exactly what was required. Word will filter to Berlin and they will see you as an ally. You've just unlocked André's prison."

"We'll see," I replied. All of a sudden, I found his satisfaction distasteful in the extreme. "I assume by word filtering to Berlin, you mean Momm. You'll tell him and he'll tell them."

He raised his glass of wine. "If you like. But I think they'll find out without the need for Momm. Nothing that transpires in Paris escapes their notice."

"Is that so?" I felt the urge to slap his face. "Regardless, I want Momm to know. I have done my part. Now, he must do his. All that paperwork he mentioned, he must file it. At once."

"Consider it done," said Spatz. If he felt my disdain, he did not remark on it. We finished our meal and I returned to my room, while he made his habitual rounds in the reception area to talk up his Nazi contacts and pretend he wasn't planning to slip around the corner to sleep with me. I was sorely tempted to bolt my door against him, permanently. Though I believed the Wertheimers had played me for a fool, I loathed myself. It was not a fair fight, but when had they ever abided by fairness? They had made a fortune from No. 5 while I had to content myself with a pittance; even their cousin Bollack had started charging me double for half the amount, citing all sorts of ridiculous obstacles to inflate his costs. Still, I knew that in seeking advantage through the new anti-Semitic laws, I had crossed an invisible line.

I had become the enemy.

When Spatz knocked at the door, I sat on my bed and waited. He tried the latch, knocked again. Then he stood outside without a sound. I could glean his shadow blocking the sliver of light under the door. He just stood there, patient.

Finally, he went away. He would return, of that, I had no doubt—but not tonight.

MY SUIT AGAINST THE WERTHEIMERS came to nothing. Once Bollack caught wind of my ploy, he resigned and fled to New York, transferring Bourjois to a French aviation corporation run by an executive with blood as pure as mine. The impetuous lawsuit I had set in motion, costing me Misia's respect, languished in the overcrowded courts, my lawyer grappling with the delays until he told me it was hopeless. No judge wanted to contend with a dispute over perfume when they were busy protecting themselves.

I stayed aloof from the Sert household as the summer of 1941 faded and the war ground on. Hitler had most of Europe clutched in his fist and declared his intent to invade the Soviet Union. In the meantime, he directed his Luftwaffe against Britain, launching devastating air raids that rained hellfire over London. Churchill had been appointed prime minister. I sent him a congratulatory letter, but received no reply. I did not know if my letter ever reached him. Germans monitored the postal service, the telephone and wireless, anything that might leak information or be deployed for propaganda. I knew I had taken a risk by writing to him, that my letter would expose me as a sympathizer. I did not care. I almost welcomed the chance to blare my defiance in their faces and ease my own guilt.

One evening as I made my way back from the Champs-Élysées, I passed a marquee over the theater where Stravinsky and Diaghilev had staged their *Rite of Spring*. An enormous banner was plastered to its façade, announcing an exhibition on the Jew in France. The banner's illustration was grotesque: a hook-nosed caricature hoarding coins as starving waifs at his feet implored him. It made my skin crawl. People lined up to attend the exhibition, laughing and chatting among themselves, uniformed Germans in their midst. I did not recognize Paris anymore; I did not know my own city. It had become a circus—a ludicrous farce, populated by ghouls and jackboots, by opportunists who sold their souls for day-old bread.

Most of all, I did not recognize myself. I had turned again to Spatz. He was my sole link to Berlin and André; the wheels were still turning, he assured me, just not as fast as I would like. Momm had filed the paperwork; we must now wait. I raged at him then, at Momm and every other German.

I cursed and threw things at the wall, until Spatz had to hold me by my wrists and clasp me to him, my wails crumbling into despair. "I'll never see him again," I cried. "I'll never see him and his wife will never forgive me. I promised to see him safe!"

That night, Spatz found out about my sedative. I suspected he knew long before; I had discreet markings on the inside of my arm that he must have noticed. But I told him anyway and he prepared my injection for me, delivering the dose as I reclined on the bed and wept.

He cradled me in his arms as blue swirled through my blood, blacking out the world. When I woke in the morning, he was gone. Staggering to the bathroom, realizing in one terrifying instant that I had revealed a secret he could use against me, I looked up from the toilet and saw he had written on the mirror with my lipstick:

Pack your bags. We are going to La Pausa.

I HAD NO IDEA how he managed it. He secured the necessary papers, the coveted *Ausweis*; he booked first-class compartments on the express train. At the station in Cannes, he had a fueled car waiting, which he drove himself to my villa.

My staff had locked up everything and departed; only a few miles away, parts of the Riviera lay in rubble from the bombings. As I went through the house, unbolting shutters and scraping dry leaves from crevices, the scent of my garden reached me, rich with jasmine and heliotrope, with the roses planted with such hope when I still believed Bendor would propose.

I expected ghosts. The house, much as I loved it, teemed with them. All the friends who had dined at my rustic table now scattered to the four winds; all the dead, like Iribe, whose collapse on my tennis court had turned my refuge into a pantheon of grief.

But I found emptiness. Only my photographs framed on the mantels offered reflections of happier times, when maintaining supremacy in fashion was the only battle I knew.

In the room where I had mourned Iribe, I made love with Spatz with the windows open, to let in the salty air from the sea and the whispers of the pines. By day, we walked in the hills or drove into the village to buy bread, fresh butter, and jam. Though the south remained unoccupied, fear stalked here, as well; the Vichy roundups had begun and many refugees were fleeing to the coast, desperate to escape.

My architect, Robert Streitz, came to see me, having heard I was back. If he had not told me who he was, I would not have recognized him. He was gaunt, unkempt, his eyes sunken and his skin like parchment. He looked as if he had not eaten a full meal in weeks, and I plied him with food, chattering about inconsequential things, avoiding any mention of the war until he asked to take a walk with me by the empty pool, to show me, he said, incipient cracks in the tiles.

I knew he wanted to get away from Spatz, who stayed behind on the veranda, drinking wine. As we paced around my forlorn pool, barren of water and streaked with rotting vegetation and algae, Streitz cleared his throat and said, "Mademoiselle, I was wondering . . . Do you have any objections if I stay here and undertake the work necessary to fix these tiles?"

I frowned. Fishing in my trousers pocket for my cigarettes, I offered him one. He pounced on it as if he had not seen real tobacco in months. As he drew on the cigarette, his eyes half closed, I glanced to Spatz's silhouette on the veranda before I said, "What do you really want?"

Streitz froze, smoke trailing from his nose. "To . . . to fix the tiles. You see, if they continue to be exposed to the elements, those cracks will eventually widen and—"

I shook my head. "Forget the tiles. I promise that whatever you ask will stay between us." I smiled to ease the disquiet on his face. "Just tell me what you want."

He lowered his gaze. "Your cellar. It is large enough to hold twenty or thirty people."

"I see." I did not ask him more, but with the subject broached, he could not contain himself. "We have many people coming here in search of refuge. We are trying to gain them passage to Italy, but the permits take time to forge. While they wait, they need places to hide. As you know, most of the villas in the area have British owners; the houses are either locked up like yours or patrolled by dogs and hired guards. We suspect the Germans are also having some of the villas watched. We cannot trust anyone; there are informants here, too. If we could use La Pausa . . ." His voice faded as he saw my quick glance again to the veranda. "If it's too much to ask, I understand," he said. "It's only that . . . I thought you might . . ."

I shifted my gaze back to him. "Are you sure my house isn't being watched?"

"Yes. I knew you were here because we've been monitoring it. But no one else seems to be paying it any attention."

I went quiet. "If you are found," I said at length, "you realize what will happen, don't you? To you and your refugees, your friends who are helping them, and possibly to me, as well?"

"I do. But we cannot look away. It's a risk we must take."

I should refuse. It was indeed a risk, and a monumental one, at that. As I hesitated, Streitz added, "I would also be using a transmitter to communicate with our comrades on the other side of the border. You should be aware of it before you make a decision. The transmitter is British, encoded to evade surveillance, but nothing is completely secure."

I extended my silver cigarette case and Cartier lighter to him. "Take these. Sell them to help your cause." I started to return to the house. He followed. Before we reached the veranda, I said, "I'm returning to Paris in a few weeks. You can stay here to fix the tiles. I'll pay you in advance. If anyone asks, you are working for me. I'll draft a letter you can show to that effect."

"Yes," he murmured. "God bless you, mademoiselle."

I smiled. After everything I had done, divine blessing was the last thing I could expect.

"EVERYTHING ALL RIGHT?" Spatz asked after I saw Streitz to the gate. He was uncorking another bottle of chardonnay; as he sniffed its bouquet,

I thought of the extensive cellars below our feet, where he had gone to fetch the wine, and my response felt strained.

"Yes, of course. He is going to live here this winter to do repairs. The pool and the gardens; I have left the house abandoned. Since he needs the work, I thought, why not?"

"Oh." He poured me a glass. I tried to drink it, but the wine turned acrid in my mouth. "Is that all?" said Spatz. "He seemed a bit . . . desperate."

"War will do that to people," I said sharply. I set the glass aside. "I have a headache. I think I'll rest awhile before dinner."

As I ascended the grand staircase that Streitz had re-created from Aubazine, I heard Spatz call my name. The curtness in his tone brought me to a halt. "Why are you lying?"

I turned around. He was staring at me. "Lying?" I said lightly even as my heart began to race. "I just told you, the tiles around the pool are cracked and—"

Spatz took a step toward me, the sound of his shoe heel on the flagstone entry as loud as a thunderclap. "When will you trust me? Because if the answer is never, we should end this now. I am not with you to be used; I get enough of that from my superiors."

"Use you?" My laugh was brittle. "Is that what you think I am doing?"

"I don't know. I have done what I can, but you obviously still don't trust me. If you did, you'd not be lying to me now." When I did not answer, my hand clenched on the balustrade, he added, "He's working for the resistance, isn't he? He wants to use the house for it."

"I think you should ask him," I said, even as I heard the catch in my voice. "But it is my house. I can do with it whatever I like."

He strode up the steps to me. All of a sudden, he looked every one of his years, a bit slack under the chin, a mosaic of tiny veins on his nose betraying his fondness for drink. "Do you think I am your enemy? Is that why you will not tell me what he has requested?"

My reply was harsh, forced out between my teeth. "You have no right to question me." As he expelled an impatient breath, I added recklessly,

"You must think me a fool if you expect me to believe you are not what you appear."

"You are impossible," he said.

"So I've been told." I turned away. He reached out, circling my wrist with his fingers. I paused, and took a pointed look at his hand before I said, "I thought you could help me free André."

"I am trying," he said. "Momm is trying. You have no patience. You expect miracles—"

"Miracles?" I yanked my wrist away. "I am tired of hearing how difficult it is, of how much paperwork and bribery are required. I'm sick to death of your excuses."

A tremulous voice suddenly said from the doorway, "Mademoiselle?" and I turned with a gasp to find Streitz standing there, my cigarette case in his hand. "You must have dropped this. It . . . it has your monogram on it."

I froze, fear hurtling through me. Spatz said calmly, "Come inside and shut the door, monsieur. I think we must have a talk." He glanced at me. "Alone. Can you do that for me?"

I almost shouted at Streitz to run as fast as he could, across the mountains into Italy or Switzerland, anywhere they would not find him, but instead I nodded and watched Spatz escort my architect into the living room. I should stay here, I thought. I should wait until I heard them talking and then creep closer to eavesdrop. All of a sudden, I wished I had a pistol; and as I thought this, I understood, for the very first time, how dangerous and complicated, how compromising, my situation with Spatz was.

I was prepared to kill him. This was how far I had come.

Reeling back up the stairs, I went to my suite, shutting the door and standing there, not knowing what to do. Finally, I perched on one of the gilded chairs by the window and stared out to the incoming dusk, burnished with the ebbing light of the sun, a seam of coral like the color of my evening gowns, deepening to mauve where the sky touched the sea. It felt like hours before Spatz knocked on the door and entered.

Without looking up, I said, "Did he tell you?"

"He did." The carpet's pile muffled his approach. "He wants to use the cellars to hide refugees and the gardens as a staging post for their transfer to Italy. He has a transmitter he must also keep hidden; I suggested he use the cellars for it, too, as the thickness of the walls will quiet any static." He stopped a few paces from me. "He also has a friend, a Jewish professor who has been arrested in Vichy. He asked for my help. I am going to see if I can arrange a release. It's not a camp; the professor is being held at the local detention center, so perhaps a bribe will suffice."

I finally met his eyes.

"Is this enough for you?" he asked.

"For now," I whispered, though in truth I did not know if it was, if anything would ever be. I had made a pact with the devil; now, for better or worse, I must see it through.

"Good." He turned away. "I'll have dinner ready in an hour; I'll call you when it's ready. Streitz will be joining us, after he takes a much-needed bath. Your brave architect stinks."

XIII

On December 7, 1941, the Japanese bombed the American base at Pearl Harbor.

I was back in Paris at the Ritz; when the news came over the wireless, there were cheers and the uncorking of champagne as the Germans rejoiced. Their anxiety about the Americans joining the conflict had apparently been eased by the stealth attack that proved America's vulnerability.

Sickened, I avoided the Ritz's restaurant from then on. A few days later, Cocteau came to lunch with me at a bistro near my shop. I was surprised by how well he looked, his angular face fuller than I had ever seen it, his thatch of hair as unruly as ever, but his person trim, with some much-needed weight on its spare frame. He lacked that agitation I had grown so used to; after years of knowing him, its absence proved remarkable.

"The war," he said, when I remarked on his appearance, "it does wonders for vices."

I took this to mean he had weaned himself off the drugs while holed up in the Côte d'Azur at various friends' homes with his actor-lover. Cocaine, morphine, and other indulgences were nearly impossible to obtain, save through a Nazi contact or Marie-Louise's thriving contraband, and cost a fortune when they were.

"You should come with me to Misia's," he said as we ate a meal that was as tasteless and gray as the city itself. "She's been asking about you, wondering how you are."

"Has she?" I forked my fillet of—well, I had no idea what it was, only that it was smothered in soggy onions and cabbage, the only two vegetables available these days. "I find that odd. I thought she never wanted to see me again."

"She says you walked out on her." He leaned over to me with impish confidence, making me lose whatever was left of my appetite. His expression reminded me of the time he had come to visit me during my separation from Boy, when he told me about Misia's addiction. "She claims you were hysterical."

I chuckled sourly, lighting a cigarette to disguise the tang of the unidentifiable meat. "Of course she did. How could anything ever be her fault? She would blame the war on me, too, no doubt, if anyone would believe her."

"Coco, she cares deeply for you." He looked forlorn, but I could not tell if it was because he truly was sorry about the discord or because he felt deprived of an afternoon of malicious gossip. He must have seen by my attitude that I was in no mood for this. "She was very upset that you had that fight, and over a German, too."

I bristled. "It was not over a German. It was something else." I paused, regarding him through the smoke of my cigarette. "Did she tell you why?"

He shrugged, though his face brightened with anticipation. "Bits and pieces. She was rather reticent, for Misia." He paused. "So, it wasn't about this new lover of yours?"

I resisted the urge to squash my cigarette into the mess on my plate and leave. "That is why I will not go to her house anymore. She has too many opinions on things she knows nothing about."

"But she said you are trying to save your nephew, that he is in a German camp and it's driving you insane. She blames the circumstances, not you."

"Did she tell you she is Jewish?" The words were out of my mouth before I could stop them and the moment they were, I wanted to snatch them back.

He went still. "Misia is . . . ?" He glanced around at the near-empty tables around us, a gesture that gave me perverse satisfaction. It had become second nature to the rest of us, this terror of being overheard; it pleased me that he, too, was not impervious. "I thought she was Catholic. She says she is. She has icons and crucifixes all over the house."

"She is Catholic. I was just wondering if she ever mentioned it."

"Not to me." He licked his lips. I felt ill. Misia had not told me she was. She had been making a point, throwing my decisions back in my face. Now here I was taunting one of Paris's most inveterate scandalmongers with a potentially deadly tidbit.

"She was trying to gain my sympathy," I said, with forced carelessness. "You know how she is. If they were rounding up horses, she'd be a lame mare."

He giggled, to my relief. As avid as he was for dirty linen to air, I had learned I could also easily persuade him in any direction. "That she would. Misia does love her martyrdom. She's become a recluse; she almost never leaves that house anymore, and she and Sert—" He shuddered. "They must hate each other, the way they carry on, but there they are, on top of each other day and night, though he has his own apartment and surely could live there if he chose."

"They don't hate each other." I motioned to the waiter for the check. "They need each other. Which," I added, "is an entirely different sort of arrangement."

"So, you'll come?" He dabbed his lips with his napkin. He had eaten everything on his plate, even sopped up the disgusting sauce with bread. "Lifar is back from his tour of Berlin; we're gathering tomorrow to hear about it. Coco, you must. We all miss you."

"I'll wash my hair and think about it," I quipped. "Come, let's take a walk and you can tell me about your new play."

It was the oldest trick I knew: ask a writer about his work and everything else flies out the window. As usual, it worked like a charm.

I DID GO TO MISIA'S, however, and I took Spatz with me. It was the first time I had introduced him to my circle and I did it deliberately, in defiance, entering her living room in my belted mink and pearls, my lips painted red and my scarf perfumed. There was a larger group than usual: some of Jojo's artist friends, a few petty cooperating officials from the regime, as well as Marie-Louise, Cocteau and his lover, the matinee idol Marais, and Lifar with his dancer du jour.

Misia looked aghast as Spatz helped me out of my coat and I smoothed my manicured, multiringed fingers over my dark wool suit. Jojo lumbered forth to shake Spatz's hand. Marie-Louise batted her eyes at him. Spatz spoke only French; we had agreed on it beforehand. French or English, but no German.

After a bountiful lunch that demonstrated where Jojo's true interests lay, I sat at the photograph-laden piano—it was in desperate need of tuning—and with Lifar and Cocteau at my side, played some of my songs from Moulins, which had so enchanted the garrison officers a lifetime ago. My voice was smoky, breaking on the high notes, but everyone applauded, and while Spatz smiled, I let go of my inhibitions and played a few more, laughing when I forgot the lyrics to one song and Lifar sprang in with his lovely baritone to override my lapse.

Misia did not say a word.

Afterward, over Spanish cognac that Jojo had managed to acquire from who knew where, someone began talking about the catastrophic losses suffered at Pearl Harbor. It did not dampen the mood; no one seemed to be paying any mind, in fact, until Spatz remarked, "The Americans do not want to get involved, but after this, they'll surely—"

"What?" Cocteau piped up. "What are they going to do? Or better yet, what *can* they do?"

"Yes," drawled Lifar, from where he reclined on the chaise lounge. "They've lost their entire fleet. They'll have to throw gumballs at the Japs."

"And Coca-Cola bottles," said Cocteau, clapping his hands. "And peanut brittle!"

As the silence thickened, the petty officials—all French-born bureaucrats who were stuffing their larders from others' misery—looked askance at my intemperate friends, until Misia directed her baleful stare at everyone and said, "Get out."

No one moved.

"Get out," she repeated. She came to her feet, glaring at us. Her crumpled jersey dress—one of mine, I noticed, though so stretched out of shape, I scarcely recognized it—clung to her heavy thighs and breasts. Seeing that no one even made a move for their hats or coats, she tromped away to her bedroom, slamming her door with enough force to rattle the paintings on the walls.

Jojo rolled his eyes. "Go see to her, will you, Coco? She's been like this for weeks."

I wanted to refuse. Instead, I nodded, taking up my handbag. As I departed, the room erupted, everyone now debating whether the Americans would enter the war, their arguments laced with ridiculous supposition and disparagement of the crippled President Roosevelt.

I did not knock on Misia's door. I assumed it was unlocked, pushing it open to find her slumped on the edge of her bed, a handkerchief twisted in her hands. She looked up through tearstained eyes before she looked away. "Have you come to gloat?" she muttered.

Shutting the door behind me, I leaned against it and crossed my arms. "How long do you plan to act like this? Because I haven't the patience for it, and neither does Jojo." I reached into my handbag and removed three vials, setting them on her bureau. "Here."

"Thank you," she said, without giving me a glance.

"That's it? Well then. You're welcome." I turned to the door.

"Coco, wait." Her voice had a ragged edge. "I . . . I am sorry, about everything I said the other day. I was upset. This war, it's . . ." She choked back a sob.

Going to her, I sat at her side and took her hand in mine. "We have been friends for over twenty years. Friends argue. They fight. It happens. I know how much this is wearing on you. I am sorry, too. I did not mean to be so angry with you. It's not your fault, after all."

She sniffled. "I'm just an old woman in a shoe. I don't recognize the world anymore."

"None of us does. But this is how the world is, for now."

She nodded, her hand tightening in mine. She finally lifted her gaze. It struck me in that moment how weathered she was, how aged. I had forgotten in the furor of our estrangement that Misia was almost seventy, and while I did everything I could to conceal my age, she had fallen into its maw with near-helpless abandon.

"He seems nice," she said. "Your friend. He is not what I expected."

I chuckled. "He doesn't wear the SS uniform, if that's what you imply. He's a diplomat."

"Yes. I can see that." She managed a weak smile. "Are you happy?"

Her question gave me sudden pause. I had not stopped to consider it. Happiness was not something that seemed possible anymore, or at least not something any of us should aspire to.

"Don't you know?" she said when I failed to answer. "Coco, do you love him?"

"No," I finally admitted. "But I need him, like you need Jojo. Do you now understand? Without him, this life would be unbearable. He makes me . . ."

"Forget." She nodded. "Yes, I understand perfectly. He's like our blue drops."

"Better. Or less expensive, at any rate." I saw her shift her attention to the bureau. "Do you want me to help you?"

She shook her head. "I'll manage. I just . . . I can't see anyone else right now."

"Of course. I'll tell them you wore yourself out and are taking a nap." I kissed her cheek. She smelled of powder and a subtle trace of something else. "Is that Number Five?" I asked, surprised.

"Every day." She cocked her shoulder, with that sudden verve of the Misia I had known. "'A woman who doesn't wear perfume has no future,'" she said, quoting one of my ads.

I laughed, rising to go to the door. I glanced over my shoulder. "I don't know if I can love a man anymore," I said, "but I do love you, Misia. I always will, no matter what."

Her smile was heartrending. "It is all I live for."

THE WAR DRAGGED ON, and dragged us along with it. My so-called fellow designers accommodated as best they could to the strict rationing of fabric, with German-ordained restrictions on lengths and hemlines that, if breached, would result in crushing fines. My finances were not under scrutiny, however. Though I had no access to my money in the bank, I earned enough by working at my shop, trying to keep my perfumes in supply, and wrangling with the new ownership of Parfums Chanel, which proved no less troublesome. They insisted on abiding by the terms of my previous contract. I had managed to rid myself of the Wertheimers but accomplished nothing else, arguing for a new and better contract to no avail.

Every week, I had Spatz check with Momm. Every week, he returned with no word on André's case, though by now I had paid Momm enough for bribes that I should have been able to secure the release of an entire legion.

News from abroad, however, showed improvement. The Americans joined the Allied powers, and by the end of 1942, Germany's disastrous offensive against Russia had incurred heavy losses. As Misia had predicted, the tide began to turn, and as a result, persecution of the French Jews increased, with over thirteen thousand in Paris alone arrested and confined for a week in the Vélodrome d'Hiver, an immense cycle track not far from the Eiffel Tower.

That summer of 1943, the heat was stifling. At night, with my room's window shoved open as wide as it could go, I sat quiet as Spatz detailed the horrors the Jews had endured, left without water or shade under the Vélodrome's blue-painted glass roof, roasting alive, until a band of protestors led by Catholic priests advanced on the site, demanding their release.

"They were dispersed with tear gas and shots," said Spatz as he paced, his hand trembling as he tried to light a cigarette. "Many were also arrested and deported with the Jews." His visible consternation drove me to him. Taking the lighter, I lit his cigarette for him.

"There is nothing we can do," I said, despising the sound of my own voice, the weakness in it, the overwhelming sense of impotency. "We cannot stop it."

He bit at his lower lip.

"We are helping all those we can at La Pausa," I went on. "You got Streitz's friend released; countless others are being sent over the border. But this . . ." My paltry attempt at an excuse faded into silence. Thousands had been removed from their homes and businesses, forced onto trains, and sent away. No, we couldn't do anything to save them, but I felt like a hypocrite for thinking it. After all, I'd seized advantage in the same laws that the Nazis used against the Jews. Misia had warned me; she'd said I would regret it. God help me, I already did.

"They are all going to die," he said quietly. Despite its audible tremor, his voice hardened. "This war will become an atrocity unlike any ever seen. It will destroy Germany for generations to come. Our only hope is—" He cut himself short, drawing on his cigarette as he avoided my stare. He had never done this before, never expressed such overt hesitation, and I heard myself say, "What is it? What else has happened?"

He went quiet. When he finally spoke, his voice was so low I almost failed to hear him: "I think my apartment is being watched. Momm told me the Gestapo arrived without warning a few days ago to search his office. He is frantic. He says they are searching for any signs of resistance within their own ranks."

"Momm is part of the resistance?" I stood frozen in disbelief.

His answer was to stride across the room to shut the window. Within minutes, the room felt like a sauna, perspiration soaking me as we faced each other.

"We have a plan," he began. "To end it now, before it is too late. But it . . ."

Fear scrabbled in the pit of my stomach. André remained imprisoned. Everyone associated with his case in Berlin must know by now that I was the one cajoling Momm behind the scenes, to follow up on the paperwork and increase the already substantial payout of bribes. Spatz was also my lover; we'd been seen together at various restaurants, and here at the Ritz. If the Gestapo suspected him, how long would it take before they decided to question me?

"What is this plan?" I said. "Tell me."

"To seek a settlement with the Allies. Momm thinks our contact may be holding up André's release because he has determined that you can play a part."

I let out a tremulous laugh, raking a hand through my damp hair. "Didn't you once tell me this wasn't a parlor game? I am not a spy. What part could I possibly play?"

"You know Churchill," he replied. I stared at him, thinking I must have heard wrong. It was the last thing I expected him to say, but as I took in his expression, I realized he was serious.

"You cannot think . . . But I only met him a few times. He is in England and—"

"He won't be in England when we need him. He plans to travel to the Soviet embassy in Tehran to attend a strategy conference with Stalin and Roosevelt. From there, he will go to Tunisia and then on to Madrid. General Franco has taken a neutral stance; he does not want to aggravate Hitler, but Madrid is still full of informants actively working to end the conflict. If you meet Churchill there, through his ambassador, you could—"

"Get on my knees and beg? Spatz, why would Churchill heed me, of all people?"

"You are the only person we have with a personal connection to him. Coco, you could help us bring about an end to the war. Momm has already made preliminary inquiries and—"

"*What?* How dare he? My nephew's life is at stake!"

"Listen to me." Spatz came to me, restraining my outburst. "I told you there were high-ranking men in the Reich who question Hitler's policies. Our contact is one of them, and he thinks this plan can work, if you manage to meet with Churchill and deliver a message from us."

I knew it, then. I saw it in his eyes, a dreadful certainty that I could not ignore or evade.

"Dear God, you *are* insane," I whispered. "You plan to betray your führer."

"Our goal does not concern you. All you need to know is that we cannot move forward without Allied consent. Our plan involves significant risks, but we'll prepare everything for you in advance, the necessary permits for travel, your booking at the Ritz in Madrid, even an alibi."

"Alibi?" I echoed, so stunned by what I had deduced, I could barely speak.

"You will meet an old friend, Vera Bate-Lombardi. She's detained in Rome, under suspicion of acting as a double agent with her husband. She herself isn't a spy," he hastened to add, "but Lombardi had to go into hiding before he was arrested. Vera has petitioned Churchill numerous times for help but his office has ignored her appeals, primarily, though no one will say it, because they cannot interfere. Vera once worked for you; we will tell the Italian authorities you wish to hire her to help you open a boutique in Spain, and see that she is released and brought to Madrid."

I looked at him as if he had become a stranger. Of course, that was what he was, but I had never allowed myself to see it so clearly until now. This man I had entrusted my nephew's safety to, whom I'd taken to my bed and allowed myself to become entangled with, whose willingness to help Streitz at La Pausa temporarily relieved my suspicions—I did not know him at all. For the first time in my life, I had taken a man into my bed who had the capacity to destroy me.

"You were once Vera's friend, too," I managed to say. "You were with her in Monte Carlo for my birthday, so you and your friends must also know we haven't spoken in years. She worked for me in London before her marriage, yes, but why, in such times, after having refused to reopen my atelier here, would anyone believe I'd hire her to open one in Spain?"

"Because she wrote to you." He reached to his attaché case, moved the dials of its locking mechanism to open it, revealing several folders. He withdrew one, set it on the bed, and took from it an envelope. "She sent this letter four months ago, asking you to intercede with Churchill on her behalf. She must believe you carry influence with him."

"You . . . you've been *intercepting* my correspondence?"

"I had to." He did not attempt an apology. "I was ordered to. I had to be sure—or, rather, my superior had to be sure—you were reliable. We also saw your letter to Churchill, the one where you offered congratulations on his appointment. It was very personable. We sent it on, in hopes that it will reach him, though of course we cannot know for sure. They have other channels for making such communiqués disappear."

"Dear God." I spun away, my dismay choking me. What had I done? *How* had I let this go so far? In a sudden flash of memory, I saw the boy perched on the crumbling wall in Vichy, his abrupt fall before his unexpected lunge for my money and fleet escape. A common thief had lured me with sympathy; now, I found myself prey to a far more dangerous one.

But it would not serve me to show any fear. Spatz needed me; perhaps I could still turn this predicament in my favor. Composing myself, I used the same tone I might have for bartering to get a better price on fabric: "This contact of yours, I imagine he does not expect me to put myself at risk for nothing. What does he offer in exchange?"

"André's release," replied Spatz without hesitation, making me want to throw myself at his throat. "He has replaced his superior; as the new foreign intelligence director in Berlin, he can push the necessary paperwork through to send André here to manage one of Momm's mills."

"Just like that, after all this time?" I clenched my hands at my sides. "I agree to go to Madrid and my nephew is set free?"

"Yes." Spatz kept his tone level, though he must have known, he must have seen, how much I detested him in that moment.

"You are despicable," I told him. "All of you, you are monsters."

"Perhaps, but those are his stipulations. You help us and he frees André. Do you agree?"

I pretended to consider, even as I took note that he didn't press the fact that I could be instrumental in bringing about an end to this horrid war, if I managed to reach Churchill. He didn't press, I suspected, because it carried significant risk, and he had sprung his trap so well, he had no doubt of my answer. Spatz knew that for André, I would do anything.

"Tell your contact yes," I said, "but not before I see my nephew first— alive."

SPATZ ARRANGED A TRIP to Berlin in September. I left under the utmost secrecy, traveling alone on an overnight train with a small suitcase, my handbag crammed with permits and my stamped passport. As the train passed through barricades and customs checks, endless reviews of documents and searches of luggage, I kept my expression impassive. No one asked why I was traveling to Berlin, which startled me. Spatz had prepared a ruse, a tale of an elderly friend, a former client of mine, whom I wished to visit; but something in my permit must have precluded any questions. All the official who granted me entry said was that my *Ausweis* allowed me two days before I must return to France.

I had never been to Berlin, yet I saw little of the city. A Mercedes limousine with tinted windows picked me up at the station and drove me to the intelligence headquarters. I caught glimpses of soot-blackened buildings with snow banked against their sides and burnt-out shells of rubble from recent stealth Allied bombings. The ubiquitous swastika flew over façades. People walked underneath it, running errands, even a few couples kissing, just like people everywhere did. If it had not been for the demonstration of Nazi might displayed at every turn—posters of Hitler plastered to walls and passing tramcars—Berlin might have been just another city in Europe: crowded and noisy, smelling of petrol fumes and coal. It was almost impossible to imagine that I had just entered the fearsome heart of a regime determined to grind us into dust.

I waited on a bench on the third floor of an icy nondescript office building for over an hour, smoking nervously until a secretary pointed to a sign above me in German and informed me that smoking indoors was *verboten*. Finally, she conducted me down a passageway echoing with the tapping of typewriters to a glass-paned door.

Inside, I did not expect to find the usual assortment of filing cabinets, of overloaded desks and ringing telephones, and other secretaries in low heels and nylon stockings going about their work. Everything was so . . . normal. So ordinary. It did not seem like the inner workings of a death machine at all. I might have been waiting in any bureaucratic office in Paris.

"If you will please wait here, fräulein," said the secretary, and again she left me to accommodate myself on a hard-backed chair, my suitcase at my feet and my hands clutching my bag. I told myself to remain calm. Spatz's contact had allowed me to come here. If there had been any danger, he would not have done so—or so I desperately wanted to believe.

About thirty minutes later, the secretary returned and led me to a far office with a window so streaked with grime, nothing outside was visible. A tall young man with slicked-back auburn hair, narrow features, and striking gray eyes awaited me. He clicked his heels and bowed; he was not in uniform, but rather wore a dark wool suit and tie, and the red-and-black armband.

"Mademoiselle," he said in accented French. "It is a pleasure. I am Colonel Walter Schellenberg, director of the Foreign Intelligence Division. I welcome you to Berlin."

My smile felt strained. I was not certain of how to proceed, waiting while he retreated behind his desk to consult a file. "You have been apprised of the situation, I presume?" he said, without looking up.

"Yes," I said faintly. "I am to travel to—"

"No, no." He held up a hand, silencing me. "Now then," he continued briskly, "this matter of your nephew André Palasse, I have reviewed his dossier at length and believe he can be of service to us. You claim he has experience in managing textile production through training with you at your atelier. Is that correct?"

I nodded.

"And you wish to see him before he is released?"

"Yes." I swallowed. "Yes," I said, more firmly. "I would like that. He is well?"

"He has been ill. Otherwise, he is as well as can be expected. I have arranged his release from detention. He will be admitted to a hospital until he can recover from his"—he checked his papers—"bronchial infection. A few days at most, and we can remand him to Momm for his new position." He lifted his gaze. His eyes were flat. "He is here in the building."

I leaped to my feet, knocking over my suitcase. As I started to bend toward it, Schellenberg came from behind the desk. "Allow me," he murmured. As he retrieved it for me, he said, "You have ten minutes. The car will be waiting downstairs for you at half past the hour. It will take you to the station for the overnight train to Paris."

"But I . . . I thought I could spend a day or so with—"

"It is not possible. Ten minutes, mademoiselle." He stepped back, dipping his head with old-fashioned courtesy. "Delighted to be of service. Have a nice visit. Heil Hitler."

As if on cue, the secretary escorted me out, back down the passageway and up another flight of stairs. She led me into a long corridor, her heels clacking on the marble floors. At a door, she stopped and stepped aside. "Fräulein, I will wait here," she said. "You may leave your handbag and suitcase with me."

I reached for the doorknob. For a moment, my fingers trembled so much I could not turn it. Behind me, the secretary said, "Ten minutes, fräulein," and I pushed past the door into a windowless room no larger than a cubicle.

A table sat under a bare lightbulb hanging from the ceiling. Its chill glare fell upon an emaciated figure, seated on a chair, who turned enormous eyes and sharp cheekbones to me.

"André," I said. Tears blurred my vision as I went to him, enfolding him in my arms as he sat silent, still. I could feel every bone in his body under his loose clothing; when I blinked back my tears to take a full look at him, I could not curb my horrified gasp. "Dear God, what have they done to you?"

He coughed—a deep, lung-sputtering clatter in his chest. "Tante Coco," he murmured, as though the very act of speaking exhausted him. "You . . . can you help me?"

"Yes." I sank to my knees, clasping his bony hands. "They are sending you to a hospital for a few days and then you will be coming home. Katharina is waiting for you, and Tipsy, too; they are both so eager to see you. We have been terribly worried."

"They are alive?" he said, his voice fracturing.

"Yes, of course they are. They are safe in Pau. I saw them myself."

He lowered his face. As his jutting shoulders began to shake, I realized he was weeping. "They told me they were dead."

I embraced him once more, pulling his head to my chest. "They lied. Your family is alive. I promise you."

He wrapped his skeletal arms around my waist. "You smell like Paris," I heard him say. "I want to go home." His whispered words plunged me back to the day I had taken him to tea at the Ritz, when he had been only a boy and his impulsive embrace caught me so off guard.

I could barely talk past the lump in my throat. "You will, in a few days. You must get well first. Take your medicines, rest, and regain your strength. We need you—"

A knock came at the door. From behind it, the secretary said, "Three minutes, fräulein."

I glanced angrily at the door, longing to yell and scream, to bring the very walls of this building down on their miserable Nazi heads. Turning back to André, I said urgently, "You must listen to me. I have to go. They will not let me stay. Please, just do as they say until they send you home. You will manage a textile mill; I have arranged everything." I cradled his face between my hands as he tried to stifle his hacking cough, his eyes growing distant, glazing over. "Do you hear me? No one will harm you. You *will* be safe."

He did not reply, staring blankly past me as the door opened and the secretary told me, "Fräulein, the car is here."

"Just another minute," I said. "Please, he is so ill. I don't think he understands me . . ."

She shook her head. "There is no more time."

"André," I entreated, but he just sat there as if he were no longer present, as if he had already fled his fragile self. I had to bite back a sob as I began to walk away, glancing over my shoulder to him, a collection of shadows and bone, until, just as I stepped through the door he whispered, "*Merci,* Tante Coco."

I DID NOT REST during the long train ride to Paris. I sat and stared out the black window to the invisible landscape hurtling past, a pall of smoke over my head and the ashtray on the side of my seat overflowing with butts, seeing André's haunted eyes; the sharp etching of his skull under his thin skin; and hearing his deep, searing cough.

My nephew had tuberculosis. I was convinced of it. Unless he went to a sanatorium that specialized in treating the disease, he would die. The Germans did not care about him. They never had. They would keep him in the hospital and then dispatch him to Paris as promised, but he could not possibly toil in a textile mill, sacrificing what little remained of his ravaged health. No, I must take him to Switzerland, to a clinic with the best doctors my money could buy.

Before I did, however, I had to ensure his safety by delivering a message to Madrid.

XIV

In January 1944, under bitter winter cold, I embarked on my trip to Spain. The Christmas season had been more dismal than usual, the privations in Paris having reached such an extreme that even those ensconced in the Ritz were starting to feel the bite of chilled rooms and persistent hunger. The war was fast becoming a détente between Hitler and his foes.

Spatz accompanied me on the train to the border, briefing me on my mission during our hours-long confinement in a small first-class sleeper compartment.

"You will arrive in Madrid and go straight to the Ritz. Avoid any sightseeing. Once you check in, go about your business at the hotel and wait to rendezvous with Vera. Do not tell her anything. She will no doubt remind you of her letter and of her attempts to solicit help from the British to find her husband; when she does, offer to assist her by applying to the ambassador for an appointment. Churchill is due to arrive sometime after the fifteenth. If all goes according to plan, the ambassador will arrange to let you speak to Churchill on Vera's behalf. Under no circumstances can Vera be there when you meet; persuade her it's in her best interests, as her presence at the embassy will rouse suspicion with the Spanish authorities, given her predicament. Franco and Mussolini are allies; she cannot be seen at the embassy lest the Spanish think she's not in Madrid to open a boutique."

He handed me a folded paper. "Here is your confirmed reservation, which is required to cross into Spain. Your visa is in your passport. Our contact in Madrid will deliver the message to you. We do not know who he'll be, so don't expect someone German. We have people of various nationalities working for us. Do not open what he gives you; just hand it in person to Churchill at the embassy after you speak to him about Vera. Until then, never let it out of your sight."

"What if Churchill won't see me?" I asked, stashing the reservation in my purse. "If he has refused in the past to intercede for Vera, why would he change his mind now?"

"Because you are the one asking," he said. "Besides, once he reads the message, he'll understand this is not about Vera. But should something go wrong, destroy the message and return to Paris at once." He went quiet for a moment. "I may need to move to your room at the Ritz. The situation at my apartment has become precarious."

"Yes, of course," I said absently, my eyes straying to the nondescript reservation on the Madrid Ritz letterhead, which seemed to stand out among my things like a beacon of duplicity.

We did not speak about my assignment after that. We dined, went to bed, and while he slept, I lay awake, pondering, as I had since the start of the war, what I was doing. Why did I not behave like Misia or so many others who had either fled or elected to sit out the conflict, hiding in their homes? How could I, a woman nearing my sixty-first year, find myself on a train rattling toward a foreign country where a brutal civil war had just taken place, to meet a man I had seen less than a dozen times, the prime minister of a nation under German attack, who had more important concerns than indulging me?

At the border, Spatz met on the platform with a man I had never seen before, clad in a large hat and overcoat. They spoke briefly, while I waited aside, shivering, until Spatz escorted me to the next train that would take me to Madrid. He clasped my hand before I mounted the carriage steps.

"Be careful, Coco. If at any time, you fear you might be compromised you must abort the mission. Spain is not safe; Franco's Guardia Civil arrest suspects on minor infractions. Do not take any risks."

"Now you warn me?" I smiled to ease the barb in my tone and assured him I would be cautious. "Besides, I am Coco Chanel. Who would dare arrest me?"

He doffed his hat, stepping back as the train began to surge into the night. I sat at my compartment window and peered past the ice-frosted glass to catch a last glimpse.

He had vanished. Only then did I realize how alone I truly was.

MADRID WAS A BATTERED CITY. The long standoff between the Republican forces and Franco's Fascist army had left the city so destitute, it made Paris look like a horn of plenty. Piles of rubble littered the streets; people trudged with heads down, bundled against the bone-shuddering cold and clutching limp shopping bags.

In the Ritz itself, however, like its counterpart in Paris, the chandeliers sparkled and an air of cultivated elegance persisted, though the hotel had recently served as a military hospital. My reservation was in order, a small suite readied. Going upstairs to bathe and change, I wondered if I should stay put until I heard from Vera. I was just starting to unpack my things when the phone rang. Vera was waiting for me in the lobby.

She wore one of my matching skirts and waist-length jackets in cream wool, her short red-auburn hair slightly waved. She did not hear me approach until I was almost behind her.

"Vera, my dear, how lovely to see you."

She spun about with a stifled gasp, as if I had interrupted her deep in thought.

I hid my dismay at the sight of her gaunt face. There was not a trace left of the vivacious divorcée, clad in red silk with camellias in her hair. My gaze fixed on her hands, which trembled as she held her cigarette. Her nails were unpainted, gnawed to the quick. As she met my stare, she said, with an uncertain smile, "As you can see, Coco, I am not the woman I was."

"Oh, it must have been awful," I soothed, taking her by the arm and bringing her to a nearby table, where we ordered two coffees that reeked of chicory. "When I heard you had been detained in Rome, I was beside myself. You poor thing; and this terrible situation with your husband—I insisted you must be allowed to help me with my new venture."

I could hear myself and knew I was talking too fast, too eagerly, my words tumbling out as though I had memorized an ingratiating speech. Years had passed since we last met; she had left my employ to settle in Italy upon her marriage to Lombardi. Though we had exchanged a few cursory letters over the years, with the advent of the war our communication, feeble as it was, had ceased. I had always liked her; her connection to everyone of important social standing had helped make my boutique in London a success. Yet I now realized she had changed as much I had—more so, in fact. She was a familiar stranger in my clothes, our past a frayed thread like the one dangling from her sleeve cuff.

She tugged at this thread before she said sharply, "I do not understand."

"You don't?" I sipped my coffee, which proved as bitter as the lies in my mouth. "I thought it was explained to you."

"It was, but I still don't understand." She lit another cigarette. "I never wanted to come here. I told them in Rome that I had to stay because Alberto, my husband—" Her voice caught; tears glimmered in her eyes as she looked about warily, blinking her sorrow back. Then she said, in a taut, accusatory tone, "I do not understand why you are *helping* them."

I sat immobile for a moment. Spatz had told me not to divulge anything, so I made myself lean back in my chair with a worried look. "My dear, I fear you do misunderstand. I am not helping anyone. This is about fashion. With the civil war in Spain at an end, it is the perfect time to open a boutique in Madrid—"

"Damn your fashion." She dropped her half-smoked cigarette into her cup. "Are you insane? The entire world is still at war!" As her voice rang out, she went still, trembling more visibly as she struggled to contain her outrage. "What in hell are you about?" She reached into her pocket, and withdrew a crumpled telegram she tossed onto the table. "Did you send me this?"

I retrieved it, scanning its lines in English:

> I AM GOING BACK TO WORK. I WANT YOU TO COME AND HELP ME. DO EXACTLY AS REQUESTED. I AM WAITING FOR YOU WITH JOY AND IMPATIENCE. ALL MY LOVE.

My dumbfounded expression must have betrayed me, for she added, "It was delivered along with a bouquet of red roses—roses, in midwinter! Who can afford that? When they came the next day and I told them I had to stay in case my husband contacted me, they forced me onto the plane here. I had to leave everything behind, even my poor dog!"

"I . . . I did not realize." The paper crackled in my hands. I became alarmed. I had not sent the telegram or roses, yet someone wanted it to look as if I had, in order to dupe Vera. Nevertheless, she had not come willingly, and judging by the tenor of our conversation, I did not think she would request, or indeed even want, my help.

"No, apparently not," she said, cutting into my thoughts, "though you claim you knew about my circumstances. I can only assume that means you did receive my letter, even if you never replied. But letter or not, I know about you, too. It is no secret you entertain Germans in Paris or that despite your willingness to be their friend, you have not reopened your atelier. You would never open one here, either, where people can barely buy bread. So why did you bring me all this way? Because even if it is true, which I doubt, I am not interested in being your shopgirl. My husband is a fugitive; all I want to do is find him."

Remembering what Spatz had advised, I said warily, "Perhaps I could be of some assistance. I might petition the ambassor for you, if you like?"

"You?" she spat, even as her eyes narrowed suspiciously. "Why would he see you? You seem to forget that you're not important anymore. You have no influence in England. Besides, I've already sent everyone I know telegrams and letters. I've been begging for help for months. Like you with my letter, they all ignore me."

Spatz had miscalculated. Vera was not an alibi. She was not even an asset. And she could jeopardize everything because it was evident she did not trust me.

"Well, if the matter is so dire . . ." I tried to force out an apologetic smile. "I did not fully understand your situation, it seems. Vera, I promise you, had I known—"

She flicked her wrist in a dismissive gesture. "You wouldn't have done anything differently. You never do. You always act as you will. You don't care how it affects others."

Her words held scalding echoes of Misia in the Tuileries: *I warned you, Coco. I told you to be careful, that there will be repercussions . . .*

I rose to my feet. "I see this was a mistake. I apologize, really, I do. Yet seeing as we are here, perhaps we can make the best of it, if only for friend-ship's sake. I'll leave you now because you are upset. We can talk later, over dinner, if you like?"

She nodded, without looking up at me. "I think that would be best."

I left some money on the table and retreated. Vera did not call me back; I had the disquieting feeling she would avoid me for dinner, too—as she did. I refrained from ringing her room, dining alone in the restaurant, and then, seeing through the windows a flurry of snow coming down, returning to my suite to pace the floor.

The next morning, I woke early and phoned the embassy to request an appointment, determined to see the ambassador before I spoke to Vera again. I could reassure her that I was intervening on her behalf, which would be partly true. According to Spatz's instructions, I could request the meeting with Churchill to plead Vera's case. If need be, I would ask that he see her back to Italy safely, as the charade over the boutique in Madrid was over. Then I called reception but no one had left anything for me. I was about to go downstairs, in case Spatz's contact had decided not to risk entrusting the message to the front desk, when my phone rang to tell me I had a visitor in the lobby.

A short polite man introduced himself as an embassy escort. The British ambassador, Sir Samuel Hoare, wished to see me, if now was convenient? I bit back my question as to how an appointment had been facilitated so quickly, letting him lead me outside to a waiting car. As the chauffeur drove us through Madrid, the man reached over from the front seat to hand me an envelope. He did not say a word, turning away at once while I hid my surprise and hastily pocketed the envelope. I had not expected someone employed by the embassy itself to be Spatz's contact; I had not anticipated anything that had happened so far. I fought back anxiety as I tried to apply lipstick while the car jolted over potholes. Had Churchill arrived earlier than expected? Perhaps that could explain why my phone call this morning had prompted such a swift response.

I was ushered directly into the office of Ambassador Hoare. He was a slender man with a receding hairline, long nose, and impeccable manners, whom I had met briefly at one of Bendor's gatherings; he greeted me warmly, gesturing to an upholstered chair before his desk. His office walls displayed hunting scenes in oils, banal depictions of aristocratic privilege.

"I trust your travels were not too onerous?" he said. I reached for my cigarette case and then paused, thinking he might not like me to smoke. When he nodded his assent, I flicked my lighter. "Everything is far more trouble nowadays," I said, forcing out a smile. "But yes, it was not as onerous as you might expect."

"And your accommodations, I hope they are agreeable?" He regarded me with a pale, steady gaze, his intent unreadable. It made me nervous, reminding me of my meeting in Berlin. Hoare seemed to know entirely too much, making me abruptly blurt out, "I do not intend to stay long, Your Excellency. I merely wish to apply for an appointment to see Sir Winston and—" I was reaching into my coat pocket for the envelope with the message from the German conspirators when I remembered I was not supposed to reveal it yet. Fingering it more closely, I realized it was too thick to contain a slip of paper. Had the escort entrusted me with crucial documents?

Samuel Hoare sighed. "I am afraid you have come a long way, mademoiselle, only to be disappointed. Sir Winston is not here."

"Oh," I said, hiding my frustration and withdrawing my hand from my pocket without exposing the envelope, though it made a crackling sound that seemed unbearably loud to my ears. "But I understand he is due here soon, yes?"

"I fear not. Sir Winston unfortunately had to cancel his visit."

I gaped at him. "Canceled? But, why?"

"I regret that I am not at liberty to disclose that information, mademoiselle." He glanced toward the closed door of his office. As he returned his gaze to me, my chest constricted. All of a sudden, I felt breathless. "Madame Bate-Lombardi is here," he went on. "She arrived in rather a state, I'm afraid." He pursed his lips before he said, "She has made serious accusations that have raised our concern. Your name was mentioned, which is why when you phoned this morning, I made time for you at once."

As I lifted my cigarette to my lips, I found I could barely inhale. "Accusations . . . ?"

"Yes. Again, I regret I am not at liberty to explain. However, it would be advisable for you to return to Paris as soon as possible." His voice lacked any hint of inflection, as though he was remarking upon a sudden change in the weather. "I'm afraid I cannot be of assistance to you, nor can I guarantee your safety should you choose to remain in Madrid."

I sat still, feeling the envelope in my pocket. I knew without looking that whatever it contained, it could not be just a message. I heard Spatz in my head: *If at any time, you fear you might be compromised you must abort the mission;* and I murmured, "I see," starting to stand, to extend my hand to him, too nervous to inquire about what on earth Vera might have said. As he shook my hand, he told me: "Sir Winston fell ill in Tunisia. He will return to England once he recovers. If you care to leave a communiqué for him, I will see that it is forwarded."

"Yes. Thank you." I hesitated, searching his eyes. Should I give him the envelope? He would forward it to Churchill; the message would be delivered. But Spatz's insistence that I should deliver it only in person held me back. "Is Madame Bate-Lombardi safe?" I asked.

"Suffice it to say, she finds herself in a difficult position. Her Italian passport carries a German visa. It will be complicated to explain her presence here, given her allegations."

"But she is here because of me!" Worry flared in me. I had not enjoyed Vera's upbraiding but she must not become compromised by dealings she had no say in. "I invited her to meet me and—"

"Mademoiselle," he interrupted. "You are under no obligation to offer me an explanation or heed my advice, though I feel it is incumbent upon me to tell you, as a friend of Lord Bendor's, that your own presence and German visa carry significant risks, as well. I suggest you entrust Madame Bate-Lombardi's situation to us and depart as soon as you can."

He guided me to the embassy door. Outside, an escort—not the same one who had brought me here—waited with a car. At the threshold, I turned once more to Hoare. "May I at least leave a note for her? We had a disagreement earlier. I wish to tell her I meant no harm."

"That would not be advisable." He inclined his head. "Good day, mademoiselle. I hope we shall meet again in better times."

During the short drive back to the hotel, no one spoke. Once we arrived at the hotel, the escort opened the door for me and said, "I am an attaché to the embassy. Here is my card. If you care to contact us before your departure, please do so, mademoiselle." He did not await my response, returning to the car. I had no idea if he was another of Spatz's unknown contacts.

In my suite, I yanked off my jacket and loosened my collar, feeling as if I couldn't get enough air in my lungs. Removing the envelope, I weighed it in my hand for several moments, hesitating. Then I tore it open, spilling its contents onto the bed. A gasp escaped me. It held banknotes in German currency, a significant amount. There was nothing else. No documents. No message.

Sinking onto the edge of the bed, I stared at the notes, utterly bewildered. Was Spatz offering to *bribe* the prime minister of Britain? It seemed outrageous. Perhaps his message had yet to reach me and I should wait another day. While I did, I would write to Churchill myself.

I HEARD NOTHING MORE FROM VERA, and no one came with anything additional for me. After tarrying a full day in the hotel, I booked my train passage home and enclosed my six handwritten pages on the Ritz stationery, an appeal to Churchill on Vera's behalf, taking full blame for bringing her to Madrid and imploring his assistance in her case. I sent the letter to the British embassy, then took my suitcase and boarded the train to Paris.

My venture as a messenger of compromise had come to nothing.

Little did I realize how much had already been set into motion.

"SHE WAS THERE, AT THE EMBASSY," I told Spatz when I arrived at the Ritz, worn-out with fatigue and irate at the entire fiasco. It had not fully struck me until I disembarked in the Gare du Nord that I had just traveled hundreds of miles on a fool's errand, accomplishing nothing of importance save to endanger a friend. The sight of Spatz in my rooms, with his own suitcases jumbled in the corner, indicating he had vacated his apartment, threw me into more turmoil. I did not want him here. I felt compromised enough as it was.

"She told them something about me. Serious accusations, Hoare said. What could she possibly accuse me of? I only told her that I'd invited her there to help me open a boutique, as you instructed." I eyed him as I spoke, recalling the telegram and roses, and Vera's fury that she'd been wrenched from Rome without any choice.

He did not speak for a long moment. He looked only a little less disheveled than I did. A fog of smoke from his cigarettes hovered above him. Finally, he lifted his weary gaze and said quietly, "She accused you of being a spy."

"What!" I flung my handbag onto the bed, narrowly missing him where he sat. "How could she even know . . . ?" My outrage faltered as he went quiet again.

"She had the message," I whispered, cold spearing through me.

He stood hastily, moving toward me until I thrust my hand out to detain him. "Coco, listen to me. There was a mix-up at the hotel. We told our contact to give it to you in person, only he feared someone followed him. After he saw you meet with Vera, he decided to entrust it to her. He instructed her to give it to you as soon as possible, but she did not."

"She took it to Hoare instead," I breathed. "She denounced *me*."

"She denounced all of us."

"But your message—it's an offer of compromise." My breath came fast, like the panting of a cornered animal. "You and your friends seek to end the war. That's what you said."

"Yes. But what we propose is too advanced, and Churchill is now ill. I only heard of his fever after I left you at the border and returned here. It was too late to alert you. I had hoped Hoare might not see you, or if he did, you'd realize the mission had been compromised. With Vera spewing accusations, our message was useless. We must now proceed, regardless."

I couldn't believe what I was hearing. "Proceed to do *what*? I wrote Churchill a letter, defending Vera. If she denounced me, then he'll think I am party to whatever it is you plot."

"It doesn't matter. You are here, while she—"

"Doesn't matter?" I was almost screaming at him. "You used us both! If Vera brought Hoare a message of a German conspiracy, then they must suspect her of being a spy, too."

"They already had. She and her husband have been under suspicion for months; bringing her to Madrid was only cover for you. We were ready to sacrifice her, if necessary." He gave me what I imagined he thought was a reassuring smile. "There's no reason to worry. André has been released; he's in a clinic, here in Paris. He is safe now. You are safe."

At that moment, my fury turned to ice in my veins. I abruptly understood how completely he had deceived me, how the seemingly disconnected pieces of his puzzle fit into place. The callousness of his betrayal crawled over my skin as I took a step toward him, reveling, if only briefly, in his startled recoil.

"You miserable bastard. There was no mix-up at the hotel. You had your contact give Vera the message on purpose. You found out Churchill canceled his visit, so you decided to use her instead because you had instructed me to deliver it in person, while she would take it straight to the embassy and spill everything. You made sure your message will reach him eventually; Hoare must forward it, and that way, you and your Nazi friends—dear God, they'll think *you* tried to stop your infernal führer, while you had your man give me reichsmarks to make it look as though I'd been paid! I was your pawn, not Vera. I am the one you sacrificed."

His expression faltered; this time, at least, he did not lie. "I had them give you the money to protect you; no one, not even Franco's police, would dare arrest a German informant. It's no excuse but once the message was delivered, I did everything I could to see you safe. I had my contacts watch you at all times to ensure you reached Paris without incident."

If I had the strength, I would have lunged at him, torn him apart with my bare hands. Instead, I pointed at the door. "Leave. I never want to see you again."

"I cannot. I have nowhere else to go."

"Then I will." I pushed past him, storming to the closet. "I'll move to my apartment over my shop. Don't come near me or I will report you as a traitor to the Gestapo."

I MOVED TO RUE CAMBON, taking residence among the cluttered furnishings already there and those transferred months before from my former suite at the Ritz. I avoided further contact with the hotel or Spatz, sleeping on a chaise lounge in my living room, hiring a personal maid and a butler to attend to my needs at home while I tended to my business. I kept myself occupied in the evenings by helping Cocteau restage his play *Antigone* at the theater and visiting André at the clinic. The doctors there confirmed his tuberculosis. I consulted with them about how to transfer him to a sanatorium in Switzerland. His wife wanted to come to Paris but I dissuaded her, citing the need for permits to travel across the occupied zone. I convinced her it would pose too great a risk to her and Tipsy. The Germans were running rampant, ordering the arrests of thousands.

On June 6, triumphant broadcasts from the BBC filtered into Paris with reports of a massive Allied landing at Normandy, with the combined forces of America, Canada, Britain, and the Free French storming onto the beaches. Shortly thereafter, Spatz came unexpectedly to see me.

I was closing up the shop, having sent my staff home early. The German tide of customers had receded noticeably in the past days. Cinders and ash drifted in a gauzy rain over the city; the Nazis were incinerating their files. In the distance, bomb blasts announced the Allied approach. I was bolting the front door when Spatz appeared on the threshold. For a moment, I debated whether to pull the blinds and leave him standing there. Instead, I motioned him inside. My wrath had tempered. I knew that if the reports were correct, he and his German friends were not long for Paris. Already, rumors raced through the city of our imminent liberation.

"I wanted to see you," he said, removing his hat to wipe a handkerchief across his sweat-dappled brow. "Before I go."

"So it's true," I remarked, not looking up as I retreated to the counter to tally my receipts.

"Yes. The end has begun."

"Good. It is high time for this catastrophe to be over."

"You could leave with me," he said. "Once official word comes from Berlin, anyone who wants to leave will be assisted. We could go to Germany first, then perhaps to Switzerland or—"

"No." I lifted my eyes to him. "I was never the invader here. I have nothing to hide."

He shifted on his feet, as if debating whether to depart. "You will not say anything?"

"Say? About what?"

"Us. You. Everything."

I gave him a pensive look. "Why, Baron von Dincklage, if I did not know better, I would think you are afraid."

"Coco, as I told you before, this is no game." His jaw clenched. "You are still in danger. The war is not over yet. You must not say anything. It is imperative, now more than ever."

"Or what?" I stacked the receipts, snapped a band around them. "You'll shoot me?"

"God, you *are* truly impossible!" He let out a sudden laugh. "I believe you would defy Adolf Hitler himself."

"Him especially," I retorted. I let a moment pass. Then I said, "I will not say anything, you have my word. Though you hardly deserve it after what you have done."

He set his hat on his head. "Thank you, Coco," and he left without another word.

I had no idea if I would see him again. For both our sakes, I hoped I would not.

AS THE GERMANS EVACUATED THE CITY, I went to see Misia. She was haggard but welcoming, her hope restored by the news that the Allied forces were within miles of us. As I handed her my last supplies of Sedol—I had mostly given it up, braving with gritted teeth my insomniac nights—she told me Arletty was terrified. Her lover had absconded in the night, along with the majority of the German high command that had held sway over us these last four years.

"She fears she'll be arrested as a collaborator, as well she should," snorted Misia, caustic now with a dose in her veins. "She's going to have to flee herself before the Allies arrive." Then, realizing what she had said, she muttered, "Of course, darling, I am prepared to defend you."

"And Lifar and Cocteau," I reminded her. "You'll need to hide us all in your attic." As she turned pale, I patted her hand. "Don't worry. I can take care of myself. Besides, what can they charge me with? I took a lover. At my age, one can hardly afford to check passports."

She gave me an unconvincing smile. She did not know everything, but she knew enough, and I repressed my growing disquiet that in fact they could charge me with plenty, if they had a mind to. Those of us who had stayed behind and attempted to survive would be among the first targeted for retribution.

"You should stay with us," Jojo rumbled from the bar, pouring tumblers of his precious cognac. "They won't look for you here."

"No." I took the glass he proffered. "I have a feeling that soon there will be no place to hide. I might as well go to my suite in the Ritz. After all," I added, downing the bracing liquor, "I did pay for it in advance. They still owe me two months."

I returned to the Ritz to find my suite reeking of German cigarettes, with a ring in the tub from whoever had been soaking in it. I had my maid clean the room from nook to sill, then transferred some of my furnishings from rue Cambon to make it feel more like a place I'd call home. Yet it did not feel like home. Paris revolted when word came that the Allies were outside the city, delaying their assault, prompting blood-soaked pandemonium; yet everything felt empty to me, still—like a stage after the play has ended, curtains billowing down upon fake painted sets, the finale more deafening than the recent applause.

I braced for the worst. It first arrived in the form of my friend Serge Lifar. For weeks as the Allies neared, the Germans had been helping anyone with the means to escape, but leaving behind everyone who did not. His latest German admirer had offered Lifar passage to Zurich, prompting him to rush to me instead. He carried a bag crammed with his resin-soiled ballet slippers, frantic as the impact of what he'd danced his way through came crashing upon him.

"They arrested Arletty," he said, huddled in my room. "They took her into custody. Marie-Louise has gone into hiding, as has Cocteau. They're coming for all of us, Coco."

"You can stay here," I told him. "I'm not going anywhere."

I wondered at my own resolve. From Jojo Sert's apartment overlooking the place de la Concorde, we watched freedom enter under General de Gaulle. The soldiers marched in procession to the Arc de Triomphe, welcomed with ecstatic cries, with caps flung in the air even as down the side streets, agents of the Free French rounded up suspected collaborators. We got a taste of what was in store when a burst of sniper fire shattered the apartment windows, sending us diving to the floor or behind doors as glass sprayed in every direction. When we emerged warily, Jojo was still on the balcony, shaking his fist at the unseen attacker and bellowing, "Try it again. You did not hit me, *hijos de puta!*" Then he turned to us with his irrepressible grin and said, "I apologize for the inconvenience," making me laugh aloud at his bravura.

By the end of August 1944, Paris was free. To celebrate our liberation, I put a placard in my shop window, offering my perfume free to GIs. The Americans, British, and Canadians queued up for hours, like the vanquished Germans before them, to partake of my generosity and secure proof that they had been in Paris on this historic occasion. My staff worked until they were faint on their feet; I myself doled out hundreds of bottles to men whose youth took me aback. They were incorrigible in their zeal, cavorting in the bistros and cabarets, seducing every woman in sight, and quite a few men. They seized whatever joy they could because Berlin still lay ahead, unrepentant even as the Nazis cowered in the detritus of their own horrors.

"They murdered thousands," Misia wept. "Millions."

I did not comment. What was there to say? What could we have done without ending up dead ourselves? How could we, a handful, have saved millions?

This was what I kept telling myself, over and over.

Even it gave me no comfort.

XV

Persistent knocking on my door woke me. As I struggled to rise, fumbling for my robe, Lifar, who slept downstairs, came to the staircase and hissed, "Coco! Coco, they're here!" I staggered down the steps in my robe, pressed my hand to his lips. "Hush!" We froze, waiting. When the knocking resumed, rattling the door on its hinges, I pushed Lifar toward the far closet. "Hide in there! Quickly."

He threw himself into the large closet built into the wall, shutting the door as I fastened my robe, shook out my tousled hair, and undid the latch.

Two men in shirtsleeves and sandals, with berets shading their stony faces, stood outside. They were without doubt members of the Free French, or the Fifis, as we had dubbed them in mockery of their brutal tactics. They had overseen the arrest of hundreds of women in Paris and throughout Vichy-ruled territories. Branded as collaborators, they were shorn of their hair, beaten, and paraded in the streets in their undergarments to sometimes lethal reprisal by mobs.

"Mademoiselle Chanel?" said the larger one, a brute with eyes like flints. Before I could respond, he added, "We are here to escort you."

"Oh?" I set a hand on my pajama-clad hip. "It's rather early in the day for visits."

"You can come nicely. Or we can arrest you and drag you there, mademoiselle."

I did not fail to notice his sarcastic enunciation of my preferred form of address. "Very well," I said. "Only allow me a few minutes to make myself more presentable, yes?"

They shouldered their way inside, compelling me to open the closet door, only far enough to grab the first items of clothing I could without revealing Lifar, crouched behind my coats. Going into the bathroom, I dressed, ran a brush through my hair, applied lipstick, and emerged in time to catch one of them idling near the closet. I had left the door ajar. If he opened it, he would find Lifar.

"Shall we, gentlemen?" I asked brightly, striding to the suite door.

I almost sagged in relief when they followed me like sullen hounds. But wherever they were taking me, relief, I feared, was the last thing I would find.

THEY DID NOT TAKE ME to the notorious prison of Fresnes, where the Free French had locked up many of the so-called "horizontal collaborators." Instead, they took me to a nearby police office that still bore the mangled outline of the swastika on its walls. There they left me in a windowless room, seated before a scarred table with an ashtray on it.

I waited for over an hour before my interrogator arrived. He did not introduce himself, instead setting an alarmingly thick dossier on the table before he took his place across from me.

"Gabrielle Bonheur Chanel, also known as Coco or mademoiselle," he said, flipping open the dossier. I did not crane my neck to see what he was reading; I felt sick as he adjusted his spectacles and cleared his throat. "Is that whom I am addressing?"

"I assume you would know," I replied, lighting a cigarette. "You did arrest me."

"Oh, no." He glanced sharply at me. "You have not been arrested. This is only an informal questioning for now, if you please."

"I see," I said. Informal meant off the record—which, of course, could change at any moment if I proved uncooperative.

He returned to the dossier, turning its pages without any discernible expression, while I smoked impatiently and feigned a carelessness I did not feel. At length he said, "Were you ever acquainted with a Baron Hans Gunther von Dincklage, commonly known as Spatz?"

It would not do to commence with a bold-faced lie.

"Yes. I knew him."

"And did he assist in the release of one André Palasse from a German internment camp?"

I nodded. "He offered his help, so I accepted. André is my nephew."

"Indeed." He looked back at the dossier, a frown creasing his brow. "Did you ever go to Berlin yourself, to meet with Colonel Schellenberg?"

He caught me by surprise, though I did my best to conceal it. Again, I pondered the advantage of truth over lies; it was evident that as secret as I had thought my trip was, someone from the Free French had indeed been watching me.

"Yes. I went to see my nephew after he was released. He was ill."

"Yet you did not bring him back with you. You stayed only one day and returned without him, after which you embarked on a trip to Madrid. Can you please explain what you and Colonel Schellenberg discussed during your time in Berlin?"

"My nephew, of course," I replied, speaking slowly to curb the anxiety twisting my stomach. "He is ill. He contracted tuberculosis. I . . . I wished to see him."

"That is all? You met with the director of Hitler's Foreign Intelligence, the highest-ranking officer in the Abwehr, to discuss your nephew's health?"

"Yes." I met his stare. "He was very ill, as I have said."

The man flattened his hands on the dossier. "Mademoiselle, why did you go to Spain?"

"To see if I might open a boutique there."

"And did you?"

"No. The circumstances were not conducive."

"I can imagine they would not be." He stuck out his chin. "Were you ever part of a German intelligence operation?"

I froze on my chair. "No."

"Really?" He did not glance at the dossier again. "Because we have information that implies you were in fact a participant in a secret operation whose objective was to safeguard German interests and carry out the elimination of Hitler. Are you still unaware of it?"

My mind raced, recalling the mysterious events surrounding my mission to Madrid and Spatz's deliberate omission of what he and his friends plotted. Had they been seeking Churchill's permission to kill the führer? Had I unwittingly been thrust into a conspiracy to save Germany?

"Of course, I am unaware," I managed to say, pulling my voice out of my throat. "Surely I would know if I had taken part in such an endeavor."

"Mademoiselle." He directed the weight of his icy regard at me. "Co-operation with the enemy, regardless of the goal, is now a criminal offense. We have several of your friends in custody; we are searching for several more. I suggest you think carefully before you answer."

"Are you asking me to betray my friends?" I retorted.

"I am suggesting you tell us the truth. We know you have not been forthcoming."

I crossed my legs, fumbling for the cigarette case in my purse. "Then you should arrest me," I said, unable to contain a hint of defiance. "For I have told you everything I know."

He pushed back his chair. "A moment please." Taking up the dossier, he left.

The moment I was alone, I let out a choked sound, half gasp, half sob. I was trapped. I could not escape this time. They would arrest me as they had Arletty, toss me into a jail, and see me hauled before their makeshift court, where they would condemn me as a collaborator, shave my head, and take me through the streets to be pelted with filth—

He came back into the room. "Mademoiselle," he said tersely. "You are free to go."

For a terrifying moment, I could not rise. My legs felt boneless, so that I had to hold on to the table to bring myself upright. Grabbing my handbag, I started to the door, passing so close to him that I smelled his distinct tang of cheap cologne.

He said quietly, "You are fortunate to have friends in high places as well as low, mademoiselle. But if you will accept a word of advice, you should consider whether or not staying in Paris would be wise for you."

I glared at him. "I am French. This is my city, my country."

He slid his gaze to me. "Not anymore."

I HAILED A TAXI to rue Cambon. My fear was peeling off me, exposing the fury that had been building since those thugs had banged on my door. Ignoring my staff's bleated inquiries, I barged upstairs to my apartment and with shaking fingers dialed my lawyer's number. René answered after several rings, by which time I was nearly apoplectic, exploding over the line about the outrageous insult done to me, dragged in for questioning by a menial of de Gaulle's new government, accused of abetting German interests and then advised that I, France's foremost *couturière*, should leave my own—

"Mademoiselle," he said, breaking into my tirade. "I think you should heed his advice."

I could hear my own labored breathing in my ears. "You *what?*"

"It's only going to get worse," he said mournfully. "I myself have already been questioned at length about my connections to the Vichy regime; they tore my office apart and took away boxes of personal and professional documents, including," he added, to my mounting horror, "the files pertaining to our case against the Wertheimers. You should consider it a warning. They do not have anything against you now, but they'll keep looking until they do."

"That worm said I had friends in high places," I exclaimed, even as I felt a strange sense of disorientation, like falling endlessly into a void. "Someone is protecting me."

"Yes, but for how long? They call it *l'épuration sauvage*, the savage purge. They intend to prosecute all those either identified or suspected of collaboration. It is de Gaulle's sacrifice to the cause. He must assure the Allied forces that we intend to stand with them once Berlin falls. Our only choice is to leave."

"But I—I did not collaborate! I only did what I had to, to protect my nephew and my business, to save my life and those of my friends."

"Mademoiselle, you need not justify yourself to me. You must justify yourself to them, and I fear they will not care. Someone intervened for you today. But whoever it was may not be able to protect you tomorrow. Were it possible, I would leave, too, but I am the son-in-law of the Vichy minister who approved Jewish deportations. They revoked my passport. I cannot go. But you can—and should."

After I hung up, I pressed a hand to my mouth to stifle my scream. Was I expected to flee from the country of my birth? Did I have no other recourse but to seek voluntary exile?

I turned in a haze into my apartment, seeing it all, the beautiful lacquered screens, the paintings and books, like a fragile mirage already fading from view. Stumbling to my desk, I wrenched open the drawer, searching for what I had left there. When I unfolded the handkerchief and held the watch to my ear, it was no longer ticking. The miniature gold hands were frozen at half past six. I frantically turned the winding mechanism on the side, my fingertips slipping over its tiny grooves.

Nothing moved. There was no sound. Boy's watch had ceased to mark time.

I knew then, with unavoidable certainty, my own time had also run out.

ONCE I MADE THE DECISION, it was simple. Not easy, never that. But simple nevertheless. I stored the belongings I would not take in my apartment at rue Cambon and oversaw the closure of my shop, paying my staff four months of salary in compensation, even as Madame Aubert and Hélène implored me to keep the doors open. They promised to oversee everything and telephone me regularly in Lausanne, Switzerland, where I had decided to retire. I'd already sent André there by private car; Katharina was renting a house near the sanatorium where he would receive treatment.

I refused to heed my staff's pleas. It was over. France was no place for me anymore.

Then, I did the one thing I had most dreaded: I went to Misia.

She greeted me at the door with a grief-stricken cry that made it obvious she knew why I had come. She and Sert were planning to remarry, she told me, pulling me onto the lumpy sofa where we had sat so many times before, to laugh and gossip, to skewer friends and foes, to argue and reconcile, more like sisters than any we had known.

"You must stay," she said, enfolding my hands in hers, rubbing them as if she were seeking to banish my permanent chill. "Who will design my dress?"

"Someone will," I replied.

"And Lifar? What of him? He is safe for now, but they dismissed him as director of the Opéra Ballet and called him to answer before the Fifi Purge Committee. And Cocteau, how will he manage without you? They need you here. All of us, we need you so very much."

I had to bite the inside of my lip then, to stop myself from breaking apart. If I started crying, that would be the end of it. We would both dissolve. I pulled my hands from her, reached up to touch her wrinkled cheek. "Serge will survive. He is a treasure, one of the finest choreographers the world has ever known. They may make him atone, but in time he will dance again. It is all he knows. Cocteau, as well; he must write. What else can he do? And you, beloved friend, you will live. You have your Jojo again. He is all you ever loved."

She was crying so hard, I had to give her my handkerchief. "I won't," she blubbered, blowing her nose. "I cannot."

"That is only what you think," I whispered, and I embraced her, holding her close, looking past her shoulder to where Sert stood in the living room doorway, his grizzled features somber. "They don't have decent bread in Switzerland," he said. "You'll hate it. You'll be bored."

"Yes," I said, smiling through tears I could no longer hide. "I know."

IT WAS STARTING TO SNOW when I left Paris—a soft swirl undulating down over the carapace of the Eiffel Tower, drifting upon the gravel paths of the Tuileries and blinking marquees on the Champs-Élysées; dusting the artists' garrets and cabarets of Montparnasse, and speckling the spiral molten-copper column in the Place Vendôme. It settled into cracks on the pavement and in crevices of smoke-aged buildings, softening the serrated edges of a city that had seen so much anguish and terror, such joy and exuberance, there was no other in the world like it.

Gentle as a gloved hand, it caressed the awning over a shuttered storefront on rue Cambon, across from the Ritz. It paused there, its white hue only slightly paler than the awning itself, before it began to melt, dripping past a bold name that was once so coveted and famous, so extraordinary, it needed only one word:

Chanel.

PARIS

Ah, the applause at last—if one can call it that. It is muted, polite but faint; already the scraping of chairs pulled aside and the rustle of coats shrugged on, the sound of hasty kisses blown in the air and promises to have lunch soon, tell me everything I need to know. All those years I lived abroad, slowly forgotten by all but my intimate friends, even as I in turn ignored the foibles of the fashion world—this is my reward: a precipitous departure and disdainful silence, which to my ears is far worse than derision.

They are disappointed. Of course they are.

Should I descend to take my bow or leave the models standing there, with their numbered placards held before them, as the herd makes its exit?

I think I shall wait. They have seen my clothes. It is the return they have waited for, argued over, pretending surprise even as they wondered if I could recapture the glories of my youth. I have shown defiantly spare dresses in my neutral palette of black, navy, cream, and deep brown, with white camellias at the waists and sloping shoulders, my flat hats with ribbons, as well as my collarless suit in signature red. None of it is excessive.

Though Dior has returned us to the torments of wire-braced corsets and yardage, of tulle and crinoline sprouting from unnaturally cinched waists, like the inverted petals of an overblown flower, I refuse to comply.

Why should I, Coco Chanel, change for them? What I have presented is independence: clothes for women who need to move, work, and entertain. In time, they will see that while Hollywood princesses may waltz through celluloid fantasies in Dior's ridiculous creations, ordinary women cannot. They *should* not. Fashion is not folly.

Now, they can do as they wish. I will not sacrifice my ideals. Yet as I stand on the staircase, hearing them depart, I feel their disillusionment; I almost hear their urgent whispers to each other that I have lost my touch. After ten years of exile, what could I expect, really? To find the world unchanged, waiting for me to return and dress it once more?

Still, the chilling suspicion creeps over me that my activities during the war have worked against me, even after all this time. Though I was never condemned by a court of law, have my colleagues and peers judged me in absentia? If so, then that, too, is something I must ignore.

As I start to turn away, to retreat to my atelier and contemplate my uncertain future, I hear footsteps below me, a tentative voice: "Mademoiselle?"

I reel about more sharply than I should, wounded by the indifference, though I know I must not show it. The woman standing at the foot of the stairs is pretty, dressed in a lovely suit. Not one of mine, I notice, and then, as I think this, I cannot resist a gruff chuckle under my breath. How could she be wearing anything of mine? She looks no older than twenty.

"Yes?" I say, with a smile that feels like a razor across my lips.

"I . . . I am the assistant to Bettina Ballard, editor of *Vogue*," she says, and the tremor in her voice gives me satisfaction. She is all too aware of whom she addresses. My name, it seems, still carries weight. "Miss Ballard had to leave, unfortunately; she's late for an appointment at our office, but we . . . we were wondering . . ."

I keep my gaze on her. Informing me that her employer has dispatched her, a hireling, to accost me, is hardly in the best of taste. "You mean American *Vogue*, I presume?"

She flushes, nodding. Her complexion is transparent, as is her expression. "Go on." I wave my hand. After today's disaster, what's a little more humiliation?

Confidence propels her up the stairs until she is on the step below me, eagerly clutching a mannish portfolio while she balances a large, rather ugly handbag on her arm. It is made of quilted leather, similar to ones I've designed, though a poor imitation. As I look at it, I think that perhaps I should update my own handbag by adding a gold-chain-wrapped strap.

The girl says, "Miss Ballard thinks your collection . . ." But she falters again. I resist rolling my eyes as she glances at my foot tapping out my impatience.

"Miss Ballard thinks your collection might show very well in the United States," she suddenly bursts out. "She would like to feature you in our February issue. An interview, along with photographs of your new clothes. The updated suit, in particular, and the black tiered evening gown with the camellias. We believe . . . that is, if you wouldn't mind . . ."

My stare unnerves her. She almost recoils as I extract a cigarette. Blowing smoke over her head, I remark, "Are you asking to take a closer look at my collection *now*?"

"Yes, please, if you would be so kind. We can arrange to return later with the photographer." She hurries after me as I lead her toward my atelier. "He really is excellent," she babbles, "one of the best in the business. Miss Ballard thinks he'll be ideal for this shoot."

American *Vogue* wants to sing my praises, as it always has. And if America embraces me, so must France. My clientele will return. Women are too intelligent to disdain common sense.

I resist a sudden, triumphant smile. Chanel is back.

May my legend gain new ground. I wish it a long and happy life.

AUTHOR'S NOTE

Upon Coco Chanel's return to Paris and her new collection in 1954, French fashion critics lambasted her for being outdated and failing to adhere to the prevailing air of the times, dominated by Dior's New Look, which returned women to an archetype of femininity as beautiful to see as it was uncomfortable to wear. Coco had refused to concede that corsets were again in style and presented simple, unrestricted dresses harkening back to her early days. Nevertheless, American *Vogue*—a lifelong champion of her work—rallied to her sustainable vision, in particular her seductive interpretation of her matching skirt, jacket, and hat. In time, the Chanel suit would become a perennial, much-copied classic that endures to this day.

Misia Sert died in 1950, five years after José María Sert, who succumbed to a massive coronary while painting a mural in Vichy. As a final gesture for the woman who was undoubtedly her closest friend, Coco returned to Paris to prepare Misia's body for her funeral.

André Palasse suffered lifelong complications from his internment in Germany and died in Switzerland in the late 1940s. Vera Bate-Lombardi survived the fiasco in Madrid and returned to Rome with assistance from Churchill's office; she died in 1948. After his ban from working in France for two years due to his collaboration with the Nazi regime, Serge Lifar took the Paris Opéra Ballet on a triumphant tour of America, mesmerizing audiences with his virtuosity. In 1958, he had to resign his directorship of the company amid renewed controversy. Upon his death in 1986, he was buried in the Sainte-Geneviève-des-Bois Russian Cemetery; his memoirs were published posthumously. Jean Cocteau became one of France's most celebrated artists, his diverse portfolio including poetry, art, novels, plays, and films. He died in 1963. In the aftermath of World War II, the British arrested and held Hans Gunther von Dincklage; after a failed prior attempt, he gained entry to Switzerland in 1949, where he reunited with Coco. That same year, she appeared in Paris to address testimony given at the war-crime trial of Baron Louis de Vaufreland, a French traitor and German intelligence agent who had implicated her. She denied all accusations and no judgment was found against her. In 1953, she sold her villa La Pausa, which she often visited in the summer, sometimes with Spatz. He retired to a Balearic island, where he devoted his remaining years to painting erotica. He died in 1976.

Ironically, Coco's relationship with Pierre Wertheimer lasted until her death. Upon his return to France after the war, he resumed control of her perfume company, leading to a series of legal entanglements that ended in 1947 when he reached a settlement with Coco that made her extraordinarily wealthy. Pierre would go on to become one of her trusted managers, financiers, and confidants despite frequent discord between them.

Following her 1954 collection, Coco went on to design several more, often updating her signature looks. Restored to international acclaim, she entertained friends and celebrity clients, as well as several lovers, defying all expectations of retirement until her death on Sunday, January 10, 1971, in her residential suite at the Ritz. She was eighty-seven. She left the world without apology, sighing, "So, that's the way one dies."

She was laid to rest in the cemetery of Lausanne, Switzerland, under a marble headstone bearing five lion heads, her zodiac sign and her talisman number forever linked. No other designer has left such a lasting impression on the fashion landscape or in our popular imagination.

ACKNOWLEDGMENTS

This novel, perhaps more than any other I have written, was truly a labor of love. Chanel first entranced me in my teenage years when my burgeoning interest in fashion led me to pursue a career in it. I hoped to become a designer myself, but soon discovered during my education at the San Francisco Institute for Design and Merchandising that many around me had far greater talent. I switched my major to marketing and embarked on a twelve-year profession that took me from San Francisco to New York and back again, working as a retail buyer, freelance publicist, vintage-store manager, and fashion show coordinator for avant-garde couturiers.

My fascination with fashion and the personalities who create it has never abated, though I ceased working in the industry in the mid-1980s. Thus, the opportunity to write a novel about the legendary Coco Chanel, whose tumultuous rise to fame and dramatic personal trajectory left such an indelible mark on both her era and those that followed, was a dream come true.

I owe the fulfillment of this dream to many people, starting with my friend Melisse, who first encouraged me to set aside my sixteenth-century obsession for a career risk. My agent, Jennifer Weltz, applauded my new venture and steered me through the inevitable shoals of change that often accompany a writing departure. My editor, Rachel Kahan, took an enthusiastic chance, fulfilling another long-held dream of mine to work with her, and her publishing team at William Morrow welcomed me with incredible expertise. I cannot express how grateful I am.

My husband supports me in all my endeavors, sustaining me through hours of solitary confinement at my desk and the highs and lows of being a working writer, as well as in our daily life, where I can, I must confess, be less than attentive when the muse is upon me. My cats, Boy and Mommy, bring us unrequited love every day, as well as reminders that there is life beyond the computer. Friends near and far, such as Sarah Johnson, Linda Dolan, Michelle Moran, Robin Maxwell, Margaret George, and Donna Russo-Morin, restrain me from becoming a recluse, as do my yoga instructors at Excelsior Yoga, who keep me nimble. I greatly appreciate all my Facebook friends and fans for their humor and support, as well as my Web mistress, Rae Monet.

Most of all, I thank you, my reader, for I simply could not do this without you.

You give my words heart.

SAN FRANCISCO
AUGUST 19, 2013–JANUARY 9, 2014

SOURCES

Many sources assisted me in discovering Coco's intimate life. She remains controversial and mysterious to this day, as adept at obscuring the truth in death as she was in life, but every book about her fits another piece into her enigmatic puzzle. I relied most heavily on the following volumes. Please note that this annotated list does not represent a full bibliography:

Baillen, Claude. *Chanel Solitaire*. New York: Quadrangle, 1974.

Chaney, Lisa. *Coco Chanel: An Intimate Life*. New York: Viking, 2011.

Charles-Roux, Edmonde. *Chanel*. New York: Alfred A. Knopf, 1975.

Galante, Pierre. *Mademoiselle Chanel*. Chicago: Henry Regnery Company, 1973.

Haedrich, Marcel. *Coco Chanel: Her Life, Her Secrets*. New York: Little Brown, 1971.

Haye, Amy de la. *Chanel*. London: V&A Publishing, 2011.

Lifar, Serge. *Ma Vie*. New York: World Publishing Company, 1970.

Madsen, Axel. *Chanel: A Woman on Her Own*. New York: St. Martin's Press, 1990.

Mazzeo, Tilar J. *The Secret of Chanel No. 5*. New York: HarperCollins, 2010.

———. *The Hotel on the Place Vendôme*. New York: HarperCollins, 2014.

Morand, Paul. *The Allure of Chanel*. London: Pushkin Press, 2009.

Picardie, Justine. *Coco Chanel: The Legend and the Life*. London: HarperCollins, 2011.

Riding, Alan. *And the Show Went On: Cultural Life in Nazi-Occupied Paris*. New York: Alfred A. Knopf, 2010.

Vaughan, Hal. *Sleeping with the Enemy*. London: Chatto & Windus, 2011.

About the author

2 Meet C. W. Gortner

About the book

4 Why Chanel?

7 Reading Group Guide

Read on

9 Chanel's Message for Success

11 Chanel's Style: Yesterday and Today

Insights,
Interviews
& More . . .

Meet C. W. Gortner

Stephanie Mohan

C. W. GORTNER IS THE INTERNATIONALLY
acclaimed author of *The Last Queen*, *The
Confessions of Catherine de Medici*, and
The Queen's Vow, as well as the Elizabeth
I Spymaster Trilogy (*The Tudor Secret*,
The Tudor Conspiracy, and *The Tudor
Vendetta*).

After an eleven-year-long career in
fashion, during which he worked as a
vintage retail buyer, freelance publicist,
and fashion show coordinator, C. W.
devoted the next twelve years to the
public health sector. In 2012, he
became a full-time writer following
the international success of his novels.
With his books now translated into more
than twenty languages throughout the
world, he was recently named one of the

top ten historical novelists by the *Washington Independent Review of Books*.

In his extensive travels to research his books, he has danced a galliard at Hampton Court, learned about organic gardening at Chenoceaux, and spent a chilly night in a ruined Spanish castle. A sought-after public speaker, C. W. has given keynote addresses at writer conferences in the United States and abroad. He is also a dedicated advocate for animal rights, in particular companion animal rescue to reduce shelter overcrowding.

Half-Spanish by birth and raised in southern Spain, C. W. now lives in Northern California with his husband and two very spoiled rescue cats. ⁓

Why Chanel?

By C. W. Gortner

WE ALL HAVE A LITTLE Coco Chanel in us. Who hasn't experienced putting on a new outfit and feeling a subtle lift in our spirits? Coco Chanel understood this: she thrived on her ability to transform how we dress and, in turn, how we see ourselves.

I first encountered Chanel when I was a child. Her little black dress was a staple in my mother's closet and I remember watching my mom dress one evening, slipping into the sheath and layering on ropes of pearls. I asked why she wore so many necklaces but no earrings. She smiled. "Because less is more. That's what Chanel says." Until that moment, I had never heard of Chanel. Later, my mom took me to my first Chanel boutique. The quilted handbag with its gold-chain strap; the nautical sweater and collarless suit; the seductive aroma of No. 5—my mother wore them all. What I did not realize at the time was how she used them to set aside her daily cares and transform herself into a woman who exuded confident independence.

I would learn. After ten years in Spain, my family moved back to the United States when I was in my teens and I struggled to fit in. On my first day of high school, I wore a cravat and pleated trousers. The other students jeered so much that I ran home in tears. In Spain, neckwear and trousers were the rule, but in the States it was T-shirts and jeans. But then I enrolled in drama class and met others like me, who reveled in flamboyant frock coats and fringed scarves, our apparel a defiant declaration of who we were. My love affair with fashion began. Like Chanel herself, I discovered that clothing could be a catalyst for self-expression.

After graduation, I hoped to become a designer. But as a student at the San Francisco Institute for Design and Merchandising, I discovered that my talent for sketching did not extend to sewing! Nevertheless, I devoted my thesis to Chanel, presenting an illustrated collection on how she revolutionized her era by creating the signature styles that endure to this day, even though she had no training as a couturiere. Her self-taught genius, her determination to succeed, and her prescient flair with textile and form all inspired me. With a degree in marketing, I embarked on a twelve-year career in San Francisco and New York as a stylist and fashion coordinator. I loved my job—and I often referred to my battered book of Chanel designs. Her motto "Less is more" became my adage.

My fascination with Chanel has never abated; in time, I came to realize that she taught me about so much more than mere elegance. In her lifetime, she demonstrated the kind of personal resiliency we all need to fulfill our dreams. As she once remarked, "My life didn't please me, so I created my life." That's good advice for all of us.

Mademoiselle Chanel tells the ▶

Why Chanel? *(continued)*

unforgettable tale of how this legendary woman created that life. The opportunity to depict Coco's struggle and success, her flaws and controversial compromises, which are as much a part of her legacy as her clothes, is a dream come true.

I hope you love reading this novel as much as I have loved writing it. ~

Reading Group Guide

1. As a teenager at the convent of Aubazine, Coco admits that "fear had become my enemy because it might take root inside me and never leave." Does she seem like a fearful person to you? What do you think were Coco's greatest fears? Did she find a way to use them as motivation for success or did they drive her to make bad decisions?

2. After nearly starving in Vichy, Coco gives in to Etienne Balsan and becomes his mistress. Was this out of character for her? Did she compromise her principles by moving in with him? What do you make of her relationship with Balsan, both in their early days together and much later in her life?

3. Coco reflects that during her relationship with Boy, "Yes, I was happy. It was not a comfortable feeling for me." Why does happiness—especially domestic or romantic happiness—so unsettle her? Does she ever get comfortable with happiness?

4. What do you make of Coco's relationship with her family, especially her siblings and her aunt Adrienne?

5. Coco says of herself, "It appeared I did not work at all, when in truth I worked harder than ever to maintain the illusion that success was effortless." Why was this so ►

necessary? Do working women today try to maintain the same illusion?

6. Is Misia Sert a good friend to Coco? Why does Coco love her so much, and what does their relationship say about each of them?

7. *Vogue* wrote that "Chanel's little black dress will become standard for the masses, much like Ford's motorcars." How many little black dresses do you own? Why has that particular garment become such an enduring classic? Why is it the quintessential Chanel garment?

8. What do Coco's business dealings with the Wertheimers say about her personally as well as professionally? What motivates her to take such drastic action, and to create such a personal vendetta? Who do you think was in the right?

9. What is the true nature of Coco's relationship with Hans von Dincklage? Do you approve of their liaison?

10. Coco Chanel has acquired a reputation as someone who collaborated with the Nazis during their occupation of Paris. Does this seem fair to you? Should she have behaved differently during those years?

11. Did you admire Coco Chanel now that you've read this novel about her life? Is she a good role model for women? ∽

Chanel's Message for Success

"A girl should be two things: who and what she wants."

FORTY YEARS AFTER HER DEATH, her empire thrives. We all know her name, as well as her style: the little black dress and pearls, the braided suit, the quilted handbag, and her bestselling perfume. But Coco Chanel, born in 1883 to an impoverished seamstress and itinerant vendor, and whose childhood in a convent sparked a fury of ambition, remains relevant today for more than her contributions to what we wear.

Chanel rose to fame in an era when women had few choices. To work for a living was déclassé; arranged marriages were common, as they still are in parts of the world, while professional women were rare and scandalous. Chanel did more than ignore convention. She defied it. She decided that to build the life she wanted, she must cultivate herself, regardless of expectations.

Today, many of us still struggle with the same messages as Chanel. Although we've come a long way, as the ad declared, we nevertheless remain fixated on appearances—a successful marriage and children are deemed hallmarks of achievement, while a thriving career should be, whenever possible, integrated into the above. How many articles have we seen about "having it all"? How many step-by-step guides on how we can bake a cake and eat it, too? And how many times have ▸

we run ourselves ragged trying to accomplish it?

Chanel wanted her own business. When she started out making hats, she had no formal training. Fashion was a male-dominated arena in the waning years of the Belle Époque, so her first customers were courtesans, women who made their own hours and earned their keep with conversation and seduction. Some were also actresses, when a job in the theater was about as acceptable as prostitution; many went on to marry and forge conventional lives.

What fascinates us about Chanel is that she never led a conventional life. She built her hat shop into a fashion gold mine, her comfortable designs in perfect timing with World War I, which thrust women of all social standings into jobs. Chanel not only taught women how to dress for work, but also showed that they did indeed have choices, one of which could be a dedication to success—a trait often reserved for men. She never married. She never had children.

Did she sacrifice fulfillment, an issue fiercely debated in our twenty-first century? She once said, "How many cares one loses when one decides not to be something but to be someone." She defined herself with her message: Be who *you* want to be. We should all do the same. ❧

Chanel's Style:
Yesterday and Today

"A woman can be overdressed but never over elegant."

CHANCES ARE YOU HAVE AT least one of Coco Chanel's designs in your closet. Perhaps not the label itself—few of us can afford it—but something she first made popular and has since become a staple, reinterpreted for the modern woman. In her lifetime, not only did Chanel inspire new trends, but her influence remains everywhere we turn. We might not recognize it as hers, but it's there. Here are some of the fashion items she introduced to the world:

Casual separates: Chanel's first items of apparel were made in an ingenious knit called jersey. Originally employed for military underwear and uniforms, jersey was not considered a luxury cloth. But her lease at her boutique in Paris initially prohibited her from selling dresses—there was a dressmaker already in the building—and so she searched for a way to circumvent her limitations. Her lover brought back polo sweaters made of jersey from the United Kingdom; she loved the ease and stretch of it. And one summer in Deauville, where she'd inaugurated a shop, she introduced casual wear for women: matching separates in jersey. Though her clientele was suspicious—wealthy women usually endured fittings for one-of-a-kind clothes in male-run fashion salons—her loose skirts, lightweight sweaters, ▶

Chanel's Style: Yesterday and Today
(continued)

and oversize coats became hits. The next time you're browsing in a department store, you're shopping the way Chanel intended.

The little black dress: Most women own at least one; Audrey Hepburn made it the cocktail dress in *Breakfast at Tiffany's.* But before Chanel, black was reserved for nuns, schoolgirls, or mourning. She once remarked while attending an event where the women wore peacock satins that she'd like "to dress every last one in black serge." She did. When her little black dress was first introduced, however, it wasn't popular. French fashion critics derided her for overstepping herself. But American *Vogue* proclaimed it "a dress for the masses," predicting it would become as ubiquitous as the "Ford motor car." The rest, of course, is history.

Costume jewelry: Jewels have always been coveted as status symbols and investments. But Chanel thought it was ridiculous to appear in public dripping in thousands of dollars of jewels. A gift of priceless pearls from a Romanov prince ignited an idea in her. Why not mix real jewels with fake ones? She went to work, setting up ateliers where she interpreted Byzantine motifs using paste gems and false gold. She herself often went out with both fake and real jewelry adorning her. She liked to joke that no one could tell which cost more. Today, costume jewelry is a billion-dollar industry and we all wear it.

The suit: Nowadays, suits are a fixture. But women didn't wear suits until Chanel made them popular. Her collarless, braid-trimmed suit was introduced later in her career and it has become a classic, copied countless times in countless ways. Chanel's original was comfortable, made to look chic while withstanding a full day on the job. Pair it with her two-tone pumps and quilted handbag, and you'll become that self-reliant, successful businesswoman that she herself was. ✨